DUSK,
DAWN
AND
LIBERATION

DUSK, DAWN AND LIBERATION

A HISTORICAL FICTION ON THE LIBERATION
STRUGGLE OF BANGLADESH

MASUD AHMED

authorHOUSE®

AuthorHouse™ UK
1663 Liberty Drive
Bloomington, IN 47403 USA
www.authorhouse.co.uk
Phone: 0800.197.4150

Published by AuthorHouse
First Edition: 11/22/2013
Second Edition: 11/11/2014

ISBN: 978-1-4918-8103-3 (sc)
ISBN: 978-1-4918-8102-6 (hc)
ISBN: 978-1-4918-8104-0 (e)

Price: £12.95, BDT 1750.00 (Includes VAT + CD)

My Gratitude

I am indebted to a number of distinguished persons for their contribution in getting this book written and published. My wife Rifat Reza and my senior colleague Mr. Golam Mostofa proposed me to write something in English about our independence struggle. Dr. S A Samad, ex-CSP, currently Chairman, Bangladseh Board of Investment, labourd a lot in improving my draft. Besides, Messers. Mark Caldwell & Peter Murray from the UK, Ekleud from Sweden, Mustafizur Rahman, Shamim Wahid, Delwar Hossain, Mohamed Delwar Hossain, Amir Khosroo, Taufik Ul-Islam, Amimul Ehsan Kabir, Imran Khan, Md. Zakir Hussain, Bokul Haider & Bulon Chowdhury from Bangladesh did extend their support in this regard. Some of these kind persons made valuable suggestions while the others did the arduous job of typing, retyping the manuscript and correcting it many times. My special thanks to Author House, London, for coming forward to publishing this book.

Masud Ahmed.

With Best Compliments for

Mr Md. Asgar

18·10·17

Masud Morol.

Dedicated to the loving memory of my Dad

PROLOGUE

In 1971, death was stalking everywhere in East Pakistan. Any Bangla speaking human being, old or young, child or woman, Moslem, Hindu, Christian or Buddhist alike faced it as they would a sniper's bullet. The assassins were all Moslems by faith, by profession soldiers of the state who earned their livelihood defending the people they were killing. It had a genesis. The Moslems started their inroads into the Indian sub-continent's gate wall from 1202 A.D. In this respect Mohamed Ghori was the pioneer from the western flank. Earlier, non-political Arab merchants also had started landing in what is now Chittagong district of Bangladesh from the 8th century. On the other hand, through the political line, Ikhtiaruddin Md. Bin Bakhtiar Khilji usurped the throne of Bengal from Laksman Sen in 1205 A.D. Foreign Moslem rulers thus inaugurated ruling a populace in the sub-continent that belonged basically to a different religion, Hinduism. Moslems are monotheist while Hindus are polytheist. Moslems being a microscopic minority ruled a vast majority successfully up to the early 16th century. Then, the Mughals, also Moslems and a central Asian royalty, came to the fore of political power at Delhi and ruled this foreign land up to 1757. History has failed to explain the reason and logic with which only a few men could rule a vast majority for more than six centuries (1212-1756). It was not just ruling but also converting hundreds of millions of the local population to their own faith. The principal reason behind this could not be fear of the ruler's sword. It was something bigger and deeper. The conquest of the English in 1757 had resulted in totally two different reactions to the minds of the majority Hindus and the minority Moslems. Hindus were happy to think that they were relieved of an alien intruder and minority ruler. The Moslems had ousted them, and now the British had ousted the Moslems. So, the new rulers were at least not their foes if not actually friends. The Moslems took the British as an enemy since they had usurped an Islamic power. Ironically the British were intruders, alien and a further smaller minority than the Moslems and less unwelcome than Moslems. Through their 190 year (1757-1947) long domination, the English brought in a political system through which all adult population learned to express their opinion on the conduct of the statecraft. This paved the way for the demand for self-rule and finally independence for India. Then the million pound question rose. Who to take over from the outgoing British? By the very logic learnt through democratic practices, it should have been the majority. The Hindus were the vast majority (80%) of the total Indian population. The Moslems were fear-stricken with this argument. They were sure that the Hindus, as the ruling majority, would avenge themselves by treating them as abjectly as possible. So what to do? Become the majority and form a new state of their own. To do that, arguments were necessary. Their leader Jinnah invented the arguments first and fast. Culturally, socially and religiously the Hindus and the Moslems are basically different from each other. To lead a life together within a united India after the British left would not be compatible for these reasons. There would be social strife, division and even riots between the two communities. Thus the two-nation theory was born. However, Jinnah did not mention one of the major differences between the two communities. This was, the Indians were followers of the Aryan ideology of abstinence while Moslems were poised to enjoy life following Moghul tradition of consumption. The British said, 'Ok, we see your point. But Moslems are spread throughout India. How can you gather them in a country or one area?' Jinnah finally said, as the momentum for the separate homeland gained, 'in that case, divide the two provinces where Moslems are predominant.' On this argument Bengal and the Punjab were divided. The Hindus found it objectionable because with the same argument the majority Hindus was entitled to rule entire India alone. But their icon Gandhi accepted it to avert acrimony between the two communities in the future. So, two Moslem populations separated from each other by a thousand miles of Indian territory formed Pakistan with an East and a West wing. Another population about the same in numbers remained scattered throughout India. These two populations had only one thing in common—Religion. Explanation of the split in 1971 has been given by many. The Begalees of East Pakistan ate rice, fish, wore tight clothing, lived in moist monsoon and looked towards

East Asia. The Punjabees, Sindhis, Pathans and Baluchis ate dates, wheat and meat, wore loose knit clothing, and looked towards the Middle East. But this was not the whole truth. As with much more distance and a lot more differences, an Asamese, Punjabee, Malay or NEFA man used to live together in her big neighbouring country with people diametrically opposite in religion, culture, food habit and so on. Mutual accusation, mistrust, deprivation and exploitation vaporized relations between the two wings of East and West Pakistan soon after 1947. The West (44% population) soon started ruling the East (56% population). There were many reasons for this. The capital city, defense service head-quarters and business centers were all in the West. Revenue earning in the East was 70% while the Government spent 60% for the development of the West. The West's share in defense, civil services and businesses were 80%. The West clamped a minority dialect on the East as the main language which aggrieved them further. The 1958 martial law intensified the exploitation and alienation of the West from the East. In the 1970 elections the Awami League from East Pakistan won 167 seats out of 170 allotted for the province and thus emerged as the overwhelming majority party in the whole country. The deeper reason of this result was possibly something else. Pakistan was born out of an 'action action, direct action' theme. So, everything in the state was 'adhoc'. The leaders did not engage themselves in a nation building policy. The minority leader, the *Nabab* of Larkana, was not poised to accept the 1970 elections result. The West-led military also supported him and decided not to transfer power to the majority for the fear that Benglaees would take retribution for their past exploitation at the hands of the west. The army government made a crackdown in East Pakistan to smash the latter's legitimate claim for power. The leader, Mujib declared independence on the 26th of March, 1971. The whole of East Pakistan started fighting a liberation struggle. With India's support the Bengalees became free on 16th December, 1971 after a colossal blood bath. The defense services people on duty in 1971 throughout East Pakistan were mostly Punjabees.They had bitter memories of suffering from communal riots during partition of 1947 at the hands of Hindus and Shikhs. Additionally there was another factor at work in their minds. Kashmir, a princely state populated largely by the Moslems was not divided between India and Pakistan when the British left. Pakistan took a part of it forcibly and expected the whole of it on account of the religion of the population. India forcibly occupied the larger part of it. East Pakistan was far away from this place. West Pakistanees did not believe that this province was sympathetic to the Kashmir cause. Thus anything Indian was anathema to them. The military and almost all west Pakistanees supported the Kashmir cause. The two countries fought a war in 1965 over this issue. The *Nabab* earned the support of the west wing by supporting the Kashmir cause. Bengalees had hardly any such suffering during 1947 and their struggle of 1971 was largely aided by India. The cruelty committed by the Pakistanee army on the Bengalee freedom-fighters and common Bengalees was caused by this factor also.

PREFACE

In March, 1971 an iniquitous war was waged on us aiming to destroy our lives, livelihood and culture. The formidable enemy sought to have a lifeless, leafless and burnt soil. Despite an indiscriminate use of fire-power with millions of guns, rifles and other weapons and goaded with an extreme vendetta, the enemy failed to silence chirping of birds, cacophony of children, or the aroma of mustard flowers of Bengal. The nightingale still continued its songs. The iron strong vow of a rising nation ultimately buried the pathological zest of the insane enemy.

This fiction of mine moves around the terrible events of 1971 in East Pakistan. I will be happy only if and when the soul of our liberation struggle of 1971 is appreciated by readers through this book.

—Masud Ahmed
3, Mintoo road,
Dhaka, Bangladesh.

I.

It was February, 1971. The lengthening shadows of the afternoon had melted beneath the pale of twilight, and darkness was setting in. The scene was reminiscent of Thomas Hardy's Wessex but it was not England. It was six hundred miles south of Islamabad, the capital city of Pakistan.

Four Gentlemen were sitting on cane-made couches placed on the expansive lawn of the most talked about garden resort in the area. It should have felt like cool but desertation was impeding that.

The shortest person present was the President of the country. For the last thirty four years he had worn military uniform. Only in the last two years had he done away with that. He was in civvies. A pyjama, 'kurta' and Kabuli sandals gave him a very relaxed aura. Sitting at his right hand was the Chief-of-the Army Staff. Across from him, one of the chairs was being occupied by the host, the owner of this resort. On the left of the host was sitting the PSO or Principal Staff Officer of the President. The host had satisfied these three guests by offering them sumptuous culinary items and drinks for the last one and a half days.

The President-cum-chief guest was born in Peshawar, a township of North-West Frontier Province in 1917. He did not have a royal pedigree but the mix of conspiracy and luck placed him on the helm of this democracy-free country. Though ethnically Pathan, his love had always been for the Punjabees and they placed him in this highest office as reciprocation in 1969. His name was A.M. Yahya Khan. He was the senior-most General in the country's massive armed forces.

Most of the one hundred and twenty million people of the country had taken him to be their king-plenipotentiary. The rest were kids, infants and adolescents. So their view on this could not be fathomed.

Since they were growing, reading stories of medieval kings and queens in their curriculum, the intelligent guessed the latter fostered a similar view about the President. Nonetheless, the President himself did not possess any such thoughts. After getting the supreme power he did not fail to see the flicker of admiration in the eyes even of those citizens whose mother tongue was different from that of his.

Since those very moments he had taken a vow in his mind, 'No, I will be a good man indeed and not an autocrat. I will mingle with their love and earn a name in history as a caring father figure of this nation.'

He was sincere in this vow.

The President's casual wear, gray hair and sedate eyes were giving exactly that look this evening. He never had any special appetite for food. Since lunch that forenoon he had consumed four pegs of whisky, cognac and fine French wine from Burgundy.

The spokesman of the President House, earlier yesterday let the journalists know the story that this team would be out here for a shoot-out of ducks, cranes and other winter birds. The reality was however different.

The host was six feet tall. This fair complexioned man with a beaming face had a questionable descent in the Asian sense of morality. People had a perception that his father hailing from neighbouring Rajputana (now Rajasthan of India) was not formally married to his wife. This was only hinted at by the press as well as by his opponents but never discussed or resolved even by the mullahs.

This country did not have the taste of democracy for many many years. The host felt it convenient to address this evening's chief guest as 'Mr. President' or 'General' and even 'brother', while the latter acquiesced without any objection. They had been having a very good relationship for many years. Their mutual communications became stronger since the national elections held in December. The President from that day also started having a new feeling. It was 'tension'. In a military profession such a feeling is alien. He understood it was giving him a sense of uncertainty and insecurity deep in his mind.

The gentleman sitting beside the President was also a soldier. He was wearing a three-star insignia on his shoulders. He was strongly built, had tanned eyes that exuded cruelty and cunning. He never tried to understand anything beyond official formalities. His sense of security was also keen. It had its reasons. He was born in Bhopal in India 54 years ago but had to leave that birth place in 1947 for good and emigrated to this country. Three days ago he raised a point of protocol about the propriety of the President's visiting this winter-resort of the host. Reacting, the President snubbed him by saying that following rules framed by others is the job of a plebeian and the riff-raff. The President's job is to frame rules for himself and not follow the rules of others.

There was another three-star General seated on the left side of the host. He also looked strong and stout. All these four people conversed the preceding night and the following day but the host was not wholly satisfied. The very purpose of his arranging this visit and hospitality was to have a clear and full assurance regarding an important issue from the President. He was about to speak his mind when the President made a query to the soldier seated on the left of the host.

—Piru, you are not talking, huh! What is the matter?

With a quick smile he answered,

—Sir, you have known me since 1947. What can I say in your presence?

The President once again realized that this man, much more intelligent than he was, was again steering away from where he sensed trouble. The President also recalled that Piru secretly maintained a good rapport with the host.

It was an impervious critical moment in the times of the Indian subcontinent. The term 'critical' was not imaginary or over emphasized. It was real. Three parties were at work. The first party was limited in its strength and so persecuted. The second party was physically very strong, lowly in intelligence and medieval in thoughts and culture. The third one was remarkably high in intelligence and that was the source of her other strengths.

The host, *Nabab* and the three guests belonged to the second party. These gentlemen were scheduled to return to Rawalpindi in the next morning. The night passed peacefully and after breakfast the team was preparing to depart for the local air force base enroute to Rawalpindi. The President rose from his seat and told the host in an assuring tone

—You need not worry. I have deep concerns and care for this country. I will see to it that the wellbeing of everyone is ensured. I wish to thank you for your hospitality during the last two days. Now we would like to call it a day.

The President entered into his room to change his cloth. There was a soft knock on the door. He opened it. Captain Maruf Hossain Atif, the President's ADC was standing in an erect posture. He saluted the President. With a furrowed forehead the President queried,

—Maruf, what has come up?

—Sir, an emergency message.

—O.K, relay it hurriedly.

Maruf gave the details of the message while the President listened to the news silently. Then he ordered the ADC,

—Alright, put me through to the information secretary.

His profession is such that most people can go up to the highest rung of the ladder by displaying sheer loyalty and obeisance. He also followed the same track. He was at a loss and so could not decide if it was advisable to break the news to his host before departure. Actually the host knew him better than he understood the host. At 2 o'clock in the afternoon the Presidential aircraft landed at Rawalpindi. Journalists were thronging in the VVIP lounge. The Military Secretary to the President informed him that they insisted on talking to the President. He agreed but was astonished to hear the nature of their queries as he was expecting that they might be interested in his tour to Larkana. In reality the volleys of questions all hovered around the news received through his ADC two hours ago.

Akbar Jang of the daily 'Dawn' asked,

—Mr. President, did you discuss the statement given by Mr. *Nabab* on shooting down the Indian airliner by Kashmiri freedom fighters in your meeting at the resort earlier today?

The Press Secretary's advice 'Don't ever show you are annoyed or angry' flickered across the President's mind. Generally the gift of smile does not visit the President's face. At this moment he tried to bring an air of the same and quickly responded,

—This statement is the personal view of The *Nabab*

—So, you don't support this?

The journalist quipped.

The President, then avoiding a direct answer, calmly said, 'It is not an official matter, we're still observing the situation.'

AFP's correspondent Fitzgerald put the next question, 'Mr. President, does your government condemn the blowing of the airplane?'

The President was about to say, 'No. The *Nabab* issued the statement without consulting me.'

After a second thought realized that, it was safe to express the official version and so said, 'My government can tell nothing further before a final and full report on what happened is available. Thank you gentlemen.'

Leaving the VVIP lounge the President immediately started for his office half an hour's drive. He could not resist brooding over what had happened through the last few hours.

The matter started this morning when he was asleep in the resort. An F-28 Fokker friendship Dutch manufactured airliner was announcing its departure from Lahore airport for Delhi. Before anybody around could suspect anything, a group of Kashmiri freedom fighters appeared from nowhere onto the tarmac, took the aircraft in their command and blew it upon the runway. They were chanting slogans, 'we want liberation of Kashmir from Indian occupation.'

After hearing from the Information Secretary the President this morning asked him to put this news into the air. He did not discuss this with the *Nabab* but when he was already on his way towards Rawalpindi the latter had issued a statement supporting the stance of the freedom fighters without consulting the President. He considered this act of the *Nabab* as cunning. He also recollected the constant interest which the *Nabab* had started showing since the last elections in the office of the President. In spite of not being the leader of the majority party, he had almost begun to ask 'Mr. President' when shall you vacate this office.?'

///

An Aryan lady, sitting in an ancient and important city across the border, also listened to the news. The word 'listen' contains the word 'silent' also. She belonged to the third party. She had a sharp nose, a slim and tall body and a fair complexion. She was the leader of eight hundred million people. Her country owned the airplane exploded earlier that morning. The civil aviation ministry gave the news to her. She was an exceptionally intelligent person and prone to take decisions calmly and quietly after a prolonged consideration of all factors. But within two minutes of hearing the news this morning, she took a decision. To give it a look of normalcy she showed a calm face and took the ruse of summoning a meeting of her cabinet to let it appear as a decision by consultation and consent.

Wise leaders usually keep wise counsels also. Otherwise they cannot stay in office for long. So each had the same thought and the chair gave assent to the decision taken. Everyone felt a peculiar pleasure in seeing such a decision but none had the simplicity to express that feeling.

The decision got typed and circulated to all the concerned places promptly. The lady in the chair was naturally gifted to see very far away issues. Right at this moment, she felt with a complete certainty that she was seeing a very crucial matter after many many years.

The *Nabab* also heard the news. The 'writer of writers' Rabindranath Tagore of India, many years ago made a poignant remark in one of his short stories. That was 'it is not a young person's job to understand consequences of acts committed by him or her'. In Asian definition crossing 50th birth anniversary is no more considered youth. *Nabab* had crossed that recently still he did not try to realize what was in the offing after he had made his statement. It was willful as he had set out for achieving a target. A realization or understanding would be a hindrance to that path. Rather he was now admonishing his own mind. In any matter of temptation, the presence of sin is inevitable. Something which we have no right to possess or something which we have not earned but are craving to have the same thing any how is called temptation. This aristocrat had got gripped by that attraction. So he put the switch of his radio off but offering prayers cannot stop floods. Likewise the switch off could not stop the news. It proceeded towards its normal drift.

The President also heard the news. The official radio news of the vast neighbouring country broadcast that she had put a ban on the flights of airplanes belonging to the President's country over her skies following the blowing up of her aircraft at Lahore airport. The reason, her own security was at stake due to the blowing up incident. However this embargo would be temporary and they were sorry for the inconvenience thus caused to the aircrafts. This news made the President excited and instantly he thought the government under the Aryan lady was guilty for this. Neither the *Nabab* nor Kashmiri freedom fighters seemed to him to be at all responsible for this. He actually did not realize the real meaning and consequences of the decision. His mind could get only a technical

understanding of its meaning. He immediately sent for the principal staff officer (PSO) and angrily muttered,

—These infidels have been opposing us since 1947 and still they are showing the same vendetta. Piru, have you thought that I will now require more time than before to visit our eastern province. They also need to see me regularly but due to this decision it will be an eight hour journey instead of the normal two hours'. What a devilish act exactly planned at this hour!

Piru was quicker in cunning than his boss. Still he also did not understand the significance of this decision of their neighbour. He feigned a smile and said,

—Sir, I think we should summon their High Commissioner and negotiate this issue.

There was a beam in the President's face. He said, 'this sounds good' and turned to his Information Secretary seated on his right hand side and asked, 'Mr. Sultan, what do you think about this proposal?

Sultan was a contended man. Prior to the division in 1947 he dreamed of just ending his career in the civil service as a district magistrate. This division elevated him to the highest rung of the ladder which was totally unexpected. For this reason or others, he was grateful to his God and carefully learned thoroughly all the nitty-gritty of his profession. Due to those studies he realized that implementation of his boss's preference was perhaps going to be quite difficult. Among these three, he indeed had the deepest understanding of the meaning of the issue. He also understood that there could still be a way out if the *Nabab* had not issued the statement. The Secretary with a smile said, 'Sir I am talking to their High Commissioner'.

Within half an hour Sultan reported that the High Commissioner had left for Delhi for consultation with his government. The President believed it but Sultan did not and realized that this consultation was not going to end soon.

The President had a moody character. He was not poised to follow rules of business. Accordingly this matter required the attention of the Foreign Secretary but alike other important matters of the state, within days, he forgot to do so. At one moment he thought it fit to admonish the *Nabab* but a little later was not sure if it was proper to do so.

//

Three days later, the President was seated in his office. A few newspaper clippings on his table reminded him of the forgotten issue. While part of these clippings praised the *Nabab* for his bravery, a few but important ones termed his statement as 'unwise' and 'undiplomatic'.

Looking at these statements the President tried to understand the meaning. He always had fostered an unfriendly attitude towards the big neighbour since 1947. That was while he was in uniform. Since he became President two years ago he had a feeling that the same attitude, especially direct dissent, was not advisable holding such a position. So at this moment he decided that the *Nabab* had not done the correct thing. Even then he had a feeling that giving a piece of his mind to the *Nabab* was not safe for his own interest as he had heard and seen the mammoth crowds in public meetings addressed by the *Nabab*. After thinking for a while he asked his personal assistant to summon the military secretary. Major General Mashhur Talpur entered.

—Sir?

—What is the situation in the frontiers?

—Latest situation report is fine. All quiet on all fronts Sir

—How about Kashmir?

—No abnormal movement is visible. I have had talks with the chief of Army staff a few minutes ago, Sir!

—Good, you can leave now.

Though a professional soldier he was always scared of wars and battles and that was the reason for his queries about this border situation. The Major General left and the Personal Assistant (P.A) told the President that Adviser Civil Affairs was waiting on the phone line from Dhaka.

—Well, put him through.

—Sir, Right away.

After exchanging pleasantries the adviser asked if the date was still unchanged. The President could not recollect what this was about but said, 'oh, yes'. The adviser hung up saying, 'ok Sir'.

The President replaced the receiver and looked with a vacant eye across the table. He thought to himself, 'what next?' Since he had assumed powers on 25th March two years earlier it had become an established system that nobody could see him without Piru's nod. Piru himself had established this without the knowledge of the President. There was a knock on the door and Piru was on the threshold. The President raised his thick eyebrows and muttered,

—What is this?

—Sir, the *Nabab* is waiting.

The President was annoyed. This man now a days had started forgetting all formalities and niceties of this office. Before the elections this same man used to wait hours together to have an appointment but for the last three months he had been meeting him every now and then without an appointment. No, this is intolerable. He thought 'no, nobody can just barge into my office at his sweet will.' The President did not have any visitors at the moment. Still he thought a message should go to the *Nabab*. He said, 'Piru, ask him to wait'.

—Right Sir.

The President ordered his P.S. to lay the lunch on the table in the anteroom. It was laid and he enjoyed it very leisurely spending about 40 minutes. Then he started puffing a cigarette and sipping black coffee from a large mug. Twenty minutes was spent thus and he realized the fact that the visitor surely had understood the value of time of his benefactor. He had the idiosyncrasy of understanding the importance of certain matters but at inordinate late hours. At this moment such a realization flashed into his mind. He felt with a sudden sense of sorrow that the decision to spend the night at the *Nabab*'s country lodge was not a correct one. Besides, sharing some of his private foibles with the *Nabab* was also not an intelligent act. Possibly that was why he had a feeling of dithering in expressing a firm 'no' to even unreasonable requests and demand of the *Nabab*. An hour's time had elapsed and he pushed the buzzer. The visitor's impulsive nature had already smeared his mind with a deep feeling of insult for this long waiting. However, he still maintained a beam on his pink complexioned face. After the intros the visitor came to business,

—Mr. President, so what tidings do you have about the transfer of power?

—We are proceeding as planned.

—But time is running out.

—What do you mean?

—I mean you have not yet made your position clear.

—You are correct. But both of you shall fix that by sitting inside parliament. Shall not you?

—Well, but can you remember some words I spoke at my country resort?

The President could not remember so after a demur listlessly said, 'yes, I can'.

—Then?

—Even then . . .

The President wished his visitor might repeat those words. The *Nabab* gasped,

—Mr. President, if that is the case then can you see what consequences shall it bring?

—I do see that but even if they don't behave we will see to that. The armed forces will still be in our hands Mr. *Nabab*.

—But what shall happen to me?

—Why? You shall just wait for five years.

—You will stage 'Hamlet' but keep the prince of Denmark off! what will that look like?

—I do not mean that. You will enter the scene only when the drama demands your role. Does not that sound reasonable?

—But Mr. President, remember one thing. They will destroy us and you long before that scene comes in by their brute majority.

—But they have committed to me that they will not do that.

—Don't trust these 'shudros'. If you do, that will be a blunder. They are basically infidels.They were converted into the Islamic faith only recently.

The President wavered. He felt he was no more on a sure ground. Once again he felt that his visitor had a better understanding of the issue and complex issues like those. So he became soft from his earlier stand. He moaned, 'Mr. *Nabab*, then what is the way out? That the leader of the majority party shall become the Prime Minister has been announced by me in public. The whole world knows that. How can I back out from that?'

—But they have been starving for many years. If they get power this time they will try to make good the deprivation in one go.

—Okay! But what is the alternative? You also do not command a position in the assembly that we could work out something else.

—I do not claim any such thing. What I am trying to suggest is this. Mr. President, take more time.

—But how? We have given a schedule and are proceeding accordingly.

—That schedule is given by you so you can also make changes to that.

—What reasons shall I put up?

—Well, you will say that we need more time for further talks to parties and to achieve a consensus. The skeleton of the constitution needs to be fixed so that assembly sessions can be avoided from being unnecessarily long.

The President listened quietly. A person who does not have a thorough understanding of an issue usually remains confused. When he listens to arguments given by other persons they appear to him to be reasonable even if they are contradictory. So the President appreciated the argument of the visitor. He was in a sudden mood of despair and realized that it had not been a proper act to decide such a crucial issue so hurriedly. He should have spent more time on it. So he calmly asked,

—What is your proposal then?

—See, taking over power is not my goal. Rather the welfare of the people is my only motto. So Mr. President, let us cut the bullshit. I suggest you postpone the assembly date. In that statement you also mention that parties will require a little more time to prepare them for this grand finale.

The President liked the vocabulary. There was good stuff in this. He suddenly had a very pleasant feeling. He thought to himself, 'Yes, there is much good in this for myself as well. Because there is a possibility of my position's being prolonged under such an arrangement. Nobody in this country believes the other though this society takes pride in believing. Who knows that I will not be fired from my top-brass position the day after power is handed over to the new government?'

Piru was also sitting next to the *Nabab*. He also did not have much faith or respect for those who were expecting to have power soon. So he felt happy about the proposal. The brooding was over. The President came back to reality and concluded,

—Well, Mr. *Nabab*, I will think over it and let you know that.

It was not an 'I will' but was an already done job. The President had decided. Piru knew that his boss would listen more to the *Nabab* and less to the Bengalee majority leader. Piru also had his own agenda and was nurturing that clandestinely. He was not sure about the alternative path but felt more safe and comfortable with the *Nabab* than with the unknown Bengalee leader. He understood that following the *Nabab* was the only way for him to rise to the highest rung of the armed forces ladder and to stay there safely as in a cocoon. Accordingly he had kept the *Nabab* in a good humour since the latter won the elections in the western provinces of the country. The visitor was an eloquent orator. He could attract people with a blending of truth, falsehood, lies, hoax, entices and promises. Besides the people of his native province Sindh, a large audience of a vast province listens to what he said, with awe. He knew how to pull them to the epicenter. Now the *Nabab* was sure that the prey had bitten the bait. He asked with a smile,

—Mr. President, when shall we hear the statement?

The President was also feeling relieved with the suggestion from the visitor. His voice was crispy. He came on promptly,

—Yes, Mr. *Nabab*, it will be soon. Don't worry. Let the visiting Polish foreign secretary get back home. I will put it on the air right away.

The visitor had much skepticism about the success of today's mission. At this moment it was not there.

—Thank you Mr. President. The nation will note their gratitude in history for this excellent decision. The *Nabab* now looked flamboyant.

The President fully trusted the accolade but Providence did not as the latter is omniscient and so can see the future. World leaders had congratulated the President by saying that he would surely have a prestigious place in history for holding the December, 1970 elections so impeccably. There was a flood of euphoria in the President's mind. He forgot that he had intended to reprimand the visitor for his undiplomatic statement regarding the blowing of the airplane. Instead he now felt that this gentleman was a patriot and had deep love and concern for his country and the citizens.

///

Eleven hundred miles away from Rawalpindi, the winter still had its tentacles on the provincial capital city of Dhaka. A tall, handsome and very fair complexioned gentleman in a white military uniform was sitting in his office chamber. He had been born in the Deccan, a faraway place, now situated in India. Many years ago, as a boy he was calm and quiet, speaking little and looking introvert and inoffensive. In a developed society those are treated as virtues and so appreciated. But his father was anxious for the son for these very traits besides some others.—As a student mediocre, in personality—lacking in manliness and finally, a Moslem in religion. Possibly he would not be able to get into any good profession. The boy found himself disqualified in getting admission to any good degree course after passing out from an intermediate college. The competition was intense and the competitors were all brilliant Hindu classmates. So both the son and the dad were in despair.

It was 1941 and the window of opportunity suddenly opened before them. The young boy saw an advertisement hung on the notice board of the college which read, 'Recruitment shall be made to the posts of midshipmen in the Royal British Indian navy. Intermediate passed males within 20 years of age may apply'. Though placid by nature, since his birth he had a propensity to military matters. As a government official of the provincial government of the Deccan the dad also knew inside stories of such issues. It was this: the British were in dire necessity of having a large number of naval officers from India as Germany must be defeated. So there was a secret memo to the war department which allowed military recruiting boards all over India to relax the entry qualifications on some aspects except the medical fitness of candidates. With such a backdrop the young boy abandoned higher studies and after a year returned home with the insignia of an acting sub-lieutenant on his shoulders.

The boy was happy and the parents felt a sense of relief. They never even imagined such success in the boy's life. The dad was further happy for an additional possibility. The movement for a separate homeland for the Moslems of the sub-continent was then gaining momentum every day. If that could reach the climax the dad visualized the son's uninterrupted success in his future career. Fortunately the boy did not have to see action. He only learned his job thoroughly at Calcutta's Diamond Harbour port under the superintendence of an English Navy Commander. And thence it was never any looking back but only the forward movement of the chariot of victory. When the dreamed homeland really ushered the young officer was already a commander and the father of the new nation picked him up as his A.D.C. He then quickly rose up the ladder and was Rear-Admiral by 1967. The present President in March, two years ago, phoned him to tell that he was chosen as the Governor of this Eastern province at Dhaka. He was immensely happy.

It was now past midday. In this place, known as the Governor's house" since 1947, Lieutenants-Governor of Bengal used to hold office and reside with their families in the back quarters. The Rear-Admiral-cum-Governor was in his mid-fifties. He made his ablution in the washroom and wiped the drops of water from his arms, face and forehead with a fresh towel from the handle and came out on a prayer mat. He was about to start his 'Johor' (midday) prayers when the red telephone placed at his left hand side came to life. The military secretary to the President was on the receiver.

—Hello?

Asked the Governor.

—Sir, *assalamualaikum* (peace be unto you). The President would talk to you.

A moment after, the voice of the head of state and government became audible,

—Admiral Ahsan, how are you doing?

—Sir, I am fine. How are you?

The President did not answer the question. He liked talking without much introduction or exchanging courtesies. He came to the main issue in coarse and direct language. The Admiral was listening with rapt attention. When the caller stopped the Admiral asked,

—Sir, any changed date?

—Nope, I have not yet given a thought to that.

—Have you informed this to the commander eastern command, Sir?

—No. You can do the job.

—So, here what is our duty now?

—Summon the leader and ask him on my behalf so that he does not make this an issue.

—Sir, are you planning to make a radio speech?

—First I will inform you and then do that. The date is still in the future.

The President went off the line. The Governor replaced the receiver and instead of starting prayers sat on the adjacent sofa.

The creator usually does not combine goodness of the heart and sharpness of the intellect in the same creature. Good persons are seldom very intelligent while intelligent fellows are rarely good at heart. The Governor was a good soul. He was not sure if his superiors ever on some occasion thought him to be a very gifted person. Still he had introspection. Sitting in the comfort of his air-conditioned chamber he looked at the series of framed photographs of his predecessors on the wall above his head. There was wistfulness in him and a sudden thought showed up in his somewhat disturbed mind. He thought 'My days here possibly have come to an end'.

He entered the washroom, made his ablution once again and stood on the prayer mat and started praying. But the introspection continued creeping into his pious mind. Memories of his personal appearances here in innumerable schools, colleges and mosques without notice, his excellent speeches in the vernacular and resultant pleasant surprise of the audience started visiting him as a celluloid. That he made an unequivocal announcement of a theft and crime free city also appeared before his eyes. He also started remembering quite forcefully the bell ringing which he had caused by a hammer with his own hands while visiting a high school in this city. He soon realized that these fond sounds and sights so long embedded in his mind were now causing errors in the prayer.

He somehow finished the prayer. Mrs. Ahsan did not have much interest in these matters. So he did not usually talk about business to her. The admiral went inside, had a quiet lunch and looked at the table clock. Time was short. His wife was out to a meeting of the APWA (All Pakistan Women's Association) at Damal court in the Dhaka Cantonment. He picked up the telephone receiver from his bedroom and dialed the number of Commander, Eastern Command (CEC). The CEC was offering his prayers in his military 'khaki'. Finishing the offering he silently picked the receiver up and listened to what the caller told him about the responsibility given to each of them by the President. Then with a cool voice asked, 'Where and when would you like to do that?'

—The venue would be mine and we may fix the time later on.

—Good, then let the two of us talk first and then tell the President, right?

The Admiral knew that the Commander was better gifted than him. He agreed and said, 'In that case Sir, can you come down to my residence this afternoon?'

—I will be there.

The CEC hung up. Usually his lunch was Spartan. A few pieces of 'chapati', lentils and vegetables cooked at the army officers' mess appeared on the menu. But at that moment he felt distaste even for those items spread before him on a table. He pushed the ring-bell and asked the subaltern to take the tray away. Actually he was feeling bad about the news received a few minutes ago from the Admiral. He felt even worse with the thought that the news was not given to him by the President himself. In the bureaucratic hierarchy of the province he was not the governor but in military rank was senior to Ahsan. He once again realized at that moment that the President did not like him much.

He came back to the couch and started brooding about the news and its consequences. That brooding had been his habit for many years. Though a scion of the royal gentry of the *Nabab* of Rampur from the Central provinces, Yaqub had developed a penchant for studies. And the quality and span of these studies were better than those of many university professors of the west. As a young major in the Royal Indian Armour corps, he attracted the attention of Lord Admiral Mountbatten, viceroy and the last British Governor General of India. He hand-picked the Major to be the chief of his body guards and also advised him to continue his liking for books.

His office was three miles away from the Governor's and had a different responsibility. But Yaqub had the same thought as the Governor. He said to him, 'Possibly I am going to be transferred from this assignment.'

He also felt that he had started liking the place and responsibility soon after his posting there two years ago. There was a sudden philosophical

insight in his mind that 'something good can't be held long in one's life. It must ebb away quickly.'

At 3 'o clock in the afternoon the two met at *Ahsan's lodge*. Yaqub in his favourite Urdu dialect asked the Governor,

—Tell me, what is going on in your mind?

—Sir, I am confused but must say that I did not like the news from the first moment I heard it.

Yaqub knew the Admiral for many years. That naval officer seated across him was naïve and sensitive. Yaqub knew that thoroughly. He also knew that simple minded and good natured people like Ahsan became easily anxious about a crisis in life but didn't know how to come out of the same. Yaqub was also honest but intelligent. Nothing could easily sway him from the correct path. He closed his hero-like beautiful eyes and thought for a few minutes and then opened his mouth,

—I am trying to figure out who might have done this? I do not think that Piru can do this. What do you think Ahsan?

Actually Yaqub was trying to understand the Admiral's mind so that they could reach a common platform and then talk together to the President. Besides, it was a civilian affair and Ahsan had the authority to handle that. So convergence of opinion was necessary.

—Sir, I am not sure but I think the *Nabab* has a hand in this. Because the BBC broadcast last night that the *Nabab* had met the President yesterday in the afternoon.

Commander Yaqub said nothing but was happy inside. He also had a feeling at the same time that his estimate about the intelligence of the Admiral was not fully correct. After a few seconds he murmured, 'I tend to agree with you but what can we do now?'

—I propose, let us approach the President and tell him that it would not be advisable to give this decision of postponement to the leader here without announcing a revised date. Actually such a step would be quite risky.

—Excellent. I appreciate your concern.

—Sir, I have been to each of the 16 districts of this province. I have mingled with the local people and talked to them. So I know what

reaction this announcement is going to result from them. They are actually not expecting this.

—Then let us talk to him.

—But before he listens he will ask if we have complied with his instruction of informing the leader and will surely rebuke us for not doing that.

Commander Yaqub had also thought about it. Still he said,

—But the President and Piru are not here and we are on ground. Why shall he not listen to our argument? Let him do whatever he wishes to. Can those people sitting so far away guess what the situation is going to be here if we break the news without any alternative proposal?

Both discussed the situation at length and at large and imagined the possible consequences. Yaqub said,

—You see, we are not going to be the President of this country. So we have got nothing to lose. We have received everything in our life that we deserved. Now this is our duty to speak the truth. As a maximum we may have to lose our job. So let us tell the President what the truth is.

Ahsan agreed to the strategy. It was 4 o'clock in the afternoon. The P.A. was asked to make the telephone connection to Rawalpindi. It was received by General Piru. Yaqub asked, 'Is the President in his office?'

Piru avoided a direct answer and said, 'you have to wait for some time'.

After a long two minute's waiting the President came to the line,

—Commander, what is the matter?

—Sir, the governor has told me about your message.

—It was an instruction, not a message, Commander.

—Yes Sir, it was.

—I made him responsible for giving that to the appropriate place. Has it been carried out?

—No Sir, not yet. I had a few words to talk about in this matter.

Avoiding the comment, the President said,

—Where are you speaking from and where is the governor?

—Sir, I am calling from Ahsan's office and he is sitting beside me.

—So what is your point?

—Sir, I think the postponement is not advisable to be made unless it accompanies a new date also.

—What? Are you trying to teach me what is proper and improper! General, mind that I am not only the President of this country but also the supreme commander of the armed forces.

—Sir, I am not of course trying to teach you anything. Still I must say that you hold your office there but I have been doing my job down here for the last two years. So there is perhaps a gap . . . we are the people who have been watching and hearing all the changes and developments taking place here on the ground . . .

The President interrupted and roared,

—What do you mean by 'we'? Is Ahsan also with you in this?

—Sir we have the same view.

—Commander, listen, and listen well. This is not a trade union but a military establishment. You can't talk like that. Are you aware that I can sack both of you on charges of insubordination right at this moment?

—Sir, you can do that but before that happens I will resign my commission. You will not appreciate the situation while I have to tackle the same—it is indeed difficult to serve under such a situation. Sir, possibly I could not make my point and the situation going on here understandable to you . . .

True to his nature by then the President's temper had calmed down a little and so he realized that replacement right at the moment might be a bad thing to do. Accepting resignation'? He thought to himself— resignation would be insulting. The better option would be dismissal. On the other hand the governor was softer. If Yaqub was dismissed Ahsan would not be able to cope up with the situation. So he decided to buy time and accordingly said with a condescending and sympathetic voice,

—OK, should a deputy chief martial law administrator think emotionally? You have never been this hot. Now give the line to the Admiral.

Ahsan spoke to the President in a different tone but with the same content. He had by nature a conflict-avoiding bent of mind and did not like putting up arguments before superiors. So the President did not take

any offense at him though he had decided about him also. He gave them consolation by saying,

—Well, Ahsan, I do realize your concerns. At the same time I know the leader. He is a man of highest reasonableness. Please tell him about me. I will invite him for consultation. The new date shall certainly be negotiated then. I am sure you will see that he will not disagree.

Had Yaqub been the listener, he would have continued his argument against but Ahsan did not do that. He heard the President's line went off. Yaqub asked, 'so what happened finally?'

Ahsan told him what the President had said.

Both of these persons were talking with piety. As kids they had seen that at work in their families. Parents taught them that one thing, 'Tell the truth, be kind, never tell a lie, be conscientious and upright. Remember you will be punished by God on doomsday if you do otherwise'. And they believed in and practiced these values even after getting to a very high office of state. In a developed society that role is taken by culture, but in a medieval Indian conservative Moslem family it was religion which had taken that role of making those two people 'good'. However the same had failed in millions of other families. On the whole Yaqub and Ahsan grew into very good fellows.

Yaqub visualized an imaginary scene. A driver had hurt a pedestrian by his vehicle and then speeded away thinking nobody or no policeman in the street had watched it and so nothing would happen. Then in order to get away from the spot hastily, he accelerated the speed of his vehicle and in the excitement he got less careful and hit another passerby frontally. If he had stopped after the first incident it would be easy for him to settle the matter right there and the second incident would not occur because he would have a cool head. Yaqub could not understand why such a scenario appeared in his mind. He still looked pensive. The governor asked him,

—Sir, what are you thinking about?

Yaqub came back to reality and replied,

I am wondering what is in the offing. I guess days of tension will increase instead of getting low.

Meanwhile afternoon had set in. There were no more words between the two and both stood on the prayer mat for the afternoon prayers.

On the other hand at Rawalpindi the President sent for his PSO and told,

—This guy Yaqub used to make speeches against the two-nation theory while he was just a cadet at the Dehradun Indian Military Academy. The British Instructors used to say nothing against him because they secretly supported such ideas. The man, now, is trying to teach me the same thing. But this is neither India nor British Raj. I will not tolerate any such nonsense here.

///

It was the afternoon of 27th February at Dhaka. A white Datsun saloon car softly pulled off at the kerb down the veranda of the Governor house. Before that, guards speaking vernacular had allowed this car through the security gates and were wondering if a salute was necessary to be discharged to the rider. There was no such instruction from the guard commander, so they watched the rider seated inside. They knew who he was and there was deference in their faces.

The chauffeur opened the left back door of the car and held it for the rider to get down. He stepped down on the cobbled path and there was a majestic aura in his gait. He was wearing a white cotton pyjama and 'punjabi'. He had a big body but was not obese. He had a thick helmet of hair on his manly head and his eyes showed affection and love. There was a strong personality exuding out of him but there was no cool pride there. He was holding a black tobacco pipe in his right hand between his right and the middle finger.

The Admiral came down the fringe of the red-carpet covered stairs and received this visitor. Yaqub stood just behind the Admiral. He never received any body except the President of this country from so close. The protocol also did not demand that. Still for some unavoidable attraction he did that and had done the same with this visitor before. Their languages were different. They were not related and their familiarity was only two years' old.

Man craves for creating history. Providence either approves it or does not. The name of this tall personality was Mujib. In the stage of this crucial time of history being made he was the protagonist. He was also the principal figure of the first party. Legally the most popular in the whole country. On account of love, the most liked person of this province. With that thought in mind the two war-leaders escorted the very special person inside the house. Outside, the weather was excellent. There was a cool wind while the sky above was blue with no signs of clouds. Summer had not arrived yet.

The hosts and the guest spent a few minutes talking about these. The hosts also eagerly made enquiries about the welfare of the family members of the very special guest. That he had to take his dinner had already been politely and formally told by the Admiral earlier.

That tall person was fully aware that the present invitation was not for the pleasure of enjoying food and drinks here. He waited. As the guest he could not initiate the discussions. The hosts stopped the pleasantries, took a formal posture on the sofa with their fingers crossed. The informal air was gone from the room.

The admiral opened his mouth, Can we talk in private?

The tall guest understood the hour had arrived. He made a sign to his private secretary to leave the room. The p.s. of the governor immediately escorted him to an outside chamber.

The room was now closed. The governor said' the President is going to postpone the assembly session scheduled to be held on the 3rd of March. Actually this is why we have sought your presence here today.'

There was no change in the face of Mujib even after hearing the words. Just as a big ocean-going vessel is not influenced when mighty waves pound on it and the vessel continues on its course Mujib wore the same look. When the two had finished he took the thick black coloured framed pair of spectacles and the tobacco pipe from his hand and put them on the center table before him.

Instead of his natural sonorous voice he quietly said,

—I am afraid the matter might get out of my control. However if the President mentions a changed date along with the announcement of the postponement then I suppose there will be no problem. You see, here people have been eagerly waiting for the session. So if they don't hear about a new date they could get annoyed and even angry.

—Still we believe you and only you will be able to handle it. As you know the President will be going to discuss with you.

—The public is not going to know that while the postponement will be made. Accordingly I think whatever harm shall have taken place immediately after the announcement. If there is not an alternative date simultaneously the situation can be different.

—Please believe us. This is the order of the President. Both of us have tried to convince him about your point, but we were not successful.

—I am happy that you tried. I wish the President will reconsider his decision. Thank you gentlemen.

The talks ended there. Meanwhile developing the dusk outside, the night had proceeded far.

///

In any society there are school-going boys who come across abandoned toy-like things on a playground or inside a bush. Some of them out of curiosity touch and open the same without realizing that these could be a camouflaged grenade or something like that and could have the potentials to killing them. But playing with such things is not becoming of adults. Even then we can see some adults around who are strongly poised to play such games.

Yaqub watched the reaction of the President's radio announcement about postponement on 1st March and, thought, 'so there are these adults who are once again playing games'.

The whole of Dhaka city exploded into unimaginable anger. Gradually news started coming in from all corners of the province which were in the same vein. There were no possible precautionary measures against such a reaction from the administration's side. So in many places government properties got vandalized by spontaneous crowds. Yakub served there for long two years and had the experience of talking to all leaders of that society. Even he had not imagined that the situation would deteriorate to such an extent.

Prior to the postponement, the public demand was for holding the assembly session. Thereafter the demand came to one thing, 'hand over power, no more need for sessions'. The police as usual came forward to curb disturbances but soon got scared and stepped back seeing the deadly reaction and determination of the demonstrators. They realized it was as vain as resisting a tidal bore by building sand blocks. The tall protagonist summoned an emergency meeting of his party at hotel Eden. It was short and decisive. He came out of it and addressed the crowd gathered around,

'Please resist from any unruly activities. Talks are going on with authorities. Until then, please be patient. You are the ones who made me to this, so you believed in me. Now listen to me and trust me.'

The effect of the short address was instantaneous. Just as the arid scorched fields of Bengal summer become moist and green with the first showers of the Monsoon, so was the transformation of the excited crowd like. Without the slightest noise they listened to him and dispersed for home. Both the admiral and Lt. General immediately phoned him expressing their gratitude and thanks for controlling the situation with such skill. Then they called Rawalpindi and talked to the President who asked,

—So chaps, what is your thinking now?

—Please fix a new date and put it on the air. Otherwise things may get worse.

—For example? How worse?

—Masses got hysteric here. They have been chanting slogans which are not very appreciable but the leader is somehow keeping them under control, Sir.

The President got impulsive and so groaned, 'What non-sense! What are you and your forces doing then?'

—Sir, the time is not especially suitable for using forces. You are not aware of the circumstances we are facing here. Actually your presence here will be required very soon.

The President was mum for a few seconds and then said,

—Well, I will come back to you later on.

The line went dead. Then he phoned the *Nabab* and the Chief of Army Staff to tell them that they should be in his office next morning. The meeting lasted only half an hour just between three of them. Usually a lousy fellow, the President suddenly became very active and told the two men before him many things about Yaqub and Ahsan. In an aside to himself he sarcastically said, 'each of those two is as impotent as the other. They will be able to do nothing. I now realize that it was my mistake choosing them for East Pakistan in 1969. The present situation is the creation of these two fellows.'

He dismissed the *Nabab* and Chief of Staff for the day and made a number of phone calls to various places.

//

An hour ago in a dormitory of the Dhaka University a strongly built student union leader was looking very nervous. Usually he had been a dare-devil. At that moment almost all the adjacent rooms were deserted. For an unknown fear students had fled to their village homes. The reason for the nervousness of this leader was that he was doing something very especially anti-state. He along with his compatriots was almost finished drawing, designing and tailoring a tri-coloured piece of cloth into a standard bearer. This was their dreamed flag for an independent motherland. They were not caring about the police or government spies who were already moving under direction of Mujib. After completing their self designed flag they saluted it, took an oath to protect its prestige. Then they folded it into a leather-made attaché case and hid it in an almirah of the room. It was post noon. They came down from the building, took a scooter and moved towards road no. 32, Dhanmondi, a posh area of the city. After a few minutes waiting they were shown in to the expected chamber. The uncrowned emperor of Bengal, Mujib, welcomed them. They told what they had done and requested the grantor of the visit to allow them to hoist it here in his residence and then replicate it to all important places. The visitor listened with patience and then affectionately said 'I admire you but we need restraint also. Let us wait. I will keep this in mind. Wait for my party's instruction.'

His influence was unquestionable. Though a little disappointed the three young men committed they would obey his advice.

At the top north of the eastern province, Asad, a student of journalism was preparing for attending his class at Rajshahi University. He was coming out from his room no. 111 of the students' dormitory to proceed towards the class room in the Arts faculty building 300 yards away. It was five minutes to 12 noon. Asad had passed his honours examination the previous September.

At that moment he heard a stream of slogans, 'Heroic Bengalees, take up arms.' He looked through the window and watched a huge procession in progress chanting that slogan repeatedly.

—What is the matter? He asked himself. There was nobody around the floor of the dormitory. There were no radios or transistor also to listen to any news. Asad came downstairs and learnt the cause of the slogan from a passer-by. He felt ashamed. He felt, as a student of journalism, he should have learnt that much before anybody. Asad's parents and only sister were at their house at Mohakhali in Dhaka. His father was an official at the government security printing press at Joydevpur near the garrison town of Gazipur.

Asad came back to his room; put his books and note-books down on the reading table. Opening a drawer of his cupboard he drew out a camera and rushed to the spot of the procession which was now nearing the Registrar's office of the university. He took a few snapshots of the scene from various angles and then went to classmate Wazed Ali's room to listen to the news on a radio there.

///

It was the following noon in Dhaka. The Governor had just finished his prayers. At Sheer-E-Bangla Nagar, Yaqub was thinking of going to the provincial secretariat to see the Chief Secretary for a piece of official business.

The ADC to the Governor was waiting behind the prayer mat. Ahsan looked at him.

—Zakir, is there anything?

—Sir, an emergency signal message.

The admiral looked at the short message and spent five seconds. The Governor's shock absorber was never very strong. His reaction to the message became visible on his facial expression ignoring the fact that the ADC was very junior to him in rank, age and was a Bengalee.The laconic signal informed that the Governor had been removed from his post. It also instructed him to hand over charge to the new incumbent the day after. It further said that Yaqub was also no more in his post and both positions would henceforth be assumed by the new incumbent Lt. General Tikka Khan, commander 3rd corps of the country's army.

The Governor was asked to report to headquarters at Rawalpindi but there was no such instruction for Yaqub. The Admiral was puzzled and could not gather which direction things were moving to. There was a feeling of humiliation in his mind also with the thought that the Chief of the country had decided that without any consultation with him. Strange! At Sher-E-Bangla Nagar the same feeling caught Yaqub. The speeding away vehicle once again visited Yaqub's mind. He saw the same driver had now overrun two passers-by and was ransacking shopping malls and houses while trying to flee away in a hurry with the speeding vehicle. He also thought what was looming ahead? What those symptoms presaged?

All their kids were studying abroad. So the Admiral and his wife had not many household items to be packed. Still valets and Mrs. Ahsan started putting necessary items into a few hand-bags and leather suitcases. The short afternoon had fallen outside on the green velvety gardens of the Governor house. The ADC came in to deliver a message. He saluted and said, 'Sir we are going to close our business for today. There are no appointments for anybody pending today. Still a lot of visitors without having any appointments are waiting outside and insisting to see you. What shall I do Sir?'

—No matter. Have them seated in the waiting room and then let them come in one by one. Also give orders for tea.

The first gentleman who entered the Governor's chamber was an elderly fellow. The Governor welcomed him asking 'how are you doing?'

—Fine, Sir. Do you recognize me?

—Of course, I do. Are you not the Professor of Bangla in a Govt. College?

The gentleman was extremely pleased but in a doleful tone said, 'Sir is the news true? What are we hearing? we feel orphaned.'

—Don't worry though what you have heard is correct. I believe, by the grace of Allah the merciful, everything will be fine.

Another teacher was the next visitor who gratefully recollected the Governor's donation of five thousand rupees for the development of his institute at Mirpur. The gentleman was almost in tears. Ahsan gave him consolation with some soft and kind words. Another visitor mentioned that his madrasah had been benefited by a tube-well sanctioned by the governor and that students were praying for him.

One after another beneficiaries filed into the Governor's office and thanked him for many sweet incidents. Those included Ahsan's congratulatory message for a boy's obtaining a scholarship or for doing well in an examination or his intervention in reoccupying a plot of land from an illegal intruder. A young man who headed a club expressed his gratitude that his benefactor had given four bundles of tin for the construction of a garage for the club.

The aged among the visitors had queries in their minds about the sudden transfer of the Governor, but then did not think it was decent to raise the same. They realized that they never dared see a bureaucrat even much junior to this Governor in their life. It was possible only for the reason that this gentleman had established the image of a simple, honest and compassionate figure in the province. They recollected that this most powerful man in the province had led a totally transparent and pious life. His visits to lowly places without notice, his offering of prayers in the secretariat mosque without any formality were unforgettable. A Principal of a degree college remembered that this non Bengalee man had mingled with all classes of people and in his own institute surprised all teachers and students by speaking in correct Bangla.

During the last month of fasting he had paid incognito visits to slums to see their life which later on came to light through journalists. He also ensured that the maximum budget was spent during his two year tenure which was highest for the last decade. None of the visitors today came here for seeking any favours from the Admiral. They were here to thank him and to express their concern for his well-being. On behalf of the assembled an elderly gentleman rose up. Many years ago he was a professor of accounting in Commerce College, Karachi, in the western province of the country. He was now the treasurer of a university. He wished the Admiral well and said, 'We were all very well with your administration. But now we have started worrying for the future.'

In response the temperate admiral succinctly said, 'Allah will take care of you. Let me express my gratitude to you for your cooperation while I was here'.

He shook hands with everyone and they went out one by one, many with tears in their eyes. Ahsan entered his lodge and started roaming through every room. His wife was moving along with him. Then they came out to the balcony and the lawn and finally the kitchen at the further end. Tikatooly area of the city became visible from that end. Ahsan remembered that they had enjoyed a Bangla movie in the newly built 'Avisar' cinema hall in that area.

Ahsan could not sleep throughout the night. The following day he went to the airport to receive the newly appointed Governor at noon. At five thirty in the afternoon the same day he once again started for the airport to catch the flight for Karachi. He looked both ways of the motorway and memories of visiting Tejgaon polytechnic school and Intermediate Technical College came strongly into his mind. He also identified the house of a former provincial minister situated on the roadside near Farmgate where he had dined on an invitation.

The luggage was put on the conveyor belt and Vice-Admiral Ahsan climbed aboard the flight and fastened the seat-belt. His wife sat beside him. The VIP flight started gaining heights through the blue skies of Dhaka city. Ahsan looked down through the window and had an intuition that there would be no coming back to this place any more. Many years ago as a young lieutenant-commander, seating behind the car of the father of the nation, he had a similar feeling. He never had had the opportunity of going back to Aurangabad though he secretly wished for the same. Indeed he had seen that good days or feelings do not repeat themselves in one's life.

///

The name of the village was Ishakhel. It was forty miles away from the sub-divisional town of Khanewal in the Punjab district of Peer Mainuddin. There were adjacent villages with similar names which took their names after the preachers of Islam who started arriving in the area in 11th century AD. They were called 'pirs', an Arabic synonym of 'mullahs'. In the centre of this village Zahanjeb Abrar's mud walled home had taken on a distinguished look and air for the last few days. A grand occasion was going to take place in this home.The familiar sights and sounds of a marriage ceremony in and outside the home were being watched and appreciated by the villagers. Zahanjeb's only daughter Lubasha Khan was going to be given in marriage on the day after tomorrow. The traditional Punjabee 'vangra' dance was being performed on the yard with colourful turbaned and loin-cloth worn professional dancers hired in from the sub-divisional town.

The groom, Amama Talal Khan was a technician at the World Bank constructed Mongla-Dam irrigation project. The groom's family hailed from the neighbouring village Toback Singh Adom. The heat was scorching in spite of the time being afternoon. Lubasha's friends attired with shimmering heavy brocade and 'Gultex' shuttin clothings were smiling around in spite of the heat because that was the most important occasion of a very dear person of theirs.

In the Eastern province there was no electricity even in many police stations. That was a tahsil which is a lower administrative unit. Still it had electricity connection which many people believed was being produced at the cost of Bengalees' wealth. So the high pitch vocal music of Mehedi Hassan and Noor Jehan were audible from a tape-recorder in the home. Those two were the favourite vocalists especially in the western wing of the country. 'Kawals' (religious singers) were scheduled to arrive for their performance. With all those and a big canopy fastened above, the whole yard of the home made the scene absolutely cheerful and festive. Tonight's guests were arriving in. In a separate surrounding, a little away from this covered place, a lot of culinary activities were going on. Blazing woods, frying pans, aroma of roasted spicy meat and onion were the elements of the scene. Zahanjeb accompanied by his wife Mobasshera was monitoring the activities of the cooks. Guests would be served from this place. The couple looked satisfied.

There was still about an hour to go before evening. A strongly built fellow quietly approached outside and asked to see the owner of the home. Zahanjeb came out. The man introduced himself as the messenger of the local tahsil, made an obeisance to Zahanjeb and held out a message from his hand. Zahanjeb looked at it which read, 'Your leave of absence has been cancelled. You are instructed to join your unit at Balakot by 1700 hours tomorrow. Signed/—Lt. Col. Ahmad Imtiaz Khan Warsi, 11th Anti-Aircraft Unit, Pakistan Army'.

Abrar, *resaldar* gunner of the unit,folded the piece of paper and signed the acknowledgement memo from the messenger.The spontaneous query which came out of the message recipient's mouth for the bearer was:

—But what shall happen to my daughter's marriage ceremony?

The bearer from the same village was surprised and sympathetically said,

—Sardar sahab, I am a petty messenger, how can I answer such a grave question?

He then came inside.

Asian women always worry about their family members. A married one worries about her spouse while an unmarried one worries about her brothers and father. Mobassherra was watching the proceedings from inside and even with her totally simple mind was sure that this messenger did not bring any cheerful news and further it was nothing to do with the gorgeous function that the family was celebrating. Seeing wrinkles of thoughts on her husband's usually brave face she asked what the message was about—Mobasherra easily read the Urdu message.She had seen such incidents before. There was no remedy to that and time was short. Plus the destination was 110 miles away. If the first train was missed somehow, her husband's trial in a court martial was inevitable. So the woman arranged the necessary things for her husband into a hold-all.

Zahanjeb had not wept for many years. The last such occasion was his father's death. This afternoon the professional soldier felt tears gushing out of his eyes. He summoned his younger brother into his bedroom, explained the situation and handed over the charge of the ceremony to him. Putting the hold-all on his strong shoulders, Zahanjeb looked at his infant grand-daughter by his son. The little baby was sleeping on an oil-cloth with a nipple in her mouth. He had planned to wear a new turban on his head during the nuptials. It was dangling on an iron hook astride the bed-stead. Wistfully he threw a glance to it and then came out of his home to catch a horse-cart to the rail station.

Subeder Hikmat Nassor Abdullah of Nawabshah was enjoying a fortnight's leave. Only five days had elapsed. The couple was going to have their first baby. His wife was managing well with her health. Still Nassor had carried his wife to a gynecologist in the nearest cantonment. The doctor had given her a clean certificate of health. In this Sindh district the heat was almost intolerable. Abdullah was reposing on a rope made 'Khatia'(indigenous bed-stead) on the yard to have some air. His mother was taking care of the pregnant daughter-in-law and sewing clothing for the expected baby in an inside room. A message came in to tell Abdullah had to report for duty at Malir Cantonment, 200 miles away. Abdullah became enraged. He thought 'what the heck is this! There is no war like situation in the country and I am a lowly soldier. Why is this summons? Surely this is a devilry of commander Shammon kanwar who made me suffer earlier also. This is sheer Punjabee cunning. I once again realize why dad advised against my joining the army. Sindhis cannot expect to fare well in Punjabee dominated armed forces.'

Likewise in many places at their private homes Major Gul Mohammad of 24th Fd.Regt. Artillery, Lt. Col. Ilahi Dad of 7th paratrooper Brigade. Rear-gunner Gulbadan Vatti of PNS Bokhtiar Khilji and Ft. Sergeant Golondaz Talpoor of 3rd Frontier Squadron received similar instructions. The formidable military police, signals and civil police ensured the receipt of these instructions at all addresses without a single deviation.

Jafrin Khan's, a J.C.O., father was in his death-bed at his Okara home. So Jafrin had taken leave from his garrison in East Pakistan.

Nayeb Subeder Yar Md. Khan went to Mithankot to arrange a wheat field with the farm cultivators. *Subeder* Niaz Naek of Dera Bugti was at his home for his son's nuptials.

Captain Monabbir Hossain Molla of Boramchal was posted at the 4th Punjab at Horoppa Cantonment in the Punjab. Here it was his own grandest occasion of life. So he had taken a furlough of 15 days. The traditional 'turmeric festival' of the bride had taken place yesterday while the groom's was scheduled this evening. But before that, a local police official appeared to inform him of the recall. Monabbir reacted by uttering a few dishonourable words aimed at his commanding officer.

Many of those had received similar orders prior to the 1965 Indo-Pak war. The situation of the country was difficult on that occasion. The whole country knew that enemies had made an attack on their homeland. Even reservists were happy to report to their units. Nobody showed any signs of annoyance. But the present situation was quiet and there was not the slightest sign of disturbances anywhere. Still why this en-masse cancellation of leave? No body found any answer to the queries raised in their minds. However following their professional edicts, no body uttered any of these questions.

In the northern Rangpur Cantonment district, second in command Major Iftekhar Chowdhury of 2nd special commando battalion had taken leave for 15 days for performing the pilgrimage to Mecca. His home was at Jampur, in the southern Punjab. The Pak mission in Jeddah started tracking him for a similar cause—cancellation of leave. But Iftekhar was already off to his home and taking rest there. On 3rd March, he was reading the 'Morning News' sitting on a couch at his ancestral home town. A plainclothed man showed up to tell him that he had to join his East Pakistan command post within 24 hours. Iftekhar caught the next flight to Dhaka that afternoon and reached his unit the morning after. He met the commanding officer of the battalion and casually asked him, 'Sir, only five days were left of my vacation. Why this emergency call?'

No sooner had he finished his query then the C.O Lt. Col. Humayun Warda pulled out his revolver from the waistband, pulled the trigger targeting Iftekhar's left foot. Iftekhar was astonished but since then had to take rest in the local combined military hospital's surgical unit with a bandage in his foot. The C.O's angry question, 'Officer, are you in command of your senses?' was still ringing in his ears.

Further down at Faridpur district in a remote village, *Habilder* Monser Fokir was vacationing. It was a pleasant noon in the last month of the Bengali year. Monser was working on a piece of handicraft made of smooth bamboo and cane weeds along with his paternal uncle Gatai Fakir. They were half-way through their labour. The village warden entered their home to tell him that he must report for duty to East Bengal regimental center by the next afternoon at Chittagong without fail.

The newly appointed Governor watched the situation for three days and then phoned the President.

—Sir, I think your presence here is required.

—Well. Since Mujib will not be in my place I have to be in his. Tell him I will be at Dhaka on the 17th of March. Until then I expect him to remain patient. Understood?

—Right away, Sir.

The Governor and the President had known one another well for the last four decades since the British rulers of India recruited them to the Punjab regiment. So they knew their respective wave lengths. Both loved talking little. The conversation did not last long. Earlier the provincial Chief Justice at Dhaka had refused to administer the oath of office to the Governor. Lt. Gen. Tikka was licking this wound every moment. So legally he was acting not as the Governor but as the Deputy Chief Martial Law Administrator. And the President meanwhile had dismissed all civilian members of his cabinet. He was proceeding as the Chief Martial Law Administrator of the country.

///

Colonel Amery was holding office at the Punjab regimental headquarters at Wah cantonment. He was looking for special persons. He had earned a name for head-hunting in this dreaded establishment of the communal state. He set aside a number of personnel files and threw them on the floor. The orderly was taking them back to the sections where they came from. It was his ninth attempt and he looked happy. 'I have seen this photograph and the man holding it. This is the fellow I am looking for'—Colonel Ameri moaned to himself as a soliloquy. He turned the file cover over and looked inside. He started reading the information inside.

Name: P.A. no. 1552 Mohamed Yaqub Malikee

Father: Banjaran Malikee. D.O.B: 1.2.1930.

Place of Birth: Hoshiarpur, East Punjab, India.

Height: 6 ft.

Colour of eyes: Gray.

Complexion: Fair.

Rank: Lieutenant-Colonel.

Corps: Artillery.

Incessant suspicion is the foundation of security in this profession. So Col. Amery, to be absolutely sure asked the telephone operator to put him through to this officer. The telecommunication system of this country was worse than primitive. High civilian officers had to wait for hours to contact persons in other government offices. But the military lines are very efficient as they are unimaginably expensive. So within two minutes the operator said

—Sir, Lt. Col. Malikee is holding the line for you.

Ameri asked, 'Malikee, where are you now?'
—Sir, at Kohat.
—Okay meet me at 4 'o clock this afternoon.
—O.K. Sir, I will.

The road and rail communication of this country were also very poor. Passengers had to sleep overnight on platforms to catch a train and even then might not be successful. But the military had special communication lines. Kohat was 140 miles towards the North-West Frontier Province. So it was five minutes to four when Yaqub Malikee with an impeccable uniform and glittering shoes reported to Col. Amery. A subaltern announced the officer's presence.

Ameri let him in and asked
—Where had you been in 1959?
—Sir, I was with the combing operation in Waziristan.

During 1959 there was a bloody event in the area. Only the best were chosen for that.

—Well, now tell me if you are conversant with Bangla language?
—Sir, I am fluent in it.
—How come?
—Sir, I had served twice in East Pakistan. Once at Jessore and once at Syedpur cantonments.

—Excellent. Now listen carefully. The infidels and their stooges in East Pakistan are in a deep conspiracy to secede the province from the center. Their aim is to destroy Islam and Moslems. You have been transferred there as the C.O. of 49th Bengal under 4th brigade. Any questions?

—Sir, what shall be my mission there?
—You will have the authority to 'size' anyone you suspect to be a part of the conspiracy. Anything else?

—No Sir.
—Good luck Yaqub. You are dismissed.

Yaqub stiffened his shoulders to attention and went out of the room. Lt Col. Yaqub had mastered a virtue. He could let feelings of pleasures appear as sorrow and vice versa on his face. At this moment he looked pale.

///

By March 6th all recalled men and officers had completed their reporting to units. Their briefings were over. Ships and airplanes carrying them were heading for East Pakistan. No writ of the provincial or of the central government was visible at Dhaka and other places in the province. Citizens had been carrying words of an invisible authority as law. The DCMLA and his aides were pretending not to see this. The reason: the President was coming. Thus the seventh of March had arrived.

The winds of the last month of the Bengali year always lead people to poesy. That day there was no change to that. High above, a totally cloudless blue sky looked like a beautiful canopy. The dazzling sunshine was still temperate. The populace of the whole province had been waiting for this day for the last seven days at the word of a single man. The tall, handsome and healthy Mujib with his traditional white cotton trouser and *punjabi* was expected any moment. He would give directions. The whole racecourse had become an impervious human-sea. The clock stuck three o'clock in the afternoon. Mujib climbed up the podium within seconds and the cacophony of the audience stopped to a total silence.

His inimitable thunderous voice became audible through the microphone,

'My brothers,

I have come before you today with a heavy heart. All of you know how hard we have tried. But it is a matter of sadness that the streets of Dhaka, Chittagong, Khulna, Rangpur and Rajshahi are today being spattered with the blood of my brothers, and the cry we hear from the Bengalee people is a cry for freedom, a cry for survival, a cry for our rights. You are the ones who brought about an Awami League victory so that you could see a constitutional government restored. The hope was that the elected representatives of the people, sitting in the National Assembly, would formulate a constitution that would assure that people of their economic, political and cultural emancipation. But now, with great sadness in my heart, I look back on the past 23 years of our history and see nothing but a history of shedding the blood of the Bengalee people. Ours has been a history of continual lamentation, repeated bloodshed and innocent tears. We gave blood in 1952; we won a mandate in 1954. But we were still not allowed to take up the reins of this country. In 1958, Ayub Khan clamped Martial Law on our people and enslaved us for the next 10 years. In 1966, during the Six-Point Movement of the masses, many were the young men and women whose lives were stilled by government bullets. After the downfall of Ayub, Mr. Yahya Khan took over with the promise that he would restore constitutional rule, that he would restore democracy and return power to the people. We agreed. But you all know of the events that took place after that. I ask you, are we the ones to blame? As you know, I have been in contact with President Yahya Khan. As leader of the majority party in the National Assembly, I asked him to set February 15 as the day for its opening session. He did not accede to the request I made as leader of the majority party. Instead, he went along with the delay requested by the minority leader and announced that the Assembly would be convened on the 3rd of March . . . But suddenly, on March 1, the session was cancelled . . . Since we have given blood, we will give more of it. But, Insha'Allah, we will free the people of this land! The struggle this time is for emancipation! The struggle this time is for independence! Be ready. We cannot afford to lose our momentum. Keep the movement and the struggle alive because if we fall back they will come down hard upon us. Be disciplined. No nation's movement can be victorious without discipline. Joy Bangla! (Victory to Bengal!)'—

With those unforgettable and passionate stanzas Mujib unravelled the deepest aspirations of the seventy five million people of East Pakistan. Who could remain callous to such diction, oratory, light and sincerity? None. The whole audience listened with pin-drop silence. Its impact was not only local. People in every nook and corner of the province listened to it with rapt attention through battery-run transistor sets. The DCMLA-cum-governor had informed the President earlier about this possible speech.

The General Officer Commanding of the 14th infantry division of the army stationed at Dhaka Cantonment in Kurmitola had sought instruction from the President about facing such an eventuality. What to do? If there was any pernicious element in the speech? The forces had instruction to remain prepared. The G.O.C. himself stood guard along with a company strength of soldiers outside the venue and listened to the speech. He hailed from the East Punjab, a province of India since the partition of 1947. An interpreter standing beside translated every word of Mujib's speech for the G.O.C. 'Good that this man had not made a unilateral declaration of independence (UDI)'. He felt he was relieved of anxiety and tension. Faraway Rawalpindi also breathed a sigh of relief.

The Governor had been a professional soldier for the last 38 years. Throughout his career, his instructions under every circumstances had been carried out without a word. So he was feeling humiliated to see civilian processions carrying sticks, iron rods and other objectionable indigenous weaponry. Besides were the slogans chanted by these people. He did not understand the meaning of these slogans but could see and interpret the wrath and air of disobedience visible in their sun-burnt faces. This was totally unacceptable and insulting to his profession. So after finishing his report on today's speech to the President he said,

—Sir, I can't forget this.

—What?

—This whole province is now being de facto ruled at the behest of a single man who is against the solidarity of our country. It is under his direction that people are not paying taxes, keeping government offices closed. The contractors have stopped supplying food to our cantonments. Besides, I have firm intelligence that this man did not allow the administration of oath to my office. How can I condone this?

—But I have told you about my program. Haven't I?

—Sir, you have but should I continue to tolerate this disobedience and audacity? Like that damn Hindu Gandhi during the 1930s, this man has given a call to all Bengalees to shun anything from West Pakistan. People are obeying his call.

In the armed forces job the Governor was senior to the President. But not that the senior most military officer always holds the office of the President. Until two years back from now the President used to salute the Governor but now the governor has to salute the President. The President's attitude to the Governor was soft and unlike the one to Yaqub's. So he was tolerant with the complaints of the Governor and patiently said

—Yes, I understand that. Even then, wait and be patient. Don't you know that armed forces are like women? They do not express their inner feelings even to themselves.

The Governor was all through a straight forward man and so could not catch the meaning of the President's remark. He was not satisfied and said,
—Sir, these rogues have been burning our national flags and stampeding images of the father of the nation on the streets before our eyes.
—I would still suggest you hold on with patience. I will be there on the seventeenth March.

Before Tikka could say something more the President's line went dead.
The Urdu version of Mujib's speech was made available to the *Nabab*. He listened and analyzed it. He himself was an eloquent demagogue capable of exuding anger, heroism and even hatred to his audience. However in his inner self he was not a very brave man. He was worried and even scared with the text and consequences of the speech. It melted down when he heard about the positive reception of the speech in his provinces through his party men. Then he talked to General Piru and asked him to fix an appointment with the President. He felt time was running out and there were many things to do. The appointment was granted forthwith.

//

Asad's university was closed down by authorities on 1st March. He came to Dhaka to his dad's house. After much imploring he had persuaded his dad Rauf to allow him to go to the race course in order to listen to the speech. He listened to the speech. At the same time Asad took a few snaps of the podium and the crowd. The waiting for the speech was like candy being boiled in a pan and then its crystallization in tubes taking place and people craving to have a piece without delay. All the people of the province had swarmed around this single person Mujib since last December's national and provincial assembly elections. The riff-raff and the aristocrats, the plebian, the middle class, the bourgeois and the proletariat were in this mingling. The personnel who were at the only official radio system of the province were mostly Bengalees. They knew this like any other Bengalee. They had approached earlier to their higher-ups, mostly west Pakistanees, demanding,

—Let there be a transmission of the speech through the radio.

—No, that is impossible, folks.

—Then we are going to shut the whole transmission station down immediately.

—Even then.

So the speech was not available on the air. Those who could get to the racecourse heard it direct. Those who could not, heard from those who were present there. Telephones were rather scarce. Still many people spread what they heard, through this equipment. From ear to ear almost every adult throughout the province came to know about the speech. Foreign correspondents and informants of diplomatic missions also heard the speech and spread it throughout the civilized world like wildfire. Many climbed to tree tops, electric light posts, or precariously dangled on roof tops and carnishes of buildings to watch and listen to this speech. In this province no gathering even on festivals like holy Eid, *Puja* or Independence Day celebration had been this big. Masses had never paid keener attention to any function of state or even to the reception which took place during the visit of the nation's father Jinnah during 1948. These were the interested groups.

Besides, there were groups of people watching this great epic-like event with another point of view. They were anxious and scared but were very much eager to know the results of the proceedings of this gigantic mass attendance. These people were scattered throughout the province since 1947. They were awaiting this day from 1st March. None of these people had voted for Mujib. During the 1964 Presidential elections, they had refused to cast votes for the sister of the father of the nation on the same ground. Rather they voted for the iron-man Field Marshall Ayub Khan. They all had come from India and West Pakistan and used to speak a different language. They never forgot in spite of living here for long that this was not their home and that they had once left their original homes. This time they had had the gut feeling that something big like the one in 1947 was possibly going to take place any time. They wore different apparels. They had long trousers and '*kurta*'. Even their sandals were different. Of them, Iftekhar Achokjai used to earn his livelihood by peddling colourful bed sheets from a basket hung over his shoulders. These were made in Peshawar. He hailed from Mardan, a district in North Western Frontier Province. He had a very small capital. Md. Talat Jabir from Bannoo was running a small cloth shop at Nawabpur area of the city.

There had never been so many voice recordings and photo sessions together in one single place ever in the province.

Kallo Shah, Bostam Khan, Ismail Khatok, Ismail Walia, Umar Bachhan and Dil Mohamed from Dera Gazi Khan, Kalat, Hossainwala, Wazirabad and Meena Bazar had been living in a mess quarters for many years. It was a tin-shed hut situated behind the Nawabpur rail-crossing. Their families were all living at their homes in West Pakistan. Those people had little education, lowly livelihoods, and simple intelligence. Still, after listening to the speech, they felt that it was safe to leave this place. Possibly the whole province was getting antagonistic towards them. So their thought was—how to get out of here to their homes more than a thousand miles away.

To board a ship was impossible. The port city of Chittagong had to be reached by an unsafe road journey of two hundred and fifty miles. Though a ticket for an airplane was costly, it was within their means. They went to the local flight office which was mostly manned by people of their language. After some supplication and solicitation each got a ticket for Karachi but with the forward date of twelfth March.

Three days were still to go. Shopkeepers had locked their shops in the afternoon of first March and had not been there since. Everywhere enraged Bangalees were in occupation of streets holding large demonstration every day. They were cautious in carrying the last cash with them on the last business day. Now the only point of worry was how to get to the airport. If they changed their traditional dress, the ethnic physical traits like big physique, sharp nose, very fair complexion and moustache could never be camouflaged. And some people were looking exactly for those.

A non-stop strike was in progress. It was ridiculous even to think of boarding a bus. There was every possibility that the conductor and helpers themselves would dare catch hold of them. Rickshaw would be even worse. In a scooter or a baby-taxi their height simply could not be accommodated. There was a stand for horse driven carts adjacent to their mess quarters. Luggage and passengers were easily accomodable into that. But this transport was slow and the airport was about four miles away. They thought it would not be an intelligent act to do so. Suddenly, it was like a lightning in the dark. How about Chevrolet taxis on hire? Those English made large cars could comfortably take all of them in fours. Those were fast and safe. So they decided they would take two of these and leave for the airport at 6 o'clock in the morning when the neighbourhood would be asleep. The flight was at 12 o'clock. So they would spend the rest by awaiting the flight at the airport terminal. They also sent letters to their families informing the itinerary.

Similarly a group of men, women and children living at Mongla and Chittagong ports and Syedpur railway colonies quietly arranged their baggage. Earlier, by very arduous efforts they had collected tickets for a voyage to Karachi. Those people also had lowly professions. They never understood politics but could sense danger right on 1st March. In the community of living beings the ant is a rather insignificant insect. However, it is this ant which can feel the upcoming earthquake before everyone else.

///

The afternoon of 8th March was passing away. Asad and Rauf were talking in their drawing room. Asad asked,

—Dad, I am wondering what is going to happen?

—I think nothing will happen. Everything will calm down soon.

—What about transfer of power?

—Do you think these people are after power? No. Are you not listening to their slogans 'heroic Bengalees, take up arms!' what an oratory! Just tell me when these people did any heroic feats in history? I must say, never. One non-descript Titumeer built a miniature barricade of bamboos against the English. And now this one. Your hero is telling us about construction of forts in every home! How sensible does this sound, son?

—Dad, I am shocked to see your utter disrespect towards this. I disagree with you. Surely Mujib is representing the aspiration and dream of all the countrymen.

—Son, you are making a mistake. Mujib did not get a single vote from the western wing of our country. So he can't represent all the people of this country.

—But Dad, you are also making mistakes. True he has not had a seat from West Pakistan but he has bagged about a million votes from that area.

—That is the same thing.

—Why it should be the same thing? On the whole Mujib is the majority party leader of this country. Right?

—Well, son. Nobody has disagreed with that fact. But that does not entitle him to talk seditious words. You have not seen the army of the Punjab. If they show up in action, these slogans will simply disappear. The agitation mongers will hide in earthen holes like rats. What a statement, 'this time the movement is for independence'. May I ask who voted him for independence?

—Dad, you have always been like this. But now I think it is time that you made some change in your mind-set. Everyone should be able to read the writings of the wall.

—That is also a slogan. There was news that the President is coming for talks to this city. Let us wait for what comes out of that.

—Dad, don't you hold them responsible for this unexpected and totally irrational postponement of the assembly session?

—No, at least not yet.

—Why?

—The time for the session has not yet run out. All parties must agree and in doing that the government will need some time.

—Enough time has been spent. Besides, those agreements can be reached inside the assembly. Many countries have done this.

—All these will be sorted out in the future.

—Dad, I will still argue that this dilly-dallying has already damaged the trust between the two wings of this country. People had an expectation that something new and good would start on the 1st of March. Even many leaders from the western wing had this optimism.

—How many seats or votes did those leaders get in the elections? So what is the value of their words?

—Then Dad, for the same logic our leader has a right to talk. Am I not correct?

—Yes you are. Of course he has the right to talk on our behalf but son, there is a but.

—What is that?

—This right of his in no way authorized him to demand secession from the center. We have never given him this locus standi.

However Rauf had voted for a candidate in the last election who lost his security deposit. It was unknown to Asad. At this point the call for 'Magrib'(evening) prayers became audible. The father and son ended their conversation.

//

General Piru had been leaking all vital information to the *Nabab*. This was against the official secrets act and so a punishable offence. The information was like this: '34th mountain brigade had left Karachi. The 14th Punjab is moving towards the left side of Ceylon in the Indian Ocean. The second Air squadron from Peshawar is almost on the skies of Dhaka and P.N.S Landikotal is only forty miles south of Chittagong.' The significance of these movements was well understood by the *Nabab* and he felt indeed cheerful. He wished to see the President and so asked,

—Piru, tell me what schedule does the President have at this moment?

—No, not much.

—Then may I come around?

—I guess you can.

The President also was in a high mood. Everything was moving according to plan. So he immediately agreed to see the *Nabab* when Gen. Piru requested for it. It is natural that even powerful men become careless when they are charged with emotion. On such moments they forget protocol. The two discussed their plan at large. The *Nabab* proposed,

—In that case Mr. President, can't we fly to Dhaka by the same plane?

Though fully drunk, the President did not lose total command of his senses. He said,

—People are already suspecting many things. So your proposal would not be a wise thing to follow.

The *Nabab* realized that he had over-shot. He recovered quickly and with a sly smile on his face said,

—Well, we will travel separately. I was actually kidding. We are actually in luck that the stiff-neck Mujib has not said or done something deadly.

—Mr. *Nabab*, don't worry about that. He would not dare do anything like that. I had got him warned by General Raja that such nonsense would not be met cheerfully. He was not that stupid. He wants to sit on this chair and nothing else. So he shall do nothing to spoil that possibility.

—But Mr. President what shall I . . . ?

The President interrupted and said with a firm voice,

—Ah, haven't I told you I am going to Dhaka for talks. Until then have patience.

Once again the *Nabab* felt uncertain. He thought, 'strange, this man sitting before me is by nature a drunkard but is quite good in his senses. I have been seeing and talking to him so many times since December, still I could not fathom what is there in his mind!' The occasion was the visit of the Romanian foreign minister. So the President withdrew and the *Nabab* went home.

//

Bostam Khan and his five mess-mates had a smattering of Bangla language. They had been listening to the local news through a second hand NEC transistor since 1st March. Later on, they always had the daily Urdu version of the news available in the evening. There was disturbing news for every person here who was not a Bengalee. So this was increasing their tension but it was unnecessary to make a new plan. Strikes were continuing every day. They were not getting out at all even for a small walk. There was enough stock of their staple food flour and lentils—to last until their day of flight. Now it was the tenth of the month. After lunch all had been sleeping. It was about dusk when Bostam woke up due to some noises outside the mess. He moved himself to a seating posture on the wooden bedstead. He could hear the cacophony of a procession. A large number of demonstrators was heading along the Nababpur road. Three persons at Malibagh and five at Rangpur got killed yesterday by army firing. This procession and slogans were in protest at those killings. The procession moved past their mess. Meanwhile all five roommates of Bostam were also awakened from their sleep. And immediately afterwards there was a knock on the wooden doors of their mess. Outside, it was already dark. No way to see who was knocking, without opening the door. Bostam asked

—Who is there?

An unknown male voice replied,

—Khan 'sahab', are you inside? This is Adil.

Bostam could not understand who this Adil was. He had a friend by the same name at Dhaka Cantonment. Since March 1st, there was no more contact with him. Bostam had been living with a feeling of fear since the 1st day of March. In his fear-stricken mind he did not realize that if the visitor outside was the Adil of cantonment he knew, he would not address him with the formal 'sahab (mister)'. With a mixed feeling of uncertainty and anxiety Bostam opened the door. With the dim light of the kerosine-lit-hurricane lamp the face of the stranger standing before him now became visible to Bostam's eyes.

A dark young man in his thirties was standing there. He was bare-footed, wearing only a sando guernsey and a white loin cloth. His dirty yellowish teeth and gums bore the marks of chewing bettle-leaves. He had lied about his name. Actually his name was Jumman and by profession a butcher in the local meat market of Thataribazar. Jumman was not alone. About twenty people were standing behind him. Many held knives, axe, iron rods, hockey sticks and other indigenous weapons. Jumman appeared to be leading the gang. He was clasping a large knife in his right hand. Bostam never bought any beef or mutton from Jumman on credit. Besides there was no reason to have a bad relation between the two. Bostam had a primary knowledge in the Urdu alphabet. Still it did not take long for him to understand the situation he was in. For ethnic reasons Bostam and his mates all possessed tall and muscular bodies. Still they never had had a quarrel with anybody. None had ever used even a stick or knife against anybody in his life. They had always gone about their own business offending no one. Jumman with a wave in his thick black hair grinned and asked,

—Khan Sahab, where are you fleeing to?

Bostam recognized the disdain in the questioner's eyes. He also realized that neighbours would not come to their help now. The time had changed. The police station and the judiciary were skilled but they were torn between satisfying a master and earning wrath from the same quarters. Bostam was scared but without showing any reaction to these he kept a smile on his healthy face and replied,

—Who told you? We have been here for many years. We are going to nowhere.

—Brother-in-law, you are telling lies'—spitted from Jumman's mouth. 'Brother-in-law' in the local culture is an abuse.

The next moment the gang swooped on Boston and the six men behind. They were perplexed. Bostam thought if someone smiles at the enemy, the enemy would become soft. It is usually reciprocal. But this did not work here. Dil Mohammad and Abu Sufian were young in age. The animal instinct for self-defense and resistance were roused in their heads. Each took a kitchen hammer to protect him. But they were no match to the organized strength of the gang. Within minutes, under repeated fustigation and stabbings the six succumbed to death. Looting their life time savings and the air tickets the gang decamped within minutes. Behind on the floor laid the six big gory corpses as a heap.

At that epoch making convergence of times, Jumman and his followers were not a mere band of hooligans. They had promoted themselves to an institute. In many societies similar moments show up when forces like these rise to this level. The French Revolution witnessed these in lots. Actually society for their own interest summons this people. But the irony is that they can't be sent back to their original dungeons when society's purpose has been served. Those who called them in also lose control over them and fail to send them back.

Two hundred and fifty miles south east of Dhaka was the port city of Chittagong. Scenario somewhat similar to the one above were taking place there through the last few days at neighbourhoods like Feroze Shah and Sher Shah Colonies. These were mostly ghettos for non-Bengalees like Bostam Khan's. Locals were keeping them besieged, cutting off water and electricity connection. Inmates could not come out for buying the groceries. It was twenty four years ago that these people had settled here to earn a livelihood. Some came from Makran in Baluchistan. Some from Kalat in the Punjab while others from Dhanbad in Bihar. Organized muggers and thugs stormed their houses, swooped on the male inmates and carried away young women for their own purposes and also looted whatever valuables the families had. None of these people was a debtor to the locals. Rather they were creditors to many Bangla speaking inhabitants. Of course the victims had not a very good relation with everyone but that was not the reason for being attacked by this people. It was simple and plain—to write off debts for good.

Outside Bostam Khan's quarters a pale moon was floating in the clear sky. Those from the simple labour class souls never had the leisure or taste for watching the beauty of a moon-lit sky. The moon light now had entered their room through the rusted window panes and spread over the corpses. A look at the effects would seem as if these were classic designs of lights and shades over a bunch of dead bodies and was the work by a gifted artiste. The large sized personal apparels of the just dead men hanging on a rope tied over the bedstead were spreading ghostlike and mysterious images throughout the poorly lit room.

A little behind the sleeping room some kitchenware laid sprayed over the floor of the tiny kitchen. A cooking pan with boiled lentils, a few tin plates, dry tea cups and a cheap aluminium mug were littered beside. Some fermented wheat flour in a wooden bucket was drying out near the kerosene stove.

While breathing his last the smiling face of his pregnant wife and the wrinkle full visage of his old father waiting for his arrival at their dusty village home on the foot of Parachina hill in the frontier province made a last glimpse in the eyes of Bostam Khan.

///

It was 12th March. Pakistan International Airlines flight number 19 was preparing to leave Tejgaon airport for Karachi. It was 11 'o clock in the morning. Almost all passengers were already aboard. The announcer had already announced the names of six passengers to report to his desk twice. Now the final call was made but none reported. He went through the passengers' list and could not make out why any passenger should be required to be announced more than once when tickets were expensive and were sold on black markets. Exasperated, he consulted his superior and took different six passengers from the endless long waiting list and issued them with boarding passes. Like, many others, these six had been sleeping in the airport from last evening for the miraculous strike of such an exceptional fortune.

On the other hand M.V. *Pakputtan's* staff could not trace about one hundred and fifty passengers bound for Karachi. Their addresses were either Feroze Shah or Sher Shah Colony at Chittagong.

//

One hundred and fifty border out post (BOP)s sprawling like a zigzag laid thread were circling the thirty-three hundred miles long border of the province. The Para-military force called East Pakistan Rifles (EPR) was the organ responsible for managing these Bops. All the other ranks of this force like *Habilder, Subeder,* gunner, Lance Nayek, Corporal, Sergeant and subaltern had to hail from the province while all officials from the ranks of Second-Lieutenant to Colonel came from West Pakistan.

That was the provision of the book for this Para-military force. Standing on duty at B.O.P no. 21 under the wing, *Habilder* Mozammel had done a dangerously risky job. He had arranged to receive a coded letter from his brother who heard the speech of 7th March. He read and destroyed it promptly. He first asked *Nayek* Barek Molla, his second-in-command,

—Are you aware what is going on in Dhaka?

—The border is quiet. That is all I know, *Ustad*(leader) What else do you have?

Mozammel then told Barek what he had received and read and suggested him to do whatever he could with this piece of news. The Wing Commander of the 7th unit Lt. Col. Manjoor Shah Quraishi had just completed his tour of inspection of this outpost. So the situation was one free from worries. Everyone maintained a normal countenance and using the wireless passed the message to all the Bops within minutes. They knew their lives could be at risk but nothing debarred them. All Bangla-speaking personnel were aware before the evening what had happened at Dhaka. While relaying the message with elation each advised the other to remain vigilant. It was one thing for the civilian population to be stirred with a political ism. It was totally different and difficult for armed services personnel to be imbued usually with such an issue in any society. But it was permeating fast into the fabric of the society's texture. That was Mujib's charisma.

MASUD AHMED

//

The airplane was on troposphere. The President asked his tour officer
—Lt. Col. Masud, where are we now?
Four hours had elapsed since the aircraft had taken off from Karachi
Airport.
Before Masud could answer his boss's question, the microphone
came to life and the pilot's voice was audible,
—Most honourable President, Ladies and Gentlemen, we are now
turning left and crossing cape Cameroon.
The place was adjacent to the coast of Sri Lanka. Lt. Col. Masud said,
—Sir, another three and a half hours to go before we reach Dhaka.
—Oh, what a tedious journey!
The President said as he yawned. In the back rows were seated
Justice Cornelius, General Piru, Deputy Chief, Planning Commission
Mahbubul Hakue, A.K.Brohi the solicitor, Sharifuddin Peerjada and
eight officials. They were accompanying the President to assist him in
the coming negotiations at Dhaka.

Today there were no locals among air-controllers on duty at
Tejgaon airport. All of them had been transferred to Karachi, Peshawar
or Sargodha on the 2nd of March. Muktar Syed Naqvi, Controller,
grade-I was in charge of the morning shift. He was being assisted by
Deputy-Controller Iftekhar Hamid and another twelve officers of the
air-force in civvies. No civilian official was on duty. Since that morning
the civil aviation authority had issued no passes to any kind of visitors.
Even porters were being kept out of-bounds by fierce looking military
security guards. Passengers were carrying their luggage and walking long
distances to and from the airport terminal.
Visitors never saw such a deserted look at the airport before. None
from the ordinary police, civil aviation security department and armed
police battalion could be seen anywhere. It was a company strength
troop of the twenty fourth Punjab who were cordoning the whole
airport, tarmac and the runway. They stood at attention, with their
newly pressed *khaki* uniform, polished boots and smile-less tough faces.
They were glaring under the scorching sun. One could easily take them
as performers of a Greek tragedy queuing and waiting for entering the
scene for their turns.

According to the schedule of the day four domestic flights were expected to depart from and arrive at the airport. After 12 o'clock all these were cancelled. The only international flight of the day had been diverted earlier to Kathmandu, Nepal. It was forty minutes past one o'clock in the afternoon. Mukhter's head phone came to life.

—Sir, the flight has become visible on the screen.

It was Iftekhar Hamid's voice.

—Well, watch and confirm.

—Right Sir.

Ten seconds later Iftekhar was once again on the phone,

—Sir, the radar system and wireless together confirming the flight's arrival.

Everyone in Mukhter's office became active in a body. Five minutes later the aircraft carrying the President landed on the runway and soon reached the tarmac. The President descended the stairs, walked past the red-carpet and reached the reception foyer. He had a furrowed forehead and a wrinkled face. A result of the merciless sun. He extended his right hand to the governor who saluted him. Then he shook hands with Dhaka Zonal Martial Law Administrator, Commodore commanding Dhaka and Air-Officer commanding, air force base Dhaka. There was not a single civilian officer present. Not even the Chief Secretary, the Inspector General of Police of the province, or the Divisional Commissioner or Deputy Commissioner or the Superintendent of Police of Dhaka. A discreet phone call from Islamabad had told them not be anywhere near the scene today. They did not question him under what amendment of the protocol was this being done. Throughout the last two years, there had always been a press conference wherever the President had made a tour. Today was the only exception to that. Journos and even the official press information department were absent. He talked only to one, the DCMLA and governor throwing a question

—What mess have you created here?

Seeing a very angry face of his commander, General Tikka dared not come up with any defense.

In any developing nation the common masses have a deep interest in certain issues and objects in spite of their abject poverty. These are the aeroplane, politics and leaders of state. They will always watch an aeroplane whenever it is visible. They would talk about politics if there were a chance to do so. More importantly they will always try to come as close as possible to their leader whenever he is reported to be nearby. A minister or the prime minister or the President draws the same measure of attention from them. They like to waive hands, shake hands, have snapshots or just watch him. But that afternoon there was no such gathering or guests. Authorities said a firm 'no' to this though explaining that was not necessary. The people of this province had started hating him from the 1st of March announcement.

The President rested for a few minutes at the VVIP lounge. Then he started for his official residence at Mintoo Road, about three miles from the airport. A dozen riders of 10th unit of the military police and a platoon of the 24th Punjab battalion escorted him from the rear and front. His touring officer started reporting the President's motorcade's progress.

Fifteen minutes later another aeroplane of the P.I.A appeared in the skies of Dhaka. The *Nabab* and his fifteen followers landed from its belly. They all started for hotel Intercontinental at the city center. It was two o'clock in the afternoon.

///

Day by day it had become increasingly difficult to be at Joydevpur. Rauf's office was here, situated quietly behind a secluded place. He was the senior most official of this purely central governmental office whose daily business is to print classified instruments of the government. Still when he got down there every day from a passenger bus traveling from his Mohakhali residence and started walking down to his office a hundred yards away, he had to face the same set of questions. There was a security check post at the mouth of the Joydevpur crossing. It had been raised after 1st March. Personnel in uniform from the regimental police of the local battalion manned this check post on a rotation basis. A non-descript man of unknown rank stalked out of the post and asked Rouf in Urdu,

—What is your name?

—Rauf.

—Where are you going to?

—To my office.

—What is your position there?

—Deputy Controller.

—Do you have an identity card with you?

Rauf showed his I.D. Still the questioner and his colleagues from the dark room looked at his face. Rauf could read the contempt in their blue eyes. Rauf did not miss their grinning also. His sense of honour was roused. But he resisted himself. He felt if there was the slightest reaction on his face to their contemptuous looks, the situation would turn worse. Rather Rauf gave himself some kind of consolation. 'Indeed, how and who should they trust in a country where the number of unruly people is so big and unmanageable? Actually those people were being rude just to defend the country's larger interest'. After the question-answer was over they let Rauf in. But Rauf had to face the same scene the following day because a change of guards had taken place.

New personnel, old questions.

His wife and son asked him,

—Can't you avoid going to your office now? Nobody around has been attending office during this month?

Rauf retorted by saying,

—You folks don't know how important a government service is. Don't talk like irresponsible persons.

—But Dad, especially since 7th March almost nobody has been going to office. Are they?

—They are not, but none of those truants is a central government employee. Please don't talk about something you do not know.

—Well Dad, you are right but it was only the other day when the army opened fire and killed eleven people near your office.

—But how do you know that those who were fired upon were not responsible for this?

—Dad, maybe we don't know that but there is other worrying news.

—For example?

—Look, talks are going on in the President's house. Still additional troops are being flown into the capital from West Pakistan. One may legitimately ask why these are happening.

Rauf did not like his son's interest in collecting these news. So he asked,

—Son, where do you get such important news from? You are a student. Why should you bother with those stuff?

—Dad, now such stuff is known to everyone in this city. Those who are working at the ports are telling these news. Those who have jobs in P.I.A are also telling similar things. They have been watching these developments before their own eyes. So how can one think that these are not reliable?

—I will still say, it is not proper for you to have contact with these people.

—Dad, have you forgotten which department of the university I belong to? Many of my seniors are with the newspapers. They are also telling the same stories. Besides people from the cantonment and the East Pakistan Rifles are verifying the news. My point is if they mean negotiation why is this mobilization?

—Son, now I am really worried about you. You have your acquaintances in such dangerous places?

—These are no secrets now. That is why everyone is raising doubts about the goal of the negotiations. Bringing in new soldiers and killing civilians when the President is present in the city are by no means good symptoms. The question now is what they are going to do?

Rauf had not forgotten his recent experience with the military just close to the outer perimeter of his office. Still he was apprehensive of his son's queries and concerns. He never liked anyone's questions about the legitimacy of the moon and green colour strewn national flag. He remembered one thing very vividly. That was, the people who were dead set against the creation of Pakistan. So with a moment's thought he said

—I think progress is taking place in the negotiations. Otherwise why should it continue? Either party would have terminated it.

—Dad, I pray your views are correct. But what about the increased military presence?

—Well we are a whimsical nation. Right? We have a strong penchant for making a mole into a molehill. Some mobilization might have taken place. Our big neighbour, who always had been against us before 1947 and since might try to look for an alibi to foment trouble on this occasion. For that reason, I suppose it has been necessary to call for one or two additional army units. Your friends in various places are possibly overstating this.

—Dad, may be you are correct. However, a high tension is being felt everywhere in this city. There was also news that Non-Bengalee civilians are selling their shops, houses and even utensils at throw away prices and leaving for unknown destinations. Heavy crowds of passengers are a daily scene in air and sea ports. Air and sea tickets are being sold on black markets in open day light.

—Well that may be true. Possibly these people are thinking that if we get power this time, their life and property may not be safe in our hands. That is why they are arranging for their security.

—Dad, still everywhere there is a hush-hush atmosphere. Especially the military's movements seem to be very secretive and frightening.

—If one is not a law-breaker he or she has got nothing to be worried about or afraid. I have worked with them for many years. They are basically good people. They are not the ones who harm someone unnecessarily. You will surely see that.

The call for *Magrib* prayers became audible from the local mosque. Rauf left the room to offer his prayers. Rauf did not have a beard previously. Since 1st March he did not have a shave. His beard had taken a good shape giving him a look of piousness and grace. Asad entered his room and switched on the family transistor. He scrambled to connect the British Broadcasting Corporation (BBC) but found it difficult. After much trouble he caught the Calcutta radio station of India. A news bulletin was explaining the political disturbances going on in Pakistan. It was followed by a patriotic song,

'*Aji Bangladesh er hridoy hote* (from the heart of Bangladesh today)'.

Asad recollected that the same song was presented by artistes the previous afternoon at a place of demonstration near the martyrs' monument at Fuller road. Meanwhile Rauf came back after finishing his prayers. Rauf caught the last stanza of the song, listened to it and then sat on the sofa. Asad commented,

—Dad, what an excellent piece of music! Nobody else but only a genius like Rabindranath Tagore could compose this. Don't you agree?

—Agreed but you should also consider another matter.

—What is that?

—How many stanzas have this favourite poet of yours written about us? I mean, for the Moslems?

—Dad, why do you bring in politics in literature and music? These should be apolitical.

—You are wrong Asad. It was this very poet who did exactly the same thing. He opposed the division of Bengal in 1905. Why son?

So that we backward, poor, and illiterate Moslems of East Bengal could not have a chance to prosper. Was he apolitical?

Asad was enthusiastic but young and not adept in history. He felt weak before the argument. The conversation ended.

//

Four days had elapsed since talks started between the President and Mujib. The governor-cum-DCMLA and other military officers could not remain present around the negotiation table. The reason was this. Political leaders had demanded that 'khakis' must not be allowed in the talks. So the President briefed them each evening about progress. Each briefing was held at the Mintoo road residence of the President. While this was going on, the PSO, General Piru told the President that a visitor was awaiting him. Learning his credentials the President asked him to come in. A slim, tall, fair-complexioned and sedate looking gentleman in his fifties stood before the President. He was the commander Eastern Command and DCMLA just three weeks ago. He saluted the President. The President pretended not to have seen it and asked,

—Yes, Yakub, tell me what can I do for you?

—Sir, I have been here for many months . . .

—No introduction is necessary. Please come straight to the point.

—I feel, for the good of the country we should do one thing.

—Tell me what it is?

—Show respect to the results of the last elections, Sir.

—We are here exactly for that purpose.

—Sir, we may proceed to that keeping in mind that this country came into being due to the support of the voters of this province.

—I fully agree with you General. Do you have anything else?

—Sir, my posting. I have been doing nothing for the last three weeks.

—Oh yes. I actually did that with a purpose. You need some rest. I will look into the matter as soon as I get back to Islamabad. Okay?

The visitor once again saluted the President and walked out. The President looked at the governor and muttered in a totally different tone,

—This is the man who refused to drink with me during a tour here on the plea that he was a teetotaler. So much for a show of honesty! But he did nothing of his duty. He spent the two years just mingling and socializing with all depraved Bangalees. Now he has come to give me sermons on what I should or should not do . . . huh!

—Sir, I also have some intelligence on this nincompoop.

—What is that?

—Without his knowledge of the basic Bangla language he was feeling uncomfortable in mixing with his Bangalee compatriots here. So he hired an infidel from the Dhaka University teaching staff, to go to his house and thus he learnt the language well. And he did this without your permission, sir.

—So that was the way how he became a sympathizer of the province.

The four star General of Bhopal was sitting beside the President. He said,

—Sir, when you are aware of so many things, why did you grant him an appointment?

—I had my reasons. If I refused it, he might have found an alibi to tell something very embarrassing or dangerous to Mujib and his aides. For the same reason I have not given any order for his new posting. Let him stay here until our work plan is complete.

—Sir, what is the progress of the talks so far?

—The bastard is not behaving.

The President didn't realize that such bad language was unbecoming of a head of state. He further added,

—I requested him to go to Rawalpindi to talk to me. He did not agree. So I came down here. Now he has been making all types of nonsensical demands. He wants everything.

—Sir, what are those demands?

—He was saying that all matters except defense, money and foreign affairs should be in the hands of provinces.

—Sir did not you try to make him realize that he was going to command the central government so it is self-contradictory if so much is given to provinces?

—I did. Brohi and Peerjada did, but he would not listen. Not only that, he further demanded that separate fiscal policy, paramilitary forces and part of foreign aid negotiation must be with the provinces so that the centre cannot exploit them anymore.

—This is too much Sir. Why then are you continuing the talks?

The President looked at Major General Khadim Hossain Raja, G.O.C 14th division and said

—So that his and your forces get enough time to mobilize. Raja, how many more days shall you need?

—Sir, the pace with which things are going on now is okay with me. The seventh division is almost landing. The 34th armoured brigade is near Calcutta. I will require nothing else when they arrive.

At that moment the governor understood that many issues were being kept secret even to him. He was not wrong. The President had not forgotten that the governor had been cruel enough to bombard an Eid congregation in Baluchistan province. The President didn't wish that an action of that extent should take place here. On the other hand no compromise could be allowed with the territorial integrity of the country. The problem as the President realized was this that Yaqub was too pliant. So he had to be replaced. On the other hand, the governor was too harsh. But at the helm, such a tough man was the need of the moment. The President with a concluding tone said,

—So you people should wait until these units arrive.

Everyone nodded and the briefing ended.

//

It was the following afternoon. The *Nabab* and Mujib were standing on the lawn of the President's residence. They were talking. The former had always been cunning and unscrupulous while the latter straight-forward and honest. Mujib knew the *Nabab's* character very well. Still he was saying,

—You must keep one thing in mind.

—What is that? Asked the *Nabab*.

—If we can't find a way out they will first destroy me and then destroy you. They will not spare you, though you are very smart.

The *Nabab* heard the words but didn't pay heed. How could he do otherwise? He had, by then taken the role of the protagonist in a Greek tragedy. So Nemesis had become his fate. How could he avoid that? Accordingly the wisdom of Mujib's words didn't touch him. Now was the time of the Gods. They were waiting to lead him to the path of sin. Otherwise, how could a tragic ending look justified? He didn't make any comment. What was happening behind the negotiations was known to him better than Mujib's. So no worries touched the *Nabab*. Even before the talks started he had demanded a strange thing. He said,

—The theory of a single majority does not hold good for this country. Two parties have become majority in the two wings of this country. So let power be transferred to those two separately.

In any civilized nation such a statement or demand would have immediately faced charges of high treason and sedition but the President did nothing against the proponent of this grotesque theory. He was in his fifties but yet not acquired maturity to understand the consequences of such words. Talks continued for the next three days. Each party appeared to be happy. In the afternoon, Mujib asked,

—Mr. President, when shall we hear your announcement? The whole nation is waiting for it now.

—Yes, of course. It will come without delay. The assembly will be in session from the 25th March. And before I announce that please sit with our respective legal advisers to agree on the draft of the announcement. Happy?

—Happy, Excellency. But when shall the statement be made?

—As I said when you agree about the draft. Then at the right hour you will hear it.

Earlier reporters had press briefings with Mujib. One had asked

—Is any progress taking place?

Mujib replied,

—Otherwise why should we continue the talks?

—So when shall we have the details?

—At the right moment.

///

Actually nobody in the province was sure what was going to happen. Uncertainties and rumors were spreading like anything. Not only the Bangla speaking people but a number of important personnel also had the same feeling. They all came from West Pakistan and were holding responsible positions in the sixteen districts and four divisional headquarters of the province. They were members of various branches of the civil services net. They spoke the same language like the President and his entourage from the west. Even then they were not apprised about the progress of talks and future plans of the government. The only reason for keeping them in the dark was their difference in profession. They were civilians. Most of them were living with their families and were not feeling good. A member of the prestigious civil service of Pakistan (CSP) Amar Saad Chawla was the head of the civil administration of Khulna division. He phoned his brother-in-law Lt. Colonel Yar Md. Khan Ansari at the Jessore cantonment. Ansari was commanding the 22nd battalion of the 47th Field Regiment artillery unit there.

—Ansari, what is the news?

—Which news are you talking about?

—There is only one news now. What is the latest from Dhaka?

—Brother, talks are going on and I know nothing else, no details.

Chawla understood that his brother-in-law was going tight lipped. Surely he knew something and was hiding it. Similarly Deputy Commissioner of Jessore Khushi Md. Khalid, Police Super, Mymensingh, Nashroom Daulatana, Jane Alam Rathore, SDO, Kushtia and Faruque Wadekar, DC, Bogra made telephone queries to respective sources at Dhaka to know what was going on there.

A revised date on the 25th of March for holding the session hung in the air. It was already twenty third but no sign to that effect. If discussions were going on or concluded? When was the President going back to the capital city? Those were the questions asked. In response nobody could say anything.

Deputy Director, official press information department, Anjum Khalili phoned his nephew Asghar Ali Durrani, Deputy Commissioner, Dinajpur district to tell something. Durrani got very worried. Khalili confirmed that members of parliament who came from Karachi and Lahore to Dhaka expecting to join the session were all going back home. Asghar immediately phoned the chief secretary at Dhaka to know if this was the case. In a very dry and official voice he replied,

—Look boy, I am not a party to the negotiation. How could I tell you what is happening?

These were distinguished and elites anywhere and everywhere in the country. No social evenings neglected them. There was a 'but' at the moment. People like Durrani had taken note of one thing since 2nd March. Many social evenings were being held in cantonments in connection with arrival of new troops, but no civilians like them were being invited. Even their pay master, the controller of military accounts and garrison engineers were also off the guest list in those functions. They were asking to each other and themselves, one—why those new troops and, two—those change in hospitality? No, nobody could provide the reasons.

Deputy Commissioner Mudassar Raja Faruqui like Yakub had earned much popularity in the province mostly with the Bengalees. In one of his sub-divisions the number of non-Bengalees was quite high. Still there had so far been no trouble between the communities. His personality had so far been enough to maintain that excellent comity. Even after 1st March no trouble erupted. Now on the morning of 23rd March, his sub-divisional officer Aslam Khuro phoned him. It was Aslam's first posting after finishing his training from the civil service college at Walton in Lahore. Aslam's home was at Shahiwal in the Punjab.

—Aslam, what is it?

—Sir, there is a bad news.

—Tell me what it is.

—Sir, tension was going on between only a handful members of the two communities. I was almost managing it when a platoon of the 7th Punjab appeared and opened fire on the eastern neighbourhood.

—Under whose order did they enter and opened fire when the sub-divisional magistrate himself was present? Was there no police there?

—Sir, the police were there but they did not care.

—Who has been killed?

—Sir, all twelve are locals. Not only that Sir, the army have cordoned the area and detaining sub-divisional police Officer Ibrahim Khalilullah. They have not yet allowed me to enter there.

—Don't they know who you are?

—Sir, I gave my identity. Still they did not let me in.

—Well stay there. I am coming.

Faruqui immediately rushed to the spot in Syedpur in his jeep. Sultanpara was inhabited by a thousand people. Reaching there he found army personnel removing dead bodies and getting the spot sealed off. He was enraged. Getting down from the vehicle he angrily asked the C.O in his flawless Urdu, 'officer, why did you enter here without my requisition?'

Faruqui was a deputy secretary to the central government and a Punjabee. The C.O. Lt. Col. Risalat Shewan disregarded this totally and arrogantly replied,

—Commissioner, martial law has been tightened from 1st March. You should know that since then the army can move anywhere it likes to.

—But, this is my area, commander.

—We are answerable only to the DCMLA and not to you Mr. D.C.

—Please withdraw your troops. I have to conduct an enquiry into the incident and file a report to the government.

—No, that duty is now ours. My troops will remain here.

Good natured but intelligent civil servant Faruqui could see that the officer was not even addressing him with the normal official deference. He also realized that nowhere in his career had he ever felt so much insulted. He was puzzled and asked himself, 'under whose orders and why are these events taking place?' He returned and reported the matter to his superior, the Divisional Commissioner of Rajshahi. He non-challantly said, 'keep absolutely quiet. The President himself is in province'.

//

The road to his office was still cumbersome. Rauf had gone to the office the previous day, though amount of business was very low now. Today is 23rd March, the national day of the country. It was an official holiday. He went to the 'bazaar' for buying vegetables and fish. He could see rows of black flags flying atop all houses and shops. He was angry. That black flag instead of the national flag!. What type of anarchy was this? Rauf was 51. He vividly remembered this day 31 years ago. He was at Dhaka city along with his father. He was then a student of the Dhaka Government College. On that day the 'Lahore resolution' had just been adopted. There was euphoria everywhere at the news. And today! What happened? There is marital law and the President is here. Before his presence! No, this is more than anti-state. He felt very annoyed and threw the shopping bag before his wife's face at the pantry. Rauf had a talk to his brother last night on these illegal activities. His brother also had the same opinion that these were more than indiscipline. His wife looked at his unhappy and disturbed face and asked,

—What happened? What is the matter with you?

—What a mess is going on around the city! I can't bear this . . .

—You mean politics?

—Yes. This lawlessness, slogans and black-flags. Though I know you have no headaches about this, you are better off!

—Correct. These are the matters of men. Let them face these. Our job is still within the kitchen.

—But I am worried about Asad. Where is he?

—He was in his room listening to radio news.

—I really don't understand how one can listen to the same news so many times! He has no faith in his country's news but what is the point of listening to those foreign sources? I have been watching him how much labour he is putting just for adjusting and re-adjusting the aerial of the transistor set in doing this.

—Remember he is going to be a big journalist one day. May be that is the reason why he is so attentive to these things.

As soon as Mrs. Rauf had finished talking Asad entered the room and excitedly told his father,

—Have you heard the news?

—You have got only one news. How many more times shall I have to listen to that, son?

—No Dad. It is really something to worry about.

—Hell, what is that?

—Moments ago the revised assembly date on the 25th of March has been cancelled. Dad, do not you think this is a paradigm shift from what was expected?

—Which news agency told this?

First it was B.B.C, and then radio Pakistan Karachi broadcast the same thing.

Rauf was not at all moved by the news. He said 'so what? Why should this worry us so much?

—What are you saying? After talking for so many days, a new date was fixed. And now they will not keep that. People everywhere were excited. Now this news will put fire to that tempo.

-May be your dear leaders have made wild demands which the President and his team could not commit. So it was not possible to arrive at a deal. It requires more time. This might have led the government to take such a decision. I can tell you facts on similar issues. After the 1954

elections there were lengthier discussions among parties and then they reached understanding and compromises.

—But Dad, you are blaming the leaders without knowing what illogical demands they really made.

—I have reasons to doubt son what they might have demanded. This is not totally guess-work.

—Well then tell me some of your doubts.

—Consider this 'writings of the wall' and slogans on the street, Huh!' Take up arms and liberate!' Do you want me to believe that these are unrelated and sporadic incidents? No, I don't believe that. Surely the top leaders are behind these. These are highly objectionable language. No government of an independent country can tolerate this.

—But Dad, this situation has not arrived in a day or two. This cancellation of the assembly date. May be you have seen the causes. I have read these in books. Who has created this situation? Did you, even today, ever blamed the *Nabab* or the government for once?

—Let me take your points son. What shall the army do? Anti-social people are chanting slogans against the solidarity of the country, burning national flags and the images of the father of the nation before their eyes. And they shall do nothing? Is that what you expect from them?

—Father, these activities have not developed suddenly. There is a long evolution. The rulers have been proceeding with conspiracy and devilry. Masses also have a limit to their patience-

—Well. Even then these activities on the streets are simply anti-state. Since there is martial law now, you are seeing army's action. If it was a normal civilian administration then the police would have done the same things. Plus why should one get so impatient so soon? Not that the government has terminated the talks.

—How about the *Nabab*'s demand? How reasonable do you think is that?

—Yes he has asked for transferring power to two wings. I believe this is a political statement only. Why should we read it literally? Politicians have to do many such things which they actually do not mean.

—But Dad he was demanding power to be transferred to him without being the leader of the majority party.

—But the President has not done that. Has he?

Asad got slightly disgruntled with his father. He knew this rightist gentleman well. He could never be moved from his position on these issues. Asad started getting interested in politics, earlier, when he was younger and studying at the college level. Whenever he talked about politics and exploitation of East Pakistan by the people at the centre, Rauf would become more vociferous and talked more offensively. Asad at this moment recollected those words.

—Son, actually you have not seen how this country came into being. That is why you are creating so many noises with many imaginary complaints in your mind. If this country had not become independent, we would never expect to sit on this sofa set. Nor could I expect to become an officer. Rather I would be dusting office furniture in a place like Tribandram or Vellore in India.

In desperation Asad said, Dad, I have always seen that you support them anyhow.

—You have spoken at length. Would you please allow me now to talk a little more?

—Okay.

—Have you noted the last part of your favourite leader's speech?

-which part exactly?

—This time our struggle is for independence.

—So what is your point, Dad?

—One cannot talk like that, standing on the grounds of an independent country. From that point I must say that the government has shown too much tolerance.

—What is your second point?

—You will dislike that even more.

—Still, let me hear it.

—In the manifesto of the election, was there the agenda of separation. Did we vote him and his party for this?

—No Dad, on both points you are correct.

—Son, I am happy you accepted these without any argument.

—But Dad, everyone has a limit to his patience. It is a simple matter that the party gaining a majority shall sit in power and rule the country. Instead of doing that they have been procrastinating since January. How long should people hold on?

—You are once again becoming emotional. Let us take up one example. A marriage has been fixed. Do you think both parties can immediately hold the functions without making preparations for a feast, booking club or hotel for holding the reception, printing cards, distributing these to guests with enough time in hand? No, it is not possible. Think of Lord Admiral Mountbatten, the last governor-general of undivided India. Even after the plan for transfer of power was okayed by the British Cabinet he could not go ahead with that right away. He held prolonged discussions with all stakeholders. Even he talked to the father of Manobendro Narayan Larma who was a tribal leader in our hill tracts area here. He was a small leader representing only a faction of ethnic minorities. Still Mountbatten asked him 'which country his voters were thinking of going to, India or East Pakistan? Everything that I am talking to you is recorded in history. Consider these matters and realize how difficult and complex a statecraft is. These are not simple issues. By hurrying one can always be criticized by either party as being partial to the one or the other. So this has to be kept in mind.

—Dad, are situation in 1947 and the present issue the same?

—Not the same but each is very important. Even in a small office one has to consider many factors before issuing a circular so that this can be implemented. You see, the British Secretary of State in India used to take years' time to draft an office memorandum. While our present issue involves 120 million people's welfare, let us wait and see. Anti-state slogans can't be the way out.

—Father, you came up with many arguments in their favour but is there a single one from them who would argue in our favour?

—Son, you are committing a mistake.

—Give me an example, then.

—How about our neighbours? Ayub, Sabera and their parents?

—This is just one single family?

—But you said there was none. Besides them, there are people who support our legitimate demand and respect our valid aspirations.

A Poshtu speaking family had been a neighbour of Rauf's for the last two decades. They hailed from Meeranshah in the North West Frontier province, a place 160 miles from Lahore. Yaseen Fakhri, his wife Farjan Mahmudee, daughter Sabera and son Ayub had been quite fond of Raufs' family. Fakhri came to Dhaka right after 1947 to take advantage of an industrial loan provided by East Pakistan Industrial Development Corporation. Industrious, honest and persevering he soon set up a Steel re-rolling mill at Tejgaon Industrial area quite near Mohakhali. Good luck soon visited him. The family became prosperous. Fakhri built a house at Mohakhali and started staying there. Members of the two families were soon intimate in spite of the language barrier at the primary stages. Each family has been visiting the other on birth and marriage anniversaries and other occasions of family members.

Fakhri's tribe was famous for hospitality. Every year during the winter, Fakhri's family went back to their village home for a vacation. While returning they never forgot to bring apples, woolen ware and almond as gifts for Rauf's family. The Raufs politely objected to this courtesy and kindliness. Fakhri reminded them of their role 18 years ago while they were having their first child Sabera.

In 1953 Fakhri was totally unknown in the neighbourhood and the number of families living around was rather small and scattered. Nor had he any relatives around. No telephone and no electricity connections were there. Mrs. Mahmudee's expected date of delivery suddenly advanced to an unexpected date and it was the dead of the night. The Raufs heard a series of sharp screams in their neighbour's house and soon rushed there. With Mrs. Rauf's help, a few minutes later, the first child of Mrs. Mahmudee came to this earth.

Thenceforth Fakhri used to tell Rauf

—To us you people are closer than any of my relatives. So don't refuse to accept if I bring something for you. Besides, in our religion, exchanging of gifts has been encouraged.

Sabera was a 2nd year student of Intermediate at the Ispahani College while her younger brother Ayub Khan Fakhri was a 1st year I.Sc. student of the Notre Dame College.

That one incident created a heart to heart relationship between the two families. The results of the 1970 elections did not cause any downstream in the relationship. However neither Rauf nor Fakhri had ever talked politics. Asad had totally forgotten about this family since the trouble started on 1st March. Now after talking to his father he recollected many sweet memories and he could not deny to himself that he was feeling very good indeed. But men hardly change. After some pause he said,

'Well Dad, no doubt this is a splendid example but it is only one and so is an exception. In any case, I have always seen that you never blame the West Pakistanees.

—Son, listen. There are many important facts about this issue which may constantly perturb your mind. It is impossible for a young man like

you to consider all those facts. So be patient. Gradually you will learn those points and then possibly you may change your views.

Rauf learnt something from a high level yesterday. He guessed that his son was unaware of it. Otherwise he would have a more aggressive tone today. Rauf came to know the members of National Assembly from West Pakistan had already gone back. No joint communiqué was issued. He was wondering, so what was going to happen? But men don't change. So Rauf's wondering was momentary. He soon came back to his normal self and rationalized by thinking that this government will do everything for defending Islam and up keeping the solidarity and prestige of this country. So whatever his son and his supporters might argue or think, he must continue his support to the government.

//

Rear gunner Zahanjeb Abrar reached his unit head quarters at Balakot duly. He put on his uniform, boots and beret and then appeared before his C.O. Major Bayejid. The Major explained why his leave had been cancelled. He further told that many of his colleagues also had been recalled for the same reason. Abrar realized that it would be pointless to tell the story of his daughter's marriage ceremony and thus earn sympathy to have the recall cancelled.

The standard procedure after reporting was to check weaponry, to grease them and to make full preparations for action. Bayejid said that it was unnecessary at this time since the whole unit would start their voyage for East Pakistan the next day.

Almost all in the unit knew very little about their destination. They had seen only a map of the place in their classrooms.

The following day Abrar wrote a letter to his younger brother asking him to give all news about Lubasha's marriage function. This should reach his unit address. These fighting people had always learnt to obey their superiors' command without questions. But, this time almost none, within their own minds, agreed with the reason for their transfer. Many of them had participated in the 1965 Indo-Pak war. Leave of most of these people was cancelled on that occasion. They were quite happy with that. There were genuine grounds. This time it seemed to be very flimsy. No signs of war with anybody. The frontiers were quiet and still those orders. Zahanjeb was particularly disturbed. At last he said in a soliloquy

'Well these are important matters of the state. If I could understand these I would be at least a brigadier or even Major-General. Now I can end up at the maximum rank of the *Subeder*. Let the big bosses think about these issues'.

Abrar had invited twelve from his own unit. They were now around him. They gave him consolation by saying, 'Abrar, don't worry, you and we have missed the pleasures of this ceremony. So what? The main thing is that your son-in-law has been an excellent choice. Be happy with that.'

In spite of being unhappy with the sudden transfer to a distant and hither to unknown place, everyone felt, no queries should be made about this. That would be unsafe.

///

Major General Raja was doing office work sitting at his 14th infantry division headquarters. It was Kurmitola cantonment at Dhaka. The second month of the Bengal spring was showing its full beauty and symptoms. It was nine'o clock in the morning. Sunrays were trying to get around the British made military office through the overshadowing thick greeneries and bushes. Groups of sparrows were flying to and fro from one green branch to another with their sweet chirruping. The General had no mind for this natural beauty around his own place. What he liked about this place was the mild heat and the dryness. He had special requirements for these things. What he always disliked about this place since his posting here in last October was the moisture, sweat and rainfall off and on.

He hailed from a dry place.

He was not on the negotiation table. Still he knew many things. Actually he had instructions to get prepared right from the 1st day of this month.

The day was 25th. Raja completed his preparations yesterday though he was not yet aware of the zero hours. After putting the file tray away, he pulled the daily 'Morning News' and started looking at the headlines. There was a buzz from the green-coloured telephone placed on his left hand side wooden 'what not.' Societies which believe they have the monopolistic prerogative of claiming a one thousand year old history and tradition of enriched culture demonstrate certain traits. One such is that a senior will never first greet a junior when they meet or talk.

The General lifted the receiver and before he could recognize the voice, the caller started talking without any greeting,

'Khadim, this is tonight.'

Khadim replied by saying' yes Sir, understood'. The caller was commander, eastern command cum-governor. Raja looked at his watch. Fifteen hours to go. He started pulling the strings of his office. Suddenly after many days at this moment he remembered his village home at Panipath on the Grand trunk road in the Indian Punjab. After 47 he had never had a chance to be there. He heard from his father that the Hindus and Sikhs burnt their village to the ground. His yellow and black coloured eyes started glowing. He thought' I have a very busy schedule to night'.

Yesterday there was no news from Mintoo Road. The official spokesman did not inform the journalists if talks had ended or would continue any more. It was Major-General Ishhaque who met the press and could not tell where the President was. At road number32, Dhanmondi, crowds were increasing. Processions were surrounding it. Foreign correspondents alike had the same questions to Mujib:

—Would talks be held today?

—Well we are expecting so. We are waiting for a call from the President house.

—What is the basis of this optimism?

—Because the President has not formally concluded it.

Everyone received the same answer from the most popular man of the province and the country.

///

At Mintoo Road the sun rays of the noon melted into a mellow softness as the afternoon set in. The President had his lunch and watched the long shadows losing their bright rays. Nobody around dared ask him if there was a message to go to Dhanmondi. It was full afternoon now as the President lifted his intercom receiver to talk to his tour officer,

—Masud.

—Yes Sir.

—I will start for the cantonment at 6' pm.

—Ok Sir.

Lt. Col. Masud signaled 24th Punjab to arrange the escort.

He drank and dined at the flag staff house at the cantonment. Nobody still knew where the President was going to and when. The President suddenly asked,

'Hamid, do you remember what a special day to day is.

Hamid was never given to introspection. He hesitated, Sir?

The President said 'Is not today our second anniversary in power?

—Sir it is. How can I forget such a memorable day?

It was 25th March 1969 that the then c-in-c usurped, deposed President Ayub and made Hamid the new c-in-c.

The reflection of high intelligence or philosophy was hardly visible in the President's face. However at this moment Hamid thought his boss was looking like a philosopher. His impression deepened further when the President somewhat sorrowfully said, all of you know, I was the G.O.C. here in 1960. I made a deal with the Bengalees here but now they are talking with a difference to me. It pains me'

The President then got up from the sofa and went out to board his car. He shook hands with everybody and said 'Khadim, good luck. Go ahead with your plans. Sort the bastards out well and proper.'

With his impetuous manner and nature he had earlier taken this decision now expressed as an order about this province.

His motorcade directly and unceremoniously moved towards the air-port. The mode of moving of this most important man of this vast state was such as if he was fleeing from his own country. His pilot car started reporting to the air-tarmac about the progress of the cars'. 'We are now crossing officers' mess, now crossing the 'signals centre.'

By the time, the President's limousine reached the air-port he was half asleep. His face looked vacant. There were no thoughts or compunction in his mind like Ahsan's.

Back in his office Khadim called in five uniformed men, handed over to them five blueprints and briefed them about their imminent duty. At 9:30 in the night five helicopters carrying one each of them left for different destinations of the province.

///

In the city the whole day was dazzling sunny. There were not the slightest signs of cloud in the blue skies of Dhaka. The bitumen on the cobbled streets turned deep black due to melting by the scorching heat.

71

All birds had returned to their nests by the evening. A half moon showed up after the sun-set.

As usual, Rauf, his wife and their daughter Jerin went to bed and had fallen asleep by ten o'clock. Asad could not go to bed. He was trying to get news from different sources, but could get nothing new. While listening to foreign radio stations some special types of sounds started disturbing his attention. Asad switched the transistor off and tried to find out what this sound was. First it came slowly and then loudly and regularly. Asad recognized the sound. These were the clatter and boom of guns nearby.

Many people were shooting intermittently and then continuously. At the same time there was sound of moving vehicles on the street. Switching off the tungsten bulb of the room Asad looked out of the window but could see nothing though outside was moonlit.

At that moment the telephone bell rang in the drawing room. Asad rushed and picked the receiver up. A close friend from Salimullah hall of Dhaka University was on the line.

—Asad, the army is conducting a crackdown.

—Then what is the result of these talks?

—Have you not still understood it? However, this is not the time to talk about this. Take care, bye . . . bye . . .

—Brother Kader, Kader . . . Asad screamed in a loud voice but the line was dead. Asad looked very worried. Meanwhile his mother and sister's sleep had been broken by the very disturbing noises. They were knocking on Asad's bedroom door. Asad switched on the electric light and opened the door. The two looked visibly scared and worried. Asad held them and asked, mom, why are you so afraid? Where is dad?

Mrs. Rauf' answered, he is awake and is coming here.

Rauf approached the room with blood-shot eyes. He did not look scared but thoughtful. Asad excitedly said' 'dad, see what they are doing. Did not I tell you they had bad plans? But you said nothing would happen'.

—What bad do you see in it? It is good enough that they tolerated this so long. Is it possible that a government in power will just see such lawlessness and will take no action?

—You are still supporting an illegitimate government. A military government.

—How come it is illegitimate?

—You tell me how can a military government claim legitimacy?

—If the civilians are inept and can't run the country is there any alternative to a martial law government? Tell me.

—So they shall start killing people instead of the expected arrangement for power transfer and assembly session? And you would like to justly that?

—Before I answer that you tell me how you know that they are killing people?

—My senior Kader told me that their provost, teachers and many students of the hall have been killed by the army tonight. Besides killing missions are active at Rajarbagh police line, Rokeya hall, Jagannath hall and Iqbal hall of the Dhaka University.

—This is hearsay. We have got nothing to worry about. If someone does nothing against the country they will never harm him. I have seen the martial law of 1958. No, even then, the army never showed the slightest rudeness to any innocent person.

Asad looked confused. Rauf gave attention to his wife and daughter who were visibly shivering with the increasing boom of the gunfight outside. He said 'You better go to bed and try to have some sleep—Asad You also go to your room. It is now time to remember Del Karnegy's writings. What is the point of being worried and having problems on our minds with imaginary things?'

Three miles south-east, at his Iskaton rest house, Yaqub also got up from his bed. He was a confirmed bachelor. He was never a deep sleeper. A particular sound stream and aroma just outside his windows suddenly broke his drowsiness. He had not a moment's difficulty in recognizing sounds and smell on the street. He had earned his salt amidst gunpowder, armoured cars and guns for thirty years. He could see that hundreds of army vehicles carrying helmeted soldiers with sub-machine guns and trucks were moving through the old Mymensingh road towards the south of the city. The gunfights were audible from the university area. He quickly understood what these people were after. Once again the image of the speeding truck driver came into his mind. He saw, the driver now was moving fast and smashing houses, people and pedestrians like a wild and lunatic elephant. From far behind a group of security men were chasing him. They were moving slowly but a steadiness and determination were clearly visible on their faces.

///

The fair complexioned and beautiful Aryan lady across the border also got this news. Her Deputy High Commissioner in Dhaka was continuously reporting the nitty grittys of happenings in the city to their information minister. The report specially noted that the major victims of this crack-down were believers in the ancient religion i.e. Hinduisim. The Aryan lady herself belonged to the same class by birth and not so much by faith. This part of the report made no special impression on her mind because the highest classes of personalities of the globe never look for religion. They never fight for this issue. Their interest lies more in the conquest of markets and establishing hegemony. As a brilliant student of history and world affairs she had earlier concluded that the Second World War also had the same target. Establishing Aryan supremacy was a phony agenda only. At the same moment she had another thought also. That was, 'I am far above average'. What she was looking for was already there in the first part of the report. Usually in her society decisions were taken on the basis of consultation with colleagues and that was leisurely. But now at 11' o clock in the night and beyond her office hours she unilaterally took a decision. The heads of her information and foreign affairs portfolios eagerly asked her, madam, what shall we say in our news media? Without a moment's demur she answered 'Tell them that a civil war has started in East Bengal.'

The chief of foreign affairs objected by saying 'Madam, the area is still a province of our neighbour. Its official name is not East Bengal, but East Pakistan'.

The information head added, besides, We do not yet know if it is a civil war or not. There is a definition of civil wars, madam. Plus it could be a routine army action like the one we are having in our Jammu and Kashmir province.

Disregarding both, she firmly told, 'Gentlemen, thank you for your opinion. However this is not a place or house for a parliamentary debate. Please do what I have asked you to do. This is the decision of my government.

Information Secretary Mohon Kumar Vatia was still not unnerved. He said, 'Madam it is the responsibility of the civil service to advise you. That is why I gave the argument.'

This Aryan lady was immeasurably superior in intelligence to all and any around her. On top of that her party's landside victory in the last elections added pride and confidence to intelligence. So she retorted, 'you have well discharged your responsibility. However it is also your duty to see that that discharging does not look similar to that of an opposition member'.

Both the top brasses felt embarrassed though at the same time realized that actually they should not do something beyond the borders of their jobs.

//

A young girl aged 11 years was sitting in their family house at Gulmarg, Lahore. She was trying again and again to establish a telephone contact with a place eleven hundred miles south-east. The name of this district town was Faridpur. Her father was working there as its deputy commissioner. Rubaya's mother had made the same attempts earlier but without success. Taj Khan Shamee, C.S.P was worried about his family as he also had been unable to talk to his wife and daughter since the second of March. Taj as head of the civil administration of this district could never imagine that the local operator of the t&t exchange had quietly damaged the vital wires of the coaxial cable connections. So he was wondering what the matter was. He had tried to ask the divisional engineer but he was simply 'unavailable' from 2nd March. However Taj khan got some cheerful news from Dhaka through acquaintances and this washed his worries away. The source said that army units were on their way to restore discipline and order. He was feeling insecure due to the callousness of the local police. The Bengali speaking personal assistant, cook and gardener were simply absenting from their duties at the Dy. commissioner's Bungalow. A lonely police constable was doing his duty at the entrance. Until 1st March, the Bengalee Police superintendent used to meet him at least twice a week, salute him and would talk law and order and social events. It had been more than three weeks that this keeper of the law for this big district was available nowhere. His residence phone was always found engaged. Taj reported the situation to the divisional commissioner. He in a grave letter wrote to him 'the situation in my office and residence 'Kahkeshan' are the same. You just wait with patience. I cannot do much to correct it'

A few minutes ago Taj took a stock of the situation in this town. He looked out of the window and saw nothing disturbing at this moment. His black telephone rang. He was happy with the thought that the phone set was in order.

District magistrate Taj Khan Shamee was moving inside to his bedroom to lift the receiver. Before his fingers were on the set, he felt a very strong thud on his chest. A very sharp, hot and painful object penetrated him through the bronchus. Taj with a 'oh' sound fell down dead on the floor. The telephone continued ringing. A blue Bedford truck was waiting across the window of the bungalow with its engine on. The assassin with a rifle in his hand boarded the truck along with his colleagues. The police super standing a little away beckoned the driver to speed away.

People throughout the province had been patiently awaiting the transfer of power for the last 25 days. Instead they heard the news at Dhaka and felt extremely betrayed. The resistance and vendetta started spreading like a wild fire from location to location. Mujib's call to 'build fortresses' was already in their minds. Nature was also exuding heat of the approaching summer. Now the fire of human hatred added fuel to it.

Towards the north at the district town of Comilla the victim was the police super Meerja Adnan. His forces, all uniformed members of the district police line had deserted him right after 7th March. He immediately sought the army's cooperation from the cantonment at Lalmai. His relative Lt. Col. Khijer Hayat told him that the time was not yet ripe for such a move. Indeed the move remained unnecessary for ever when to night his local cook, orderly and three unknown persons hacked him to death in his residence. He did not get any chance to put up a resistance with his eleven years experience in the much feared enforcement service.

The retaliation hit not only the high-ups. It spread like a locust on the human crop field on whoever spoke Urdu, Poshtu or Punjabee. Now locals were doing the same as the non-locals had done with their Bengalee neighbours a few days ago at Syedpur. Self organized groups in hundreds started a killing spree as the news of mayhem from Dhaka reached them. There was not much enmity between the locals and the settlers. Still within two or three days a few thousand dead bodies of men, women and children all wearing traditional pyjamas and long *kurta* or *kamij* were floating along the rivers around Khalishpur at Khulna,

Vairob at Mymensingh and Syedpur at Rangpur. Some of them hailed from Peshawar, while others came from Lahore, Landikotal, Quetta or Makran. They used to earn their livelihood by doing menial jobs like masonry, fruit selling or usury. Killing and rampage were accompanied by looting of their belongings and putting fire to their houses.

Besides the President, the governor, the G.O.C and Chief of the army staff, one particular gentleman did not hear the screams of these victims. He was the *Nabab* of Larkana. Sitting at his luxurious suite of the hotel Intercontinental, Dhaka, amidst army guards he looked at the star-studded moon lit sky of the city. He could clearly hear the sounds of army's gunfire near the University not far from the hotel. There was deep satisfaction in his mind. He felt, the impediments to the seat of power had all disappeared. He noted down in his diary 'God saved Pakistan.' After a few moments thought he decided he would write a pamphlet on the present crisis of his dear country. So he gave a title to the future write up. This was 'The Great Tragedy'.

It was past midnight. A new date and a new day had appeared in the equinox, 26th March, Friday. The President's plane was now three hundred miles away from Karachi. It was hovering smoothly along the coast of the Arabian Sea under a white sky. He was listening to the progress of the mission ordered by him at Dhaka. Like the *Nabab* he also looked satisfied. He pushed a button on the handle of his seat to call in an air hostess who appeared within moments and asked,

—Sir, what can I do for you?

The President said—Put me less water and more whisky in this glass.

Both he and the *Nabab* were husbands and fathers but tonight both remained totally indifferent to the screams of thousands of families around the city of Dhaka. .

At his Dhanmondi residence Mujib was shocked by the treachery. The shock was momentary. He had his plans for such an exigency. At the moment an anonymous voice made a phone call to him to say that a commando unit had started for his residence to take him into government custody. It was a confidante of his.Mujib asked a radio operator to bring in an East Pakistan Rifles wireless set before him right away. It was thirty five minutes past midnight. He took the mouthpiece of the wireless in his right hand and spoke in Bangla and English "I, Sheikh Mujibur Rahman hereby declare the independence of Bangladesh'.

Within seconds the declaration spread through the ether. Few people could hear Mujib's declaration at that moment.

Earlier on 23rd March a plan had been chalked out at Comilla cantonment to arrest Mujib. Lt. Colonel Zahir Khan, C.O. 3rd commando battalion flew in to Dhaka by a C130 military plane and soon met Colonel S.D. Ahmed at the cantonment. He picked up captain Syed and Major Belal and made a recce of house no.172 on Dhanmondi's road no. 32. That unostentatious house had already become the lighthouse of the seventy five million people since the 18th day of the month in the ocean of its struggle for independence. The team under Major Belal now at 40 minutes past 12 in the morning quietly destroyed the brick-walls of the house and entered it through three sides a minute after Mujib had finished his declaration of independence. Belal's team whisked him in a military jeep to the Adamjee Cantonment college of Kurmitola, housed him there with the purpose of transporting him to West Pakistan a day after. A Bengalee EPR officer caught Mujib's message in his wireless set and immediately recorded it into his personal tape recorder. He was sitting in his office at Chittagong where the details of what happened at Dhaka was kept secret to the army units. The officer learnt a summary of this also from the EPR headquarter at Pilkhana, Dhaka. The number of soldiers under his command there at the port city was small. The epicenter of defense activities here was the regimental centre at the cantonment. There was not a Dhaka like army action plan for this city. That was why the whole city was calm and quiet. Dwellers were dead-asleep.

The Bengali speaking second-in-command of the regimental centre, a Major, was riding an army vehicle towards the port-area. He was under instruction to unload arms and ammo from a vessel named M.V. SWAT for the armed forces. He had instructions from his commanding officer to make a report to him the next morning on completion of the unloading work. The EPR commander sent a wireless message to him. He said 'do not commit any wrong now. This is possibly a historic moment. Try to understand the demand of the times. Just for a slight delay in decision making, may be both you and we will lose our lives at their hands.'

The major was undecided. The news of the crackdown on Dhaka and the advice from his senior helped him taking the correct path. He abandoned the idea of arms unloading and drove back to the city centre. The Major looked at his wrist watch. It was Four thirty in the morning. He reached his unit headquarters and before any non-Bengalee personnel could suspect anything he disarmed all of them. They were taken into custody. The residential quarters of his C.O. was a mile away from the office.

At his Halishahor quarters, the commander of the regimental centre Lt. Col. Habib Fatmi had just put on his uniform. With his beret, the just polished shoes and a clean-shave he looked very manly. The belt of the waist was not yet in its place. He sat on a sofa in the drawing room and was awaiting his second-in-command to report to him any moment. Fatmi's home was in a village of Sheikhupura, a district town, 80 miles south to Lahore. He was promoted to his present rank in January, 1969 and was posted in the East Pakistan military base. A hater of Benglalees and this climate since he came here, Fatmi, however started liking his 2-i-c, after observing him for some weeks. Gradually that liking graduated to a deep trust and love. The 2-i-c had two kids and wife. They were staying at Dhaka while he lived in the officers' mess here. Fatmi told him to bring his family and live with them in a family quarter in this duty station. The Major politely informed him that due to family reasons that would not be possible now.

Fatmi gradually felt that his feeling towards this young major was almost brotherly and the latter had earned this feeling by his demeanors and personality. So he proposed 'so long you have to stay without your family here, you can have breakfast with me. Then we can go to the office together, okay? The major said 'ok' when he felt that the wife of his C.O. was also pleased with this arrangement. Since then they have been breaking fast together. The Fatmis were married twenty years ago and had no children. The major realized that. Yes, even tough professionals need company. Fatmi was a Punjabee but pious and simple minded. It had been his strong believe that if he could rely on a single local, it was this major. Fatmi's rank was not senior enough to know what really happened at Dhaka last night or what talks went on between the President's and Mujib's partners.

The only news of note here in this city was that a local brigadier was quietly taken off from his duty. A few days ago a Major-General flew from Dhaka and took the Bengalee brigadier in his helicopter to Dhaka while the Inter services public relations explained it as a routine transfer. He read no changes in the atmosphere of the city or people's mind. The city was tranquil.There had been no reporting of any trouble about the unloading of the arms in the port. So Fatmi looked free from worries and happy. Nothing crooked had a place in his straight-forward and credulous mind. However keeping him in the dark his superiors had by this time silently killed one hundred fourteen Bengalee soldiers at jetty number 17 at the EBRC centre.

Still half an hour to go before dawn. Fatmi heard the sound of salute by sentries from the guard-post at his residence gate. Then a jeep pulled to a stop. There was the familiar knock on the door. Fatmi, while fastening his service belt through the loops of his trouser's waist said 'Come in'.

The young major came in, saluted Fatima and said 'assalamualikum' to Mrs. Fatmi seated on a corner of the sofa set. Fatmi said,

'Take breakfast and let me hear from you about M.V. SWAT.'

The major slightly moved towards the left side of the sofa. His right palm was descending from the saluting position to the right side of his waist. He pulled out his service revolver hanging from his waist. Within seconds the small but deadly weapon's nozzle was looking like a cobra straight at Fatmi's chest. Fatmi was still to buckle the belt. There was a sharp scream from Mrs. Fatmi's mouth.

'What type of joke is this?'

Though looking a simpleton, during the 1965 war Fatmi had killed 34 blindfolded enemy soldiers. After the 1969 martial law Fatmi had experience of killing civilians of his own district as normally as shooting games. So the posture of his 2-i-c did not seem to him to be any kind of joke. He sprang to his left side but the safety catch of the 2-i-c's revolver was off. Besides, in moments of changing epochs, only either of the plaintiff or adversary can survive. It is never the both. The major was prepared for that. Three pieces of molten lead hit Fatmi on the chest before he could do anything in full view of the incredulous eyes and shriek of his wife. Simultaneously outside, the driver of the major took the lives of the sentries inside the guard post as soon as he heard the shootout inside the drawing room. Within moments the major reported the incident to his EPR boss. The Chittagong mutiny started then and there. All Bengalee soldiers immediately joined them. The EPR commander told him 'the matter was not a military one but totally political. We should report this to the political authority'.

'Yes Sir, as you deem it fit. I never intend to understand these complex matters. May be it is not possible to understand also. However I have jumped into the fire.'

Then they reported to the local leaders. Having discussed everything they were advised to wait for instructions. It was further decided that Mujib's declaration of independence as caught here in the EPR wireless would be further transmitted from the local Kalurghat radio station.

///

At 4 o'clock in the morning Asad could hear the clatter of guns gradually dying out in the city. He then fell asleep. Meanwhile the news of civil war had been broadcast over the air. Asad could not hear it as the transistor set was off. It was 9 o'clock in the morning when he woke up. He felt very tense and anxious and immediately switched on the radio. After many days this was the Dhaka station. A news bulletin was being repeated for the fourth time. A non professional voice was announcing in Urdu, English and Bangla alternately.

'Here is an emergency announcement. Curfew has been imposed in the city sine die. All officers and members of the staff of all government and semi government departments are ordered to join their duties without any delay. Non compliance will meet severe punishment.'

Asad smiled to himself. He thought, surely, this man might be anything but a media man. His coarse, uncultured tone, voice and vocabulary were unmistakably non professional. Possibly that man's knowledge of Urdu and broken English was the only reason for the authorities to pick him from the street and to order him to sit before the microphone that morning. Asad turned to a different foreign radio station and immediately heard the news about the starting of the civil war in East Bengal. He could not contain himself and rushed to his father's room,

—Dad, have you heard the news?

—No, which news?

—Listen, here is it.

Asad brought the transistor set to his father's room and raised the volume. It was still being repeated. Rauf listened intently and then asked

—Whose news is this?

—Have not you heard whose news it is?

—Well. Tell me what is the definition of a civil war? Remember you are a student of journalism and you are a good student.

—A civil war is a fighting among internal groups within the same country.

—As a primary definition yours one is no bad. Now tell me how many gunshots have taken place in this city? We are living here yet do not know about this detail how could that foreign radio come to know this so soon? How could they conclude that it is indeed a civil war? I suppose you have accepted the news right away as you have a wishful thinking in this. Is not that correct son?

—But do not you agree that at least something grave has happened?

—Something grave and a civil war are not the same thing. By the same argument of yours what has been occurring in Kashmir is a civil war. Has that news agency of yours ever admitted that they have been fighting something there, like that?

—Dad, that is an internal affair of theirs.

—I agree and by the same argument what has been happening here is also a domestic issue of ours. Accordingly they should not make such propaganda about it. Actually you and supporters like yourself have very strange arguments. That is why you talk like this?

Actually people of your age did not see how strongly this power opposed the creation of Pakistan in 1947. If you had seen that, you would not be so happy today.

Asad kept mum for some time and then giggled, dad, the Moslems were a minority and still ruled a vast majority for 650 years. Again on what logic they demanded Pakistan in 1947 is itself a question and an iniquitous thing.

-Son you are talking like the British viceroys and Hindu leaders while you have been a beneficiary of Pakistan.

—Well Dad that is not an answer. Let us come back to what we were discussing. The B.B.C. has been giving the same news. How about them?

—I have not heard that one though I trust theirs.

—So how do they have a similar interest or point of view?

—Because they ruled us for 190 years and they also opposed the creation of Pakistan. They gave all out support to our big adversary and neighbour in this on the argument that they were the majority. Finally only on the face of invincible arguments given by Mr. Jinnah they agreed to divide the sub-continent into two separate countries. And even then they intentionally kept the Kashmir issue unresolved while leaving India

so that the two countries would have continuous trouble and the British and their allies could sell arms here.

Asad looked a little disconcerted since these facts were not known to him. Then he managed to argue, but dad so they shall make propaganda on fake issues now?

—Yes they will because they want Pakistan to look weak and discredited before the eye of the international community. Do you know son what used to happen when the education system before our independence was such that candidates' name had to appear on the examination scripts up to 1941?

—No Dad, I don't,

—Moslem students' success rates were low. But when on the basis of demonstration and demands, only roll numbers were allowed to appear, Moslem students started doing very well in the examination. Can you explain it?

—Yes, you know these facts better. Still don't you agree that the government did not inform the public if talks had concluded? They also did not tell where the President is. And instead these are sounds of a heavy gunfire. Don't you think these are for killing men? Further if this is not something big how could the world powers come to know this so promptly?

—I can answer your queries. We are Moslems. The powers you are referring to are not Moslems. They don't like to see our unity or prosperity. The non-Moslem interests have always been against ours and that is why they have become vociferous so soon. The same powers have said nothing against the Kashmir issue.

—Even then what do you think happened last night or is happening now?

—I think the army has taken some action which they should have or could have taken earlier. A whole province is trying to forcibly secede from the centre and the government will be silent spectator to that! No, that cannot be. Accordingly some firing, even counter firing is not abnormal which is being exaggerated by those media people around.

Asad thought for a while and then said,

—Dad, seems you are correct but we are the majority. Is it normal that the majority would like to secede from the minority?

Rauf got slightly shaken by his son's last argument. He never thought his young son was so mature. Still he did not show the nervousness. That would embolden Asad more. He said.

'You are correct son. The matter should be the opposite one. In spite of the theory, that the majority is now striving to get away from the centre is correct.

—How Dad?

—Otherwise how could that 'the struggle this time is the struggle for independence' come out from such a responsible leader's mouth?

—That was rhetoric only and he actually did not declare independence on that day.

However, now tell me what will happen?

—Son, let us see what happens. The President is going to address the nation tonight. Let us wait for his version.

Asad was startled by this news. He was not aware of this. He asked.

—Dad, where did you get this news from?

With a thin smile Rauf answered

'Son, why do you forget that I am an official of the central government for the last twenty years? I heard this in the morning when you were sleeping.

Asad once again admitted to himself that he always knew less. While he had heard almost all the major radio stations ransacking the brands of the transistor throughout half of the night he had missed this important news. The official radio since the public uprisings in 1969 had always been an anathema to him. He understood that that very radio had surely been the source of the news.

Rauf went to his room to wash. Asad started tuning the transistor. An announcement was made about a relaxation of curfew. This was a Friday. The gunfire had stopped now. Rauf finished his breakfast and dressed himself. His wife watched this and asked in a surprised tone,

—Where are you going to on such a day?

—Why? To my office. I am of course not going to my father in law's house for pleasure.

Rauf's tone was full of humour.

—But we heard there is not even a street dog out there. Can't your attendance be avoided this very day?

Rauf fastened the straps of his shoes and answered,

—There is no excuse. I have to go. You are worrying for nothing.

—Ok, but take care. First see if buses are at all plying today.

Physically Rauf was always sturdy. Mentally he was a brave man. He had two postings at Karachi and Islamabad. His command of Urdu was excellent. Still when he walked out of the gate of his house and approached the walkway he felt something like scared. The whole street looked deserted. No rickshaw, scooter, buses, pedestrians were visible anywhere. A particular type of vehicle and people were dominating the familiar street. These were the groaning olive coloured military jeeps and lorries moving from Mohakhali towards the north to his office. Somber looking helmeted soldiers with green camouflage and machineguns pointed to the front direction were boarded on these vehicles.

Rauf walked for three minutes to reach Mohakhali bus stop. There was not a single civilian around. A familiar man who used to sell cigarettes and matches with a blazing rope hung around an electric pole on the stoppage was also not there. The usual sights of beggars, peddlers and passengers around the stoppage were also totally missing. The men in uniform aboard the vehicles did not pay any particular attention to Rauf. Rauf was looking ahead but no buses were coming from either direction. Seven minutes elapsed. He was also looking for somebody; he could ask if buses would be available today. None was there. He was not one to lose heart quickly. His duties at the office were in his mind. He looked at his watch, 10 minutes past ten o'clock. The heat was rising. At this moment something added to his anxiety. Very close to the side of the walkway exactly opposite to Rauf's, a military vehicle screeched to a halt. In the front seat an officer was sitting along with the driver. Behind, about ten soldiers were seated all with protruding fire-arms. One of them swiftly got down from behind with something which looked like a tool-box. Rauf felt his heart-beat rising. Immediately after, the man seated on the left side of the driver also opened the door and jumped down on the street very close to Rauf. Rauf looked at his face but due to the netted helmet on the man's head Rouf could not read his face. Rauf then saw the name plate on the left side of the man's uniform's breast-pocket. The inscription was 'Didar'

Rauf felt his palpitations rising. He was almost sure that this man was a Punjabee. Such names were common with them. Rauf was cautiously looking at the shoulder badge of the man and recognized the man as a captain of the Pakistan army. Meanwhile the soldier was taking out some metal instruments from the box.

There was a flat tire along the rear side of the military vehicle. Captain Didar examined the trouble and watched as the soldier stooped to fix it with the tools in his hand. The soldiers gradually got down from their rear seats to ease the repairs by reducing the weight of the vehicle. They did not look at Rauf and looked at the repair work. Out of a sense of self-security Rauf felt that it would not be wise to walk away from this place right at the moment. He was also not feeling at all comfortable standing thus. The repair work was half-way through and the captain stood up and was coming closer to Rauf. Rauf felt scared. Rauf was wondering how could he let his face look as normal as possible. He was sweating. At that moment suddenly but very quietly captain Dinar glanced at the red identity card hung on Raff's chest and asked 'Where are you going to? Rauf could not believe his ears. The captain was speaking perfect Bangla. Rauf much surprised and relieved of his fear, stated his destination in a voice as calmly and as normally as possible. The captain said in the same voice, 'I think no buses or other vehicles will be available today. There are no passengers anywhere. It is better you go back to your home.'

Meanwhile the repairing was complete and all the soldiers had boarded the vehicle.

Rauf did not miss the deference in the captain's tone with which he made the suggestion. He liked that. He felt a very intense interest in making a query to the captain. He was going to ask him if he was a Bengalee. Meanwhile the captain also had boarded the vehicle. Before Rauf could ask the question they were gone towards the direction of Tongi.

Within minutes Rauf walked back home. His wife and daughter asked about the reasons of his return. Asad also joined them soon. Rauf realized that those three very dear persons of his life would have a score with him if he talked to them about the actual cause of his return. So he edited the reason slightly and said in a normal voice, 'Today the number of plying vehicles is limited as the conditions of the road are somewhat abnormal. That is why I decided not to attend office.'

Asad reacted by saying

'Dad, what will happen if your boss suddenly makes a phone call from Islamabad and discovers that you are absent without his permission?'

Rauf said 'Well this is only once in a lifetime. He knows me. I will take a day's casual leave.'

Rauf looked at the apparently innocent eyes of his son. He did not at all doubt that his son, for the first time in his life was actually teasing him for his pro-government attitude by that question.

//

At twelve thirty in the afternoon the call for the Friday 'Jumma' prayers became audible from the mike of the local mosque. Rauf was sleeping. His wife asked,

'Shall you not go to the mosque?'

Rauf woke up and said,

'Yes. I will. By the way did anybody call me from the office?'

—No, but our neighbour enquired about us.

—What did they say?

—We should not worry and that we should not hesitate to give him a call if we need anything.

Rauf was always self-reliant. He helped others and never accepted assistance from others. Still he felt better after these words from his neighbour. Rauf went to the bathroom, took his ablution and then dressed himself for the prayers. While getting out of the house he asked his wife,

'Where is Asad and what is he doing?'

—He is in his room, possibly taking rest.

-Good. Make sure that he does not get out. It is also not safe to use the telephone unnecessarily. I have a feeling that the present matter is perhaps not going to be resolved easily or soon.

The mosque was just across the Mohakhali railway crossing. It was a three minute walk from his house. Rauf found only two men wearing caps in the whole street proceeding to the mosque. Rauf could see that they were very old men.

The black-top road was abandoned. The sky above was emitting heat and a dry air around the environment. The familiar place was looking more spacious than usual due to the total absence of any traffic. The walkway also had the same look. Rauf's eyes caught two corpses lying on the rail track. Both were adults. They did not look like cut down by a locomotive but shot to death. A little further down two dead dogs lay sprawled on the stairs of the mosque. There was nobody to put these unholy beings away from such a sacred place. The cemented place looked blackish with the dried up blood smear of the animals. Rauf was surprised that even the mullah of the mosque dared not do anything about this sacrilege. Rauf entered the prayer place. Prayers would start very soon but the congregation was only eight old people strong. Not a single young man was there. A chill feeling went through Rauf's spine.

The familiar young Imam was not there. The *muajjin* could not tell his whereabouts. The eldest among the assembly was requested by the others to take the lead in the prayers. He agreed and read a *Khutba* for the military in a tone full of fear. A '*Khutba*' must always contain a prayer for the unity of the country along with its well-being. Rauf thought, so the fear of the military is deadlier than the fear of Allah!' The prayer finished very quietly and promptly. Nobody uttered a single word about politics or society. Rauf returned home.

The lunch of the family went by quickly. Asad looked somber. His mother and sister looked morose while Rauf looked as usually comfortable. Everyone was waiting for something.

//

A few minutes before eight'o clock in the evening Asad switched on the transistor. The family sat around him. A male announcer with a grave tone made an announcement alternatively in English, Bangla and Urdu. 'This is Radio Pakistan, Karachi. Dear listeners, now the most honourable President of Pakistan General Agha Md. Yahya Khan will address the nation.'

Immediately the national anthem started playing '*Pak Saar Jameen saad baad* . . . . ended and the sonorous voice of the President followed . . .

'My dear countryman, *Assalamualikum*. It is with a heavy heart that I have appeared before you. You are aware that my government and I have been giving relentless labour for the last two years to hand over power to a civilian administration. With this end in view an election was held throughout Pakistan on the basis of one man one vote. It was praised by the whole world. After that I held discussions with all the political parties so that a constitution could be formulated and power transferred. In this regard I received unflinching support of the countrymen. For this, I thanked all of you. So that there is no trouble in the national assembly session I had a plan. I consulted my legal advisors and tried to reach a consensus with the political parties beforehand. My goal was to reach a formula about the transfer of power. But it is a matter of great sorrow that the majority party did not render any co-operation regarding this. Rather they remained uncompromising on certain demands. These demands are against the unity and solidarity of this country. We could not reach an understanding due to the obduracy and lack of compromise of Sheikh Mujib. His illogical demands and conduct have led me to be convinced in one matter, that this man and his party are enemies to Pakistan. This time they will not go unpunished. So long I will remain the President of Pakistan there will be no compromise about the territorial integrity and unity of the country. However, after the control of the central government is restored, my government will continue to work for transferring power to the elected representatives at the right time.

Khoda Hafiz. Long live Pakistan.'

Again the sounds of the national anthem were audible. Asad instantaneously switched the transistor off. He almost screamed and said,

—Dad, have you seen what a big devil he is! Neither a single word about killing men nor any blame against the *Nabab*. He put all the blame on us! Did you listen to the diatribe he used against Mujib?

Rauf hurriedly stopped his son and anxiously said 'Asad you are endangering us and you will also be in danger.

—Why Dad? What have I done?

Asad asked still in an excited tone.

—My son. Please lower your voice. Even the walls have ears—is not there a saying like that? Someone might watch that you are criticizing the speech of the President. That may not be good for us.

—Well you are correct. Actually I was astonished with the speech. Now tell me in this speech where is the truth? Where are the facts?

—Not that there was nothing in it. The President mentioned that after authority of the government is restored power to a civilian government will be transferred.

—What contradiction! Power will be given to those who have destroyed the governments' authority?

—About your use of the word 'diatribe' may I also remind you the patience the President showed to the jeering attitude of the political activists shown to the army during the month of March?

About power transfer I see your point but may be the President meant there will be fresh elections.

—Do you suppose people will vote otherwise? Which party is here except the Awami league?

Rauf was a devout Moslem and against anything opposed to Islam. His belief in Pakistan, Islam and Moslems was deeply rooted in his inner psyche.

He replied,

'Well, totally different results may not be an absurd idea if there was a free and fair election.

Asad was indeed surprised by his father's words He said, 'Dad, I think you are capable of leading many seasoned politicians. What you want to say is this that the last elections were not free and fair. So this is not reflecting public opinion?'

—You see. Many false and exaggerated ideas, promises and information were given to the electorate during the election campaign. They cast their votes accordingly.

—You have stunned me father!

—How?

—As you said voters were fed with lies. The President himself confessed publicly that the centre had exploited us for long twenty three years. Though today in his speech he was lying and blaming us.

Rauf was about to tell that the President was a castrated ox. Otherwise how can a head of state be so undiplomatic and frank? On second thought he resisted himself as such indecent words cannot take place between a father and a son especially in a conservative society. Besides that argument would go to Asad's favour. So he said 'It is true some deprivation of the Bengalees has taken place. That cannot be made good overnight. They have to be given quite a while to balance this inequality'

—I admit that you know many things better than I do. You are experienced. Still given what happened last night, do you think that we two wings will still stay together or it would be proper?

—If there is no intervention by a third power we will remain together. And there is no question of 'should not'.

-Then what happens to this declaration that the struggle for independence has started. World powers are also disseminating the same—So what are these for?

—Son, I will be frank with you. This propaganda is just hocus-pocus. These will not last long. These Punjabees are such a martial race. If they chase and beat us for a few days, which they will do indeed, we will not hold long and will back out. Without knowledge, skill and preparation how can a liberation resistance be put up. Plus there was no such big issue and the fighting is like a same side.

—But Dad, the radio is saying that the EPR, Police, faction of Bengal regiment and freedom fighters are fighting heroically. Are all these events fiction?

—That radio is of your choice. A freedom struggle can't be fought with a few 303 rifles. Besides we have always been a fissiparous nation. You will see that within a few months factions will raise their heads for leadership and hegemony.

The clock by that time struck nine. Gunfire though not as intense as last night had started in the city. Mrs. Rauf and her daughter so far did not speak a word. Mrs. Rauf rose from her seat and said,

'You have had enough of politics. Now get up, have dinner and relieve me of my kitchen duties.'

The family took their seats around the small dining table. Mrs. Rauf served the meal and everyone started eating. Rauf looked normal and he ate like a hungry man. The sound of gunfire outside was becoming louder and more frequent. The mother and daughter looked scared. Rauf watched them. They were not having a morsel but just moving the food with their fingers. Rauf affectionately asked,

—Honey, feeling scared?

With ashen faces both answered in the affirmative.

Rauf reassuringly said,

'Why? Did not you live with these people for six years at Rawalpindi, Karachi and Islamabad? These are the same people you socialized with. Now, why should you be afraid of them?'

Rauf was smiling but the faces of his wife and daughter remained unchanged. Asad also looked thoughtful and did not eat much. The dinner ended up without any further words. Mrs. Rauf entered the kitchen and started cleaning the dishes with the maid servant Gulenoor.

This house was a two-storied building. Rauf's family was occupying the first floor. The ground floor was used by a long standing tenant. He was a young gentleman but the tenancy was old. Rauf was preparing to go to bed. Rauf heard someone knocking on the door of the drawing room from outside. Everyone except Rauf became scared. Asad was a brave man though not as much as his father. Still the sound on the door did not seem good to him. He took up a thick iron rod from the kitchen and stood on the corner of the door. The knock was continuing. The mother and daughter's face looked anxious. Rauf loudly asked 'who is there?'

There was an answer. 'This is Shakhawat Hossain, your tenant from the ground floor.'

Rauf recognized the voice and opened the door.

He asked 'Mr. Shakhawat, what is the matter at this late night?

Shakhawat looked scared. He was holding a shopping bag in his right hand. He whispered, 'Uncle, may I borrow some rice or perched rice from you?'

Mrs. Rauf comforted him and replied,

'First do come inside please. Then we will see what can be done.

Shakhawat came in and closed the door behind him. Shakhawat worked in an electrical company near Gulshan, a place not far away from his residence. About a week ago, sensing trouble he had sent his family away to his village home at Mymensingh district.

He explained, 'I usually do my shopping weekly on Fridays. Last Friday was fine. Today I could go nowhere. All the shops around are closed. I have got nothing in my kitchen.'

Rauf said 'don't worry young man. I have never been scared like you that I should send my family to village home for safety. No, why should I? This is an independent country. We abide by the law. Why should I feel panicky about our own country? No, I will not flee from them.'

—Uncle, what are you saying? Don't you know how many people the army has killed during the last forty-eight hours? They have killed all in the university, Rajarbag and Pilkhana areas. The Punjabees are going to finish us this time.

—How many of the incidents you are telling me about have you seen with your own eyes, Mr. Shakhawat?

—See, Uncle, these things are now known the world over. How can I watch these with my own eyes?

—You are talking like my son . . . The Punjabees are destroying everything. Actions are going to be taken only against those who have done something wrong or illegal. Can you show that they have done anything against you or me?

—Then why are people fleeing from the city? Tell me why this city is getting abandoned?

—These are called whims; you people often repeat one thing that the army is Punjabee. Why? Don't we have our Bengalee people in the armed forces? Even today amidst army action I met a Bengalee captain. He spoke to me so courteously and sympathetically!

Shakhawat did his Master's in business administration from the Punjab University at Lahore. His age, intelligence and experience were more than Asad's. He was almost going to tell his landlord that the BBC does not do their business by eating grass. His age made him control such coarseness—It would not look nice also. He toned down and said, well uncle, now we will gradually come to know what actually is happening but the public is panic stricken. In such a state of mind even cautious persons tend to believe anything that is coming in to the air. But now how can we save our lives?

—You just move about normally. If the office is open attend it. And never talk politics with anyone. By the grace of the almighty Allah everything will be fine.

Even with these words of an elderly gentleman Shakhawat did not get any reassurance or comfort in his mind.

Some memories of his student-life crossed his mind. His Punjabee classmates always used to talk and behave offensively with him. They also blamed East Pakistanees for not being good Moslems.

Meanwhile Mrs. Rauf packed some rice, perched rice and curry for Shakhawat and told him that so long as shops were closed he was free to have his breakfast, lunches and dinner in this house. She further told him 'we will be able to run a month with the stock of foodstuff we have now. So do not worry.'

Shakhawat thanked the Raufs for their hospitality and went back to his house. The boom of gunfire gradually increased outside.

A vernal equinox was in progress. A big moon was floating on a clear sky. The vacant roads were glittering with the shining moonlight. Curfew would continue until seven o'clock in the morning tomorrow. All the doors and windows of this house were shut. The roads had only one continual sound from plying military vehicles at prolonged intervals. At a faraway place a dog was barking.

In their bedroom Mrs. Rauf and her daughter tried to sleep. Asad in his bed tried to listen to a news station at a very low sound level. Now he had started listening to the Islamabad radio station. A news bulletin was telling that the President's speech that evening had been praised

from all quarters. The felicitators had congratulated the President for his statesman like role in the crisis. Khan Abdul Quyaum Khan, a veteran politician from the N.W.F.P. had expressed his satisfaction saying that the present army action had successfully eradicated all anti-state elements. Besides, the nation had found a new direction about its future course from the President's speech. A mock smile surfaced on Asad's face as he listened. Rauf was sitting on his bed. He was brooding something.

//

On the day of final call Zahanjeb Abrar wanted to know the name of the place of his new assignment. A sergeant told it was Allen Bury. People around pronounced it as Alan Bari. 'Bari' means 'home' in the local language. Most of them did not know that actually it was magistrate Allen Bury of Dhaka after whom the place was named. He left India after 1947 for his home in Britain. The place was near the only big airport at Tejgaon area of the provincial capital city. It was the third night that Abrar had been on duty here. Duty meant just watching the fireworks from light arms taking place in the southern part of the city. Abrar had orders to remain seated on his anti-aircraft gun all through except for ablution, prayers and toilet. He was waiting to face enemy aircrafts but found no such signs and so got disappointed. In 1965, he remembered, he continually shot in the sky at Rajouri sector and brought down three enemy aircrafts. Later on, commanders told him that a few pilots from the falcon fighter-bombers were captured due to his successful gun fire.

This area was within the Dhaka cantonment board and was quiet. Besides Abrar's 47th field regiment artillery, 11th Baluch Regiment and an infantry company were in full attention position here. Abrar knew nothing about this area. He knew this much that people here were basically idle. They had no fighting qualities in their history. Two persons from this area were with Abrar's unit. One was Awlad Hossain who was the unit's cook. Another one was Kalachan. He was a mechanical transport driver.

Twenty four hours had gone since the crackdown. Abrar was thinking about just one issue. Authorities said the unit had to be fully prepared for action. Action means shooting enemy aircrafts. Where shall the Bengalees get air-crafts? There were no foreigners or Hindus like in 1965. The briefing could not answer his question as to why a civilian

population would attack its own army or an airport. Abrar could not avoid a thought which was running persistently in his mind—for nothing had his daughter's marriage ceremony been turned into a totally merriless function without the father's presence. What non-sense is this?'

The 9th Baluch regiment was camping along the military court no. 8 at Nakhalpara near Allen Bury. The C.O. of the battalion Lt. Col. Najar Hossain's father was a famous lyricist of Uttar Pradesh in India. The world-class Indian maestro Md. Rafi and legendary vocalist Lata Mangeshkar immortalized many of his lyrics by giving their golden voices to these lyrics. Najar however had no liking for music. His lookout was for murder, blood and the kill. His unit, like Abrar's was sitting idle as no order for action had been given to them.

At one thirty in the morning Najar was sitting in his camp and was listening to the results of action from his colleagues and friends units' through his wireless set. With each news of a Bengalee casualty he was jumping with a morbid satisfaction and excitedly telling people around 'the history of these sons of bitch is like this. If you give them a good thrashing they will behave. Otherwise they will climb on your head. This time they have received such a good beating that there will be no uprising by them in the next five hundred years.'

His battalion major Nasser supported him by saying 'Sir you are absolutely right'. Najor got further inspired and said 'I failed to appreciate why the President gave these infidels so much time right after the speech on the 7th of March.'

Across the camp in another building the chairman of summary military court no.8 Lt. Col. Gulistan Badaiunee was also releasing his version for the locals of this province. He was saying 'I said right in 1967 that the allegation of Agartola conspiracy case was totally founded. Why should the defendants be given an opportunity for self-defense?' His 2-i-c was listening and asked 'Did you suggest anything?'

-Of course I did. I said, let us stage-manage a trouble in the court by govt. agents on a day of their hearing. Then in the melee, have all of them shot by brush-fire. If my advice was heeded things would not move this far!

Major Farhan Tanvir asked 'Sir, what did the big bosses say about your proposal?'

—Tanvir, I was a mere major then. Who would listen to me? Major General Rao Farman Ali stopped me with a heavy snub. He said such works are to be carried out slowly. Now we are seeing the results of going slowly. After so many years, by Allah's grace my wife is going to give birth to our first child. But she is at Daudkhel and I am here 1200 miles away from her. Only Allah knows when shall we see each other and if that will happen at all.

—Sir, why are you saying 'if at all?'

—Listen, such news can never be kept secret. Do you know how many and who have got killed so far?

—No, Sir, I don't know. I never imagined Bengalees could ever have the capacity of killing us, Sir.

—Mohammad Khan of commando battalion, Shakil Durrani of the 7th Frontier force and Hossain Kuli Khan of 4th cavalry are among those who are very close to us. They are all gone last night. Plus there are so many which we don't know personally.

—What a strange news! When did this rice-eating lousy people learn how to kill and more so military people?

—Haven't you heard about commander Moazzem, Col. Osmany, General Wajid and Brigadier Majumder? These bastards have trained them on fire arms. So our thought that the trouble would be sorted out within 48 hours does not appear to hold good now. I don't think everything is going to be cooled down so soon. On the other hand the thought of getting a transfer under such a condition is unimaginable.

—Sir, then what are our forces doing?

—They are killing without pause. Even then you must bear one point in mind when you are in a war. Suppose you are the elephant and your enemy is an ant. You can beat him but you must tolerate the sting of their bite. And in our present case we should not think they are ants.

Major Tanvir was posted out here a few months ago from Nawshera cantonment. He had little idea about people here. So he said,

—Sir, our intelligence sources say that there is hardly a gun in any home around here. Plus they were never known to be a martial race.

—Even then. Don't forget that those who put up the resistance battle at Khemkaran sector and defended Lahore from inevitable fall during the 1965 war are now stationed in this province. They are fully armed. Have you forgotten 8th Bengal regiment's action in that war? Besides, the EPR has joined hands with them along with their arms. All of them have deserted the B.O.P.s, you know that?

—Sir, then it is indeed something which can't be taken lightly. But . . .

—But what?

—Our academy has always taught us to be optimistic and never to be a defeatist.

—We will show that but there are further worrying factors. Can you guess that?

—Not exactly?

—Those that instigated the Agartola conspirators from behind have now become active once again. They are supporting these depraved Banglalees direct and without any camouflage. Did you miss their radio news bulletin on the 25th of March? How could they determine so soon that we are in a civil war here in this province? The matter on the whole does not seem to be a good one.

Badaiunee was known to be a radar of military and political issues. So Tanvir understood what he was telling were mostly true. He said,

—Sir, I was not much aware of these realities and so was happy. Now I am getting anxious.

—No, don't worry. So long our unit is not called into action we should not have a heavy mind. When there is a call we must be ready to die any moment. The very duty of our profession is either to kill or get killed. There is no option except these.

—Sir I am absolutely prepared for that but I will be sorry if that consequence befalls on us from such an inferior race.

Badaiunee looked like a reflective man as the dim light of the camp fell on his face. He said,

—It is an offence in our profession just to imagine a defeat. Still I will say no body can tell who is going to defeat whom.

Badaiunee was a junior officer at the Punch-Shakkargor sector at the Punjab—Sindh border during the last war. He remembered at this moment that the government had told many lies about those wars which were concocted glories of victories. He then decided that these should not be shared with a junior officer.

PNS Zahiruddin Md. Babar was anchored for the last four days at the Chittagong Naval base. Lieutenant-Commander Makhdum Shah commanding the ship was born in Gwalior, India. He joined the Pakistan Navy in 1961. This was his first transfer to East Pakistan. This port city and even this Bay of Bengal were alien to him. Earlier he had spent three postings at Hull and other ports of the U.K. and Debal port

in West Pakistan. During the last war of his country he was commander of a Frigate. Before his ship could fire a single bullet, two enemy bombers bombarded and sunk his ship within five minutes. Makhdum managed to swim up eleven miles away to a coast and make a survival somehow. His experience in war was limited to this much.

He remembered all the instructions of the briefings given half a week ago at the naval base, Karachi. He was watching the city skies and the bay's southern flank with a pair of binoculars in his eyes. Nothing worthy of taking any action so far caught his attention, except a theoretical threat of the briefing. Makhdum did not have any other thoughts about the rebels. A tough man by nature Makhdum was not feeling any poesy in his mind in spite of a beautiful moon on the sky, the salty breeze and silvery surfs of the bays around him. His front gunner Mubarok Kasuri asked him,

—Sir, may I ask a question?

—Go ahead Kasuri.

—I was wondering where these rebels of Bengal have arms from that they can use to fight a sea battle. I know about these fellows. They have never boarded anything other than country boats in their life.

Mubarak was attached to *PNS Bakhtiar Khiljee* when it was anchored at Mangla Port here in this province in 1966. At that period he gained a basic experience in the local boatmen, boats and environment.

In the military profession there is no scope for a senior to show any ignorance about anything to a junior. Makhdum promptly said,

'These crooked fellows will infiltrate your vessels in the garb of stevedores and torchbearers and from underneath the sea water. They do not have the courage to come frontally. So we have to keep an eye to that direction. All civilians, contractors, porters must be kept on the suspect list. Mind that, they can sink a ship even by subterfuge.

Mubarak could not believe his boss's words. How can a French made destroyer be infiltrated and destroyed by unprofessional people? He asked himself. However, there was no scope to raise such queries and start a debate with a senior. Mubarak with a salute turned his head around and started thinking about his old parents, children and wife living in a small village cottage near the Wagah border.

///

It was 05.00 hours, 27th March. The white rays of the dawn were becoming visible through the glass window panes of the Easter Command head quarters. The Commander lifted the receiver of his telephone and demanded,

'Khadim, when shall I have the final report?'

—Sir, at six-thirty.

—No, make it 6' o clock.

—Ok sir.

The commander hung up.

A scion of the Greeks when they conquered the Punjab in 300 B.C., this commander did not have any sleep last night. With full battle gear on, he was sitting in his office at Sher-e-Bangla nagor.

At 6' o clock his phone buzzed.

—Yes, Khadim.

—Sir, it is 4000.

—What? In two nights only four thousand! I demand a break-down.

—Sir, police 490, EPR 50, 600 at the university dormitories, about 2500 in old Dhaka including Awami league activists and Hindus. The rest were in the slums. Plus 1760 EPR soldiers have been disposed of at Chittagong.

—No. This is not acceptable. Don't you know the price of a bullet? Didn't you ever work in the ordnance depot?

—Sir, we had to give some time to screen. My units were the best but many of the targets fled before my boys could get them at their address.

—I don't give a damn for your alibis and procrastination, man. Launch a combing operation. I have said it earlier. I am repeating it now. Listen and listen well. Capture those who burnt national flags, hoisted their own and shoot them then and there. Am I clear?

—Sir, give me a little more time.

—No, you don't know these people. If you can't show terror right now, our mission will be delayed. We can't allow them time to get organized.

—Ok Sir. I will do my best.

The commander replaced the receiver.

Nobody had even seen him smiling.

The only expression on his face was toughness. Known as the notorious butcher of Baluchistan, this very tall fellow never blinked. When he put a beret on his head he looked quite close to Hitler's companion Himmler. He thought over the figures received a few minutes earlier, and in a soliloquy whispered' If I had orders on the first day I would not let things go this far. I wish I could hang that ruffian in public.'

//

Mrs. Rauf watched her husband dressing up. She asked
'Hello, will you try to attend office today?'
—Indeed because it is Saturday. Tomorrow is the weekly holiday. Yesterday I was absent. I think I should go to see if there is any news or information.
—But how shall you be there? There is no movement of any traffic yet.
—They have relaxed the curfew until six' o clock in the evening. I hope I will be able to manage some transport. Let me see what I can find.
Asad came in the room and heard the conversation. He proposed 'Dad, can't you make a phone call instead of going there on such a risky day?'

His sister also joined him in this proposal. Rauf replied, 'no kids, I am the head of the office. If I abstain myself in this way, I might have to face some trouble in the future.'
—Ok Dad but please be cautious. Take care.
Rauf took an umbrella, spread it over his head and reached the bus stop. The sight was not normal but much different from that of the previous day. He found many people on the streets. Army convoys were also doing their rounds. Men, women and children were walking or boarding buses, rickshaws and baby taxis. They were also carrying heavy baggage. Many of them appeared to be of the gentlemen class. Rauf's bus for Joydevpur was yet to arrive. He asked a head of a family, may I know where you are going to? The gentleman said 'to my village home at Netrokona district. The army has shot many people and will kill more. Last night at Arjotpara, where my family was staying in a hired house they killed at least twenty people. Now we are trying this way to save our lives, by going to the village home'
Arjotpara was not far away from Rauf's residence. He had not heard any sound of shooting from that area last night. Rauf did not believe in the news. Rauf found another man in his mid fifties leading a family to get a transport. They appeared to be a lower middle class family. Rauf put

the same question to him. He replied in an emotion charged voice 'the military has killed thousands of innocent civilians, university teachers, students and women around Nilkhet and the University dormitory areas. My home is at Azimpur. I am going to Mirzapur of Tangail district to my village home. Only Allah knows if we will be able to make it. Already the army has checked my baggage twice while coming to this bus stop.'

This information also could not disturb Rauf's usual tranquil mind. He thought this half-educated man was exaggerating. Rauf boarded a bus and got off at Joydevpur stoppage at forty-five minutes past nine.

The security check-post of the army meanwhile had been beefed-up. It was now being commanded by a commissioned officer. As Rauf arrived in the area a soldier approached him and started checking him. Seconds later a tall, black and stout man with the insignia of the '4th Cavalry' on the shoulder of his uniform appeared and stopped the soldier from checking Rauf. He very politely asked Rauf who he was and where he was going to. Rauf introduced himself. The man made an obeisance very close to that of a salute to Rauf and said in clear Urdu, 'Please proceed on your way.'

Rauf noted the particulars of the man showing him such respect. His name plate showed him as 'Gulbahar' and the insignia was that of a Major. Rauf tried to remember these facts. He did not find a single soul on the expansive road along the International Rice Research Institute leading to his office. Usually there was a great hubbub every day. Within minutes Rauf entered his office premises. The guard, orderly and his stenographer were still absent. With the personal copy of the key Rauf unlocked his chamber and entered there. His table and chair had a quarter inch dust cover.

He sat on his chair after getting the dust cleared by a member of subordinate staff and talked through his intercom to his assistant controller in the adjacent room. Nobody answered it. He asked the staff,

—How many are present today?

—Sir, eleven.

—Show me the attendance roll.

Rauf put his initial on the roll. The real operating business of his office took place at the printing press which was about a hundred yards behind his office. Only nine out of nineteen officials had reported. Out of the absentees, 4 were non-locals. No-one had sent any application for their leave of absence. Rauf summoned his superintendent, got an application for his recent absence typed and ordered him to send the paper to the controller's office at Islamabad.

Rauf listened to the noises coming out from the printing section for sometimes and estimated that if there were no new work orders soon, he would have to stop the press section some four days from now. Rauf sent a situation report to his head office through the teleprinter. At one forty five in the afternoon Rauf started for home after offering his noon prayers. At half-past two he reached home, had lunch and went to bed for a rest.

//

At Dhaka cantonment a briefing session was in progress. Commander Eastern command, was conducting it. Across to his left was seated Brigadier Khalid Abdullah Tasneem, C.O. 27th infantry brigade. Tikka looked at him and asked 'you have not had a war or battle since 1965?'

—True sir.

—Where had you been before Kharian cantonment?

—We were at Jampur and Shahiwal sir.

—Well.

Now he looked at Lt. General Sher Ali Bajj and said the deployment shall be as follows:—36th division-Bogra-Rangpur, 14th division-Faridpur, 9th division—Mymensingh, 16th division—Rajshahi, 29th division—Sylhet and Chittagong.

General Bajj said 'what about support units?

-Shall be deployed when felt necessary.

-Sir, is that all?

—Yes, for now. You can leave now. You now complete down the line briefings in your respective units. Remember what I said at the beginning of today's session. Forget what was said to you before coming to this province. I am in command here. Nothing or nobody can be more important than what I say here, Right?

In almost unequivocal terms, he today at the beginning of this session had told the commanders 'Kill them all whoever you feel like . . .'

This was the first briefing since the authority of the army had been established at all sub divisional levels. Tikka visited this new command post to conduct the briefing, after it was established on 30th April.

Officers from the ranks of the highest to brigadiers and equivalents were allowed for this purpose. Tikka emphasized that the success so far was fully satisfactory. To sustain that, operations must be conducted from then on at the grass-root levels. The high command was convinced that was the only way to resolve the problem the province was in. None of the commanders asked anything further and filed out of the room one by one and went back to their units. Only a very few thought, this would be too much. Most accepted it as a normal thing. Under their thick moustaches they smiled which made them look like Dracula.

Having finished the briefing Tikka went back to his office at Sher-e-Banglanogor. He thought 'I have given them a piece of my mind. Now I will see how they behave and what results they bring in for me. The bosses in Islamabad or Pindi don't know how to rule this land and its miscreants. I have done similar things before with my own land and with my own people. Nobody can preach be better than I.'

//

Lt. Colonel Yaqub Malikee was a perfectionist. Men whose very physical survival has been significantly threatened since childhood have to be perfectionist. Yaqub, holding his parents hands had made a hair-breadth escape to Pakistan dodging severe communal riots along the path from their family's home from Hoshiarpur to the Lahore border in 1947. He was then seventeen and so time did not efface those horrible gory details of man-slaughter, arson, loot and inhumanity of fellow human beings. Anything Indian, Hindu or their sympathizers made a deep impression on his mind. As he landed at Tejgaon airport Yaqub briefly thought of those past but unforgotten canvas of his life. He also recollected the earlier occasions when he had worked here in two army units.

Never a votary or reader of Shakespeare's Yaqub still held his 'tongue less and lent his ears more'. He was still examining a military map of the Comilla cantonment brought from his West Pakistan office.' Fine, I will enjoy it' he said to himself.

The plane stopped. Yaqub disembarked and was received by an ISPR major and they right away started for Comilla by road. They reached his unit HQ at 3:00 clock in the afternoon. Late that night Yaqub sat on

his office desk. His hither to acting battalion commander and now 2-i-c watched him sitting in front him across the table.

Ninety-five percent of the other ranks of this army unit was local. All *Subeders, Nayeks, Habilders, Habilders* Major, Lance *Nayeks*, Corporals *Subeder* and *Nayek Subeder* were from West Pakistan. Yaqub scanned through each of those names and titles very carefully. No, not a single familiar face. The British were responsible for this gap. They said the social and positional superiority must be maintained between the leaders and the led. No, democracy or egalitarianism must not have any place in this profession. Yaqub completed his scanning and told the man in front,

—I will meet the unit, day after tomorrow. Make arrangements accordingly.

—I will Sir.

That morning dawned on 6th April, 1971, Sunday. The morning exercise and breakfast of the unit had been complete by 7.30. Yaqub Malekee with a ceremonial uniform had been sitting in his desk since seven o'clock. All soldiers and officers were waiting in a single camouflaged shed along the playground of the cantonment. It was going to be not only an inspection by the newly appointed battalion commander but a 'durbar' also. Anyone can talk, exchange views and make petition to the C.O. on such occasions. That is the army rule. The clock struck thirty five minutes past seven. Major Ishrat Fardin entered Malikee's room, extented a smart salute and said.

'Sir, the whole unit, men and officers are ready to give you the guard of honour—your permission is being sought for that.

—Allowed, proceed Major.

—Proceeding, Sir.

Malikee left his room along with Ishrat, walked past a rear gate and both boarded a vehicle. The vehicle started and within a minute reached the main gate. Both got down from the vehicle and immediately a smartly turned out contingent of the unit staged a guard of honour for the C.O. The two finished the inspection and entered the shed. The four hundred and fifty six strong unit was seated in 38 rows and 12 columns on the floor. All rose as the battalion C.O. entered. Ishrat beckoned *Subeder* Hamja Khan, the guard commander. Hamja made a war cry to his soldiers,

'Attention, the armed salutation will now be taken. Turn right, arms down.'

It was a smart scene. All soldiers obeyed him, released a full-throated sound of honour and made a sign facing their palms towards Yaqub. Yaqub took the salute. Hamja said 'Turn left, stand at ease.'

Yaqub and Ishrat proceeded towards the stage of today's ceremony. The traditional chair of the C.O. looked very special. Carved in the manner of a throne the credit for its craftsmanship went to a skilled carpenter in the pay-roll of the military engineering services department. With the polish of varnish and brass clippings the Burma-teak made chair looked majestic. Again the same mindset—the Commander must look superior. Lt. Col. Yaqub Malikee said 'in the name of Allah' and sat on the designated chair. His Arabic was clearly audible to everyone in the shed. Then he made a sign to Isharat to sit. Yaqub said 'Please take your seats' in Urdu. Everyone except the guards at the four entrances folded their knees and complied with the command.

Yaqub's eyes were perfect. In the armed forces medical corp's ophthalmologist's scale, the measurement was 6×6. He threw a glance and could clearly see even the subtlest expressions on the faces and eyes of the men seated before him. He also understood the meanings of those expressions. During the last two days he had collected necessary information about these uniformed men from the unit intelligence officer. The report said nothing to worry about. These people did not yet know what actually had happened in Dhaka on the night of 25th and 26th March. The only thing is, these men were somewhat tense because of the overall condition of the province and the country. Yaqub smiled inside his own mind with the thought that even this stupid intelligence officer also was not aware of what had happened in Dhaka. Malikee now looked very tough. Putting his lips close to the microphone and using pure Urdu, he suddenly asked the audience 'Can you tell me who are responsible for the trouble that this country has been facing since 1st March?

Most of the audience had an 8th grade education. Still they knew under the service rules, such a question should never be answered by any of them. During their training period and even later on it was repeatedly told to them that involvement in any type of political activities was severely punishable in this profession.

So they remained silent. Yaqub's physical strength was visible through his gorilla like posture. His thick jet-black moustache, broad muscular arms and palms covered with black whiskers, blood-shot eyes and deep voice sent a fearful chill through the spines of the assembled men. Looking at his crew-cut hair and the kohl smeared cool eyes they felt that this commander indeed meant business and would surely be ruthless in dealing with the slightest deviation of discipline.

They had some vague information about the situation of Dhaka since March. They also knew through the state news agency that disturbances created by anti-social elements had been quelled by the army on the 25th and since then government authority had been established. From the content, style and tone of the question they guessed that their commander himself would answer it and in that he would surely blame the Benglaee secessionist elements for this trouble of the country.

They waited for it while Malikee also watched them with his fiery eyes. Ten seconds passed and Malikee opened his mouth.

'I am giving the answer.'

The troops were somewhat surprised at the voice and vocabulary of their commander. It was soft, mellow and sympathetic. That fire was gone and more surprising, Yaqub spoke in Bangla.

-None but the *Nabab* and his party men are responsible for this.

Malikee was almost smiling now. His sincere tone once again came through the microphone.

-I know what you are thinking about me. Being an army man, I am talking about politics. Am I not? Yes, it is not proper, but there is a but. Under special circumstances every law is to be changed. It requires to be changed. The word 'officer' was almost in Yaqub's lips but on a second thought he preferred to use the word 'man' so that the troops in front of him would feel more akin to him. Now Yaqub looked at the faces of the men to see the impact of his words.

The men actually felt a relief. They never expected this. The tense air inside them, which is normal before a commander, was gone now. Yaqub now took the pickup off from his head and kept it on the table. He looked happy and at ease. Then he continued 'You see. The President himself has admitted that the Bangalees were deprived. They have been exploited by the centre and who have been at the centre? Always ruling people from West Pakistan. So even though the Bangalees have chanted an objectionable slogan or two during the last month, they can't be blamed for that. It was out of frustration and due to the sudden postponement of the expected assembly session which was normal. Political problems must be resolved through political means and never by military might.'

Malikee paused and did not miss the total pleasant surprise in the men's eyes. The reason for this was Malekee's fluent Bangla and sincerity. Abdul Ali from Cherag hat, Rajshahi district thought, 'before this I saw only one such good fellow. He was Azam Khan. Eleven years after, today I have come across another one. All praises to almighty Allah.'

Lt. General Azam Khan was the governor of this province in 1960 when Ali was recruited as a soldier in the army.

Yaqub's voice once again became audible.

'These issues are not taught to you because you belong to a disciplined force. But now, a time has come in our history when you need to know these things. This country of ours came into being by the support of Moslems of East Bengal. They were and still are the majority population in Pakistan. After wining in the last elections they have earned a natural right to sit in power. The President himself has recognized this right. So you should have no qualms about this in your minds.

A sepoy named Dhonai Fokir aged 40 years of Faridpur district was the oldest in this unit. He had questions in his mind about the genuineness of Yaqub's straightforward speech. In the soldiers' mess he could never like the offensive dealing of Havildar Bahram Vatti. So he thought how could a senior commander be trusted? What could be the meaning of the matter?

At the same time he also felt good, because such a big shot was speaking their tongue. He recollected that Dy. chief martial law administrator Yaqub and governor Ahsan of this province used to give their speeches in Bangla in the radio. Plus they had been known as good persons. So there was a connection between these two scenarios.

Meanwhile Malikee started talking,

—In spite of this reality the Bengalees have been blamed for the recent disturbances. Is it fair to blame the whole population because one or two of them have committed a minor folly or two? Those who, sitting at Pindi, think like this, do not know many things. Do you know who composed our national anthem 'Pakistan *Zindabad*, Pakistan *Zindabad*'? He was Nazir Ahmad, a son of this soil. Who tuned this song? He was also a patriotic East Pakistanee' Abdul Ahad. Is it possible for someone to compose and tune such a song unless he has a very profound love for his motherland? No it is not. And may I remind you who defended Lahore in 1965 war? They were the heroic soldiers of 8th Bengal from this land.

The story of the 8th Bengal was true and known to the soldiers. So they felt happy. The information about the national anthem was not known to them. Even then it pleased them.

Malikee continued. 'Hafiz Jalandhorie, the lyricists of the Urdu version of our national anthem and Nazir Ahmad-both great musicians are citizens of the same country. They laboured for the whole nation like the 8th Bengal. You also had been at Sindh. Think about myself. Out of sixteen years of my services in the armed forces I spent a whole seven years at Chittagong and Jessore cantonments. And my father? He was a teacher in Pogose High School in the city of Dhaka where he used to teach Arabic. I have also studied Nazrul, Tagore and Iqbal in my school just like you people. The father of the nation Mohamed Ali Jinnah said that in Pakistan there was nobody called a Moslem, Hindu, Baluch, Punjabee, Bengalee or Pathan. There was only one identity—that is Pakistanee. Now all of us should remember this great saying. I know we do have that in mind otherwise our brothers from here would not defend Lahore. Likewise Major Tufael would not also sacrifice his life to defend Comilla borders in 1966. Tell me if I am speaking the truth? Major Tufael hailed from Jhelum in the Punjab, did not he?'

The men seated in front did not say anything but had to agree with their commander. But there was a dilemma in their minds. They felt it might not be proper to raise it. The question was 'where the majority party leader is now and how he is doing?

There was a flash of a renewed smile on Malikee's face and as if he read the minds of his troops, Malikee slowly spoke 'the leader, so dear to us. Sheikh Mujib, whom the President himself has declared as the future Prime Minister of this country, is in good health. For reasons of security he has been taken into safe custody by the government. I know everyone has an interest in knowing absout him and his welfare. I can tell you there is nothing to worry about him. The President's speech about him and the Awami League on the 26th evening was diplomatic. It had to be diplomatic otherwise there would be pressure from the leaders of the western wing. The President had to appease them by his speech.'

All soldiers felt a flood of happiness engulfing them due to the sincerely of the commander. They were also happy with the thought that such a superior officer spoke so fluently in their own language. Surely even amongst Punjabee or West Pakistanees they were not all bad but some good ones also. They also felt they could say something in response but this was never permissible in this profession. There was not a single exception to this in the last twenty four years.

The C.O. started again, 'it was necessary that I talk to you on these issues given the emergency situation in the country. I strongly believe that the 49th Bengal will co-operate with the nation as it has done before. One thing, can you tell me why I chose this very day to address you?'

Everyone looked at the speaker but did not say a word. Yaqub said, because this is the raising anniversary of the regiment and Major Goni, the founder of this regiment is a son from this Comilla district. That is why I thought I should not make any delay in meeting and knowing you better. I am confident all of you will be behind me in resolving the present crisis of our dear nation. Pakistan *Zindabad*.'

Yaqub put on the pickup on his head, held the stick under his left underarm and stood up from the chair. The troops also rose to their feet. Yaqub came down from the stage and started shaking hands with everyone. He made enquires about the welfare of their wives and kids. Then he exited from the shed along with Major Ishrat. Many had tears in their eyes. They never expected such kind dealing even from any East Pakistanee officers. They had always seen and felt the social and provincial distance and the coolness of their commanders. What happened today was totally unexpected. They said to themselves, an angel-like man. He is a handsome fellow and at the same time is very broad-minded. Many of these people never saw Azam Khan who was a *Pathan*. They heard about him. They said 'our commander is surely a relative of Azam's. Otherwise how can one be so good? Such nice command of the Bangla language in spite of being a Punjabee! It would be impossible unless he had a deep love for the Bengalees.'

With those nice thoughts in mind the troops went back to their barracks. They had their lunch and slept for sometimes. They could not deny the fact that most of them had ambitious thoughts during the whole month of March and until yesterday of April about attacking and killing all Punjabees in the unit and take possession of the unit arsenal. After meeting their new C.O. today, all these plans melted away. Many of them even felt ashamed for such illegal and immoral thoughts.

The afternoon passed by with routine games, sports and exercises. The C.O. appeared to be a good volley-ball player. He played for the 'Punjab' company against 'Yamuna' company. 'Yamuna' won. Yaqub in a half-sleeve sports white jacket and shorts looked very cheerful.

The April chrysanthemums were fluttering their branches against the waves of breezes along the play ground of 49th Bengal. Two hours had elapsed since evening. Street lights around the battalion except those for security gradually faded out. From his officers' mess room Yaqub looked through the window and watched the flowers and the trees. His batman Moidan Ali and body guard Sulaiman Koreshi stood guard outside on the balcony. At 9' o clock they saw darkness falling in their commander's room.

Soldiers are usually light sleepers. But 49th Bengal never participated in a war. The unit had some tensions and uncertainties about the country's situation throughout March and until yesterday. With the commander's honest words all these evaporated from their minds. So most of them were having a worriless slumber. Sepoy Jonab Ali of Alfa Company first heard the noise. He had a chronic itching problem in his left foot and so he slept less. The dermatologist of the army medical corps was treating him. In spite of his inexperience, Jonab Ali recognized the nature and sound of the noise. Training in such a profession is not easily forgotten. He slowly opened his eyelids while still lying in his rope made bedstead.

Seated on a skylight of the barrack, *Subeder* Zikrullah Kiani was spewing fire from a berretta sub-machine gun onto the sleeping local soldiers. Jonab Ali instantly rolled himself out of the bed and hid beneath a hold-all on the floor. The gunfire was increasing. It was going on in all the barracks at the same time. Those who were young tried to reach the arms *cote*, but could not cross even the quarter guard. These simple minded and lowly educated soldiers had not the slightest idea when the 8th Punjab battalion from Chittagong cantonment had reached and cordoned off the barracks. Within a few minutes and half-understanding the treachery the four hundred and twenty five Bengalee soldiers were dead. A few managed to escape. Those fortunate were M.T. driver Atosh Ali, Batman Kalom gazi, sepoy Omar Ali Matbar, Kailash Chandra, military police Alek, Nurul Islam, Milon and Shamsel. A flawless plan executed with a high degree of efficiency ended quickly.

It was four' o clock in the morning. Major Ishrat, 2-i-c went in to make an inspection of the results of the mission. There was no change on his facial expression when he passed through the corpses of his long known sepoy Afser Molla, Eshak Fokir, Kadom Ali, Saijuddin and Alefuddin. He came across the blood-spattered body and smashed head

of his former batman Dhanu mia and gave it only a casual look. He then made an oral report to his c.o. Yaqub who looked pathetic.

It was 5 O' clock now. The call for morning prayers became audible from the battalion mosque. Yaqub meticulously completed his ablution. First he cleaned his palms and fingers, then washing the mouth and nostrils, then the arms and face, head, ears and finally the legs. He wiped the limbs dry with a fresh towel. The afterlife prizes would be more if the prayer was made in festival attire. Malikee was not unaware of this dictum of his religion. He put on a freshly pressed white *kurta* and pyjama made of finest *'tossor'* fabric from Mardan Textiles of N.W.F.P. Then he stood on a colourful prayer mat spread on the floor. The image of the holy shrine of Mecca *Muazzema* was embossed in the middle of the velvet prayer mat. Before starting his prayers he could not forget that he had told lies the previous morning about his father's profession, the anniversary of the regiment's raising and the name of its founder. In the official history of the country the name of the founder of the regiment was mentioned as Fd. Marshall Ayub Khan. The date of its raising was also a different one. Yaqub's father never worked in East Pakistan.

Yaqub now looked at a photo frame placed above a wardrobe beside his bed. Two faces were smiling in the photograph. One was his wife Zubaera and another one, his daughter Najofi. There is a dictum in his religion on the 'dos' and don't's while offering a prayer. One prohibits thoughts of the terrestrial life while in prayers. Still Yaqub could not resist a few thoughts rising from his mind. Those came with some of the questions raised by Col. Amery a few days ago at Islamabad when he was chosen for this appointment.

—Will you be able to tell lies nonstop?

—Do you think you can signal in one direction but then move in a different course?

—Would you be able to mingle fully with the enemy?

—Can you manage a smile when one is not actually coming up spontaneously?

—Will you be capable of nipping something in the bud?

Yaqub smiled as he remembered the answers he gave to those questions. As a ritual Yaqub lifted his palms to the level of his ears. With those same hands Yaqub had shot fifty tribal rebels in 1959 near

the home of the then President. Then he started his prayer by 'Allahoo Akbar'

With an expensive Jinnah cap on his head, a bright and clean prayer dress on his handsome body the prayer engrossed man looked like a sacred angel in a beautiful dawn. Yaqub Malikee had an excellent education in Arabic language from the best teacher of Lahore. With a very good pronunciation the verse which Malikee now recited meant 'and this is the path for the simple and easy going people.'

//

Ten days had elapsed since the crackdown. General Tikka was looking through the figures of achievement after his last briefing six days ago. His face expressed no emotion but he was happy inside. This happiness was increasing as he was turning the pages through his files. There was nobody in his room at this hour. One by one he finished scrutinizing the papers and muttered to himself,' can one rule without fear and the stick? What an excellent result has come up here just after an hour's snubbing that day! This is what I was looking for. I am not here for any stupid love making with the Bengalees.'

He folded the files closed and put them in a drawer of his desk marked 'top secret'. He then made a few phone calls to his zonal martial law administrators. It was noon. He pushed a button on his left hand. A subaltern came in. He ordered 'ask the mess *habilder* to come on.'

—Yes Sir.

Mess *habilder* Dorya Khan appeared.

—Sir.

—Is your meal ready?

—Sir, absolutely.

—Can you bring it here?

—I can, Sir.

A bearer with a silver tray followed the *havildar* into the commander's room. The commander washed his hands and mouth in the adjacent washroom and sat before the dining table. What he had finished studying a few minutes ago were all facts and figures of people killed in cold blood by his troops all over the province. The circumstances of the deaths were unthinkably cruel while the numbers were enormous considering the time line in which these were carried out. After studying these for hours no normal man could have the guts or taste to enjoy any delicacy. But the commander started studying the menu laid before him as intently and artfully as a connoisseur of food and drinks. He started eating and easily swallowed *dohibora*, four *chapaties*, beef steaks and a pair of mutton *kebab* within minutes. He then devoured two *tandorrys*. After drinking a mug of chilled water he sat with a cup of Lipton tea. As he sipped through he felt very satisfied with everything. He took down his diary and wrote 'my brave boys have fulfilled their target very efficiently. I will congratulate them in the next '*durbar*'.

Eleven hundred miles away in Islamabad and stooping on his desk, the President was also studying the same statistical reports. He had been commanding a brigade at Gurudashpur in 1947. That was inside Indian territory. One of the bloodiest communal riots was raging in that area. He was charged with the responsibility of quelling the riots between the Hindus and the Moslems. While his forces were resisting rioters by indiscriminate shooting and arrests, twenty thousand souls from both communities were killed in the riots. The situation was altogether different from the one now going on in East Pakistan. By the time his soldiers could kill three of the rioters the rioters themselves had killed five hundred of the opposite community. So speedy and fierce were they.

But today seeing the figures of civilian casualties, the President was surprised. What had his forces done in East Pakistan! In his profession it has been a normal spectacle for him to come across human blood, wounded limbs, smashed heads or watch people getting shelled or shot to death in seconds. 'But what is this I am watching now in these reports? No, no doubt, surely my commander has committed excesses.'

He lifted the hot line receiver. Tikka said,

'Hello Sir?'

—These reports of yours are indeed frightful. I instructed you people, when I left Dhaka, to restore law and order. Should that mean you will kill twenty seven thousand civilians within a week's time?

—Sir, there was no alternative.

The President barked 'What the hell do you mean there was no alternative? Listen General, my instructions were never like this. Who told you to kill university teachers, women, children and old people? And why have you ousted all foreign journalists from the province? Now after

exclusion from the province, they are reporting all kinds of nonsense in the world press.'

—Sir, as a local commander some discretion has to be applied.

—Your damn discretion is tarnishing the image of me and my government. I plainly asked you to tighten martial law but you have misconstrued that. Do you know now the whole world community is suspicious about us and what we are actually doing inside the province?

The commander was trying to say something more in self-defense. The President shouted, this is crap and bad enough. General, stop this non-sense. I now realize what a mistake I have made!'

The President on the spur of the moment was going to scream, I forgot there was a charge of patricide against you.' On a second thought he decided not to mention it.

Without any pleasantries or goodbye the President put the receiver down, and moved to a sofa in his room. With his head down, he was brooding. He remembered that some good people had advised him that as the head of the state and government he was expected to nurture a good image in the minds of the public. For that he required to show an ameliorative attitude to people. Following that he had done things in that direction. He remembered he had shaken hands even with lowly people like a boatman while crossing Buriganga river at Dhaka. He paid visits to such remote areas of the country where none of his predecessors ever thought of putting his feet. 'And with all these, this is what had happened in one of my provinces!' In a flash of sudden remorse he thought that the *Nabab* was a very cunning and crooked fellow. By listening to his insistence the country now has this image. He said to himself, I never had the slightest imagination that the fall out of postponing the assembly session would be this bad.' He thought for a minute.

The President was known to take even important matters of state casually. So without any further consideration he asked his military secretary (MSP) to come inside. He instructed him to contact a certain officer at the General Headquarters. Within a minute the MSP told him, that the official was not available at his desk, as he was outside his station in a furlough. Attempts were being made to locate and connect with him at his leave address.

This non-descript small village called 'Balokhel' had been in existence since time immemorial. Along the bank of the Indus river this was the last flank of the Punjab district Mianwali. The weather today was quite hot and dry. Fifty three years ago this village gave birth to a strong male child. Eighteen years after that, the village became boastful of that child turning into a young man when he became a second-lieutenant at a British-Indian regiment stationed in Dehradun. Five years ago he became a Major_ General. Since then he was a VIP and the only VIP of the village. The six-feet tall, very strongly built man with a falcon like nose used to cause quite a stirring among the communities and villages around whenever he was on a visit to his native village. Elderly and young alike assembled in his drawing room and court yard to pay their respects.

On such visits people used to say that 'Tarik bin Ziad' had come here. This title was conferred on him by the villagers. The reason for bestowing these honours was that he was the only Lieutenant-general of this village and the district. People believed that he had arranged about seven hundred local people getting recruited into the country's army. These beneficiaries were not only from his village or district but also from the neighbouring districts of Ludhianwala and Faisalabad. With such a high credentials he had always felt flattered. Now he had been here for the last two nights and had already enjoyed the pleasures of those rituals extended by the villagers. There was a third reason also. He successfully fought two wars and survived both. The one was the campaign at Burma in 1947 and another one was the 1965 war with neighbouring India.

This was a Friday. It was past noon. Ziad had just returned from the village mosque after offering his *jummah* prayers in a congregation of half a thousand devout Moslems of the nearby *mohollas* and villages. He was preparing to sit for lunch along with his two daughters, wife and old mother. Moslem women usually have to pass a long period of their lives as widows. The main reason for this is they are given in marriage to men much older than themselves. Ziad's father died two decades ago. The old mother was very happy because of her son's visit after about a six months gap. He will get back to Rawlpindi after four days. Plus the daughter-in-law and two grand daughters' presence made her very active in spite of her age. She had spent a lot of time in the kitchen. Today's menu is tempting for any Punjabee family. *Tandoory, Sikandari nan, Nali Kebab,* and sweet *lassy* were laid smartly on the dining table. Her

daughter-in-law and a maid were arranging the table ware. Ziad was glancing through the daily 'Nawai Wakt 'a daily news paper in Urdu.

The telephone set placed inside the drawing room of this village home sounded a ring. Tarik's batman Khurrom Khan Hashime received it and hurried to where his boss was seated on the courtyard.

—Sir, you have a phone call.

—Where from?

—Sir, from the President's office.

Ziad received the call. The military secretary was on the line. The President joined in within seconds.

—General Tarik, how are you? How is everyone in your family and how are you enjoying your vacation?

—Everything and everyone is excellent. I am going fine. Thank you sir. Can I do something for you sir?

—Yes, General, I am thinking something about you. I am going to make you the new commander of the Eastern Command.

—Sir, may I say something?

—Of course, you are allowed

—Sir I cannot disoblige you but in the seniority list I am the 13th.

—So what?

—My colleagues and batchmates will feel jealous about my appointment because the appointment is so prestigious.

—Do not give a damn to what people think. Leave that to me. You were the c.o. of the 14th Punjab at the Dhaka cantonment. That is a good point. I have seen your records. Those are simply excellent.

Ziad was already melting with the commendation and flattery of the President. One holding such senior rank can express his preference or reservation about such appointments but Ziad felt euphoria and did not think for a moment to enquire what was happening in East Pakistan. Actually on account of intelligence, temperament and personality he was close to the President's. Shallow in thoughts, his moods used to change frequently. He decided important issues without enough analysis or proper considerations. Actually Ziad had watched with intense interest the two martial law regimes of his country. In none of these was he invited to take any role by the junta. Except in war time the military had no power but a martial law regime provided that to many of his colleagues, seniors and juniors. This was their opportunity to wield a stick over civilians which made many in uniform rich and prosperous. He only had a British cross on his uniform in 1946 after the end of the 2nd world war. This was a below mediocre and almost throw away military award. So he used to vaunt this to any one he came across in society. He was looking for power and to be the chief of a province was surely going to give him this. The initial modesty he was showing to his boss today was not real but pseudo which is the usual culture of sycophancy of underdeveloped societies. So he jumped up saying 'Sir, I will obey your order.'

The President felt a great relief. Because of his same casual personality he simply forgot to mention the reason for his choice and the removal of the present commander. He, within the last two years in his office had not created a system which could advise him on important decision making issues. He never realized the meaning of the saying 'two heads are better than one'. Before his regime there was a sort of advisory system. On the advice of Piru and the *Nabab* he simply put that away in cold-storage. It was to the advantage of the trio. Piru advised him that statecraft is as simple and as straightforward as the armed forces where an order issued is considered carried out. He used to forget to instruct his aides to take notes or records of the decisions taken by him. As a result, these decisions were unilateral. These were neither of the government's nor of the state's. Everybody around him thus got an alibi to disown the decisions and their consequences.

The President thanked Ziad and hung up. Ziad was elated. He now remembered the non-descript medallions and awards he received like *Helal-e-jurrat, Bahar-e-risallat, Sitara-e-Pakistan* and *Sitara-e-Khidmot* during the last twenty four years. He felt these were not enough recognition of his prowess and merit and now he was on the verge of getting the highest military award *Nishan-e-hyder.* Possibly that was not far away now with the good news of today but he never spent any time to thinking about what was happening in the place of his new assignment.

His mom and family were eagerly waiting. His mom asked 'the President himself is looking for you. Son, what is the matter?'

Ziad respectfully touched the feet of his mother and with a wide smile on his broad face replied 'it is a very good news, mother. I have been

appointed the deputy chief martial law administrator of Zone 'B'. From now on I will be the chief of the eastern garrison.'

The son at least had some vague news about the army in East Pakistan. The mother and the family were totally ignorant of that. The government never discussed this with the public in the western wing. Ziad's mom and family were also happy to learn the news and said 'all praises to Allah.' To whom they addressed their gratitude is omnipresent and omniscient. He sees the future and controls and determines it. He was not happy and remained silent because He has given 'free will' to his best creature.

The following day Tikka received the phone call from the AHQ General Staff Officer (GSO) 2 of the chief of the General Staff. He simply informed him the commander had been removed from his post and transferred as a corps commander to the western theater.

The next day the hero of Balokhel, Gen. Tarik bin Ziad reached Dhaka and assumed the tasks of the new commander. It was after many days that the civilian press was allowed to enter the cantonment.

The new commander talked to the journalists at large on issues here since 25th March many of which he himself was ignorant. After entertaining those with high tea and a lot of talk Ziad led them to a balcony under a tin-shed building in the cantonment. He addressed them by saying 'Gentlemen, I am so happy to be here once again. Here, under this very tin-shed I was the commanding officer of 14th Sherdil Punjab battalion in 1954. Do you know what that word means? It is an Arabic word meaning 'the lion hearted'. This is my second home. This is the Tiger road and this road was named after me.'

///

Rauf was now attending office regularly. He was also listening to the news of the state radio. This was a Sunday. Rauf was listening to a news bulletin. It said 'all anti-state elements and depraved people in East Pakistan have been taken into custody. They will be tried according to martial law regulations. Arsons, vandalism and harassing innocent people have stopped now. The situation is under full control of the government. Patriotic elements are helping the government—Life has returned to normalcy. All educational institutes in the province are open now. Students are attending their classes.'

Asad was also listening to this. Rauf asked 'This is the 15th of April. Your imaginary liberation struggle is over now. Why are you not going back to the campus to attend classes?'

—Dad, I am also following the news. These claims of the government are all bogus,

—Do you know what punishment there is for labeling the government as a liar?

—I do not know because I have not had any government job. You believe in this official news but I know that the classes being held in my campus are only in two departments. Two students of Arabic and three of Urdu are attending classes. Otherwise the campus is vacant.

—Son your answer is significant and intentional. I can't miss the point that you are slyly criticizing Islam and the Moslems as usual as those two languages belong to them. Tell me what is happening in the other departments?

—What is happening in the others can't be termed as teaching or learning. In some there is no teacher while in some others there is no student.

—But remember what the government has said. They have warned that those who will remain absent will face an exemplary punishment.

—Is the governor a chief justice or at least a judge? Otherwise how does he know that a student for being absent from a class can be severely punished under the law? Is there any such provision in the law?

—Son, you are correct but if someone is punished under a martial law regulation there is no recourse to any appeal. I am, therefore, worried about you.

—Okay, Dad, I will get further information about the condition of my campus. Especially the situation of the dormitory will be important for my stay there.

—That is good.

—I will go back and attend classes though I fail to understand what is actually happening in the country. Our radio is broadcasting that there is about a totally normal situation while foreign news sources are contradicting it. Even this noon, West German radio from Bonn was reporting that the army is still killing civilian population in many parts of this province. It also said at Shetabgonj sugar mill, troops shot about eighty labourers and officials in cold blood.

Rauf pondered. He also had witnessed something similar while returning home from his office. A few days back the army lined up people in front of a Tongi factory and then shot them. Rauf had concluded they were Hindus and so the act was justified. He said,

—The army might do this with only those who are not loyal to this country. A state can't be run with mercy and undue favour. Read the history of this sub-continent. You will find many such examples. The Moghul emperors kept their fathers and brothers imprisoned for many years on political grounds and were having wars with cousins and possible adversaries to the throne.

—Has anyone thus been able to protect himself in the long run?

—May be some could not but one has to try it. Do you know what cruel deeds have been perpetrated in the very recent history of the country of your supporters you are so fond of?

Asad had no idea about the issue. He did not get his father's point so asked 'what are you alluding to?'

—The most powerful man of that country publicly used to call an important person as his best friend. Later on, just for the political interest of his country this person was held in prison for fifteen years.

Asad understood which country Rauf was referring to but not the person. He asked,

-who was the person?

—The chief minister of Kashmir. This is called politics and state.

These facts were unknown to Asad but his father's convincing tone told him these were unquestionably true. So he felt dejected. In such condition of the mind men try to be defensive. A fact seen by him two years ago did this job at this moment. The scene of an army firing killing a renowned teacher inside his campus before his own eyes angered Asad right now. Emboldened and convinced he argued'

'I know you and people like you supporting the Muslim League will never agree but tell me one thing. Is there any doubt that the EPR troops shot and killed Dr. Shamsuzzoha, Reader of chemistry, almost in front of my eyes? What is the argument for it? And only a month ago the same forces killed Faroque at Rampura without any provocation . . .

—Son, listen.

—Dad, I have not yet finished. They killed Sergeant Zahurul Haque at Dhaka cantonment. Is it civilization to kill someone who is under their custody and trial? Should or can these acts be tolerated? You often blame the British for the Kashmir issue. Still would this happen in their country?

—I would not say these are acceptable or reasonable but one or two will usually face injustice when you are doing justice to a hundred. Or this could be put in a different way. When you are punishing a hundred culprits; you inadvertently punish one innocent or two. Be a magistrate and then you will find if you can resist such deviation happening in your own office. It is one thing stating an ideal or theory and another thing to act accordingly.

—Agreed Dad. Still I will say they are committing excesses.

Rauf did not make any comment on the son's opinion. Then with a wrinkle of thoughts on his face Rauf said in a serious tone,

—Let me tell you one thing. They have already established their control in the country. Now troops have started patrolling neighbourhoods. I feel they will find out those who are working for the break-up of this country. So I suggest you should not listen so much to foreign news agencies. We may make us unsafe by doing that.

—Dad I agree with you but don't worry. I listen to news, but I am very careful in this and keep the volume of the transistor very low.

The situation appeared to be better now with the increasing number of people in the streets and shops. The national flags had replaced all black flags from 27th of March atop houses, offices and commercial centres. The excessive show of loyalty to authorities was source of jokes. In a developed country this would be termed as a very serious offense and the offenders would be punished promptly. The issue was the uninterrupted hoisting and position of national flags. That these must be brought down everyday immediately after sun-set is an international convention but this was being flouted inadvertently in all cities and localities of this army occupied province. The exhibitionists did not know the law while the army had never thought of it as they were too busy with other important issues around.

It was the 18th of April. Asad was preparing to leave for Rajshahi within the next week. Rauf was on an official holiday. The father and the son were talking as usual. Everywhere, though in a hushed tone people were talking about only one issue. That was politics. Asad told his father

'Dad, a provisional government has taken oath. Though I know you will not like or believe in it.

Rauf said with a smiling face, tasty news indeed. Tell me where this government is seated and who are the ones who got portfolios.

Asad gave the information as he heard from his favourite sources. Rauf smiled and asked

—Do you believe that this place is somewhere inside our country?

—Dad, four internationally reputable news agencies have confirmed this. How can I disbelieve them?

—Well, in that case why are your government and the ministers not coming to this capital city and having their offices down here?

—The capital is under occupation of the enemy. One day they will evict this illegal occupation and then have their seats over here.

—Bravo son, bravo! You have started thinking your own army as an enemy. Surprising indeed.

—Yes indeed. They are our enemy since we have started a liberation war against them.

—May I know what the number of this freedom fighters is? How and where could they have their training so quickly that they are fighting a highly professional army?

—These people are members of the E.P.R and Bengal Regiment soldiers.

—So far, how many cities and ports have they evacuated from the occupation forces?

—They haven't yet but will do in due course. They have just started.

—Good. I suggest you return to your campus and resume studies and let the war continue. But I want to give you an important information.

—What is that?

—That is, you have no idea as to how efficient and ruthless our armed forces are.

Providence whispered, 'you are also unaware of it' but Rauf did not hear it

Rauf further told,—I never wish my son ever to have that experience. It is good that you are sharing this only with me. Never ever do it with anyone else. One thing is certain. They will do anything they feel necessary to protect this country, Islam and the Moslems. They will never compromise with this mission. So Allah is with us. Now it should be the duty of any patriotic citizen to co-operate with the armed forces.

—Dad, I understand the reasons for my mom's support to them. Her father was killed in the riots during the partition of 47. My maternal uncles had to leave all their properties and flee here just to save their lives. So that is reasonable for them. I never understood why you also support these inhuman people?

Rauf's paternal home was at Calcutta but he used to stay at Dhaka since before the partition along with his father. Rauf had never been to Calcutta. His education and profession all had been at Dhaka. Rauf quietly said 'in course of time you will understand the reasons for my support. It would be better if you could measure just the difference between where we are now and where we would be had this country not come into existence. My parents or brothers did not suffer from the riots. Still I can see and understand the matter indeed clearly. Those who opposed us in 47 are the same people who now have become active once again. Someone who has not seen those days is not expected to appreciate this reality, so I don't blame you for your simplicity.'

Asad once again was at a loss as to what to argue further.

It was neither Asad's wishful thinking nor exaggerated pictures given by foreign news agencies. A provisional government had indeed taken oath at a border village west of Meherpur subdivision. The vice President of the government made a declaration on behalf of President Mujib distributing portfolios. It said the warring nation was divided into several military sectors under the overall military command of a retired colonel from Sylhet district and that the struggle must continue until all Pakistanee occupation forces were routed or crushed to a defeat.

Rauf also heard the news earlier but did not admit it before his son. He came inside their bedroom and told his wife, 'look, people who don't have the caliber of holding any position higher than that of a *habilder* or *Subeder* have now become sector commanders. A bunch of dreaming warriors in an imaginary war! Is this not the situation like?

Although his wife supported him on these issues whole-heartedly she seldom talked about this. Her support was spontaneous. The memory of the communal riots, her father's murder and loss of a life fortune were still fresh in her mind though two eras had elapsed since.

Their daughter also listened to her father's arguments and opinion but did not talk much. She had been one of the best debaters in the university. The student leaders often had tried to make her an office bearer of the Union. She always politely declined because she was opposed to the political trend of the union for the last two years. However, she never told the reasons to them. She was fearless like her father and a staunch supporter of the country's solidarity and unity. Her love and respect for her father were also deep. In the last elections she cast a vote for a candidate running with the rare symbol of a sword. All five candidates running with swords suffered so miserably that each lost their security deposit. Nobody in the family however knew that. Everybody used to respect the personal preferences of the others but Asad.Rauf felt the pulse of his wife but was curious about his daughter's view on this issue. Such special circumstances of the country but her daughter was still mum !

He now approached his daughter and lightly said, 'Sweetie, your brother and I discuss so many issues, but you seem to have no interest in those. What is the matter mom?'

-Dad, what do I have to say? Rather you tell me one thing. We have got three hundred MNAs in the national election and 550 legislators in the provincial assemblies. How many of them are women?

Rauf was struck with surprise by his daughter's query. Indeed she had focused on a rare important issue. Jerin again said,

-We females are a little less than half of the total population but none of the laws, conventions, govt. or society appears to admit this reality. Was there a single woman running the election independently? Given this what can we or I have to say? And who is going to listen to that?

Rauf said, "What a wonderful observation my dear daughter! Surely one day you are going to be a bar-at-law from Lincoln's Inn.

-Dad have you noted another thing? In that meeting at the racecourse was there a mention of us?

Asad was away from home for shopping. So he missed the conversation. Rauf said,

Well Jerin, I feel fine that I don't need to worry about you. I could not make out how your only brother has a totally different stand on these issues. Any person from the western wing of our country is simply a hated being to him. He can't tolerate them at all.

-Dad, actually my brother has been seeing many incidents in his campus since 1967. He has told me about a few of those. His firm conviction is this that those are gross inequities, planned and carried out by the rulers. And so can never be acceptable. He feels that any Punjabee is a devil incarnate. And now the hour has arrived to destroy them.

-So he talks about this to you also?

-Yes he does, but it is always unilateral. He speaks while I listen and say nothing. One interesting point dad, during the last election fever he wanted to know who I was going to cast my vote for. He also said it was useless to implore dad and mom on the issue. But at least you tell me what you are going to do.

-What did you say?

-I said the ballot was a secret instrument so let this remain a secret. Nobody should know that.

-I see, he is so much politically conscious, and that is always unipolar. Leave that for now. Now tell me something about the progress of your studies, the condition of your dormitory and lectures.

-The dormitory is empty because after 25th March, no student has returned. Though a few lectures are taking place. I am thinking to attend may be from the next week.

-There is no question of thinking my dear child. If you do not attend classes regularly authority might be putting some pressures on their guardians. The government has been doing everything to normalize the situation. Even then if we do not render our cooperation to them, that will not be proper.

The clock struck eleven 'o clock and Asad returned home with a shopping bag. Rauf in the meantime heard the news about the formation of the provisional government but did not mention this to his son.

//

The briefing by Tikka's own initiative to commanders down the line was not forgotten at all. In the military profession things like those are not forgotten or even diluted unless revised instructions follow. The President's shock on seeing figures of civilian mayhem was compatible with his nature and so momentary. He made the replacement and then forgot about the purpose of the replacement. So the same operations continued wherever the army was in command.

//

It was the month of May. The lunar eclipse was due tonight, but the name given for an army operation at that hour was 'moonlight'.

In spite of being evil forces of darkness the planners had a penchant for the word 'light'. On the 25th March they titled the operation as 'searchlight'. Since then they felt goaded with success. Brigadier Mukhtalib Rana had been in charge of Sylhet district since 1st of April. Like Lt. Col. Yaqub Malikee, Brig. Rana was transferred here with a special purpose. Sitting in his desk since early morning today he studied a lot of documents. He never worked in this province before. Still with an exceptional drive and initiative Rana had completed a plan after analyzing the voter list of this district. The implementation of that plan was scheduled to start and finish tonight. Brigade Major Omar Khaiyam Zilany was seated across from Rana. After sifting through the list finally, Rana felt sure that there was hardly any difference between the contents of the briefings at Kurmitola and AHQ on the one hand and the ground realities on the other, here in this district. So he felt happy. In spite of clear instructions about tonight's operations Rana was given special and additional powers as the local commander. This thought made Rana more confident and cheerful. He now looked at Zilany in the face and asked,

—Zilany, have the battalions taken positions?

—Sir, they have and it is according to plan.

—Revisit the schedule.

—The first battalion at Srimongol, the 11th at Habiganj, 6th at Moulvibazar, and the 2nd at Sylhet are fully prepared for action, Sir.

—Well, they must follow the list, clear?

—Absolutely clear, Sir.

Brigadier Rana hailed from Ganganagar district in the Rajputana of India. The year was 1941 when Rana arrived at the age of 18. Major Roger Allenby was holding an office of the armed services board in a camp in that city. Rana made an application for an appointment to the Royal British Indian Artillery. A recruiting board was conducting an interview to select candidates. It was Rana's turn. After a few questions Allenby asked him,

—Do you see a dog in this room?

Rana saw a dog chained to one of the legs of the wooden table before Allenby. He said,

—Yes I can see one.

—Do you think you could kill the dog with this gun on the table?

Without a word Rana took the revolver in his hand and shot the dog to death. Major Allenby noted a classified observation in the file about Rana, 'this candidate is a born-killer. He will kill without remorse'.

After a few days, this young Rana got a commission as a second lieutenant in the 41st British Indian Artillery Regiment.

Brigadier Rana and his HQ Lt. Col. Ikramullah Saadakat were working for quite a while on a mission soon to be accomplished here. They were working on a map of all the sub-divisions of this district. Bigger concentrations were marked with red ink while those with less got black markings under their skilled fingers. The charts of the names of people under the scope of the mission were almost completed flawlessly. Field commanders duly received copies of the same. Instructions in detail accompanied the charts. These maps showed everything their bosses at AHQ had been looking for since 1947.

Finally yesterday Rana checked the latest intelligence reports. He was satisfied and decided no changes to the plan and schedule were necessary. Now this was the longest day of the month of June. It was about 7 o'clock in the evening when the last sunrays faded out in the west skyline. In the sub-division, there was no arrangement for electricity at the periphery except at the government officials' quarters and offices of the central government. People lit their houses with kerosene-run lanterns and indigenous torches. Since March, even this so far easily available fuel had become scarce and the price expensive. Dwellers everywhere finished their evening meals by seven thirty and though they did not go to bed immediately they put off the lamp, keep awake for some times talking about family matters.

The big house at the backyard of Islam Saw Mill of the township of Srimongol-Moulvibazar crossing was an affluent one. Since one and a half century ago it had been the abode of a well-off Hindu family. Mrinmoy Mitra was the present inheritor of this landed gentry. Under the mix of little light and more shadows and mosquito bites the family had completed taking their dinner half an hour ago. Rakhi Mitra, a daughter of this family, aged eighteen years old had passed the Higher Secondary Certificate examination last year. Then she had to drop out from the higher class due to typhoid infection for a month. She accepted the loss and was now planning to get herself admitted into Srimongol

Degree College. Rakhi lying on her bed under a mosquito net was talking to her father. In a faint and scared voice she told her father,

—Dad, how long shall we stay under such a condition? I can't even sleep with so much fear and anxiety in my mind.

Her father told, 'There are many check-posts of the army all along the border. How can we cross it? Plus where shall we go? We have no relatives across the border. They will ask us why we are crossing. Surely they will doubt our loyalty to the government. We may get killed or abducted before crossing it. I know how deeply you are scared with the sounds of boots of the patrolling troops so near our home. Still is not there at least one good point in staying here instead of the risk of crossing the border?'

—What is that Dad?

—By staying here we are at least managing a survival and a demonstration of our loyalty to the army government my child, are we not?

—Dad, still I feel very nervous all the time.

Similar conversations in hushed tone were taking place in many families around Hospital Quarters of Hobiganj, Dhaka Road of Moulvibazar, and Municipal Road and Nabiganj areas of the big district. Besides the middle and lowly castes, aristocrat Hindus like Mukherjees, Banerjees, Duttas and Senguptas were also having similar feelings about the daily life.

Vabani Mukherjee was the Chairman of Sreemongol municipality. Hindus and Moslems taxpayers alike of this small township voted him to this prestigious local-government position. His wife Debojanee was a staunch believer in two things. The first was her religion and the second, an untarnished homage for Mohandas Karamchand Gandhi. A painted portrait of this deliverer of India from the British rule had always been hung on a wall of the family's drawing room since 1947. Debojanee, never forgot to bow before this inanimate replica every morning before starting the daily chores of the household. She wiped its front and frames clean respectfully with her own cloth. Vabanee, hearing the news of trouble and shooting at Dhaka on the 25th March, asked his wife to bring the portrait down and throw it under the water of their family well for drinking water or burn it in the oven. That this photo would not be a source of special appreciation for the authorities now a days was keenly known to this local leader. Debojanee, a votary but illiterate, was shocked and retorted, 'what a monstrous proposal! You are asking me to burn this?' Vabani replied, 'Look, honey, this is a time when we may think of doing a sacrilege of eating even beef just for survival but you are bothering yourself with the maintenance of a photograph! Our life is at stake now. You must realize that. Besides, we now have to put all idols of our belief deep under the earth.'

That portrait was a fond and respected item in almost all the houses of this community around. Many of them were not sure about the nature of the danger they were in. Still they were now hiding the portraits underneath their mattresses.

The kids were already asleep. There was no more household work to do. Now the Mukherjees retired to bed.

A little away, from his jail road residence, Municipal Commissioner Amiyo Sengupta was the first to see the dazzling lights. He was a lawyer of the local bar-council. He was still unmarried. He just finished feeding his mother, a paralysis patient for the last five years. With an indigenous hand-fan he was trying to give some cool and comfort to the old woman amidst the hot and moist weather. Even well-off people's houses here were usually constructed with bamboo fencing and with a roof of spinned hay. Concrete buildings were rare. Some were made of wood and asbestos. Amiyo put the hand-fan down on his mother's bed and rushed towards the portico exclaiming, 'What's the matter? Why is such a flood of light out there?'

He swiftly opened the door of the drawing room and watched the outside with panicky eyes. All houses of the neighbourhood were ablaze. Before understanding who put this incendiary into action, he saw the spiraling waves of the blazing fire engulfing everything very fast. The adjacent house on the left belonged to Askir Chowdhury. Its torched wooden frame and structure of the roof were now falling on Amiyo's house. It was devouring the dry hay, fencing and wooden structure. There was only one thought in his mind at this moment, 'Mother must be rescued'. He turned round with a scream, 'mom' from his mouth and started for the bedroom. Now to the hissing sound of the flames, a new type of noise was added. It was the clatter of gunshots. Amyo had not much heard this noise in his life since his days so far had passed mostly in rural towns and countryside. He could not quite make out where it was coming from and what it was. Amiyo frantically raced for the inside but could not get far. The wooden ceiling had caught fire by now and the whole structure fell on his head. Simultaneously pieces of swinging hot lead from a roaring submachine gun pierced Amiyo through the vertebra-column. He fell down then and there and died

The next hour was hell brought down on earth? Spewing bullets and raging fire continued their wrath through the jig-jag, red and blue markings of Rana's chart, burning houses and destroying their inhabitants. Those who tried to come out to save their lives were gunned down immediately. A few were fortunate to avoid gunshots. However they faced a more painful death. Soldiers standing on exits bayoneted them to their end. Some were in deep slumber. They were burnt to their skeletons within minutes. Not that the possibility of tonight's events had never appeared in some of the victims' imagination. They knew that their communal identity was always a point of suspicion in the eyes of authorities. They were believed to be the main supporters of the break-up of this holy land of the Moslems. People like Vabani and Amiyo had destroyed all their idols of worship, wiped signs of vermillion from the foreheads of their womenfolk to avoid any fatal dangers. Still this carnage could not be avoided. The weather during this time could be different. There were green lushes around which could make it cool. Above all a heavy downpour from the skies could have assuaged the heat of the environment. But that night an inclement Nature was colluding with the fireworks by her dry and hot temper.

In some places houses were locked from outside and then set on fire. Inmates were roasted to death. The reason for this was that some of the commanders were not in favour of spending a costly item like bullets for killing these infidels. Torched young people were trying to come out from the locked houses. The helmeted Punjabee barbarians clasping firearms in their hands were watching the scenes and saying with a grin, 'treachery to the motherland? Now test the punishment!'

The hate and death campaign continued like a serial drama. Rana's forces had been recceing this concentration of the dissenters for quite some days. The present action was the successful implementation of those recces.

Adjacent to the sub-divisional township of Sreemongol was a village named Baromchal. *Nayeb Subeder* Sher Bakht Jung Majari of the 1st Punjab battalion was in charge of this ethnic cleansing operation. A big family, Roy Chowdhury living here had about thirty members. They were known as the socially most respectable family of the area. The neighbouring houses were already blazing. There was no resistance from anywhere. Captain Ataullah Shah, Majari's supervisor, had completed his inspection of the progress of this operation a few minutes ago. He had asked, 'Is everything going on according to instructions?'

With a salute Majari replied, 'Sir, absolutely'.

Ataullah was satisfied and sped away with his vehicle in another direction. The entrances and exits of this big house were all duly locked earlier. Now Majari ordered his troops, 'Set fire to this house!'

Instantly flames were shining around. Majari watched the rising flames and looked satisfied. He then said, 'Soldiers, this is good work. Now you people move towards the back of the shunting yard of the rail station. Quite a number of Hindus have fled in that direction just a while ago. Chase them and kill them.' It was actually a concoction made by Majari.

All the eight soldiers rushed towards the dark. In the mean time, groans and screams were coming out from Roy Chowdhury's house with the expanding fireworks. Majari cautiously looked around. His colleagues were all engrossed in murder and looting inside the houses around. Majari moved towards the entrance of Roy Chowdhury's with a sten-gun pointing towards its lock. He started firing intermittently aiming at the lock. The lock dangled out on the attached iron rings and the two parts of the door swung open. Now Majari entered the house.

Two women with kids on their laps and an elderly gentleman who appeared to be the guardian of the family saw Majari. They were ready for death either by fire or by bullets or by both. The heat inside was already unbearable and their attempt to come out of the house was so far unsuccessful. So they thought it was now the turn of the bullet. The family since March had managed a smattering of the Urdu dialect knowing this might be of some use for survival. The old man now raced towards Majari, prostrated before him and implored in broken Urdu, 'We have got a kilogram of gold in our possession. Please take this and everything else. Let us go away just with our lives. We have never done any harm to Pakistan though we are Hindus by faith.'

131

Majari looked towards one of the kids on a woman's lap. He looked as handsome and fair complexioned as the Hindu God *Gonesh*. His hair was disarrayed. He had woken up from sleep a few minutes ago. With his innocent eyes the child was looking towards Majari's gun in spite of the scorching heat. Majari in a mix of broken Urdu and Bangla smilingly said, 'I don't require gold or any valuables. Do not be afraid. Please get out of here as fast as you can through the pond behind.'

With disbelieving eyes, the family, emerged from the certain death row and hurried out of the frying pan like silhouettes into the dark. Within seconds, the flames spread out to all directions. Majari came out of the house and shut the door with the broken lock hanging on it. He stood in front and fired a few shots out of his sten-gun now and then and muttered, 'O Almighty Allah, just now I have not been true to my salt. Still accept my supplication and pardon me for the offence. You saved my parents and me in 1947. This evening I tried to repay that.'

Nayeb Subeder Majari was born in Hissar district of the East Punjab. After partition by the British, news soon spread that the area would go to India's side. Rioters were looking for such information. A band of Sikh and Hindu hooligans immediately pounced on their Moslem neighbours like hungry wolves and started killing them and looting their possessions. Majari's neighour Kishen Damodor Charanwala heard that rioters were approaching his village. His immediate neighbour, Majari's parents and kids became his prime concern. How to save these very good neighbours who had never ever given any offence to any one belonging to a different religion. Charonwala quickly consulted his wife. Then he advised Majari's father, mother and the kids to put on dresses of housemaids and daily labourers working in his courtyard with cow, hay and fodder. Then he set fire to a part of Majari's father's house with his own hands. When the rioters came in, ashes, smoke, charcoal and other signs of the incendiary were still visible on the house of this Moslem family. To the queries of the rioting bandits, Charanwala told that another Hindu-Shikh gang had done this and the family had somehow managed an escape or were missing.

Majari, now standing on an alien area of his country, remembered this with gratitude towards his God Allah and to Charanwala, whom he never saw since 1947. He felt happy. Never in his life did he have such a profound feeling of satisfaction. Looking at the still blazing flames around he thought, 'in my small capacity as a non-commissioned officer I have done the ever best act in my life. I realize that repayment is an act a hundred times better than retribution.'

However unlike Majari's reminiscences and moralization his comrades in arms around were taking satisfaction from a different scene. Flames and gunfire from point-blank range were devouring houses, hearths, men, women, children, cattle-heads, chicken and even the moon and star studded national flags on rooftops indiscriminately. This spree ended a few minutes before dawn.

At 8 o'clock in the morning Brigadier Rana sat in his office. He went through the reports of 'operation moonlight' and a significant smile surfaced on his face. It was happiness all around. He opened his diary and scribbled down, 'not a single incident of resistance anywhere. Good. It is indeed a great victory towards the target of achieving ethnic cleansing. In our holy Moslem nation, there is no room even for a single infidel or treachery. Those minorities are the very people who joined a party whose only agenda is to break the country into two pieces. No, that can never happen. I will not allow that.' Suddenly Brigadier Rana had a strange feeling. He thought he was the inventor of a new kind of gas chamber. Rana now ordered his brigade-major to collect all locals who supported and cooperated with the army in this killing mission. The collaborators had identified the victims and their addresses and gave that information to the army units. They all gathered at 10 o'clock in the morning on the parade ground of the brigade head-quarter under banners of 'Razakar', 'Muslim League', 'Al Shams' and 'Al Badars'. Rana thanked them for their patriotism and told the gathering that in due course they would be rewarded with appropriate awards, like titles, commendations and credentials by Major General Jamshed, Commander, East Pakistan Civil Armed Forces.

Brigadier Rana looked happy and thought 'What Tikka did at Dhaka will now look rather pale compared to what I have done here just last night'

With the advance of the day, Commander Eastern Command also came to know about the mission results, at his headquarters. For the last few days this imaginative Lt. General was spending most of his time in reminiscences and sweet down memory lane visits of his earlier tenure through 1954 and 1955 in this cantonment. After reading more than half way through the reports and data of Rana's, something struck his mind.

He thought, of what instruction's follow up is this one?'

Tarik saw nothing of the bloodshed of the 1947 communal carnage when the British were partitioning India and Indians. His home district Mianwali was far away from the just drawn frontiers. There were no riots and Hindus and Sikh neighbours were freely and peacefully moving towards India facing no violence from any Moslem. Brigadier Rana's reports on the massacre of Hindus in Sylhet created no repercussions in the tranquil mind of Tarik. However it posed a totally different query which was egoistic and official in nature. 'When was the order for this mission issued and who authorized it?'

His careless mind did not consider for a minute that asking such a question to his juniors in his own command area would neither be wise nor would look good. Such a question would mean an admission that 12000 people got killed in his own area but he was unaware of the same. It would undoubtedly give a very incredible image about the General. He gave no thought to it. Having finished the report Tarik picked up the telephone and asked Rana who authorized this mission. Rana said, the plan was conceived and authorized by Tarik's predecessor. It took a few months for drawing up the implementation and action plan along with identifying the targets. After having this reply Tarik remembered that before assuming charges of his present position, he did not take any briefing from his President or from his military seniors. Prior to his joining here he called on the President. The President told him briefly, 'Please try to win their confidence both by soft and hard ways. Tikka was too harsh with them. Good luck General Tarik. Now proceed to the Eastern theatre.'

Tarik followed this and looked at nothing else. Immediately after sitting in his office he had started mingling with the press and civilians regularly. He reminded everyone that this was not his first posting in this province. He used to pay regular visits to rural schools, colleges, madrashas, bazaars and rail-stations, collected people there and assured them that there was nothing to be afraid of. That his mission was to quell the miscreants and then hand over power to the chosen representatives of the Bengalees in due course. And for this mission the sincere cooperation of the civilians was essential for him. To demonstrate his sincerity to the press, a few days ago, Tarik walked into a newspaper office near Tikatuly area of the city which had been burnt by the army on the night of 25th. He told the owner that the press would be rebuilt fully at government cost and that the army was sorry for its excesses committed in that office during the hubbub of that night. At this moment these fond past memories could not comfort him. Tarik replaced the receiver and started fumbling through the files, 'who can tell me where, in which file was this instruction given?'

Tarik had been a student of military campaigns and history. Still it did not appear to him that this type of instructions is ever recorded on a file. The order and discipline of record keeping of this office was equally untidy as or even worse than that of the President's secretariat. The Eastern command was actually not certain about the target of their mission though the briefings were quite detailed while the targets were rather vague. So here also Tarik found no notices for meeting, minutes, attendance rolls, relevant files and necessary documents through which this important office had been running since the adjournment of the assembly session. Exasperated, Tarik ordered Brigadier Siddique, his chief of staff, to see him immediately. The brigadier also could not say or show when this mission was ordered. Tariq once again realized he had accepted this assignment rather hurriedly. Even after joining he had not contacted the President even for once. He also never looked into any paper of his own office nor talked to his predecessor or men and officers under his command. He also remembered that he also had not briefed any one so far down the line.

Tarik was worried now. He asked his staff officer to get him through to all divisional headquarters and martial law administrators of the province. One by one each of the officials came on line to tell him those missions similar to that of Sylhet's had been carried out in their respective zones with comparable results. The death toll was four thousand and they were minority groups and suspected to be anti-Pakistan. Tarik was sweating now.

His press assistant entered the room to turn his tension into a deep anxiety. He told his boss that representatives of the 'News Week' and 'Herald Tribune', two internationally reputed news magazines, were awaiting him for an interview. They had prior appointments with the General.

Men who are dull in intelligence tend to think that with the pink warmth of the heart difficult problems can be sorted out easily. A better or tactful person would have chosen a different course of action about the occasion. But Tarik did not do that. He did not prepare himself nor

did he cancel the appointment. Without realizing the significance of the media muff he thought he would not take recourse to any ruse or cunning but would be straightforward and sincere with the journalists. The General asked them to come in.

One of them played a recorded report from a foreign news agency before him and then asked, 'General, what comments do you have on this?'

The recording said that special ethnic groups known as Hindus were being indiscriminately killed by the Army. Their homes and properties were being burnt. As a result about two hundred thousand citizens of this civil war torn province had crossed its north-eastern borders and taken refuge in the neighbouring country. While crossing the border these panicky people were being persecuted by the security forces. Other members of the interviewing group joined in and flabbergasted the General by their very incisive queries. Tarik understood that he had committed a blunder by agreeing to this interview and thus letting those smart people ask any questions they would like to. Tarik, always a civilian and Bengalee hater, never cared for his public relations department. There was no press adviser for him who can always manage a cunning smile and talk in a manner before journalists by which even untarnished lies appear to the listeners as absolute truths.

Tarik portrayed a simpleton's smile on his face and said, 'Well, Gentlemen, I am a simple soldier. I appreciate your questions and comments. That is why I have invited you to this session. You see my predecessor ousted all foreign press from this province while I have opened all information systems for them. Now let me address your questions and the recorded report. My forces have been conducting a campaign only against those who are secessionists. Some ethnic groups are especially attentive to working for this. So some action against them is not unnatural.'

—What would you say about the refugees?

—The army has got nothing to do with this. Not only in this province, it is a normal phenomenon throughout the subcontinent that people are crossing the border without having proper documents. The reason is simple. In both parts across the border people have relatives. It is the same for the Punjab, Bengal, Assam, Sindh-Rajasthan and everywhere.

—But why has it increased so dramatically during the very recent months?

—How can I answer that? You better ask the intruders and bring them before me. Only then shall I be able to answer your query.

Brigadier Baqar was watching the interview and he thought 'circumstances sometimes cause an increase in one's intelligence and presence of mind. This has now happened to someone whom I thought to be an unintelligent fellow.'

Without any alarm, Jack Moribuax of the 'Herald Tribune' suddenly slung a question to the General,

—There are reports that your forces are raping women including many Moslems for their belonging to a particular political faith. How would you respond to this?

—At least no Moslem soldier can do this?

—Do you have a big number of non-Moslem soldiers amongst your troops, General?

—If not many, there are of course some of them. May be these few are actually doing these bad deeds and thus trying to tarnish the image of the majority of soldiers, by shifting the blame on their shoulders. I can assure you that if the anti-Moslem practices are proved to be true, the offenders will be punished. Now I cannot take any more of your questions. Thank you gentlemen.'

The time limit for the conference was over. The military police personnel escorted the press men out of the General's office. Now Tarik had a different feeling. It was an attraction for certain vocabulary. Those who are weak in character and prey to temptation, like these words. Earlier he had not known anything about molestation of women by his troops and officers here. He heard it just today in this conference. He thought, 'so my men are enjoying this pleasure. Lovely thing to do in a war-torn area. I have never been callous to this in spite of my usage of 'Islam', 'Moslem' or 'the Holy Quran'. I am not going to ask who authorized this practice.'

A few days later Tarik started doing this himself. Opportunities wait for those who look for them. He found many local women were lobbying in his office for their husbands' release. For real or imaginary offences his troops had arrested them. Tarik started making a trade-off between releasing some and enjoying the company of their spouses. In doing these the innocent faces of his two daughters never used to disturb him.

Young years usually give in to old ones. Asad never agreed with his father's logic of still supporting a united Pakistan but to keep his father and the family safe before the eyes of the authority he agreed to join his campus. He reached Rajshahi without much inconvenience though he faced an easy interrogation on a ferry while crossing the mighty Jamuna River. His fluent Urdu convinced the junior level interrogator and he was allowed to proceed to his destination. Then Asad faced check-post routine questions while entering the city. An EPR captain asked him where he was going to. He answered and then his baggage passed through a routine check by a soldier whose nasal tone told Asad the man was from Barisal district. After a few minutes Asad entered his dormitory. The heat was almost unbearable under a dazzling sun. The surrounding environment reminded Asad of a poem read many years ago in a childhood text book,

'Sweat oozes out in a summer noon,
There is no water in the torn and dried canals
Nor in the ponds anon'

Asad found the green grass field along the dormitory had turned into a pale yellow. It was half past five in the afternoon. Asad climbed up the stairway and walked down the locked doors of his room. It was the fifth from the left. The scene reminded Asad what he had told his father about normalcy of the campus. The first three rooms were all locked from outside and the fourth from inside. No, there was no student on this side of the floor except in one. The occupant was a second year student of Arabic. He was an activist of a reactionary student union of the university. Asad had little intimacy with this student. Asad now unlocked the door and entered his room. With the first look he realized that it had not been ransacked by any one. He changed his clothes, went to the washroom, cleaned his face and hands and then decided to see his buddies living on the fourth floor. With this in mind he sat on his bed to rest for a while. The body was tired through the long road journey from Dhaka. Unawares, he soon fell asleep.

Asad realized the length of his resting when he woke up at eight o'clock in the evening to a knock on his door. It was Borak Ali, an old guard of this dormitory. He saw Asad entering the campus in the afternoon. He also used to work as a part-time assistant in the students' dining room. Asad opened the door and the two exchanged greetings. Borak Ali asked, 'Will you have your meals tonight at the dining room?'

—Yes I will

—How about breakfast tomorrow?

—I will take that also and will regularly stay here to attend classes from now.

—Okay. No problem.

—Now tell me something about the situation here.

—Well, some classes are going on with a few students.

—How is the attendance in the dormitory and dining hall?

—The figure might be a little higher if non-resident students are added to it.

—Good.

Asad felt he could ask this lowly employee some more questions about politics and law and order here. On second thought he decided that would not be proper and safe. So he bode the man good bye.

The most reliable person for Asad in this dormitory was Fakhrul, a student of physics. He was older than Asad and was the first to join the freedom fighters' forces. Asad heard about this from Dhaka. Now he was in a war camp inside India undergoing military training. The last meeting these two had had was on 2nd March. This well-wisher of Asad warned him, 'Now is the time to test one's fidelity and credibility. Be careful. Don't open your mouth to unfamiliar people. You must know that spies will be all around to gather intelligence. They will inform authorities about who is on which side at the present crisis.'

Asad felt he should inform his parents about his safe arrival here. It was too late to make a phone call from the provost's office. Asad decided he would do the job tomorrow from the local General Post Office (G.P.O.) situated outside the campus. Asad came out of his room and entered the dining room. The boy who used to serve the meals from inside a cemented counter was still doing his duty. About ten students were eating. None of them appeared to be familiar to Asad. So he remembered the advice of Fakhrul and resisted asking questions about the military operation in campus and in the town to these boys. Listening to news was as normal to him as having a cup of tea in the morning. In some of the students' rooms a radio or transistor set was available. Considering it risky Asad abandoned the thought. While eating Asad could not avoid listening to tidbits of some of the conversation the boys were having around the tables. These were about the liberation struggle, torture by the army at some Hindu houses and the ludicrousness of some collaborators of the army. Asad wondered how daring or careless these boys were that such grave issues were being talked about openly in such a place. Even a name or two of those from the university who had joined the freedom struggle entered Asad's ears. Finishing his meal Asad came back to his room.

With a refreshed body after a long rest and not so bad meal, Asad sat on his bed and looked out of the window. There was no activity there. An empty play ground, pale and gray trees stood there with a look of emptiness. The sky above was pitch-dark. After a long day's heat, a gentle breeze now touched Asad's body and mind. Still something was itching in his mind. Slowly Asad understood what it was. The conversation of the students in the cafeteria, his own quest about the liberation war and his hatred for the ruling clique and the crackdown were silently at work in his mind. And the ignition today was provided by the boys' comments.

Asad stood on the floor, checked that the door was shut safely and then sat on the only chair in the room. He lit the reading lamp and carefully removed the cloth and old newspaper covering his reading desk. From under the cover he brought out a manila envelope and opened it. There were two photographs inside. He looked at the first one intently under the light of the lamp. A beautiful and young girl with her big and simple eyes was looking from it. As he looked at it, his eyes moistened. The name of this girl was Minoo. She used to live with her parents in their house near Harian rail station, not a faraway place from this campus until 25th March. Asad at this moment could not be sure if she was still there and she, her parents and the house were safe. Correspondence was dangerous now. There were no alternatives to obtain news also. Asad looked pale and pensive. From another envelope under his mattress Asad now brought out a few pieces of paper. In a neat handwriting and poetic diction Minoo in these papers gave replies to Asad's love overtures. Asad remembered their first meeting only a year ago at a picnic and excursion arranged by the University Registrar's office. Thence, none knew how they gradually came closer and closer till 28th February this year. Now excommunicated Asad had often thought of one thing. This affair with the girl was not known to his mother. His only sister suspected it without proof. So what will be their reaction if they really come to know the relationship and see this girl? After fighting the initial hesitation Asad wrote a letter to this girl. Then exchange of letters started. Asad tried to figure out if she was attending classes. Then he concluded possibly not as no female students were participating. Asad lifted the love letters with his hand and pressed them softly against both of his cheeks and then replaced them.

There was a change in his looks now. The glow of love and softness were gone and toughness replaced those expressions.

He took the second photograph out of the envelope and looked at it without blinking. The holder of this photograph was a man in his late thirties. His eyes would tell anyone that he was rough, tough and a cruel guy. His eyebrows were thick. He looked extremely healthy and mighty. The photograph was in black and white but developed on a silk paper. The resolution and features were very distinct. The man was in his *khaki* with a pick-up on his head. Asad now read the name plate fixed on the left side breast-pocket of the man's uniform. During the last two years he had done this same thing many times. Asad never had enough information on the meaning of shoulder badges worn by security people. One day a person having good knowledge about the workings of the armed forces told him that the man in this photograph was a Major of the Pakistan army. This man, when photographed was appointed in the 21st Wing of the East Pakistan Rifles deployed along the Rajshahi border. Asad put the photograph inside the envelope and replaced it inside his cupboard.

Now he was planning to go to bed. As he was arranging the bed-sheet and pillows a bad feeling started engulfing his mind. He had had this feeling many times even earlier through the last two years. Usually Asad had seen that his father's impressions and experiences about many issues of society or politics were riper than those of his, so in arguments he could not defeat his father on most of these issues. Even then he was never poised to lose respect for his father but at this moment the sight and memory of this photograph generated a deep sense of anger against his father. Asad controlled his emotion, put off the lamp and soon fell asleep.

The next day after getting up from his bed the first thought which struck Asad's mind was the whereabouts of Minoo. It had struck him actually as soon as he entered the campus yesterday. He got out and took a bus to the Harian rail station. The familiar neighbourhood looked cheerless and deserted. Asad approached a petty shopkeeper, bought a cigarette and cautiously proceeded through the alley where the fond little house was situated. There were almost no passersby or children or peddlers around. An old gentleman asked him what he was looking for.

After Asad answered the gentleman informed him that the house along with the adjacent railway staff quarters was burnt with petrol on the 1st of April by the army and their collaborators.

The scene hit Asad's soul instantly. The bricked semi-pucca house did not have the familiar appearance. Charcoal, ashes and black signs of burning were smeared all around it. With a dejected mind Asad asked the shopkeeper in a hushed tone,

—Did you witness the scene?

—Almost.

—How did it happen?

—They came in and looked for particular Hindu men. Asked Minoo's father about their whereabouts, then they shot him, took Minoo away and killed the other members of the family. Finally looted their belongings and put fire to the house.

—But her father was so intelligent. Why did they remain here?

—May be he thought it was so far away from the cantonment or the township and it was almost a village. They would not come this far. You know, he was my customer.

—Thank you indeed.

Asad felt an intense pain in his chest and thought he was going to have a heart attack but a memory flashing in his mind stalled the feeling. The memory was of the photograph of the mighty man in uniform of last evening. Asad's despondency was soon replaced with a diametrically opposite feeling. It was revenge. With moistened eyes but with a determined mind, he again thanked the shopkeeper and returned to the dormitory.

///

The President was not feeling good enough but that was not physical. The elegantly built Presidential palace was indeed a peerless edifice in this country. It had always attracted him. Besides the inner luxury, every blade of grass outside on the expansive lawn was imported from abroad which gave the place aesthetics of a Moghul garden.

Such bad feelings of the President used to show up when the effects of wine were gone. On such moments he sent for a vocalist. However, his attraction was more to the vocalist's beauty than to her tune or voice. This young song-star had a very sweet voice and she was enjoying an international reputation for that. She could pour her soul into the lyrics very adroitly. She was fair-complexioned and her Aryan beauty was the source of jealousy to many women in the country. She was not a slut or an ordinary type of courtesan but her social respectability was questionable. She used to take up the role of a stallion for the President. When he was horny he called for this woman or even visited her place. His name thus became slurred but he didn't give a damn to it, and asked his wife not to meddle in it.

On the advice of the information secretary the President usually gave one standard statement in seminars and meetings like, 'we have a thousand year old and enriched cultural heritage.' Then he realized that he himself was not sure about its meaning. On a different occasion like inaugurating the exhibition of an oil painting of an eminent artiste he said, 'one can smell the soil in the artistic creations of this maestro Mukarram Khan Kijilbash.' A question soon rose in his mind 'How can one find soil in the sands of Kalat desert?' He was unable to find an answer to this and thought that the language of these sly civilians and intellectuals were so dubious and equivocal. How can I figure out what the hell they mean by these vocabulary? However, whatever the meanings were, these are to be told. Without these, the country and society's image can't be made brighter.

About this song-star the President did not have any hesitation as to her quality and attraction. He knew she had a million votaries especially in the western wing of the country and secondly he could find solace with her very presence. This intimacy was no secret even to the family members of the President. One of the most popular songs sung by this artiste started with the diction, 'O lal mere (O my red)'.

The reason for his not feeling good was his thoughts about the crisis in the Eastern wing. This morning he received a report from the Eastern theatre. The new commander in that report informed that a total of seven hundred and twenty eight personnel starting from the rank of ordinary soldiers to colonels had been killed since he took command. These were the acts of anti-state miscreants and most of them could not be apprehended by the army. Earlier the President went through a number of paper clippings placed before him on his table. These clippings gave detailed photographs and reports of people tortured by his troops and their exodus to the neighbouring country. The reports further said, those same people were getting fire arms training, coming back and then shooting government soldiers resulting in the casualties of men and officers.

It was only a few days ago that the President chastised Tarik and asked for an explanation for the killing of minority men, women and children. In response Tarik said that this was done on the authorization of his predecessor. The President could not remember if he had given any such instructions to Tarik's predecessor. On the other hand these white men dominated world press were so devil like efficient that they were printing every detail of time, spot, date of the killings along with photographs of casualties. None of them could be denied or explained away as fabricated by the government. As soon as he instructed his commander to avoid excesses and pursue a tolerant policy with the rebels, casualties of his own forces were on the rise. The incidents of bombing power stations, blasting away military convoys, bridges and culverts and frontal attacks on army units also increased.

The President now looked at the eminent lady and asked her, 'Nuru, can you tell me what I should do now about all these problems? I don't know what a task I have laid my hands on!'

Though a high class performer, this artiste did not use to roam in the air or move on emotions only. She knew the President's mind-set intimately and she exploited that to her own material advantage. Three years ago the present President was the chairman of the powerful capital development authority, an organ responsible for developing and allotting very expensive plots of land at throw away prices to privileged applicants. When he is in a drinking spree, the President is not in command of his normal faculties. During those hazy hours it is possible for opportunists to get very important government orders, papers, sanctions and files approved quickly. The half-clad dancers display their talents and bodies, vocalists render their songs and the President, a connoisseur of these luxuries expresses his satisfaction in high pitch Urdu like 'keya bat, keya bat(what is the talk about)'. At such hours he can't say 'no' to any applicant waiting for his favour.

Nuru had made adroit use of these weak moments of the chairman and had been allotted scarce plots of land for herself and all her relatives. The artiste felt very sorry for her votary. She thought what a big position but what a simple man! What is he doing? Consulting so important a matter like politics with a woman and singer who knows nothing about the issue. There was nobody else on such an issue! Nuru realized how happy she was and felt it was much better to be a common citizen than to be the President of a country. Then she said, 'why should you burden your head alone? There are advisers and people enjoying power. Let them share the labour and the headache.'

The President relieved somewhat at the comment, said, 'you are correct. Usually the impression around here is such that the responsibility is only mine.'

His basic nature was at work and he ordered more for music, songs, dances and wine.

Six hundred miles south of this place the *Nabab* was seated at his resort. He also came across the press publications and was reviewing the same. More than three months had elapsed. The whole world was becoming increasingly critical towards the situation in the Eastern sector. Many of them were now directly condemning and protesting the army atrocities there. May be a few hundred got killed due to the army campaign there, while the western press were overstating the deaths as a few thousand. But they have credibility to the international community. So gradually his country and government were becoming marginalized in the eyes of the comity of nations. A normal person, i.e. someone with a burden of conscience would have thought like this and would have a feeling compatible with the thought. The *Nabab* was not such a person. On account of personality and character traits there was hardly any match between him and the President. He never suffered from a sense of shame or indecisions. Actually he was getting impatient. He was thinking about only one issue, 'how long shall it take to capture that very thing for which I have labuored so much and waited so long with such fortitude?'

The fact that incidents of genocide were causing condemnation for his country was not touching him at all.

The *Nabab* now summoned his political secretary. After a few minutes talk he ordered him, 'book a seat for me on a flight to Islamabad. I am going to meet the President'.

Another month passed away. It was the 15th of June. A very special person was waiting to see the Aryan lady in her office. He was granted an appointment for today a month's time ago. He was the chairman of All Indian Federation of Chamber of Commerce and Industries and Trade. His interests in the petroleum, airplanes, mines and steel sectors of the country were worth two hundred crore rupees. He was the chairman of a group of companies where the number of working chartered accountants was thirty. The stock exchange traded his company's shares almost daily. He was waiting for half an hour. The clock struck 10 'o clock. Assistant private secretary-I Mr. Chandanlal Shindhia entered the waiting room and showed the visitor to the doors saying, 'Mr. Varodaz Khandwala, please do follow me.'

He entered the room, made a bow and said,

—Good morning, Madam.

—Good morning, Mr. Varodaj, how are you doing?

—I am fine Madam, how are you?

—I am fine. Now tell me what I can do for you.

The madam spoke very little. Often her visitors had to take the role of talking. The visitor knew this very well though it was their first meeting. He started talking,

—Madam, you know that our business and trade have actually been suffering from various impediments since 1947. There was a great deal of difficulty in sending goods from one part of our own country to another. The main reason for this is the existence of an enemy state in between various parts of our country. The seven states have a lot of difficulties in this field. Still we were pulling on somehow. Now after March this year this difficulty has increased more than double. Every industry is under higher risk now. Production had to be reduced, as there has been a great slash in turnover. Already many production plants have been laid off. If this situation continues which I am afraid, it will, unless your government does something, we will be under heavy pressure in the near future. The owners will not be able to pay back their interest on loans to the bank. Many will become simply bankrupts.'

The visitee instantly understood the significance of the words she heard just now. Positioning the pair of spectacles on her alkyne nose she asked, 'Well, now tell me what your proposal is.'

—Madam, I hope your government will consider the present situation and take measures accordingly. Besides, we as business people think if we can reach a nearby market for selling our goods and services we can avoid this hassle and expenses of approaching ones which are far away. My federation has considered this option that we do have an opportunity at the moment. Politics is yours while business is ours. May I suggest we try to avail ourselves of that rare opportunity?

—Okay. Understood. Anything else Mr. Khandenwala?

Time was extremely expensive to this visitee. This visitor knew that well. He once again understood the point of the last question. He quickly said, 'Madam, I have to bear the pressure of quite a big number of stakeholders. You know I am also the elected representative of Ex-Punjab association. Actually today I came in here to make a request that your government, which is very popular, will take the necessary steps as soon as possible. I have nothing more to say.'

An aide of the host was taking down notes of the discussion accurately sitting down on a nearby table. She looked at him and made a sign that he could get out now. Then she said, 'Mr. Khandenwala, I am happy with the patriotism of the body you represent. I can tell you my government is fully conscious of the gravity and urgency of the situation. We will not make any delay in taking appropriate measures in this regard at the appropriate hour. Thank you gentleman.'

The visitor went out. The host reflected that all refugees from the west Punjab support today's visitor. During the last elections in which her party won a landslide victory, members of this association acted as a big vote bank in her favour. She now summoned the aide inside and thoroughly read the recorded notes and said, 'Forward these notes to the commerce minister right away'. With a 'yes Madam', the aide made an exit.

Her principal secretary entered with a knock and said that another visitor was waiting. He was Mr. Subramaniam Swami, currently the director of national defense institute. There were few persons who did not require an appointment to see the madam. Mr. Swamy was one such. He spoke little, thought and studied more. Most of his time was spent on research and writing. He stepped inside and the two exchanged greetings. Earlier he had been instructed to submit a report today. The host never read anything while a visitor was sitting in front of her. She usually talked to the visitor and then bid them adieu. But today she asked the visitor to sit before her and she started reading the report brought by the visitor. It took about half an hour's time to finish the report. She used red and blue pens to mark some parts of the report. She liked the contents of the report deeply but did not show any such expressions on her face. She then invited the visitor for tea and snacks and spoke. 'Mr. Swamy, I will arrange to place your report before the defense sub-committee of parliament so that it gets due consideration.'

In the present parliament her party's majority was such that anything could have an easy passage without any material impediment from the opposition. When tea was finished she told the visitor, 'I may request your presence once again, when necessary.'

After the visitor left the room she asked P.S-I to come in. He was carrying a bunch of papers on the situation yesterday. These papers detailed the entry and location of refugees which was now about half a million strong in the three states of Meghaloya, Tripura and West Bengal. She glanced through the papers, returned those to the official and said that she would now do paper work for half an hour before the defense sub-committee meeting at 1 o'clock in the afternoon. There were reasons for this verbal communication with staff members. In the highest circles of powers, certain issues are never printed. The defense sub-committee met at 1 o'clock. Khetlal Pandey, its chairman opened the discussion. He was aided by Bipin Mukherjee, Gauro Govindo Nando and Iqbal Ahmed Khan, all members of parliament. Three of those belonged to the treasury bench and one to the opposition. The whole matter under consideration today was totally military in nature but civilians had an unconditional supremacy in it. At one corner were seated Lt. General Amornath Raghupati Raina and Major General Rustomji. Madam listened to everyone and then asked General Raina,

—What would you like to say on this issue?

The General was very straightforward on such issues. He replied,

—Madam, this country has been a constant headache for us through the last 24 years. There has never been and still not anything called a government in that country. The whole country and all resources there are all for one institute. That is the military. The military is their government and it is their country also. We must punish them and this is the right moment. This is an interface of politics and the military

The General could not avoid staring at the lady's eyes. What he saw there was wrath and fire. He became afraid. Madam looked at the General with her cool eyes and said in a stern voice,

—General Amornath, listen. You have no right to dabble in politics. The military in my country has no prerogative of making speeches on political issues. That job belongs to the government and the party in power. Allow us to do that. Now answer my question.

—Sorry Madam, I said that as an introductory remark. However, we recommend the implementation of the proposed plan. If we do that we will have a net annual savings of 400 crore rupees on account of the cost of maintaining our border along the eastern sector. Plus the tension now suffered by our armed forces will be reduced to a great extent.

—Would you please furnish a little more details, General?

—Yes Mam, under the changed circumstances 12 infantry battalions, 8 BSF battalions and 3 cavalry regiments will not be required to be deployed along this border. Besides, a proportionate strength of support units will also become unnecessary.

Madam had a thorough understanding of these figures. She was happy and was almost going to say, 'very good'. She controlled herself and instead said,

—Gentlemen, I wish to thank you for the labour you have put into these exercises. My government will consider this proposal. Now you can leave.

The room was now empty. The lady was not one who would be satisfied easily. Still she had some preferences and likings. It does not look nice if someone expresses her own preferences. It is better if others do this. In today's meeting she bagged support from three different quarters on issues she had preference to. These were the military, parliament and the opposition. So she felt very pleased. She was a genius as a chess player since her school days. She knew the best hour for playing a bout. So she decided, 'the hour has not yet arrived. The game can be had at the appropriate time. I shall have to consider some more things before that.'

///

The Bengal season Monsoon had set in. It was the month of July. The movement of human and transport traffic had become a little more normal. Intermittent rainfall, heavy moisture charged air, sweltering heat under a cloudy sky had become the normal weather every day. Rauf's daughter was doing her classes in the campus. She had told her father once or twice that students' attendance at the classes was often thin. This was making her slightly scared in the campus. Rauf comforted her by saying, it would get normal gradually.

Now a days it was difficult to make a phone call from Rajshahi University as the telephone and telegraph lines were mostly occupied by the army for communication throughout the province. Asad informed his parents that he was keeping well, by writing a letter through the official postal department. His education was also progressing.

While Rauf was in his office and her daughter in her classes, Mrs. Rauf still did not feel so lonely. After completing cooking and washing along with the housemaid she had started visiting her neighbour often. Mrs. Farjana was also visiting her neighbour more often than before. The Fakhris assured them by saying, 'don't worry or get scared. These abnormal days will not last long. A solution and a good one will surely be reached. We know how nice people you are. Don't hesitate to contact us if you feel anything bad!'

Rauf couldn't talk much as Asad was away. Rauf was very cautiously listening to foreign news agencies. They were giving the same types of news. The number of refugees was increasing, security forces were continuing genocides and especially the religious minorities were becoming their victims. Rauf listened but believed little of what he heard. He told his wife, 'these are exaggeration. Why is there no emphasis on what Israel is doing in Palestine? How can one believe that you have very much sympathy for human suffering?'

It was a Monday. It had been raining cats and dogs since dawn. Rauf was unwilling to attend his office but it was the opening day after the weekly holiday on Sunday and a lot of work was lying pending in the office. Rauf took an umbrella and reached his office half drenched with rain water.

After one o'clock in the afternoon Rauf stood on the prayer mat on the left hand side of his desk and started praying. The door of the room faced westward. While he was through to the compulsory part of the prayer it seemed to him that two men entered the room and sat on the visitors' chairs placed in front of his desk. There was no carpet or mat covering on his office floor. If someone with a boot steps in his room the sound is easily audible. His orderly Tahfiluddin had orders not to allow strangers in like this. These questions rose in his mind but Rauf concentrated in his prayer.

Having finished he stood up from the mat and seated himself on his designated chair. Earlier Rauf had suspected the reason for the intrusion. Now looking at the two men in front of his desk he realized that there was nothing to chastise the orderly for. These two strangers were military officers. Instantly Rauf thought he should ask them why they entered the chamber of the head of an office without appointment or permission. Someone and something inside him cautioned him not to do so now. Rauf extended his right hand to the men. They shook it but Rauf felt from the way they did it, that they had no intention of doing so. One said that his name was Major Asam Walia while the other introduced him as Captain Ameer Hamja Butt.

Hamja opened his mouth, 'Mr. Deputy Controller, we need to have some talks with you.'

—Yes, go ahead.

—Is there any anti-government fellow in your office?

—Look, this is a pure government office. I never allow anyone here to talk politics. So there is no question of having any body like that.

—Don't you have an employee union here?

—No it is a security printing press. Law does not allow that kind of organization here. What we have here is only a welfare committee of employees.

—Does the union have a registration?

—I told you there is no union. The welfare committee has a registration

The major was not talking. He was looking away and listening. Hamja remained silent for a few seconds and then in a very casual manner asked,

—Mr. Rauf, where is your residence?

The captain could be slightly older than Asad. Rauf did not like the way the captain asked the question. Rauf had always been a very honest

officer and never accepted any bribes. He also never committed any illegal or improper act in his office. His controller, though a Punjabee, trusted him as a very good and efficient officer and gentleman. At Islamabad, officials of the establishment division who dealt with promotions of all government officials often said that Rauf was going to be promoted any moment to the post of additional controller. He was a staunch supporter of the pro-government Pakistan Muslim League though he never expressed this. Rauf's courage was a source of fear to many normal persons. Rauf decided not to answer the captain's last query and asked the captain, 'May I know the reasons for this query of yours?'

There was a flicker of smile from the captain's face. Through the series of white teeth the captain authoritatively told, 'the army reserves the authority to ask any questions to anyone since the whole country is under martial law now.'

Rauf gave his home address. So far the conversation was in English. Now Major Assam joined and asked in Urdu, 'Where had you been on the 19th of March?'

A matter of a few months back. Rauf could not remember immediately. He quickly looked at the official red calendar under the glass cover of his desk and said,

—I was in my office.

—Can you recollect the incident happening that day?

—Which incident?

—The army came under attack from the civilians quite close to this place.

—I heard about that.

—Was there anyone from your office?

—No, there was none.

—How are you so sure?

—Each of the employees of my office is personally known to me. They were all on duty throughout that day.

The major flashed a broad smile on his face and said, 'We are happy to know this. Look, you are a government official. If you come across any anti-state employee please inform us immediately. The security of you and your family is our responsibility.'

The officers rose to their feet shook hands with Rauf and then both made a sign something close to, but not exactly, a salute and walked out of the room. Rauf thought over the matter for a while. Then he put on his shoes. It was quarter past 2 in the afternoon. It would take half an hour to return home. Two assistant controllers rushed into Rauf's room followed by his orderly and personal assistant. The two officers eagerly asked,

—Sir, what's the matter?

—Nothing important. They just came to see and talk to me.

—Sir, we were scared. We were not sure if we should enter your room.

—Why were you scared? Has anyone amongst your sons or family joined the so-called freedom fighters' groups?

—No, the matter is not like that Sir. Still these military people's faces are such that one gets scared even when they are smiling.

—Believe me gentlemen. I fail to understand why one should be afraid of our own army? Tahfil, lock the office. We have to go home now.

Assistant controller Abdul Matin thought that only a very few people in this office might support this view of Rauf? He wished Rauf had not expressed these views here.

///

The name of the training camp was Kalyani. Captain Muruli Dharan Joshi of the 3rd Maratha Light Arms was in charge of the camp. He had been training Bangalee freedom fighters how to use light arms since last April. His headquarters from Delhi instructed him to complete basic training to batches of freedom fighters as fast as possible and then release them for campaign in the field. Joshi was a small talker. Before the partition of 1947 his parental home was at Songhar district in Sindh, now in Pakistan. He was a lad of eleven years on that historic year. He remembered everything he saw happening around his village. There was not a single incident of communal tension in their district or even an altercation between the Hindu and Moslem communities. The Moslems shook hands with their Hindu neighbours intending to cross the border for India. Even many poor Moslem cart-pullers carried luggage of Hindus intending to cross the Rajasthan border and charged no fare for the labour or the bullocks. That was why captain Joshi was

wondering since his posting here, about the reasons of the present crisis in East Pakistan. He was watching the daily increase in the number of immigrants intending to join the liberation war and thinking what could have happened inside that province. He was puzzled to think why hundreds of thousands of people who were so nice with people belonging to a different religion were taking up arms against their co-religionists and undergoing unbearable hardships with smiling faces?

During the initial days Joshi could not speak the language of his trainees. Gradually he picked it up to make the lessons easy. Now he talked to the trainees in their language while teaching them about fire arms. He had been getting along with these foreigners well. One day a person named Mumtaz appeared in front of the camp, met Joshi and expressed his interest in joining the war. Captain Joshi immediately felt something very special about this applicant. He was sure this stranger was one in a lac he had trained so far. Joshi asked,

—What were you doing to earn a living before crossing the border?

—I was a lecturer.

—In which institute?

—At a public university, called Rajshahi University which is not even 50 miles from this camp.

—My God. You are surely a great person. It is surprising that you abandoned that honour and comfort to take a totally uncertain and dangerous mission!

—Why are you so surprised captain Joshi?

—Because I have hardly come across anyone amongst my trainees here who has your status or education.

—Actually there are many. May be not in this camp but in the others along your borders.

—Would you mind telling me what was the bone of contention between the central government and East Pakistan? Actually I am confused about the reasons.

—Well, then I will tell you what led to this. You see we have always been the majority since 1947 but they ruled us always except for a very short interregnum. They imposed a minority language on us. That is why we were angry in 1952 against that decision. Then in the last year, 1970, they allowed an election, where we became the clear majority. After a long talk they refused to hand over power to us and treacherously started this genocide.

—What is the target?

—To destroy us as a nation, impose Urdu once again and then continue to exploit us as before.

At this point it came to Joshi's mind that in his country only a few people's mother tongue was Hindi and in spite of it that was the official language of the country. Nobody had spoken against it. Again, the people of Calcutta or West Bengal also had never been clamorous about establishing their mother tongue in their state. And exploitation? Where on earth was that inevident?

However Joshi said, 'that is why your whole nation has risen in such a beautiful way. I really get surprised to see that boys not yet adults with a myopic minus seven lens in their eyes are coming down here with an application that they want to fight this war. One of them said, 'please recruit me, I will kill at least one soldier and then die.' Another one with a limply leg appealed to work as a cook for the freedom fighters. Many others, who I can say are unable even to carry the weight of a fire arm, are looking for an opportunity to fight this war and liberate their motherland. It is really touching.'

Mumtaz got emotional and said to Joshi,

—Do you know what else they have done with us?

—To be frank, very little. You know the nature of our job is such that there is no scope for us talking national or foreign politics. It was only after your liberation struggle started that our government allowed us to listen to or discuss these issues. Yes, you wanted to say something.

—Yes, their inequities started right after 1947. We Bengalees of East Bengal brought about Pakistan by the strength of our majority votes. The first thing they did was the establishment of the capital at Karachi. Then in 1958 a martial law government took power and shifted the capital to the Punjab. Our revenue earnings are much more than that of the western wing but they always spent more than 70% of the income for their development. Everywhere in military and civil services, business and trade they are the overwhelming majority. All benefits of the military rule accrued in the west because almost all the cantonments and military expenditures have been made there. We still accepted that. The first premier was elected from East Bengal but he could enjoy only a short stay in his office due to the clique of the west. Still we held on with patience. The present President admitted that we were exploited and assured that

would be duly compensated. He appeared sincere and that meant a lot to us. But now see how he has backed out from his commitment after staging a farce of negotiations at Dhaka. One special mention of their insanity must be told. They have always treated us as if they are the pure Aryan Germans and we are the Plebian Jews. This is a continuous insult to a nation who has a thousand year old culture and history.

—These are indeed important issues.

—You see what type of human beings they are. Do you know what Sher Ali Buzz, a Lt. General of the army has said about their present mission?

—No. I have not heard that but I know this much that he graduated from our Military Academy of Dehradun in the Uttar Pradesh.

—He has directly told the army, 'We want only the soil of East Pakistan and not the people.'

Captain Joshi though young understood that he should not involve himself too much in these issues. He just listened. Mumtaz continued,

—The present issue is not an isolated one. Millions of people across the border are flooding into your camps. Most of them are not Hindus. Rather the number of Moslems is much more than the Hindus. It is surely known to you under what condition a people take up arms against their own armed forces. The members of civil and military services, students, peasants and intellectuals all have joined this movement. Not only that, where in history have you read that about four hundred and fifty elected legislators of a country made an exodus in a body? May I inform you something more on this?

—Yes please go ahead.

—These Punjabee-led military always played the 'non-martial' fiddle against us too much. That was not correct. Tell me who defended Lahore city from falling in the 1965 war? We Bengalees fought against India and defended it.

Joshi felt embarrassed with the fact that these people were against India during that time and now they are fighting the Pakistanees taking refuge inside Joshi's country.

—You are a scholar. What you are saying is surely correct. However let us now talk about business. Fire arms, military training and warfare are indeed very difficult and painstaking matters. I always use to give this warning first to people who come to me for training. Besides the end of this war is also quite uncertain.

Mumtaz got very stiff and retorted,

—Captain Joshi, you may not be certain about the end or consequences of this war but we 75 million Bengalees are. The reason is if this became a failure our death as a nation will be inevitable. So we are determined about its course.

Captain Joshi felt slightly disconcerted by the firm words of Mumtaz. He recovered quickly and said, 'Well, now let us start our talks on training.'

///

The President became furious as soon as he saw the *Nabab*. In spite of allowing him a priority appointment to see him earlier this morning he kept this important visitor waiting for an hour unnecessarily. He did not have much work on the desk but feigned than he was too occupied. The *Nabab* sat in Piru's room but did not lose patience. The President always suspected that the two had extra legal relationship and exchanges but did not possess the ruler like qualities necessary to take action against General Piru for this. Like many other issues of his office, he had also taken this one lightly. After avoiding the greetings of the *Nabab*, the President said,

—It is due to people like you that the situation of the country has become like this.

The *Nabab* was as cunning as Machiavelli's prince. In 1965 his ill advice to another military President pushed the country to the brink of a grave crisis. The country unnecessarily involved itself in a war beyond its affordability and was going to suffer a humiliating defeat. The international community mediated to stop it when a debacle seemed imminent for this country. At that time the *Nabab*'s agenda was to show the President as discredited to the common people of the country as possible and gradually pave his way to power. In spite of his instigation and unsound advice the *Nabab* could not be brought to book and stood innocent after the end of the war. He now knew well that the present President was less gifted than the previous one. So he decided not to show any reaction to the accusative tone of the President and calmly said,

—Mr. President, the supreme authority of the government of this country is vested in your hands. I am not even a cabinet minister. So I really do not understand how I can be in any way connected with this situation of the country.

The President boomed and said,

—Please hold your tongue. This is you and your party who have time and again influenced me not to transfer power to the majority party. I am a military person. We are trained to look at things in a straightforward manner. So I did not realize the magnitude of the issue. Now I can see that I committed a mistake. I spoke to the nation on last 28th of June with all sincerity. I have feedback that almost the whole world has disregarded it. If I had not given the order for military action on the 25th of March. I am sure; the situation would not be as bad as we hear today.

—Mr. President . . .

—Don't interrupt. Let me finish. A personality like Mr. Harold Wilson, the ex British Premier, has personally told me over telephone something which is very serious. He informed me that our troops and officers alike are not only killing civilians in East Pakistan, they are raping women also. Where did they get this news from? I got my training and commission from SandHurst. I have seen their news is always almost correct. Do you want me to believe that they ruled us for over one hundred and ninety years by eating horse fodder?

—But Mr. President what could I do in this matter and what was my responsibility in this? That is why I suggested power to be transferred specially to the two parties in the regions where they got majority votes.

The President remembered how considerate he had always been to this visitor. He also realized that the situation now had become like one where a transaction has already taken place and he was the creditor in that while the *Nabab* was the debtor. Instead of discharging the debt and giving thanks for the benefit, he was criticizing the creditor now. He understood that now there was no chance at all of having the money back. On the contrary the relation between the two was possibly going to take a turn for the worst as a borrower or beneficiary in this society always becomes ungrateful to the benefactor or lender. The President said, 'you are correct that you had no legal responsibility in the matter. But you and your followers made me and my government nervous with the threat of organizing agitation all the time from Khyber to Teknaf.'

Usually though a man of mediocre and limited capabilities there were moments when the President demonstrated some dazzling reflections. Now, he was in such a mood. In a considerate and temperate tone he said, 'nobody advised me before the results of the elections were brought before me. As a man truthful to his oath I accepted the results given to me by the chief election commissioner Sattar and allowed their release before the nation. I should have said there were charges of vote rigging by over-enthusiastic activists. So investigations were necessary before determining the position of the parties. Had I done this, they and the world community would not be able to show the courage they have been showing now. Even you could have given me this advice. Could you not? At least about the Awami League? You see, on the contrary I made no delay in congratulating them and announcing the name of the fellow who was going to be the next premier.

—Mr. President, Piru and his staff advised you to do this. Not we because we were also a party in the elections.

—You are right. What I mean is civilians like you who have a better understanding of political issues could give me a sound opinion. And now once I announced that, all of the democratic forces of the world are pressurizing me to hand over power. They do not believe that a majority party can be anti-state. My story of discrediting Mujib and his party is not being supported by the western powers. On the other hand we are so indebted to them since our independence. We can't be tough to these creditors and donors. I must further say that when Mujib was campaigning for their low representation in the civil and military services, none came to help me to face these allegations with arguments, neither you nor your party, even . . .

—What argument could be given before the leader of that brute majority party, Mr. President?

—Why? We could ask, how an East Pakistanee who did not try to be a 2nd lieutenant in 1947 could be made a Lieutenant General alongside a Punjabee or west Pakistanee who took his commission. The same could be applied for someone in the civil service. If one does not start his career as an Assistant Secretary, how can he expect to be a Secretary to the government? Similarly, I could argue why it was not possible to bring parity in industrialization of both wings. The Bengalees hardly took the advantage of taking loans from EPIDC and establish enterprises like

their West Pakistanee businessmen. These are not matters which could be solved overnight or within a year or two.

The sly *Nabab* never expected such intelligence from the President and so was surprised. The President again started,

—Actually we should have started talking some more issues gradually. One of the best things for addressing social dissension and mutual mistrust is the bondage of marriage. We, as a policy, should have patronized and encouraged inter-wing marriages. That would surely reduce the possibility of conflicts and increase amity. Only a few CSPs or other highly educated people of both wings have inter-wing marraiges which is peanuts. If an Assamese can marry a Rajput or a Bihari can have a spouse from Malayalam and be happy why can not a Punjabee or Baluch do that with a Bengalee?

The *Nabab* looked thoughtful but calculated that his own prospects would be reduced under that scenario. He quietly said, 'Indeed these sound good but I doubt if Mujib would allow this . . .'

The President retorted, 'But we have not tried this at all. Nobody, no civilian ever advised me that I should address the common men on certain important issues. I should have asked them if they would like to stay with us or if they would like to go to the clutches of the very cunning people from whom they were separated after the bloody riots during 1947 and leave us behind? If this would be any good for them? Unfortunately, it is due to people like you, that I did not have any scope or time to address these issues.

—But, Mr. President, you dismissed your civilian cabinet long before the negotiation with Mujib's team started. So who could render such advice to you?

—I know this is the very style that politicians talk during troubles but I am indeed worried about the situation we are in. Only God knows how and when we can get out of it.

Though the President's comment on politics and politicians was not palatable, the visitor swallowed the insult. He knew this man was still in the chair and so must be kept in good humour. Otherwise the destination he was targeting would be more difficult to reach. Accordingly the *Nabab* feigned a beam on his handsome face and reminded the President,

—You have all along assured the nation that after transferring power to the politicians you will go back to the barracks.

—You are right. Let the trouble ease a little. I am thinking of forming a civilian cabinet.

The mental make-up of the President was such that he couldn't maintain his temperament on the same scale for long. It changed frequently. If he was tough on someone he became soft soon even before the intended message was delivered well. At this moment such a changeover was taking place in his mind. It appeared to him that his words today with the visitor were too harsh. This man had bagged crores of votes from his supporters. They were waiting to see him in power soon.

Then he shall have to salute this man. What guarantee is there in this incredulous society that then he will not fire him? So he made his voice softer and said in a conciliatory manner,

—Please pray to Allah so that with His infinite mercy we may come out of this uncertain situation. After '47, our nation has never fallen into any crisis like this one. The clouds now shrouding us are indeed thick which have never visited before. Pray, may Allah deliver us.'

—Yes, *Inshallah.*

A number of globally influential magazines had pointed their fingers to the *Nabab* for his responsibility in the present crisis of the nation. In his excited state of mind the President had decided he would show those reports to the *Nabab* today. He now decided not to do that as his temper cooled down. Rather a different thought gripped him. It now seemed to him that for this crisis the responsibility of the leader of the majority party was much more than the *Nabab*. Though not a Punjabee, the *Nabab* was a Sindhi and at least an aristocrat by birth. People with noble lineage can't be that bad. Besides most of the armed forces and General Piru have a liking for this person. Therefore he should not be annoyed. The President quickly said,

—Don't worry. Not that the civilian cabinet will be formed without you. And we will do that indeed quickly.

—Thank you Mr. President for your time.

—You are welcome. Let us call it a day then.

Officially the army spokesmen were denying the existence of anything called freedom fighters in the province. What they admitted was 'act of miscreants' at the maximum whenever there was an incident and casualty of troops or officers anywhere. Actually the army units were not getting any time to sleep whenever there was the slightest presence of the freedom fighters. There was also an instruction that whatever casualties there were the information must not be circulated to other units. Spreading panic must be avoided. So only the sufferers were experiencing the might of the freedom fighters. Potential ones were unaware of the exact nature of possible exigencies.

Charged with training, equipped with arms and above all imbued with patriotism, and readiness for death or anything else the freedom fighters were making the troops' life restless by their unpredictable attacks. The troops and their commanders had some leisure only during day time. They were under orders to keep awake during night bearing the stings of mosquito bite and irrespective of the presence of moon light or darkness. The attacks usually used to come sometimes between evening and sunrise.

The 31st Baluch regiment had its camp at Nalitabari, in Mymensingh district. Hikmat Nasar Abdullah belonging to this unit was experiencing 'war' for the first time in his career. He however did not agree to regard this as a war but something a little higher than skirmishes. He had a feeling that not even a sub-machinegun should be used against these amateurs of Bengal who claimed themselves as freedom fighters. Of course he did not have the authority to take such a decision.

It is human nature that good news brings the recipient happiness and energy. He had received a letter in which his parents informed him that his wife had given birth to a male child. It was now a week since Abdullah found himself floating in sheer dreams since getting such good news.

During the day time his duty was to recce about a 10 miles radius of the area with a band of soldiers following him. He had so far felt no necessity of taking special precautionary measures as a follow up of the recce. His estimate was that an ambush might result in the death of five Bengalee miscreants and one wounded on the army side.

There was an incident like this yesterday. So the neighbourhoods were reeking with the stench of dead bodies of miscreants killed in yesterday's action. It was still entering the nostrils of troops in this camp as the dead bodies were not buried. Who shall bury them? The mosques of the neighbouring villages were empty, and the mullahs of the mosques were absconding for fear of the army. Abdullah was thinking that after the heavy beating by the army yesterday, no local amateur would dare staging any further drama with the army. The sentries were on duty around the camp. Abdullah, lying on his camp bed was dreaming about his baby son. How did he look like? Fair and soft like his wife Najli or manly like him? Yes, a manly child was better otherwise how will he be able to join the military when grown up and fight the infidels to create a country for all Moslems?

An hour had passed by since the sun set today. Abdullah had no sleep today. He did not realize when he fell asleep while dreaming for his home and family far away. His sleep was broken by a soft purring sound. Immediately he thought this was coming from some moving animals. May be dogs or foxes eating up the dead bodies outside the camp. Still, he was a soldier. Within the next two seconds his fingers reached for the trigger of the sten-gun laid along the right hand side of the camp-bed. He was about to call sentry Mukeem Khan and ask what it was when a very sharp article stabbed him through the left side of his chest. He could make only a suffocating sound from his throat and fell down with a thud while his fingers got loosened from the trigger. His eyes still saw the killer and recognized him.

This afternoon when Abdullah and his troops were on a killing spree in the nearby Ram Chandrakura weekly bazaar, this man was peddling onions. Prior to this there was no sound of shooting. Now it started from all the corners of the camp. All twenty troops were dead by stabbing and bullets of the freedom fighters.

Only survivor wireless operator Bachhu Khan from his underground trench started sending messages through his set, 'my camp has been attacked by the freedom fighters. Please rescue us.'

Almost at the same time, Major Gul Mohammad of 28th Field regiment artillery camped at Kendua police station in the same district faced death from an unknown bullet. He was seated on a chair in front of his tent. His body guard *Nayeb Subeder* Rostad Hoti got shredded into pieces by a bren-gun firing, midway while he was rushing to save his commander's life.

Through the last two months, Captain Golondaz Naqvi of 29th Frontier force had been on duty with a platoon strength. His assignment was to protect the Fulchoriori-Bahadurabad ferry station. His troops covered an area of 10 miles on a patrolling duty. The people of this area were very pious and docile. Naqvi himself was also very God-fearing. He had given a standing instruction on his own to all of his men and officers that he would show no mercy to them for offences like molestation of women and loot. He also said that he was aware many in uniform were doing this and were in the temptation of doing that further. Naqvi completed another job after being posted here from Rawalkot. Captain Didarul Alam, his batch-mate hailed from this village. Both got commission from Kakul Military Academy the same day. Didar was now posted in paratrooper unit-I at Attock fort in West Pakistan.

Naqvi found out the address of Didar's village, met his father, conveyed his son's greetings to him and then assured him, 'Uncle, you or none of your village has got anything to be scared about from the army. Nobody is going to receive any wrong treatment at our hands. But there is one thing. Anyone doing anything against the country's solidarity will not be spared.'

So far neither Naqvi nor any soldier of his troops had fallen into any ambush from the freedom fighters. After evening, Naqvi was offering his prayers. All his soldiers were standing behind him in the offering except sentries guarding the camp. This camp was inside the office of the local union council, a branch of the local government of the province. The devout soldiers were going to bow for the 2nd stage of the prayer with an 'Allahu Akbaar'.

At this moment, a group from the 3rd Bengal regiment cordoned the whole camp under the dark shades of a cloudy twilight. To the sentries it appeared as if these fighters landed from the skies, such was their quiet and skill in doing the job. The sentries simply surrendered their fire arms without any noise in the face of nozzles of gun pointed at their back by the Bengal fighters. Naqvi and the forces finished their prayers. He looked at the leader and was wondering what these people were after.

Abdul Ali Mondal, Lance Naik, pointed a light machinegun close to the nose of Naqvi and said, 'We intend no bloodshed, no shooting but just want the firearms and ammo, right?'

Naqvy estimating the situation, ordered his 2nd-in-command to comply with the demand of the Bengal deserters. The firearms all gradually accumulated on the ground. Mondal was hesitating about the next part of his assignment as he had planned earlier. Seeing his delay, Angur Mia, *Habilder* of Sonapur, Noakhali district, spoke in a low tone in the vernacular to Mondal, 'It is dangerous to spare even their eggs when you come across snakes.'

Immediately the firearms of the Bengal men whimpered together and twenty two large lifeless bodies of Naqvi and his troops fell like coils on the ground. Before breathing his last captain Naqvi could manage to vent his wrath with a word, 'treacherers!'

With the memory of thousands of his innocent villagers getting killed and women and children raped at the hands of similar uniformed men working in his mind, Angur Mia only told, 'the treachery of your colleagues on us has been fifty times as much as the one we have done now. So no regrets.'

Angur Mia would never know it was far from poetic justice. Naqvi, in spite of being a rough and tough soldier had never perpetrated any such misdeeds in his career or life. Alas! War is neutral of morality and immorality, equity, virtue or sins.

//

This was the last Sunday of August. Being a weekly holiday Rauf went to the municipal fish and vegetable market at Mohakhali. Then he went to a hair-dressing saloon and had his hair-cut. After lunch he made several attempts to place a trunk-call to Rajshahi to talk to his son. Being unsuccessful he decided he would make a phone call to the direct line at the house-tutor of Asad's dormitory later and request him to call his son for a minute's talk. This also failed. The operator gave him the same news that telephone exchanges were constantly being used for the army personnel for most of the time. Civilians would need to wait longer before expecting to get a connection. He then planned that he would make the next attempt later tonight when the lines were expected to be less occupied.

It had been ten days that he had the last communication from his son. He was thinking about him although Assad had told him that he was having no problems with his studies or health.

Now reclining on his bed, Rauf remembered something about his daughter also. It was yesterday that she told him something. She was coming back home after attending her classes. She hired a baby-taxi from the exit of the public library situated at the north end of the campus. After a few minutes on the road with a light traffic she sensed that a

Willy's jeep, the army's olive-coloured brand vehicle, was following her scooter though keeping a distance. She was sure about this when she reached home and saw the jeep moving away in another direction. One *khaki* clad man was seated on the front seat beside the driver. Rauf asked his daughter,

—Did anyone try to talk to you?

—No, Dad, nobody got down from the vehicle.

While thinking about this Rauf fell asleep. He woke up when the time for evening prayers arrived. He quickly completed offering his prayers. A few minutes later he asked the maid-servant Gulenoor to serve the evening tea. The family usually enjoyed the evening tea with snacks and cookies sitting in the drawing room. The cookies usually came from 'Maruf Sweetmeat' a confectionary at Farm gate area. Rauf was munching a biscuit and sipping from his cup holding it in his right hand. His daughter was also enjoying tea seated face to face to her father on another couch. Inside the kitchen Mrs. Rauf was giving instructions to the maid about this evening's menu for dinner. There was no separate entry door for Rauf's floor from the stairs below. It was common with the tenant on the ground floor Shakhawat. Up to 25th March a boy servant used to do the duty of guarding the entrance sitting on a stool at the mouth of the staircase. Since then his whereabouts were unknown to the family. He simply disappeared without taking even his pay or belongings. Rauf did not look for a second one as all kinds of thefts or robbery had simply stopped after March.

Rauf told her daughter to switch the television on. Before she reached the TV set a light knock became audible from outside the door of the drawing room. Rauf approached the door. There was no key hole on the door. The only push button electric calling bell was also out of order since many months. No electrician was available to fix it. He asked,

—Who is out there?

Rauf could not hear any response to his question. This door was made of high quality Burmese teak and crafted by a highly skilled Hindu carpenter famous for this type of craftsmanship throughout East Pakistan. Rauf now opened the door. Three men were standing on the step. Two were tall, fair and handsome. One was short and dark. All three were wearing recently pressed crispy uniforms. Rauf looked at the insignia on their shoulders. He recognized one as a lieutenant-colonel, one a major and another one to be a junior commissioned officer. All three were wearing woolen berets. The service boots on their feet were dazzling due to the fine polish. The bright brass clips of the insignia made a flicker of light inRauf's eyes. The tallest one said, 'Assalamualaikum', extended his right hand to Rauf and then introduced himself in English,

—This is Lt. Col. Babar Laek Abbasi, 7th field intelligence unit, Dhaka Cantonment.

Rauf without asking them to enter, said dryly,

—What is the matter?

—We need to talk to you.

—But why during this time and at my residence? Give me a call and meet me at my office.

—Look, we are officers and gentlemen. Considering the situation of the country, we have no schedule of duty now. Can we now maintain official decorum? That is why we are here at this odd hour.

As Abbasi answered, his face was all smiles and humility. Rauf said,

—Ok then, come in.

The two officers entered and they asked the JCO to stay outside. Rauf noted the name of the Major. Umar Raja. He asked,

—Tell me what it is?

Abbasi, in response talked about the general law and order situation of the province and the city for some time. Then he asked,

—How many kids do you have?

His daughter was sipping tea and listening to the conversation. Rauf told the truth. Abbasi asked,

—Where are your son, what is he doing?

Rauf stated the facts.

—And your daughter?

—She is right there. She is a student of Dhaka University.

The two watched Rauf's daughter on the sofa. Rauf also watched the two. Suddenly he noted that none was wearing any sign of the abbreviation of F.I.U. or field intelligence unit anywhere on their uniforms. Then he remembered another thing about this matter that intelligence people

possibly can't wear any uniform except for official ceremonies. So he wondered why these people were not properly clad. Abbasi now asked,

—Is your son involved in some kind of politics, I mean student politics at the university?

—No, he is not. He is a good student and he is attending his classes there regularly.

—OK. Who was singing in this room before we entered here?

—My daughter.

—A sweet voice indeed.

Major Umar Raja was so far silent. He was studying everything about the drawing room and the young girl seated on the sofa. Raja looked like a strongly built ox attired with a military uniform with a pair of yellow cruel eyes, a heavy set eagle like nose and a fearless countenance. His appearance seemed very close to cricketer Imran Khan Niazi's but without his cinematic softness. A small firearm inside a white cambish cover was visible on his right waist. He was sitting beside Rauf and Abbasi. He now rose whispering a stanza of one of the popular songs of Mehedi Hassan's, proceeded towards the sofa where Rauf's daughter was seated. He softly sat beside her and asked more softly,

—What is your name?

—Jerin.

—Do you speak Urdu?

—I speak English.

—Which subject are you studying in ?

Jerin made an answer. Mrs. Rauf was standing on the dark passage leading from the drawing room to the kitchen. She watched the talks and scenario of the drawing room and was about to ask her daughter to withdraw and come inside. Major Umar meanwhile had seated himself close to Jerin. Mrs. Rauf listened to their conversation. She did not sense any danger but there was something like an uncomfortable feeling brewing up within her mind. She entered her bedroom and quietly dialed the phone number of her neighbour. Mrs. Mahmudee received the call.

—Hello, what is the matter? Mrs. Rauf.

—Not bad, but is your husband at home now?

—Yes, he is. Why?

Mrs. Rauf described the situation of their drawing room and requested if Mr. Fakhri could come in to her house now.

—OK. Don't worry. He will be right away.

Within three minutes Yasin Khan Fakhri's knock was heard on Rauf's door. He entered and sat on a sofa. The dresses, shoes and wristwatch worn by Fakhri were quite expensive. His handsomeness was unavoidable and he looked like one of the most popular cine heroes of this country. He was the elected 2nd office bearer of Dhaka Chamber of Commerce and Industry, the biggest trade body of this province. When the President is on tour of this province Fakhri always received an invitation to all the luncheons, dinners and receptions held in honour of the President.

In underdeveloped societies personalities are more important and powerful than systems as is subjectivity than objectivity. Powerful and important people, by pulling a few strings of the power structure can solve many problems which otherwise have hardly any solution to the commoners. The rule of the law is still an airy slogan in such societies. Fakhri possessed all these qualities. One could easily feel the strength and attraction of his personality. Rauf introduced Fakhri to the army officers.

Pakistan, especially then was for the Punjabees, of the Punjab and by the Punjabees and not for anyone else who belonged to a different ethnic group. The army officers dismissed the credentials of this guest because they had correctly identified him to his origin. Just as an experienced man never mistakes a wolf to be a tiger, Abbasi and Umar were sure that Fakhri was a Pathan and not a Punjabee. Fakhri told the officers,

—You see, Mr. Rauf is a very nice gentleman whom I have known for the last two decades. He is a patriotic Pakistanee. I am his closest neighbour.

Umar ignoring these words and the personality and credentials of Fakhri rudely asked,

—Who are you to meddle in a case where the army is involved? Besides we have all the intelligence with us about those who are enemies to this country. Nobody can throw dust in our eyes.

Actually Abbasi was telling lies. There was no adverse report with them about anyone of this family. The purpose of those damn lies was to oust the Pathan. Umar now joined Abbasi. He said,

—These people were against the partition of India and the creation of Pakistan. They supported faithless people like Gaffar Khan and named him as the 'Frontier Gandhi'. During last March, their leader Gaffar Khan's son Wali Khan also demanded the transfer of power to Bengalees. And now, once again they are supporting the rebels.'

Abbasi supported Umar. As the talks between the two went on in Punjabee dialect neither Rauf nor Fakhri understood the content clearly. Umar added in Urdu, that the army had every authority to interrogate anyone in this province or country because martial law was running the country. Fakhri still put up some arguments but he appeared weak and fragile in spite of his sincerity. He comforted Rauf by saying that he should rely on Allah and got back to his residence. His wife eagerly looked at her husband's worried face and asked,

—What has happened?

—Nothing has happened but I am afraid something bad might happen.

Then Fakhri described the situation he had seen at Rauf's house. His wife said, 'you have friends and relatives in the army. Look for them immediately.'

Fakhri had already started with a telephone list by his bedside. His futile attempt to pull a string five minutes ago was sapping his confidence as he remembered that the people in the army he knew in Dhaka Cantonment were all from his province or tribe. The need of the hour was a Punjabee who knew him well enough to intervene on Rauf's behalf. Beads of sweat appeared on Fakhri's fair forehead as he scanned the names. The telephone system responded uncooperatively. Fakhri continued his attempts as his wife watched him.

Meanwhile back in Rauf's drawing room Lt. Col. Abbasi told Rauf,

—Actually we are here to propose something to you.

—Then why have you not said that so far?

—How could we tell you that? See how your neighbour interrupted and wasted our time? Well, what we are looking for is the cooperation of your daughter.

—What type of cooperation?

There was a note of surprise in Rauf's tone.

—It is like this-your daughter will accompany us to the cantonment and encourage our patriotic soldiers by her songs.

—She is not a professional or eminent artiste.

Rauf's tone was sombre.

—You see, everything can't be performed by professional people. All radio and television artistes from East Pakistan are fugitive now. Some of them have been killed while carrying out anti-state activities. Altaf Mahmood is a good example. On the other hand our soldiers are getting killed and maimed every day in defending the sacred motherland at the hands of the local miscreants created by you people. They are also suffering the moisture and uncomfortable climate of an unfamiliar land. So can't we expect such a small favour from you in return for the hardships our soldiers are suffering?

Abbasi smiled like an innocent child and continued to say,

—By the by, can you imagine the pains of a soldier who has received a bullet in his knee-cap?

—No, how can I? I am not a surgeon and there is no role of any members of my family or me in the creation of the local miscreants you are telling us about.

At a small distance Major Umar Raja had now touched Jerin's cheek with his left palm and slowly said,

—You are very pretty Jerin.

Jerin was angry and told,

—What are you doing Major? Get away from me.

Rauf watched this scene as he talked to Abbasi. Now in clear English, Rauf told,

—What you are saying and doing here is not becoming of an officer or gentleman. Listen, I will make a complaint to your commanding officer as well as to my controller on this matter. If necessary I will also let everything be known to the defense secretary. I will request you to consider the consequences.

These words brought no changes to Abbasi's face. Abbasi looked at Rauf in a like manner of intelligent adults patiently listening to a kid's dreams and idealistic talks. He released a deriding sound through his lips and said with a smile,

—OK, if we have done some wrongs or have faults, you may complain to the defense secretary. If necessary even to the President. Besides we know that your elder brother is a senior leader of the pro-government Muslim League.

Now Rauf rose to his feet and told in a decisive tone, 'We have had enough. May I ask you to relieve me for today?'

By this time maid Gulenoor had silently stood behind Mrs. Rauf in the dark passage and was watching the proceedings of the drawing room. She was a very brave young girl and the daughter of a constable in the East Pakistan police force. She had been an employee in this house for the last sixteen years and seen her employer's only daughter growing up.

Major Umar Raja opened his mouth and with a deep humility in his tone said, 'Mr. Rauf we will be deeply hurt if you do not allow Jerin to accompany us.'

Then he turned to the young girl and told, baby, let us move out of here. Ask your dad to stay nice and calm and make no drama.Actually I detest any kind of trouble'

Raja was now clasping Jerin by her waist. The grip of Raja's left hand pressed so hard that Jerin felt her bones were going to crush soon. Golenoor stepped back to the kitchen. Raja brought out the small machine pistol out of the cover from his waistband and smilingly said, 'I promise you will not have the least harm from our hands. To be frank I am actually a music-crazy man. Baby, please, hurry up.'

Jerin had always been a meritorious student and keen observer of life. At this moment, all memories of her life started rolling like a celluloid before her eyes. Even at this very critical moment her mind asked her, 'How was I raised in this society? How have I grown up? What ideologies have I seen since I was a kid? What have I learnt about my own country, ideology, men and civilization and what am I watching now? Are all my beliefs and dreams then, myth? Is this my country?'

Jerin attempted easing the grip around her waist but could not do anything. She felt as if a pair of big pliers was clutching her tightly. Lt. Col. Abbasi stood up from the sofa. Rauf watched her daughter's predicament and thought what to do. Never in his life had he ever shown any sign of helplessness. He never thought today that the situation would turn to this. This was the first moment after five months of the crackdown that

Rauf started believing the authenticity of reports that many young girls were being kidnapped by soldiers. The men in the armed forces known to Rauf were all posted at West Pakistan garrisons. Suddenly the names of Captain Didar and Major Gulbahar flashed into Rauf's mind. He thought for a moment if he should refer to these. At the same time it also seemed to him that these strings were very thin, weak and loose indeed.

Mrs. Rauf came out of the passage, stepped ahead and implored Abbasi in Urdu to spare her daughter. At the same moment Gulenoor forged ahead from behind Mrs. Rauf. She was holding an iron-made sharp and long indigenous weapon in her right hand. This was heavy and was used daily in the kitchen for slicing meat and big fishes into small pieces before cooking. Before anyone understood anything she tried to hit Umar's head with the weapon.

Umar's eyes caught the shadow of something closing towards him and moved his head away instantaneously. At the war of Ran of Katch along the Indo-Pak borders in 1966, Major Umar had killed about twenty enemy soldiers. He also had so far killed civilians, here, since the crackdown whose number was known only to him. He sprang into action. With one move of his right hand he snatched the indigenous weapon from Gulenoor and hurled this down on the floor. Immediately, with a swing, Umar sprayed several bullets from his pistol at Gulenoor, Mr. Rauf and Mrs. Rauf's bodies, in very quick succession. After a painful twirling they collapsed on the floor, into smashed and gory heaps of flesh. A little later lifting unconscious Jerin by his left hand, Umar opened the door of the drawing room. Abbasi followed him and both got out of the house.

Lt. Col. Abbasi said with an appreciative smile,

—Umar, your action is always so quiet and neat. I like that.

Umar reciprocated and said with a smile,

—Sir, I never like trouble, you know. I had no intention of spending these bullets unnecessarily. What else could I do? Guys of this province are such knaves that they would never listen to any good advice. Actually I used to feel an itching in my hands since the martial law of 1969 and wished I could punish a large number of these knaves. But I am an officer. How can I take the law into my own hands? So I held my patience for a long time. Then what a good job the President did on 25th March! Now I do not have to be patient any more. And since then, Sir, you might know how many people have I disposed of.'

Abbasi asked,

—I suppose it would be around five thousand?

—Sir, a little more than that. Do you know what my opinion about these Bengalees are?

—Tell me, what it is?

—Sir, it is my firm belief that there is nothing like the Awami League or the Muslim League that they support. They are all alike. Bloody anti-Pakistanee; and so should be punished without discrimination.

Abbasi with a pat on the back of Umar said, 'You are very enthusiastic. The salvation of this country depends much on loyal and dutiful men like your good self.'

Umar said, now the system is also supporting achieving that target. What fun, that there is no judicial or legal system here which can try us. We can play around and do anything we like. I learned that our bosses are also doing the same thing, sir.'

The conversation ended as the pick-up carrying them started for the cantonment two minutes later.

It was the 11th day of the moon. The weather had been hot until this afternoon. After the evening it became temperate. A comfortable zephyr was flowing over the deserted streets and above the roof of this house. The lime washed rooftop was looking whiter with the moon light from a clear and blue sky. Today's laundry of the house was gently clipped as usual on a metal wire for drying up washed by Gulenoor this noon. They were softly dangling with the flow of the wind through them.

At a faraway place called 'Tando Mohammad Khan' in its principal mosque, the last prayers of the night had just concluded. Major Umar Raja's home was in this town. His father, the chief *mullah* of this mosque was leading two hundred God-fearing Moslems of the city in the prayer. With both hands held above the chest, he was saying 'O Allah, the all-powerful, please defend Islam, protect the Moslems. Destroy those who have staged a rebellion in the Eastern wing to dismember this country. Amen'

//

The night continued reckoning the hours and proceeded as usual.

Many years ago three people abandoned all their belongings in West Bengal of India and started for a new homeland. The dreams of these three now were lying lifeless on the floor in a pool of blood inside this modest house. Blood from their wounds had stopped oozing out half an hour ago. A little behind this floor, inside the kitchen, three aluminum utensils was holding some vegetables. These were brinjals, ladies fingers, potatoes and a *hilsha* fish knived by the maid into slices this evening for cooking the family dinner.

Alike the dead bodies inside, these inanimate objects started perishing in the moisture and the heat.

The tenant on the ground floor, Mr. Shakhawat, had watched with fear charged eyes an army pick-up halting before Rauf's house just after evening. He also saw three men climbing up the stairs to his landlord's floor. He watched for long through his window but did not see anyone coming down. He missed the noises of the gunshots because a similar cacophony was a normal thing in the city every evening.

At one point of time he saw the pick-up had disappeared. Shakhawat still waited another half an hour, watched the adjacent area very cautiously and then walked up the stairs to his landlord's floor. The doors of the drawing room were wide open. He did not require to get in, rather he could immediately see the bloody scene in front, standing on the threshold. He came down. Nobody was around or in the alley. He went up the neighbour's house and informed the Fakhris what he had just seen. The couple and son Ayub rushed to Rauf's place. Mrs. Fakhri broke into howling tears. Then she went to her house and came back with two bed-sheets and wrapped the three dead bodies with the sheets.

Shakhawat asked, 'I fail to understand where Jerin is?'

Mr. Fakhri replied, 'Mr. Shakhawat, you are a nice and simple fellow. That is why you do not know how depraved and inhumane these Punjabees are! I can imagine where Jerkin is. They surely have kidnapped the girl after killing her parents. They have been doing this at many places in East Pakistan.'

Mrs. Fakhri asked Shakhawat if the telephone number of Rauf's sister-in-law was known to him. Rauf's sister in law lived at a place called Jigatola with her family. It was about four miles from this area of the town. Shakhawat replied in the negative. Ayub proposed to his parents that they should search through the family telephone directory. Fakhri said, 'yes, though it is immoral to dig into the private information of people, we have no alternative. Ayub, you look for the address and

telephone numbers. I remember Rauf's brother in law's name is Abul Hossain.'

Shakhawat said, 'it is already summer and the heat is on the rise. These dead bodies have started decomposing and the process of rigor mortis might have set in. The burial has to be carried out as soon as possible.'

After some searching under the telephone set Ayub found a hand written note-book containing telephone numbers. There was only one Abul Hossain and it did not take long to find it. Curfew now a days started from 7 o'clock after sun-set. It was nine o'clock when Abbasid's team left. Now it was ten o'clock before Abul Hossain could be contacted over the telephone. Shakhawat introduced himself and told Abul in a guarded language what happened to his brother-in-law's family. Abul was afraid with the thought that his wife was going to know this soon though she was not around at the moment. He spoke briefly and said he would be at his brother-in law's house by 7 'o clock next morning when the curfew would be lifted.

Mrs. Mahmudee went to the washroom, performed an ablution and then sat beside Mrs. Rauf's dead body. She started the recitation from the holy Quran. With tears in her eyes she in her mother tongue Pushtu made a prayer to God saying 'O Allah the best of the judges, you can never pardon those who could kill such good fellows. I fervently wish to see those murderers punished on this earth and here in this life.'

Fakhri made a phone call to her daughter saying her they would stay here for the night. Ayub went back to stay with his sister. Shakhawat and Fakhri also joined the recitation from the holy Quran sitting near Rauf's dead body.

Suddenly Fakhri noticed that the faces of the dead bodies were positioned skyward. Islamic ritual demands this to be westward i.e. towards the holy Kaaba. Fakhris changed the direction towards the west with some difficulty as the bodies had started stiffening. Good luck that rigor mortis of the corpses had not fully set in. Then it would not be possible at all.

The soothing sound of the recitation from the holy book continued inside. Outside, moving military vehicles and barking dogs continued to break the tranquility of the night.

At the other end of the city Rauf's sister-in-law Marufa Begum was in the washroom when the phone call from Shakhawat came in. She heard the bell ringing but not the first part of what her husband spoke on. While coming out of the washroom she caught up with the last part. She asked him, 'Who called at this late hour of the night? Where did you say you would be going to in the morning?'

//

Asad's afternoon class on Mondays started at 12:30. Yesterday Asad tried twice to talk to his parents and sister in Dhaka. After booking for a call from the G.P.O. and waiting for an hour, the operator again said, the line was not available. Feeling disappointed Asad returned to his dormitory. He was thinking about the role of student union leaders in matters related to students' interest and welfare. They were in politics but did not so far plan to have a telephone connection installed somewhere at the dormitory or at the registrar's office.

Students could then easily make phone calls in an emergency and be spared from the trouble of going to the G.P.O. A few Provosts or House Tutors of the dormitory occasionally allow a few students of their liking to make a call from the phone set available in their offices. That was exceptional only and Asad did not like that much. After yesterday's failure, Asad decided he would make the attempt today after breakfast and before the classes. If his home could not be connected he would try to talk to Rauf on his office number. At 9 o'clock Asad entered the G.P.O. He was as courageous as Rauf. Still his initial instinct as he stepped inside the post office was to step back immediately. It was too early in the morning for clients. Only one of the counters was open for service. Two men were standing before that counter. Both were of large and tall physiques. With their 'Khakis' and Chinese rifles strung along their broad shoulders, two fair complexioned and very handsome soldiers looked like photographs of royal gentries usually seen hanging on the wall of a museum. Asad calculated and took a decision—it would not be safe to come out now. He managed a normal look on his face and stared at the counter as a customer.

The attending clerk from inside the counter threw a glance at Asad. The men in uniform also moved their heads towards this last customer. Their looks reflected no special attention but casualness. The clerk while working on some papers on his desk, said, 'Let me complete this first, please wait, I will then attend you.'

He was scrutinizing a form or paper with a pen in his hand. With furrowed brows the man then said in Urdu to the two, 'The form has not been filled in properly.'

One of them replied, 'This fault is not exactly mine. This is my boss's job.'

The clerk said in a reassuring tone, 'Well, there is not much problem here. I will correct the information. Tell me the correct name of your boss. It has to be written properly. Why is here so much scribbling? The recipient of this money order must know the name of the person sending the money. Right?'

'Ok. No matter. My boss's name is Major Iqbal Ghori. Do you require anything else?'

'No, nothing more. Please put a signature here'

The clerk spread a money order form through the slit of the iron grill of the counter. One of the soldiers put his signature at the bottom and returned it to the clerk.

Asad heard the name perfectly clearly. As it entered his ears he felt as if he was going to be electrocuted. A sudden emotion and an unexpected excitement brought in additional blood flows into his fair complexioned face. He cautiously controlled himself and now carefully looked at the shoulder badges of the two soldiers. The inscription '48 Punjab' on the glittering brass plates caught Asad unmistakably. Now after putting some seals and signature the clerk returned a part of the money order coupon to the soldier and turned to Asad.

'Yes, what can I do for you?'

'Please put me a trunk call through to this telephone number at Dhaka. Here are the numbers. Try either of these. I tried this yesterday also but was not successful.'

'Oh yes, I remember having seen you yesterday. Are you not Mr. Asad? Please take a seat and wait.

The two soldiers had left the room. The number of clients was increasing with each tick of the clock. The cacophony of men buying postal stamps, envelopes, money orders, reply coupons and registration was gradually increasing. Sitting on the bench Asad remained deaf to all these. Only one name he heard five minutes ago continued to ring in his ears. Twenty five minutes passed by when the clerk drew the attention of Asad by a knock of his fingers on the wooden counter. 'Hello, you have got the line, please talk to Dhaka'.

Asad rushed to the counter and held the heavy and black telephone receiver. Before he could say 'hello', a male voice which Asad couldn't recognize immediately said 'Asad, this is your uncle Abul Hossain'.

'Good morning uncle but how could the line go to your place? I asked for a connection to mom or dad in his office!'

'You are correct. The line has not gone to me. Actually I am speaking from your residence, I mean from Mohakhali. The call came in while I was here.'

'What is the matter uncle? This is the business hour at your office.'

'You are right Asad.'

'Uncle, would you please give the line to mom or Jerin.'

'My child, first listen to me.'

Abul Hossain spoke and Asad listened. However Abul remained mum about Jerin.

In many backward societies of the globe the same had happened. Pakistan, the holy land of the Moslems only, was also under the same jet black cloud now. During such dark times, hooligans of the state establish such a reign of terror that its normal citizens are scared even of mourning for their near and dear ones' death as that might bring for further terror. Asad wept silently and, then, without much consideration said,

'Uncle, I am starting for Dhaka.'

'What the hell are you talking about? Asad, listen, you are quite intelligent. Don't rush. You are already in luck that you could reach the campus safely. Now a young man like you will have to pass scrutiny through 24 security check posts before entering Dhaka city. I should not elaborate anymore on the telephone. I believe you understand what I mean. Besides, curfew will be on from 7 p.m. You will still not arrive. We cannot wait for the burial that long. The dead bodies have already started decomposing. So just be patient and pray to God. Now, your aunty is waiting. Please talk to her.'

'Yes, aunty, I heard everything but where is Jerin?'

'Oh! We have put her to sleep by some medication. She is yet to absorb the shock. She will talk later on.

Something flashed in Asad's mind. He took a crucial decision. He thought for a moment and then told,

'Aunty, would you please give the line once again to my uncle?'

Abul Hossain came on line.

'Uncle, who did this?'

'Didn't you understand who did this? Should I put our life at risk by uttering it?'

'No Uncle, I did not mean that. I mean any names?'

'Are you crazy? What shall you do with that?'

'You never can tell. I can't tell you what I came across this morning here. So of course, if you tell me it might be possible to put those to very important use. Please uncle, just the names.'

To prevent the conversation from being lengthier Abul Hossain gave the names he heard from Yasin Fakhri. Asad with no more words disconnected the line. He was still sobbing. Some aged customers watched it. It is a familiar scene in such a society. They thought may be the poor boy's old parents have passed away in their village home-The postal clerk also listened to Asad's sobbing and decided the same. Asad paid the phone bill and got back to campus. He did not attend the class. Putting his face down on the mattress Asad wept loudly now. Even the lunch hours at the cafeteria passed. All memories of his parents, since he was a kid now started rushing towards Asad with an invincible force. Asad's mind whispered,

—Dad, I started getting worried about you since 1st March. When I came to learn that the freedom fighters were organizing themselves I took it that they would be looking for you and surely take your life. That you were still a staunch supporter of united Pakistan and the government Party Muslim League would not remain a secret to anybody though you have been a very cautious man. On the other hand if the army had the slightest knowledge of what I have always believed I would surely have been killed by them long ago. What a strange reality! I am alive. Whereas the very people for whom you always extended full support, murdered you in this way? People who are originally from this part of Bengal never believe us as supporters of this freedom struggle. They feel that, as we have once come from a different land to a new country, we can never go against it. We can think nothing beyond Rawalpindi or Islamabad. And you really were one of those. Still what happened? Now where shall we go to seek justice? The state ensures trial of murders and inequities but now she herself has turned into an assassin, killing its own citizens! Only for honouring your wishes did I agree to come to the campus. I had something very different embedded in my mind which did not materialize. Thousands of boys of my age are joining the struggle every day. Whereas I have not still forgotten the memory of a teacher of this university getting killed two and a half years ago, how can I forget yours and mom's?

With these thoughts Asad got up. He shook away all indecisions with a determination in his mind.

'No, no more looking back. This crude and insensible beast of a state must be destroyed. I must participate in this struggle along with millions of freedom fighters to do that. I am ready to die for that.'

The first Nobel laureate in Bangla literature, poet Rabindranath Tagore wrote in a prose that, 'one can not lament for the dead for long. After burial one has to go round for procuring provisions like fuel for the oven and strap for shoes.' The ache in his stomach and the thirst reminded Asad of this wise saying. He remembered he had not eaten or drank anything since breakfast at the cafeteria in the early morning.

Asad quickly washed his face and mouth, took some bread and banana from his shelf. Before he started eating someone knocked at the door. He opened the door and found Salek standing outside. Salek was his classmate for the last four years from his college days and was a resident of the dorm on the third floor. Asad asked him to come in. Salek watched his classmate with a curiosity and asked,

—Hi, friend you did not attend classes today, and now eating these things. What is the matter? Are you not feeling well?

Salek was someone who could be trusted. He was an office bearer in the student's league town committee during the anti-government movement of 1969. Later on, a severe *Kalaazar* attack partially crippled him. Since then he walked with a slight stoop on his right leg. He had dropped out of the committee. Though new students were not aware of his role during the Anti-Ayub movement, Asad did not forget that. Asad replied,

—No, my health is not bad. Actually my parents died recently so I am sometimes forgetful.

Asad did not tell the reasons of his parents' death.

After the crackdown, Salek absconded to his village home for two months and then came back to campus. Giving solace to his friend. Salek said, still you are better off because your parents died recently. Remember I grew as an orphan since childhood at my maternal uncles' home'.

Salek threw brickballs at EPR (EAST PAKISTAN RIFLES) troops after Prof. Shamsuzzoha was shot dead by them. Asad suddenly remembered this role of Salek after so many days at this moment.

Asad was thinking even before Salek came in how to make a way for joining the freedom fighters group. After some more talks Asad took the initiative by asking, 'Salek, actually I remember your spirit in spite of your leg. So when I did not find you in the campus when I came here from Dhaka I thought you surely had crossed the border.'

He thought, what luck, this man right at this moment is at my doorstep!

Salek said, 'I did not . . . 'Then without finishing went out of the room, carefully looked around to see if there was anybody listening out. He came back and started.

—Even from my village hideout I used to keep track. Many of our class friends, juniors and seniors from the campus have joined the struggle. Our teacher, lecturer Mumtaz also crossed the borders. When I heard that there was no trace of you in the campus after April and even May I concluded you surely had somehow joined the war right from Dhaka.

-Why did you think I would do this?

-You see birds of the same feather flock together. Many may not know but I did not forget that from behind you used to be the think tank of the central students union of our University. So you must support our present struggle.

—Then I find there is a problem in it. It means that my position is possibly known to many others as like to you. It is risky, even dangerous to be in such a position. Suppose some pro-government elements or the collaborators like Rajakar or Al-Shams tip-off the military about us?

-Just do not give a damn to those flies and mosquitoes. I do not count them even with my short leg and you are a dare devil. Let death come whenever it wishes to. Now tell me what your plans are?

Several faces both dead and alive at this moment flocked into Asad's mind.Those were his parents, Faruk,Prof.Zoha,Iqbal Ghori and Minoo's. He thought for a while and then with finality he said,

-Friend, I know you can help me in this

-Let me know how?

-Well, I want to cross the border and join a freedom fighters' training camp

-Ok. Let me see what I can do for you. I will let you know.

Three nights later it was raining. Salek told that this job was better if done during such weather. The troops from West Pakistan were unfamiliar with this. They preferred to stay within their camps and barracks during such time. Their homes were usually in an arid and dry land. Mud, moisture and rainfall were not to their liking.

Asad and the guide provided by Salek came out of the dorm at half-past seven in the evening. The Sonamosjid border out post was just half a mile west of the outer campus. Salek's guide showed Asad the way across. Asad took out a fifty rupee note from his secret pocket. The image of the father of the nation was authentically printed on this pink parchment. He extended the note to the guide but the latter politely declined.

Slightly confused, Asad said, 'Is it an under payment?'

—No. Not at all. I do not do this for money. Do you think this is a time for making profits? Nothing is required. Please don't waste your time. Quickly get in. A searchlight of the army is not usual at this hour, still why should we take risks? Who can tell?

Amazed, Asad said, 'Really this is called patriotism and self-sacrifice. Pray so that I may take the training, stay alive and kill at least a few occupation soldiers and then die.'

—Don't worry; I have been sending people for the last three months. I recognize people by looking at faces. You look brave and intelligent. I am sure you are going to make it.

—Well, thanks. Good bye.

The two departed from one another. Forty minutes later and after a thirty minutes' walk under a drizzle, Asad reached Kazipara training camp.

//

General Tarik was sitting on his desk. He was counting the pages of the red colour government calendar. He sighed and said, 'Oh exactly five months since I took charge.'

Earlier in his career or personal life he never used to write a diary. At this time, since last May, he had started doing this. He noted the 5th month in his diary.

The intercom rang. It was Brigadier Pasha, his Principal staff officer. Tarik said,

-What is it, Pasha?

-Sir, you have an appointment at 10'0 clock.

-I can't remember it. Tell me what it is?

-Sir you wanted to see some replacement troops and officers who recently came from the western cantonments.

-Oh, yes. Every zone is clamouring for troops. Are they ready?

-They are ready.

-Have you talked to them?

-With every one Sir.

-Ok, you first come in to my room. Then ask colonel Roper Vatti to send them one by one to me? What is their number?

-Sir they are seventeen at the command level?

-Ok. Let us start the business, Pasha.

No sooner had the first man entered and saluted, Tarik looked at the red beret and green flocks on the man's head. He was surprised and asked, what is your Name?

-Faiaz Gool, Sir.

-Why is your cap and uniform like these and which Punjab battalion do you belong to?

-Sir, this is not a Punjab battalion. We are the Gilgit Scout battalion. That is the reason of our dress, Sir.

-Ok. Where do you hail from?

-Sir, Khyber.

Khyber is a district in the North-West Frontier Province.

-I also find it difficult to read your rank, man?

With the interrogation the twenty three year old Pathan was already losing his guts. Nervously he replied,

-Sir, I am a group commander, equivalent to that of a second lieutenant in the military.

-O.K. Faiaz you may leave now.

The next man with an unfamiliar uniform was Faek Ali. He answered to Tarik's queries that he belonged to the Lahore Rangers and was a captain. The other commanders he saw one by one were an Assistant Superintendent of the Punjab Police, an honourary captain, a Dy. Director of civil defense and fire brigade.

Annoyed and angry Tarik pounded his mighty fist on his desk and shouted to Brigadier Pasha, what Joke is this? Ask them to stop this nonsense. Are these called replacements?

Are these people soldiers? Now what is left? Deaf, dumb, beggars, coachmen, pimps and band pipers will be the next to be sent by them here for fighting this war? These Bengalee freedom fighters are killing my soldiers every day while the big bosses are sending in these duffers? Pasha, what do you think?

-Sir, actually the condition here is the same as in other cantonments also. My coursemate Rawal Khan is in charge of receiving new soldiers from ships at Chittagong port. He was telling me that many of those who are disembarking do not have any semblance of a soldier. The uniforms are queer. Someone was wearing a torn cap, some other a worn boot or even personal shoes, while another one was wearing a belt which was not a service one. What duty shall they perform?

-You are correct. The few I saw today seem to be worse than the East Pakistan civil armed forces.

Before they could talk further the daily news papers from West Pakistan were placed on a tray before Tarik by an orderly. Tarik took the 'Dawn' published from Lahore. Earlier this morning his public relations officer showed him news clipping from the same daily. Tarik now started studying it in more detail. The report was saying that about four hundred women clad with *hijabs* had simultaneously staged demonstration with processions yesterday. Those were organized in the cities of Lahore, Shahiwal, Montgomery, Multan, Shialkot and Islamabad. They were chanting slogans to know about the whereabouts of their husbands. These men were all in the service of the armed forces and now posted in East Pakistan. For the last two months their whereabouts had been simply unavailable. Personal letters written to them by those wives and other relatives did not so far have any replies. Separate applications much on the same issue to the commanders in the unit addresses also remained unattended. Meanwhile these women had seen the arrival of a

185

coffin or two daily from the same province in their neighbouring villages. On enquiring they learnt that the coffins carried corpses of officers only.

Tarik pushed the page away. He was already perturbed. He thought, how could this news and photographs get printed in spite of heavy press censorship? Tarik felt, whoever did it was not a proper job. It was only yesterday that Tarik took part in the burial services of colonel Nawajish Lodi posted at Chandpur, a river port city, who got killed by anti-state miscreants. His coffin had been sent to Lahore yesterday by a cargo flight. But soldiers were getting killed five times as much as officers. How could they be sent home? Tarik, a few months ago, made phone calls to an official in the army welfare directorate to know where this expenditure would be made from. The official could not answer his query. He then looked for the head of that office to learn better but that Major General was not available. He was on a tour. Tarik thought, the war is going on in my province but why is the man touring in the west. Tarik had some funds under this head of expenditure. All of that was exhausted by April. Tarik then consulted the military accounts office to know if there was any other source. They told him that there was none until the next budget as reappropriation for the present fiscal year had also been spent fully. Exasperated, Tarik then went through his military manual's chapters on defense burial and post burial services. Yet he could find nothing.

He thought of the defense secretary. This duffer could say nothing except that, under a martial law regime his office had hardly any power on issues like this. Tarik then decided to inter dead soldiers' bodies in military graveyards. Thence Tarik started thinking that the issue was thus resolved for good.

Today's news brought that back to life. He now asked his personal assistant to connect him with Brigadier Arham Suleri. Suleri was the head of ISPR at Dhaka. Tarik asked him, have you seen the news of 'Dawn'? I wonder how this news got to the press. Do they think over there that we are passing our time here in frolicking? Who gave these women permission to organize processions? Have you thought of the problem, these pictures and news are going to create for us?

-Sir, I realize that but I am not responsible for that as I am the head here while Brigadier Khaldun is the head there.

-But tell me, is the war going on here or there? Incidents are of this place while the news will be printed there and we will be in trouble for that. Is it not your responsibility to co-ordinate when something about our activities here is going to be printed or released? You people are behaving even worse than the civilian bureaucrats whose right hand does not know what the left is doing!

Suleri did not like this thrashing but he still managed to say that he would talk to Khaldun about this. The line was disconnected by Tarik. Suleri in a soliloquy said, Tarik, you cannot talk like that to me. Legally I am not under your command.

Brig. Suleri was a member of the army education corps and had a master's degree in journalism from a reputed University. His origins were also lofty. With this superiority complex he used to look down upon almost all officers of the armed services as none of their education was beyond the Intermediate College level.

Suleri took the phone and talked to Khaldun at Rawalpindi. Last night Khaldun was at a night club and came back home at 4 o'clock in the morning. His hangover of drinking and accessories was still there in his tone as he asked Suleri,

-Why is Tarik so unhappy about this picture and news?

-There is censorship and still how could this go to the press?

-What headache or problem does Tarik have due to this? We have not flashed anything about his area. So how does it affect him or you?

This man's stupidity did not allow him to understand the problem. Suleri then said'

-We, here, are denying that there is any war, no casualties of our soldiers. The news like yesterday is telling a different story. That is the problem.

-Well I will talk to my boss and see what we can do about it.

With no more words Khaldun hung up.

//

In a thick forest of the Sundarbans two young men were talking. It was a hideout. Before March this year, they used to change this frequently but since then they had not. One of the two was the boss. He said, perhaps now we are in a very secure condition. Do you have any idea about the reason?

Selim, who had the highest scores both in his school and college final exams replied

-I have a clear idea about the reason.

-Tell me what you think

—I do not think the police have ever been so comfortable in their job in the last fifteen years' time. They are now totally free from the worries of chasing fugitives, thieves, muggers and even dissident politicians. That is why we, after so many days, have been able to meet in such an open place.

-You are indeed brilliant, Selim. Now tell me another thing. Do you have any faith in the present liberation struggle?

-What are you asking leader? We are communists, while the war is going on between the petty bourgeois on the one side and boot-lickers of America on the other.

Is there any room here for the labour, peasants or the proletariat? No. So how can I have faith in it?

-Well. Do you have a thought about our role in this war?

-Our role is very clear. The masses have no linkage with this struggle. This has been waged by the socialist-imperialists also. People emancipation will not come out of it. That is why we did not participate in the 1970 elections.

—You are correct.

-But while we are opposing the petite-bourgeois in the war what shall be our role about the Pakistanee troops?

-That is a good question. We must kill them wherever we come across them.

These two were members of an underground political party. Extremism was their manifesto. The party's membership during the last 23 years could not extend beyond fifty. Police and the white clothes men of the government had always ensured that such parties cannot meet anywhere or organize a meeting or procession. Since March the circumstances changed. After observing the situation up to the crackdown, they gave a name to the crisis. It was the fighting of two dogs.

This meeting as usual took a decision. The struggle for establishing proletarianism against capitalism shall continue.

The leader now looked at the other members seated on the floor in front of him, and asked,

-Does anyone of you have a different opinion on this decision?

There is no room for difference of opinion in the struggle for communism. Accordingly nobody said anything though the doubts about the possibility of establishing the 'ism' by the barrel of the gun raised doubts in a few minds present here.

An activist from Khulna, asked,

-Brother Selim, may I ask a question?

-Go ahead.

-Should I give a thorough thrashing to Sub-Inspector Jotin of the special branch? This is only due to this policeman that I could not meet my mother for months. Do you remember how he tortured our co-activist Joinal taking him to the police station.

-I also have the same feeling but where shall you find Jotin? He must keep away now a days from the army only because of his name. The army will not spare a Hindu, anyway.

-Brother Selim there is an interesting game now. Jotin has a lot of information with him about anti state elements. That is why the army is keeping him alive. This morning I saw him talking to an army officer at a bazaar near Churipara. He had a smiling face.

-I see your point now. Even then Jotin is not a big fry for the army. Neither is he a capitalist for us. So you will see that when this interest is fully served the Punjabees will finish him off.

The mind-set of these underground activists was determined by reading the books of comrade Lenin and Mao-Tse-Tung. Besides they always lived in hideouts. The result was a stereo typed and insecure mind. During election campaign through 1970, Mujib's manifesto of socialism did not miss their ears and eyes though they were doubtful about its sincerity. The man suddenly asked.

-Leader, suppose this province really emerges as an independent country and socialism is established then what happens to our party?

The leader answered, this party can never be a believer in socialism. Hence that is not going to be implemented by them. So we will continue to annihilate peoples' enemies. Our role will not change.

A silent activist named Boltu was listening to the conversation. Before the elections he was confident about the rightness of the party's path. After the results of the elections Boltu could not remain unmoved. So at this moment he was thinking how reasonable was it to consider a party as people's enemy which had had a landslide victory in the elections. Boltu also remembered that this same leader now standing before him had told, voters would boycott the elections, because they would prefer to have the right of bread before the right of ballot. Actually things turned out differently. After the results the leader still maintained that the results would not be able to emancipate the masses. Boltu felt he could ask this questions but he resisted himself. The result of making such questions was always only one. The questioner's mutilated and dead body would be lying on a public road or field. For the same reason Boltu despite having thought repeatedly about deserting did not desert the party.

///

Marriage Registrar Haji Abdul Quader was absconding from his office and residence for a few weeks after the army crackdown.Then, after collecting information, he felt somewhat safe and came back to his office. He left his family in his village home. He was sitting in his office with little work. Marriage registration, conflict resolution and adjudication of dowry were his main responsibilities. It was 10 o'clock in the morning on a wet day. A gentleman in white pyjama and full-sleeve Hawaii shirt in his late fifties' appeared before him. He introduced himself. Quader felt happy thinking the day was auguring well. He greeted him.

-Yes, what can I do for you?

-You have to go to my residence Mr. Quader, this noon.

-Why do you say 'have to? And why do you look so nervous?

-Because it is an army matter. They have sent me to fetch you.

-My God! Tell me what it is. Is it something to do with my office? And how are you involved? I am really confused.

-Well let me cut the bull-shit. The matter is like this. I fathered my only daughter 18 years ago. Now an army personnel claims he has fallen in love with her and wants to marry her. And the boy appears to be good.

-It is indeed dramatic. Do you mind telling how all it happened. This is an exceptional marriage proposal.

-Well. After 25th March many of our neighbours went away to their village home but we do not have any village home. Where could we go?

-Why, where do you hail from?

-My paternal grandfather came from Ara district in Bihar. In 1947 he came to Dhaka and built this house at Nakhalpara near Tejgaon airport. We have been here since then.

-Then?

-My grandfather and father have been dead long since. I stayed back along with my wife and daughter and thought we would make a survival

DUSK, DAWN AND LIBERATION

by giving our origins as Biharees to the army. None of our neighbours ever misbehaved with us. The local ward commissioner also told us that we could survive together along with them. Days were going not so badly. My daughter Samia was attending her college at Tejgaon by ricksahw.

I don't know where this army man spotted her. One day, with full uniform he came to my residence and said he would like to marry Samia.

-And you agreed?

-What else could I do? He could have forcibly taken her away. He rather preferred to put the proposal gently. One of his paternal uncles was with him while making the proposal. He is a major in the legal corps and posted at the Summary military court at Allen bury.

-It sounds indeed like a fiction. Then what happened?

-The boy visited us off and on with five to six soldiers. They stay outside and the boy pays my wife and me respect, talks for some time and then goes away. Since his first visit other army units stopped coming to our neighbourhood and people were happy and feeling safe.

-What is the rank of the boy?

-Lance Corporal.

-You said they sent for me?

-Yes I mean they said it is the bride's father's responsibility to arrange for the registration.

-Well gentleman, I must say that since 1st March I have not had a single marriage registration in my office. Some parties, made appointments but then none turned up to take me. But this is something exciting.

-Are you scared?

-I will not say that. Even then what is the point of being scared? They can easily take me by force. So I will be there.

The following Friday. Monowar Ali's daughter Samia was wedded to Abdur Rahim's son Abdur Raual Chowdhury of Jhelam. This was the first marriage of this area during the last seven months.

Under a serene noon and in an almost deserted neighbourhood only twenty people including the marriage registrar witnessed the ceremony.

///

The President had not had any conferences for many months since March. General Piru never advised for it. Others dared not. Considering the reports of his commander Tarik from Dhaka and international sources, the President realized, discussions were necessary. Instead of having a quick solution to the Bengal crisis it was getting worse day by day. It was October 12th, 10 o'clock in the morning. He was conferring with his governors in his office. The meeting started without any welcome or formalities. The President was addressing the gathering.

-Gentlemen, I invite your suggestions on the East Pakistan crisis. So far my Eastern command and I have conducted the business there but we need your support.

Lt. General Atiqur Rahman, governor of the Punjab took permission and said,

-Sir, I think you need to go to Dhaka.

The President, after this proposal, looked at the governors of Sindh, Baluchistan, NWFP and East Pakistan one by one and asked,

-What is your opinion on this proposal?

-We think the following steps should be taken after consulting with the governor of that province. They gave a list of doables in a somber tone but with a tongue in the cheek-manner.

-That sounds reasonable but I doubt if that dude is giving me the real picture over there. With the flurry of complaints of committing excesses against the Bengalees there I changed Tikka and posted Tarik there to get better results. I find he has produced nothing of the kind so far. He is making almost a weekly demand for fresh troops. Do you have any suggestion on this? Under the present circumstances what can I do? I formed this civilian cabinet so that you could advise me.

The Prime Minister Mr. Nurul Ameen was from East Pakistan.

He said,

-Sir, consider if you could visit the province, meet people and talk to them and tell them that power would be transferred to people's representatives at an appropriate time.

You may also tell them that with that end in view the present civilian cabinet has been constituted.

The preimier was one of those very few MPs not belonging to Mujib's party. Out of 170 positions for the province all 167 were elected from Mujib's party.

He thought about the PM's lonely standing in the province and said in his mind' how many men do you have in your party and how many of them will you be able to gather in a meeting?

Externally he said, every day my troops are getting killed there. Under that situation what can I do by going there? I have never addressed a public meeting in my life. The Muslim League has not a single MP from that province.

Even if they support me how can I suddenly address a public gathering? Besides, I cannot speak their language.

Hamid, Piru and the other Generals said nothing on this comment. The *Nabab* was now holding the foreign minister's portfolio. He said,

-We have been able to let the world believe that we are a victim of a grave conspiracy of our big neighbour from two sides of our borders. We did not do any wrong with them. Rather they have wronged us. Mr. President, you remain firm. Victory will surely be ours.

The President had his last glass of champagne last night. So his head was clear now. He watched the Generals 'support to what his foreign minister said and also noted that they kept mum when he said something. Nonetheless the President asked the *Nabab*,

—On top of everything the diaspora is a problem. I have been reported by the UN High Commission for refugees that in the repatriation camps set up for receiving returning refugees, none has reported and only some stray dogs are sleeping there.

What is the reason?

-Mr. President that is also a plot to discredit our country and government. The same enemy of us is impeding return of willing refugees.

—But the UN Official is telling me Tarik's troops are torturing the intending returnees and Tarik is spending his time in nightclubs and merry making. Plus the harrowing experiences of refugees are being believed by the foreigners while the droning of our official radio about appeasing religious minorities is falling on their deaf ears.

The President once again read disapproval in the Generals' eyes. The foreign minister said, yes what you are saying is not totally base-less. Troops can be better controlled by a civilian authority. That is what democracy is for and that is why you held the elections. For this same reason I have been constantly advocating for a transfer of power to a civilian government. They will be able to handle the refugee issue also. In 1947 they managed the mass exodus of refugees from the Punjab better.

The President once again felt the sting of remorse. He felt he was dealing with a very sly fellow and that he was helpless before this person.

He emotionally said' I can't pay my soldiers now. The military accountant—general has sent a note to me telling me that situation. He said that his budget was finished.

The *Nabab* suggested, you could consider issuing debentures for addressing this. Even Britain did this during the last war.

-Do you think financial matters are so easy? M.M. Ahmad has told me people have no faith in those instruments. They think those are not worth the papers they are printed on. This war has dragged me to such lows.

—The military action was the considered option of the government, was it not Mr. President?

-Yes but nobody advised me about the practicalities. For example, how to fetch soldiers from a 2300 miles roundabout? Besides, nobody told me how to deal with Mujib. I had a deal with him much earlier but he started showing cold shoulders to me. I did him a great honour by beleiving in him. Mr. Ameen told, 'there are many things in life which cannot be proved. You have to take those on faith.' The President said, somebody like you could tell me that I should have addressed public meetings telling them how much money I put in in East Pakistan. And in doing that what problems did I have from the policy formulation milieu from the west wing people. I really could not figure out that there would be this backlash following the army action in March. Had I been advised properly I would have looked for other options. In every country the PM or the President has the prerogative of consulting the civil services. But here they have taken a stand-off position. How strange?

The PM understood that this President had no basic understanding of these difficult issues. He also did not believe in the foreign minister's words but knew he was also looking for a share in the booty as an elected MP. So he said, 'Mr. President, let us be optimistic. I believe the clouds will dispel in due course.

The President concluded by saying, 'Well gentlemen, I urge upon each of you to discharge your respective responsibility. I am going to talk to the President at the white house. I bank on your support.'

Everyone present understood that the meeting was over. None of the civilian secretaries or military Generals reminded the President that many items of the agenda were still unfinished. One of the items was to have a negotiation with the government now housing the refugees. The President wished he could personally talk to that country. During the last two and a half-years many such meetings had ended in the same way. As a patriot and true to his salt, each of these VIPs should have thought that ending important meetings like these in a half-baked manner was neither wise nor responsible. Here, as before, each thought otherwise—'I am not liable for this. The responsibilities of this office are not mine, it is the President's'.

//

-Asad, you told me that you never had used even a small fire-arm in your life.

-Yes indeed.

-But your progress in this training has been commendable considering the short length of time.

-Thank you major. Now what else is yet to be finished of this course?

-Actually nothing, you have finished.

The conversation was taking place at Kalyani training camp. Major Raghupoti Kundra of 22nd jath Infantry now told Asad,

-I am really happy with you. I wonder what a brilliant officer you would make if you joined the army.

-No, I am not going to join any such thing; rather I will kill members of the occupation army as soon as I get an opportunity to. So tell me what is your plan is for men like us?

-Let me correct you, young freedom fighter. This is not our plans. This is the plan of your government. Outstanding men like you will support our regular forces from the rear or fight independently in some selected operations. Now as a routine and with that purpose an officer will brief you. He is Captain Amjad Ali Fokir of the 3rd Bengal regiment. From today he is going to be your commander.

A few minutes later captain Amjad entered the camp, shook hands with Asad, and ten others who completed this training today. Of them, four were familiar with Asad. Some were Asad's classmates in the college while the others at the University. Amjad exchanged a few words with everyone while introducing himself. Having completed the intros captain Amjad addressed the team,

-Let me tell you something about our mission. So far I have fought the enemy along with the very active support of boys like you and we came back alive. Our operation area has been Gurudashpur, Godagari,

and Akkelpur police stations. So far we have had six battles. Why am I telling these facts to you? To boost your self-confidence and mind strength. Let me cut it short young fighters. We are going to conduct our next mission tonight.

Surprised, chaps? No do not do that ever. War is such a thing that anyone's call may come any moment and so we need to be on our toes so long we are alive.

Any questions/comments?

Nobody said anything.

-Okay. This is going to be like this.

Amjad took a white chalk and started writing and drawing lines and signs on a blackboard. He used his thin stick and started explaining. Within forty minutes he was done. Every one saluted their commander and started filing out of the camp one after another except one. Asad still sat on a bench. Amjad asked, What is the matter?

-May I ask you something in private?

-Well, why not? Go ahead.

-I will be straightforward.

-You need to be because in war, time is very costly indeed.

-Ok. Do you know an officer called Major Iqbal Ghori?

-Capt. Amjad was startled hearing the name but he suppressed the reflex and said, yes, he was my instructor at Pakistan Military Academy at Kakul. Later on in 1969 he was posted to EPR wing deployed along the Rajshahi borders.

By the by how do you know such a man?

—What do you mean by 'such a man'?

—I mean he is a deadly man.

—As I told you I am a student of journalism. A fond teacher of mine used to tell us it is not only for a good reporting but also for good pictures that journalists are recognized the world over. Many of them got prizes like the Pulitzer for taking world-class pictures. From then I set a target I would also try to do something in this field. The anti-Ayub movement was then in its climax. I could have such an opportunity on a street. Exactly in that week the incident of professor Shamsuzzoha's killing took place in my campus. And as good luck would have it I was moving very near the spot carrying an expensive camera with me. Trouble was brewing up from that morning. Students were demonstrating about army excesses in Dhaka. I thought possibly I could have the opportunity of having a few snaps on the procession, brick balls throwing or on smokes when students were putting fire on flat tires or the images of the President. And suddenly I saw a uniformed man giving orders to shoot Dr. Sahmsuzzoha.

The uniformed man was much nearer to me than the professor and I took the photograph without losing a moment's time.

-It is wonderful. He was so near that you could see even his name plate?

-Not quite. Actually I enlarged the photograph later on and then the name was clear.

-It has been a remarkable deed. One thing. This job done by you was not due to a good camera only but due to your exceptional courage, young man.

-Well you could say that but I was not alone. I was in the line of journalists; the EPR people might have watched us but possibly did not single me out. Perhaps they took me to be one of the photo journalists. Do you have any idea about the present location of this Major Ghori?

-He was working around Rajshahi zone possibly with the army and no more with the EPR.

The scene and conversation of the G.P.O. vividly visited Asad's mind at this moment.

Asad felt very good at the reply of Amjad. Amjad, on the other hand, was not happy. He had long working experience in the field interrogation and intelligence unit of the Pakistan army along the Kashmir border. There he had discovered how adeptly clean shaved Shikh army men infiltrated the Pakistan army and collecting vital information about the enemy's defense secrets. So Capt. Amjad had a thought working in his mind. Is this young trainee actually a double agent of the Pakistan army? The story of journalism is a fake one?

Amjad maintained his smile and asked,

-Asad, where is your father and what does he do for a living?

At this question Asad could not hold back his tears. He was speechless. Amjad realized it was genuine. He gave the boy some minutes to calm. Asad said, 'they killed my parents even after knowing of my father's being a central government officer.

-Who killed them?

-Have you not got it? Pakistan army. Major Umar and Lt.col.Abbasi

-I am so sorry Asad. Major Raghupoti told me you have done excellent in the training course. After seeing you also I thought you would be a tough man but now I see possibly you are soft and emotional also.

-I think you are getting me wrong. Not only Umar and Abbasi, I am sure I can kill this Ghori in cool blood and with a smiling face.

-That is what is required of a soldier. Plus this is our only duty now, considering the treatment they have been giving us. But you have joined this war from a sense of personal aggrievement. Would it not be better if we can expand that target?

-I agree. A nation's aggrievement is the sum-total of innumerable individuals' anger. In any case could you recognize Abbasi or Umor?

These names are in hundreds in the Punjab army. Since you are telling they were from the F.I.U. possibly a bell rings in my mind. You have not seen them. If description about their appearance or colour was known I could be certain. Even then, suppose these are the people who killed your parents, what can you possibly do?

Asad felt he could tell that his will power was very strong so it may not be impossible to do something. On a second consideration he told,

-I don't know what I can do. Still I wish I could see them once.

-Chances are very little that you will ever come across these killers. Better, let us try how to kill not such one or two men, but thousands of them and how we can manage a survival in doing that.

//

The Aryan lady had an appointment at 10 o'clock in the morning today. The visitor was a V.V.I.P. as usual. He reported exactly on time. He was the chief of Staff of the army. By faith he was a worshipper of fire. She made this selection very discreetly. The prime consideration was this man's amoral attitude to things. Field Marshal Sam ushered in as the doors were courteously opened by a guard for him. He was accompanied by the border security force Chief General Rustomji. They saluted and greeted her and got themselves seated. She asked,

-How are your preparations?

-Madam, all our branches are fully prepared. We are capable of attacking from all sides. We are awaiting your orders only.

-And you have not been ordered.

The field marshal heard something in her voice and realized he had overstepped. He said,

—Sorry madam!

-Marshall I know that your principal adversary, though a long time ago, worked with you in the same unit.

-Yes your information is correct madam.

-How is his character? I mean what possible reaction you expect from him.

-When he was a lieutenant-colonel at Hoshiarpur Cantonment, I was his C.O. He possesses nothing called determination in his character. He wavers all the time. He is brittle.

-If that is the fact why is he not moving for the last eight months?

-He would have moved but a few Generals are not allowing that. Actually power now a days hardly rests in his hands. These Generals are now pulling the strings. So if we can create a panic at the first onslaught, they will not show any resistance.

-How do you conclude that?

-Madam, have you forgotten how they begged for peace at Tashkent during the 1965 war? Now we have an additional plus point. The common masses of that country are against them.

-Don't speak so undiplomatically.

-We are professional soldiers.

-Field Marshall, you are talking to your Prime Minister. Have you forgotten that?

-Pardon me madam.

Actually she felt happy with the frank expressions of the Marshall. She got what she was looking for. Earlier, her defense analyst also gave a similar opinion.

She realized a strong possibility of materializing the very dream that she and her followers had dreamt about this neighbour for the last 24 years was there in the near future. It was going to be easy for another reason as the majority people of that country was craving for the same thing. Accordingly if she played her cards well nobody would be able to blame her. Still showing an air of cool officialdom she concluded,

-The number of refugees spreading over four of my provinces has now exceeded 10 million. Our treasury is suffering a great deal of pressure just to house and feed them somehow. This liability can't be continued

indeterminately. My government will instruct you to do something about this at any moment. You can leave now.

-Thank you madam.

The Marshall was gone and madam started studying some maps from her desk. These were about the north and north-western areas of her country. She was exceptionally capable of understanding these issues. Besides she could see such things clearly which most of her cabinet members could not guess. She then talked to the defense secretary and listened to the possible climatic conditions in certain areas of the map in the coming November-December period. Then she in a very low voice told some invisible being,—Dude, I am going to have you really soon.

///

In spite of the daily possibilities of death, bullets and suffering, Asad never forgot a certain issue. Still he had never raised it so far because the purpose of coming here was to take training and fight the enemy. Instead how nice would it look if he wanted to satisfy something which was very personal. But by this time he had successfully participated in a few campaigns and returned to the base safely. The next two days were free for his team. Asad was sitting under a big mango tree outside the camp a little later after the day began. He liked this particular act. The scene, the air, the blue sky and the total environment took his mind to Tagore's unforgettable lyric

'O my Bengal of gold,
I love you
Forever your skies, your air
Set my heart in tune
As if it were a flute' . . . .

. . . .

. . . .

Tagore's juxtaposition of mango trees, its green leaves and aroma in this inimitable lyric stirred Asad's mind and he thought of his parents. Their memory once again aroused the interest suppressed earlier in his mind—surrounded from all sides by mango trees, that little house on a green rice field. How far was that from this place? Asad had also heard from his mother that white pigeons used to flutter through the bamboo trees in the middle of the yard of their sweet and happy home. The name of that village was also different. Asad decided he must ask somebody about this today. Major Raghupoti was also free now after finishing a training class. He lived in an adjacent camp.

Asad approached him and asked, is there anyone here who is a Bengalee or can speak Bangla?

Raghupoti became a little shaky and replied, 'why? All your comrades in arms here are Bengalees and they speak Bangla.

-No, actually what I wanted to know is slightly different. I am looking for someone local.

Raghupoti was now surprised and he did not try to suppress that expression. Putting his service cap on his head correctly he said,

-Actually we, I mean Indians have grown up as a nation. We don't count who is a Punjabee or who is a Rajput. We are taught to think ourselves as Indians. However my vehicle driver is from this province of west Bengal. May I know what you are looking for from a Bengalee?

-Well, this is personal. I am looking for a particular address which dates back to even prior to 1947. Could he tell me where the village named Dipon under Naldanga Union of Bashirhat Sub-division is ? I guess that should not be too far away from this place so far as I heard from my parents.

-No problem. I was stationed at that sub-divisional headquarter when I was a captain in the Border Security force. Still I did not get a part of the answer to my question.

-My maternal grandfather's home was in that village.

-I see! Nothing is strange in that. I hailed from Shanghor district in Pakistan and you hail from West Bengal in India. What a panoroma. I have come across so many of these people throughout my life.

The central government had enforced a standing instruction to all government agencies that all refugees and freedom fighters must be treated courteously and kindly.

Accordingly it took only a day and a half to locate the address and the route. Observing the formalities of depositing fire arms Asad started for the destination on the next morning. He boarded a bus from the local Kakonpur bus stoppage for the thirty-five mile long route.

Heard many times from mom still Asad could not match that now with what he saw of his root. Ramlochon Hazra, the Chairman of the local government body was a ward member twenty four years ago. He

immediately recognized Asad's grandfather and maternal uncles when Asad revealed his mother's name. He happily said,

-So you are his grandson. Very good, this liberation struggle of your country is bringing in many people almost every day who have some linkage to this whole province of ours. Now tell me, what or who would you like to see? So far I know none of your maternal uncles or any other close relatives is here. Some left during partition while others later on for East Pakistan.

-Actually I am not sightseeing or looking for persons. My only purpose is just to see the home where my mom was born and lived for some years.

-Young man, I understand that urge deeply. You see, two of my daughters-in-law are originally from Dhaka and Chittagong. They have a similar story to you. Ok, go ahead. My staff will help you to be there. Please do not hesitate to ask for anything you might need.

It was eleven thirty when Asad got down from a vespa scooter and saw the inscription 'Dipon'. He was disappointed. Lushes of expected greeneries were gone with the encroachment of the cobbled road and brick works all around the place. A famous poet of Bengal wrote,

'Our village is picturesque . . . .
While its bed is sprawled with jems'

Asad at this moment could not agree with the poet. There were no trees, no bamboos and not much water even during this monsoon. Township had eaten up all naturalness and the prime beauty along with it. Neither could he find the poet's description of the village as one where

'Passes the cart and passes the cow
The two sides are steep while her slope is low.'

Nope, there was no such river or even canal in the village. Tagore's forecast that

'The cow shall graze while the cowboy will play on the field' was also not visible. An engine driven tractor was tilling the field and a diesel-run deep tube well was watering it.

At Rajshahi, Asad had enjoyed picnics and excursions in the adjacent villages of the campus. The construction of those houses is such that a visitor has easy access to them. Here he found the situation different. The houses were small and the entrances were locked from the inside.

Asad came to his precise address and knocked on the door. A middle aged gentleman named Shurendronath with a loin cloth and a half-sleeve home tailored shirt opened the door. He was the present owner of this property. Asad stated his purpose. The gentleman shook Asad's hand continuously and said,

-It is only twenty four years. I can recollect everything. Your maternal grandfather and maternal uncles were very good persons. What can you or I do? This is all politics. Actually the decision to partition Bengal was a wrong thing. You were not born at that time.

Asad was happy standing on the very soil where his mother once lived. However he did not like what Shurendro told about the partition of Bengal. Still Asad was overwhelmed and said,

-Please leave that behind. I never saw those events. Possibly I could never have had an opportunity like this to see this place in my life. I have only heard about it from my mom. Now this liberation struggle has given me an opportunity to visit this place.

-I appreciate your emotion about this. My maternal grandfather's home is at Narail from Jessore district in East Pakistan. And you know how difficult it is to obtain a visa for Pakistan. Still I have so far gone there four times. This attraction for the birth cord? At least no Bengalee can forget this

-You are correct. May I have a stroll through this house?

-Of course. Why not?

The gentleman took Asad through every room and corner of the old house. He said,—look, this was your grandpa's living room, which people now-a-days call bed room. That big one was where visitors used to meet him which is now a days called a drawing-room. And this is the pond where my sons are cultivating fish.

-Don't you have mango trees here?

-Yes we do have those but to let a house out here is more profitable than having trees. That is why people now a days are felling the trees and building cottages for renting out.

The so long dreamt of hay, bamboo fencing, mud walls, tin roof, bamboo branches and fluttering pigeons had all been replaced by brick walls and signs of urbanization. Still a deep feeling touched Asad's soul. He imagined, my mom, in her teens surely frequented this courtyard and used to play rope-jumping with her school friends. This was the entrance through which she used to go to school and return home. The sound of her laughter and talks is still roaming in the ether of the air around this place and home. As if I can hear that. I can see her.'

Surendronath, though emphasized the deep soul to soul relationship among all Bengalees irrespective of religion, caste and creed did not offer Asad a lunch. Asad did not miss this point and realized the difference in culture between people of two parts of Bengal. Anywhere in East Pakistan this was still unthinkable. Even a poor peasant there would surely offer a meal to such a stranger. Surendro's wife carried a small melamine tray and put it before Asad. It contained a glass of cool water, a few pieces of guava and a homemade piece of sweetmeat. Asad ate the sweetmeat. It tasted delicious. Having finished his journey down his mother's memory lane, with a mixed feeling of pain and pleasure at 3 o'clock in the afternoon Asad started his return journey to the camp.

///

-Asad, in every war and battle there is something called a grammar.

As Capt. Amjad spoke Asad could not avoid listening to and looking at his eyes. There was something in his tone close to dissatisfaction if not anger. Asad asked,

—So, have I broken that grammar?

-To some extent, yes. I instructed you only to recce the army deployment on Arani bridge and come back. You killed three collaborators which were neither authorized nor necessary.

-How many people have they killed? How many have they kidnapped and taken to their master for torturing and killing! Have you thought of that?

-Yes I have but the job of thinking is mine, not yours. I am in command here. Your group and you have carried out many good assignments. As a senior I have appreciated those. At the same time it is also my responsibility to show your faults.

-Well, I will be more careful in the future.

-Good. Your next mission will be to blow up the Arani bridge. If you can do that the patrolling capacity of the enemy will be reduced to a large extent. They will gradually be marginalized within a smaller circle. Our plan is like this . . . .

///

On the basis of an intelligence report Asad's group had no operations for the last few days. This was an afternoon. Asad was sitting under the shade of a mango tree. A co-fighter Anwar was also sitting beside Asad. He asked,

-Anwar, does this tree ring a bell in your mind or ears?

-Not quite Asad. Tell me what you mean.

-We used to talk so frequently about the sweet *Maldoho* mangoes. Even East Pakistan has a liking for this fruit. This tree is of that particular species. I remember having eaten this so many times from the fruit market at Mohakhali, you know?

-Yes indeed. Actually when I saw you here I remembered having seen you earlier somewhere in Dhaka city. But you said you are from Rajshahi University.

-Both are correct. My parents' home is in Dhaka city. By the way, where are you from?

-My parents' home is in a neighbourhood named Chairmanbari near Mohakhali Market.

-I see. I heard in your area the army has conducted a lot of massacres

-Yes. In a big family very close to us, they killed six brothers and one of their brothers-in-law. The irony is that three of those were working with the army and one was a pilot in the Pakistan international airlines. What a tragedy. Six from a single family! I heard about that. That incident took place in April. I heard another story from a cousin of mine who lives very close to that area. He is a tenant on the ground floor. In the same house the owner was living with his family on the 1st floor. He told me he almost witnessed the killing of that house owner, his wife and the kidnapping of their only daughter by the army. Their only son was away and so escaped because he was a student at the Rajshahi University.

Asad got panicked and asked 'do you know the name of the gentleman who got killed?

-No but I remember he was a senior officer at the security printing press near Joydevpur.

-I see. What is the name of your brother-in-law?

-Mr. Shakhawat Hossain. Have you heard about him?

Asad pressed his forehead with his fingertips and suddenly became silent.

Watching, Anwar asked,

-What happend? Are you Ok?

-No I am not. I am wondering how much pain and suffering these bastards will give us before we can finish them off.

Asad wept for his only sister and told the compatriot what the matter was.

Anwar tried to give consolation and said, I heard from a teacher a quotation from the west. That is 'facts are stranger than fiction.' And today I realize how deeply true this saying is and how intelligent these western guys are. I never understood the full meaning of that before. Now I realize that. I know how deeply you are aggrieved and shocked. Still I find something to our benefit.

-What is that?

-Let us sharpen our determination further and continue to destroy these Pakistanee butchers.

Asad said, I cannot talk now though I have the same motto.

///

It was the last day of October. Monsoon winds were still in plenty in the weather. It was raining. At this hour of the night an impervious darkness had enveloped the surroundings. Major Mongolam made a report to Capt. Amjad about the movement of enemies in a certain area. Capt. Amjad accordingly postponed the Arani bridge operation for a few days. Instead, another mission was planned which would be led by Asad. The target was to blow away Nobirpara Railway Bridge. Asad also got some information from his own sources for another target. He was happy thinking of the possible additional benefit if this mission could be conducted successfully. This would give him the opportunity of killing two birds with one shot. The operation was scheduled for tonight. Asad was having rest in his bed inside the camp. Eight other freedom fighters were sprawling around him. Out of these, two were from the campus, one, an employee of the registrar's office and the rest were students from various disciplines of different colleges. Ehtesham, a 3rd year student from Chemistry department, told Asad,

-I have a question about the second part of your mission tonight.

-Go ahead.

-We are surely behind you. Still we need to be certain about one point.

That point is, what type of instrument do the army use for their regular communication with the headquarter? Is it something other than a wireless set?

-What are you going to do by knowing that?

-If we don't know that and suppose we capture our target alive, then we will be in danger.

-Could you explain it a little more?

-Yes, suppose we capture them, destroy their wireless set but still they have other instruments to contact their headquarters of which we do not know. Then what happens? Head Quarters will try to rescue them by locating us and that campaign of theirs may be highly risky for us.

Montoo, a student of physics department, said,

-Brother Asad, my maternal uncle is a Major at Sialkot signals centre in West Pakistan. Last February he came to Dhaka on vacation. I then heard from him that they use only wireless sets and field telephone for communication. So if we can destroy those two instruments then we see no problem about proceeding according to your plans.

Jamaluddin, a student of electrical engineering of the University of Engineering and Technology informed the others, in our textbook we have come across a communication equipment. That is called GPS or global positioning system. Persons, airplanes or ships fallen in danger can be rescued with the aid of this equipment. They can give exact information about their location in terms of altitude, longitude and angular positions.

Montoo said, you have raised a very good issue. My maternal uncle also mentioned this and said that this is very expensive. In Asia only Israel is in possession of this state of the art equipment.

Asad understood once again that two heads are always better than one. Now he took the floor and said, it is impossible to collect confirmed information. I have told you everything so far known to me. The decision whether or not to participate in this war is totally voluntary. Right? There is nothing like a court martial here for enforcing discipline. I have a motive in this mission while you may not have any. A freedom fighter named Khoka said, you have not so far told us the motive in this part of the mission.

Asad told the gory details of his parents' and only sister's life and death. Then he addressed them,

-We know that if even each of us can kill five of these murderers our motherland will still not be free. But still we will proceed this way. We may not be able to go near those who killed our near and dear ones but this will be a retaliation of any one killed by them who we do not know. So please be frank and tell me if you would like to join this mission or not.

Rafique, a student of Botany, surged ahead and told, I have the same opinion. A handful of us can't liberate this land but we must kill them as long as we can. We have joined the liberation war for this purpose and I am with you.

Farid, a student of Bangla language and literature became the next to give his idea and he said, I had a will to become a freedom fighter. However I never felt I had the guts to do that. I was always into poetry, drama, recitation and songs. I loved these things. Even then an incident took place and I decided to join you.

-What was that?

-It was avenging an insult. On a noon I was coming back from the campus of the Engineering College after passing some time in a friend's room there. Just before entering our campus there was a security check-post. As soon as I approached that a soldier asked me where I was going to and he asked to see my ID. I was a resident student. I showed it. Then he demanded that I must give proof that I was a Moslem. I recited all the faith incantations in good Arabic. He still insisted that many Hindus were now a days doing this to save their lives. I then asked in what further way he would be satisfied. He, holding a gun and with a grin in his face told me 'put off your trousers and show me your phallus.'

All my blood went up to my head. Still I controlled myself and did as he asked me to. Right at that moment I took an oath that I would kill at least one Pakistanee soldier before dying. And so far I have killed six of them and still surviving. So I am going to be in your mission. Asad had earlier given briefings about the mission to this group. Now once again he said 'you understand that we will ambush at Nabirpara. Are you clear about the distance between Abdulpur and Nabirpara?

Farid told, yes. My village home is only half a mile north towards Abdulpur railway station. So I know the spot as good as my palm.

Asad said, 'so the location and objective of the mission are clear to each of you?

Everyone said, crystal clear, boss.

Then Asad explained the secret part of the mission clearly. He explained the spot they would take the captive to, the people who would help them in this and the possible alternative route and method if this part somehow turned into a fiasco.

Then with a somber tone he said, boys, anyone who does not agree to this plan may step out now. There is no compulsion. Right?

Listening and awaiting under the dark shades of the camp the young people understood one thing. That is, the secret part of this mission was perhaps not approved either by captain Amjad or Major Mongolam. A strange thing! Bangla speaking people have always demonstrated failure in co-operatives or doing something together. Even the best of the Bengalees, Rabindronath Tagore, noted in his diary, 'the curse of the Gods is inevitable in any collective initiative of the Bengalees. Factions will soon show up their heads and each will try to dominate the other.'

But now at this moment it was different. None asked Asad about the mystery side of the mission they were going to embark upon within hours. Even none thought that he would divulge this secret to Amjad or Mongolam and thus gain favour while posing as a good boy. There were reasons for this positive change. It was the best of times for this yet to be born nation even in a deeper sense than that of Charles Dickens's usage in his 'A Tale of Two Cities.' And the centrefold in this exceptional unity and determination was only one person.

He was Bangobondhu Sheikh Mujibur Rahman who on the 7th of March declared the destiny and destination of the nation in his impeccable poetry. He was at that moment imprisoned at Lyallpur district jail in West Pakistan, 1100 miles away from this camp. He had then bonded almost everyone in this land on a single issue in such a way that the only a handful of men were exceptions. Human nature cannot be changed but he had then brought in a total positive transformation in the mindset and mode of conduct of millions of people. A populace known as intensely quarrelsome and fissiparous since time immemorial was then marching ahead as one forgetting all differences under the charisma of this one leader. In their mouth they had a lyric 'We do fight for letting a flower live' tuned by that leader. For the same reason enormous poor people were being fed gratis by even poorer peasants. Poverty stricken boatmen were ferrying thousands of passengers free of cost with smiling faces. Freedom fighters arrested by occupation troops were not giving in any secrets to their captors even under inhuman physical torture.

//

Asad's troupe slept for two hours. This is a standard procedure before an operation. The purpose is to give full rest to the body and mind of the fighters and prepare for a confrontation with the enemy which may be deadly. A lunar eclipse and rainfall were on outside simultaneously. At midnight Asad and his co-fighters came out from the camp avoiding Godagari B.O.P by the two mile eastern flank.

They made a border crossing and reached Tetulia at one o'clock in the morning. A team of thirty freedom fighters joined them from this hideout. The leader of this latter group was Hazrat Ali. By profession he was a Primary School Teacher. He informed Asad that the patrol train was scheduled to make its upward journey from thirty to forty five minutes past one and the downwards journey by two o'clock in the morning. Thus they would cross the Nabirpara railway bridge twice within a half hour's interval.

Asstt. Railway Station Master, Rajshahi, Helaluddin had been working as a source for Hazrat Ali's team. He confirmed today that this would be the schedule for tonight. Asad considered the report dependable. Still he asked 'but tell me if our target will be available within the patrol team?

Hazrat Ali answered, well there is ninety nine percent possibility of his being present because Punjabee army are usually straightforward in their dealing. They have a single track mind. He will be in the inspection.

-How are you so sure'

-Because their nature is tiger-like. Their minds are not wrapped in many layers. If they had a fox-like character then they would think of changing their strategies frequently. I have been observing them for the last six months at least.

-I tend to have a feeling of laughter even in this tough and dark situation where our life is at a stake every moment.

-Why brother Asad? Have I said something funny?

-Funny but realistic. I mean your comparison of the tiger and the fox and I am wondering how you keep your mind so jovial. Generally I am a dare-devil type. Even then when I hear or think something about the Punjabee military men I feel a chill passing through my spine.

-You are honest indeed. I also admit that. I get scared but I try to keep well by smiling.

After these small talks the team sat on a bench of the local primary school and divided themselves into two groups. Each took positions in the two approaches of the bridge very silently to install one anti-tank mine at each approach. There was a small watch-room at each side of the bridge. According to Railway works manual, written by the British, these watch-rooms were used by railway guards.

Now Hazrat Ali found a few collaborators in one of the rooms. On the other one the situation was the same. They were asleep. Hazrat Ali seized two of them easily while one of his aides took care of the 303 rifles of the collaborators. Gorjon Ali and Baset, two freedom fighters, also had done the same with the collaborators on the other side.

Hazrat Ali asked Asad, 'should we dispose of these bastards right here? I feel it is not cost effective to use bullets for these renegades. A knife should be enough for them.

The collaborators realized who the leader was and made a supplication to Asad,

-Sir, please do not kill us. Believe us we are here just for one hundred and fifty rupees per month.

Asad replied, knaves, we will look into your matter later on.

Angrily Hazrat Ali said, Rascals, selling your motherland for this much!

He then ordered them to be tied around a tree beneath the watch-room and put clothes inside their mouth. With a big torchlight in his hand Hazrat Ali now entered the watch-room to signal the team. After twenty minutes, the headlights of a locomotive became visible from the eastern side of the rail track. Hazrat Ali gave the predetermined signal by a few movements of his torchlight. Everyone then took a final position.

Asad put his fingers on the knob of the detonator of the bombs jettisoned earlier as the locomotive's front wheels moved on to the bridge. The bridge was about 150 yards in length. Within half a minute the whole rolling stock moved half way through the bridge. Asad now pushed the knob down with his full strength.

In a scene of the celluloid such a scene usually looks a little different from what Asad watched now. Film directors design the scene in a way so that the exploded culvert or bridge first moves up into the air, hovers there like a toy for some moments and then starts descending. Here immediately after the detonation, the age old railway bridge crumbled down into two pieces from its mid-point. The locomotive and the dummy boggy started moving down slowly along with the rail track, wooden sleepers and stones. The dummy boggy submerged fully while the nose of the locomotive stooped fully into the waters of the river below.

Helaluddin's information was that all the eight soldiers and their commander of the 48th Punjab usually stay inside the locomotive while on patrol in the area. Before detonating Asad was sure that there was no rear guard bogey after the engine. He made a calculation about the strengths of both parties. He was leading 48 people while the patrolling team should have no more than 10 including the driver. He thought it should be easy to defeat the enemy if a skirmish became inevitable.

He also instructed Hazrat Ali's team not to shoot first after the explosion unless there was any firing from the locomotive's side. As the locomotive proceeded on its descent Hazrat Ali moved along with his forces and surrounded the locomotive. It was already a dark night given by the weather. It was even darker as the head lights of the engine fully submerged. There was no sound or movement as a few seconds passed by. Hazrat Ali got slightly impatient and so pointed his torchlight at the locomotive. Immediately there was a reaction. A few soldiers clad in rain coat broke the thick glass of the engine room and attempted shooting from their sten-guns targeting the rays of the torchlight. The locomotive had not yet completed its descent on the soft mud underneath the water. Its curved position was not giving the soldiers any opportunity to shoot properly as they were unable to stand on an upright position on the edge of the engine. Corporal Walker Naoman Shah was seated immediately behind the driver's. He felt something wet getting up into his shoes. It was very quickly rising up towards his knees. Hailing from a district in the north-east Punjab Naoman had hardly seen a river in his life. It was only during his first posting here that he came to know how big and devastating a water body could be. He yelled at the patrol commander and said,

'Sir, we are getting down into water. We must get the hell out of here really quickly.'

The commander and his five exhorts were fighting tremendously against the pull of the gravitation just to make a stand on the passage along the engine-room.

Gradually they felt that this effort was futile. Meanwhile the pull already snatched firearms of some of them from their hands and flung those into the water around the nose of the engine. Initially, they did not realize the situation. From Naoman's yelling and then the inability to hold on to the fire arms due to the pull from beneath, they sensed that they would have to die either way inside or outside. So they decided it was better to get outside. The survival urge had already shattered the command structure of the unit. By the time Naoman took the decision to come out, the water level had risen enough to engulf him. By a stumble, sepoy Bahlool Lodi also followed Naoman. The remaining six, from behind disregarded the screaming of Lodi and stormed out of the open window and broken glasses of the door and jumped into the open dark. Instantly they took out the grenades from their waistband. The rain and darkness were blended outside. Only one of them could open the safety pin of his grenade. A follower from Hazrat Ali's group had meanwhile extended his torchlight to the enemy group and Hazrat Ali did not miss what the man with the grenade was doing. He was actually prepared for anything. It was only moments earlier that Hazrat Ali saw the head of Mozammel a childhood friend of him getting smashed into pieces by bullets fired by one of the soldiers. He did not lose a moment to give them any chances. Hazrat Ali with his sten-gun put six bullets into the grenadier soldier's head point blank. The soldier died instantly. There was no other option still he was anxious to confirm whether he had killed the very man that he was instructed to take alive. Meanwhile ten fighters from his team had taken five soldiers alive into their strong grip.

The name of the soldier killed just now was Jaan Mohammad Khan. Minutes later, this 6 feet tall rain coat clad and blood stained dead body started floating into the downstream of the river Padma. Far away in the central Punjab at a village of Multan district, Khan's mother was sleeping. It was the holy month of fasting and this old woman was deeply tired because of that. In her sleep she was dreaming. She saw her son Jaan Mohammad had come home on vacation. He was holding a big sack bag in his hands full of beetle-leaves and *Hilsha* fish from East Pakistan. The uniform that her son was wearing was studded with some new medallions of heroic feats in the war.

Asad and his forces were on the other side of the bridge. They could not still see what happened here. They now waded fast and met with Hazrat Ali's. It was almost one thirty in the morning now. As per the plan made previously, the team took the dead body of Mozammel and the five captives and then boarded a boat. Asad reprimanded Hazrat Ali saying 'why did you use the torchlight? This could endanger our whole mission and screw up the operaton. Please be careful in the future. Everything cannot be briefed to you as we are not professional soldiers. We must use common sense every moment.'

After half an hour's rowing they landed at a big well-off house. The owner's name was Shudhir Dutta. Sudhir had crossed the border along with his family immediately after March. People around knew that this home was since abandoned. The name of this village was Digha.

//

Lt. General Tarik bin Ziad was basically a quiet man. He was a simpleton also. There was hardly any difference between what he liked and how he actually worked. He was unlike Lt. Col. Yaqub Malikee of the 49th Bengal. He had a fair complexion, a boy like face, and his pranks were also childish. Even then if a man works in a profession for thirty years he can manage to memorize the jobs of that office. Accordingly Tarik had learned the average businesses of his position. Through the last few months he had toured all of the districts of this province and most of the B.O.Ps. He met people and soldiers in these places without pomp and ceremony. Everywhere he spoke direct and vaunted that the province would be defended to the last inch with the last man and last bullet. He told this to civilian congregations also.

One could read his dullness in the verbose style as he spoke. On the last 14th August, which was the nation's independence anniversary from British colonial rule, he showed a special camaraderie to soldiers of six rungs below him in the professional ladder. This was by wearing a joker like frock-coat and dancing with the soldiers, holding their hands in his before the celebration gathering at Dhaka cantonment. A senior diplomat watching it sitting in the front row said to himself, this man will be able to give a good performance as a buffoon in an English Court drama! However, for fear of extradition he never shared this view with anyone.

Tarik usually tried to be happy with himself. But now on the 7th month of his assuming command he was becoming shaky and nervous as some unavoidable phenomena had started disturbing his mind. He had already learned how to compromise with image and avoid public relations due to his soldiers' manslaughter and molestation of women. After these

an issue much more serious than those of press reports or censorship was showing its unpleasant face before him demanding prompt solution.

This was the third week of October. Tarik was attending office today after a lapse of three working days. Rainfall was receding and the weather was becoming arid. The flows of rivers and waterways throughout the province had dried up in many places.

His soldiers were feeling comfortable in their movement and engagements. Even then Tarik was not feeling well. On his last working day the number of letters and messages lying on his desk was fourteen. Today he counted and found the number had increased to twenty. He was almost sure about the subject-matter of these papers. Tarik stayed at his residence all through these three days. He instructed his staff officers not to disturb him by giving him any telephone connection unless it was from the President or the chief of staff. The staff told him today that neither of the two had made any phone calls.

Tarik opened the mail box and started feeling worse. His presumptions were correct. All these communications were letters or petitions from his battalions or brigade commanders. The contents were also the same—'send in fresh troops. We have individually contacted the army headquarters for the same; they have not made any response or taken action. Please sir, intervene on our behalf. Your high office might be able to accomplish what we have so far not been able to do.'

Today he once again realized how difficult it would be for him to keep up his commitment for defending every inch of this land with these demoralized lechers. Tarik's smiling air started fading out as he studied the mails more. Some sector commanders had given rather dismal pictures about their situation. Earlier he used to hold staff meetings with those reports but those bore no fruits. He also used to send the reports to the centre but the centre then started blaming him commenting Tarik was not smart enough to manage the situation. Tarik put forward counter-arguments claiming those were the misdeeds of a few miscreants. He also used to ask his p.r. to continue their propaganda inside this province. The authorities did not buy this for long and demanded to know how a handful of antisocial elements could kill professional soldiers in broad day light?

Tarik started using the *alibi* of a shortage of the required troops. Tarik then opened another envelope. The letter inside informed him that the number of soldiers killed since Tarik assumed command was

officers—250 and men 2800. This figure reminded him of yesterday's incident at Malibag near the police line. At 10 o'clock in the morning unknown assailants killed 2 of his officers and 3 men inside a van through a shoot and run method. None of the shooters could be captured.

On the other hand the situation around the frontier was getting worse every day. Various unidentified armed assailants were crossing the B.O.Ps, killing his troops and decamping after looting arms. Commanders doubted that those people were actually professional soldiers of the enemy country. Such was their speed and efficiency. However so far it had not been possible to prove this doubt.

Tarik wrote several letters the previous week to his seniors. Today he found none of those had been answered. He also made phone calls to the same very influential persons but none was available. Tarik lifted the receiver and told his P.A. Hatimtai Mughal 'put me through to Gen. Hamid'

His Ps was connected within a minute. The man said his boss had left the office a few minutes ago without telling him anything. Tarik asked Mughal to look for PSO Piru. A brigadier, next to Piru, received the call and said Piru was in a meeting in a different room. He advised Tarik to contact a Major General in Piru's office. Tarik agreed but this officer was not available at his desk. His staff officer told Tarik that General Ukailee was accompanying the Adjutant General in the corps anniversary cash raising function now being held along the Sindh-Rajasthan border.

Tarik tried to be patient and asked Mughal to see if the President was available. A few minutes later he informed Tarik that the President's line was engaged. Tarik slammed the receiver down and uttered an abuse in Punjabee. He said, what is their business about?

My men are being murdered in broad day light. I am craving for soldiers. They are not minding this but holding meetings. On what the hell issues?

Before his soliloquy was finished the phone buzzed into life.

-Sir, Major General Iftekhar Fahad is on line-2. Fahad was the commander of Rajshahi-Bogra-Rangpur axis.

In an annoyed tone Tarik asked,

-What is up Iftekhar?

-Not so good, Sir

-Come straight to the point

-Sir the B.O.Ps of Vurungamari and Lalmonirhat are almost gone. The Hindus and *Muktis* have killed 64 of our men and officers there.

Colonel Ali Jan Beg also died in this action.

-What the hell did your forces do?

-Sir they never thought that such an attack could come in that dead hour of the night. Many died inside their bunker even before opening their weapon. Now I need reinforcements just to guard the B.O.Ps. However there is one piece of good news.

-What is that?

-We captured three of the Bengal Lancers by our counter offensive.

-Ok, but where shall I find troops for you? When the situation was the same at GhoraGhat, I transferred men from Hilly. Only minutes later my whole unit at Birgonj was destroyed. If I weaken my defense at one point by withdrawing troops they make my position in another flank precarious. I have no place from where I can send in anything for you.

-Sir, what about reserves?

-Where do you see reservists?

Now you have to fight side by side with EPCAF and volunteers who we can't afford to provide even with uniforms. You are dreaming of reservists?

-Well Sir. Then what is your instruction in this situation?

-Listen. There should be no HQ or ad hoc units. You must fight until up to seventy five percent causalities. Then you solicit my instruction.

-Sir, Understood.

-Good luck Fahad.

Tarik replaced the receiver and felt his temper was getting hot. He remembered that as the chairman of recruiting boards he never allowed the entry of any Bengalee into the army. By written and unwritten ways he had always prevented their admission. The incident of the Bengal Lancers reminded him of his role in recruitment. He got doubly convinced at this moment that his decision was absolutely correct because these black and short knaves could never be good as soldiers. Otherwise how could they take up arms against soldiers of their own country?

Surely many of his seniors and colleagues in the name of showing so-called inter provincial brotherhood and mitigating deprivation, inducted many Bengalees into the armed forces. That was totally wrong. That wrong has created the very adverse situation which was gripping the country now. Tarik, while sending requisition for troops in the recent months made one thing clear, that there should not be any Bengalee element in those fresh units for East-Pakistan. Even there is a problem. There is no such army unit now a days which is absolutely Aryan. A unit is 'Baluch', 'Punjab', Pathan' or 'Frontier' only in its name. Actually inside every unit Bengalee soldiers and even officers are present. This phenomenon was due to the stupid liberalism of the present President. After assuming power in 1969 he issued an order to the Defense Head Quarters. In that order he instructed all commanders to create and increase inter-provincial amity. He ordered that all defense units must have a blend of troops and officers from all areas of the country. Which meant a Punjab battalion would never be wholly manned by recruits from the Punjab only. Likewise every unit will have Bengalees, Sindhis, Pathans and Punjabees irrespective of the title of that unit. For formalising this mix the President instrcuted formation commanders to organize pompous and colourful ceremonies inside every cantonment. Tarik never liked this work of the President. Similarly he also disagreed with the introduction of one man one vote and the creation of the five provinces by the President. He took all these important decisions alone and consulted none before implementation. Now the whole nation was paying for those errors while the President was enjoying a comfortable life at Islamabad. He also went to Iran a few days ago to participate in the celebration or 3rd millennium of the Royal Pahlovi dynasty relishing much carousal and fun fare of that function.

Tarik's mind got sorer as he thought all these things. Now he asked Mughal to see again if the President was available. After a lapse of ten minutes Moghul told him that General Piru was on the line. Before Tarik could say anything Piru said in a unwelcome voice,

-Why do you people bother the President so often?

The tone was such as if he was Tarik's boss. Tarik was about to explode but remembering the *Nabab*'s rapport with Piru he suppressed his anger and responded softly,

-See, my situation here is very fluid. It gets down to such a low that even a whole district is on the verge of falling to the enemy. Nothing is happening about my requisition for new soldiers which I demanded a month ago. There are no signs of their coming. What else can I do but disturb the President?

-Does the President dispatch troops? You better talk to the chief of staff.

-I have been trying that for the last fortnight but he was never available. He was always busy with meetings. So tell me where I should go.

Piru did not say anything about this last question and continued talking in a style as if his office was pretty occupied with graver issues.

Tarik listened and wondered if a war was going on here. What else could be more important there that they are so busy with? Piru asked Tarik to make the call ten minutes later but did not say if the President was available or not.

Immediately a call from Brigadier Zahanjid Khan Ansari from Jessore Brigade informed Tarik that their cantonment was under a defacto siege from three sides by miscreants. The deserters of 1st Bengal were also with those miscreants and they were holding at least ten men and officers of the 32nd Punjab. Tarik's nephew Mohammad Khan Niazi was also among the hostages and due to this factor Ansari's forces were not opening fire on the miscreants. Tarik told Ansari that he was busy talking to Islamabad and instructed him to talk later on.

This epithet 'later on' was actually vague and indeterminate. Nobody knew when he could get a second chance to talk.

Piru was on the phone now. He said that the President would talk to Tarik. The President asked,

-Tarik, what is the matter?

-Sir, I need troops. I have been sending signals after signals but nobody is responding to them while miscreants are conducting raids inside Dhaka city.

The word 'Mukti' was the vernacular for freedom fighters. Many army officials were using it but Tarik was careful in avoiding that and so used 'miscreants' instead. He knew that the authorities at Islamabad did not appreciate the vernacular much. The President, COS or Piru thought that there was nothing called a 'mukti' and use of this word was unbecoming of a soldier. There is no alternative to high morale for a soldier. Actually the situation was such that soldiers were scared of putting uniforms on because they could be easily identified as soldiers if these were on. That was making them easy prey to snipers' shots any time.

-You better talk to the Governor. I have authorized him to come to your aid in any way.

The President did not refer at all to the signal messages.

-But Sir, he is a civilian. What can he do about providing soldiers?

-Look, commander. I know who is doing all this. Who is sending here soldiers inside your territory along with the local miscreants and conducting almost an undeclared war against our country. I have tried to talk to the prime minister of that country and settle the issue. That woman has refused my proposal. Washington and Peking gave me some pledges but so far I have seen nothing of those either. Given the situation what can I do?

-Sir, with this small army what shall I do? How much can I do? On the other hand I am getting no co-operation from the local populace. A few Muslim Leaguers tried to extend their support to me. They are being killed by unknown assassins. I am under serious strain just to guard the 3300 miles long border.

-You continue to fight with whatever you have at your disposal. I am asking the governor to help you. Let the Almighty be with you.' The President put the phone down.

For a mysterious reason unknown to either it did not take long for the Aryan lady to learn that the President of the neighbouring country had referred to her with the derogative 'that woman'. Still she was not excited out of any sense of self-respect. The reason for not getting excited was not that her culture and tolerance levels were very high. Rather the reason was that her stake of interest was quite big. She always believed in one thing-

'Small men talk about people. Medium men talk about events and big men think about ideas'.

She belonged to the big ones and so she was proceeding with a big goal. Besides there is a type of people on this earth who hit their enemies direct on the head and kill them right away. There is another type which is few and prefers to maim their enemies instead of killing them so that the enemies may suffer the pangs as long as they are alive. This Aryan lady was of this type.

Now Mughal told him about a number of phone calls awaiting him meanwhile. Tarik dismissed them. He had a subdued voice now. Even after the fasting month started Tarik keeping in touch with his boss used to say, by the grace of Almighty,

We will cross the border and offer our Eid prayers at the racecourse field of Calcutta. Our valiant troops are taking preparations accordingly'

Within a few days he felt the strength of his vow was getting lower. Though simple-minded Tarik started realizing that the possibility of crossing the border was not that bright.

Tarik had much similarity on many accounts with the nature of his boss. He usually made plans to talk on many issues in a single go but always slipped some important ones. He now remembered after getting the chance to talk to the President, that he forgot to ask him why soldiers were not coming or what was the problem in getting that done.

With the dismal talks he had had Tarik's depression was on the rise when Major Usman Chawla, his staff officer-2, entered the room and told him that C.O. Combined Military Hospital, Dhaka, was insisting on talking to him. The issue was very urgent. Unwillingly Tarik said, put him through.

-Sir. I usually don't bother you much. Do I?

-No, you don't but tell me why have you chosen this exact hour to do that? Brigadier Azizee, am I a doctor like you? What problems do you have that you have called me? Don't you know the situation I am already in?

-Sir, what shall I do? The war is here and you are the commander.

-OK Mr. Physician, go ahead. At least you are not going to make demands for soldiers from me.

-Sir, I have got only eighty hospital beds here. The number of wards is twenty. Those facilities can accommodate the treatment of a maximum number of four hundred officers and men. But at this moment I have got 1200 soldiers. Some of them are getting killed by snake bites as they are sleeping in tents in the courtyard. Another two hundred are gasping for life inside my courtyard, godowns and garages. Medicine is far away. Even items like bandages, tincture iodine and hydrogen peroxide are running short. All local suppliers have been absconding since a long time ago. How long can I run my show in this way?

-So how can I solve this problem of yours, Azizee? Why don't you talk to DG, medical services instead?

-Sir my point is different. I am requesting your intervention so that no outstations send in any more wounded soldiers or officers to me for treatment. They should go to Comilla, Jessore, Chittagong and Rajshahi CMHs.

In his usual dullness and without fully understanding the point Tarik replied 'well I will do that'.

In reality the shortage of treatment facilities was being faced even at outstations due to the increasing number of wounded soldiers reporting

in daily from fronts. They were imploring Azizee to increase the facilities. Azizee also said to them 'what can I do for you? Not much.'

Tarik replaced the receiver. He called for one of the staff officers to draft the replies to the letters and signals he received from the cantonments of the province. He remembered that most of the letters written by him to the centre had not received any replies. A few had that honour but those were also full of slyness, diplomacy and equivocality. Even most of his phone calls were not attended. In the military academy even trainees were taught that all calls must be replied to at the first available opportunity. Now even many junior officers were not extending that courtesy.

At the same time at Rawalpindi, the chief of staff also was conferring with his staff members on the letters and signal messages received from East Pakistan. Hamid was telling the Dy. Adjutant General and Dy. Quarter Master General seated before him,

-See their demand. The way they are requisitioning for additional troops suggested that I have established a factory for producing soldiers here. If I can read Tarik's words it would seem that building barracks and hospitals for troops is a very easy job to do. I do not really understand them. Folks, you are fighting a war there. What the hell are you going to do with so many barracks and hospital beds? Am I sitting idle here? I have publicized notices for recruiting soldiers in all the districts like Kohat, Bannu, Mardan, Gujrat, Lahore, Khemkaran, Wagah, and Jhung. They will be selected, trained and then sent to Dhaka. Do they not understand that these efforts require time? How dare Tarik send me repeat messages? Does he think I don't understand what a war is? Have I become a Lt. General by being an ordinary soldier? Does one require so many hospitals and soldiers to win a war with a non-martial race? No. It requires proper planning. Let this be informed to them.The staff officer asked, Sir what exactly shall I convey to them?

-Tell them they should make the optimum use of troops and resources on a best effort basis—Understood?

-Understood, sir.

-You can leave now.

Within the next half an hour Tarik received the message in his office. 'Chalk out a sound plan of action and act accordingly'.

Tarik copied the same message to all his units throughout the province. He further added 'the commanders should no more bother him sending messages or making phone calls'. They must know that he was not spending his time in fun making or by watching films of heroine Neelo or hero Wahid Murad. He did not also feel happy about his superior's message. He thought 'if they think I am here for merry making why don't they join me too'.

Tarik put his beret on his head, took the stick and left his office for the Governor's house. He should be briefed about the latest situation. This dentist-cum-governor was the only one who listened to what Tarik said. Whether he understood an issue or not, at least he supported Tarik.

///

-Hazrat Ali
-Yes brother Asad.
-Listen. Eight members of your group will guard the outside. If they see anything suspicious, any person or boat or anything they should inform me without any delay?
—Consider that done.
-Very good. Now let us attend to our main business inside.

The freedom fighters were sitting in the big bedroom of Sudhir's house. While leading the blindfolded captives to the boat half an hour ago Asad suppressed his curiosity with a difficult temperance and patience about knowing if the special person he was looking for so eagerly was indeed among the captives. Now inside the safety of their hideout Asad looked at the face of each of the captives. Seen two and a half years ago but memorized almost every month through the photograph Asad felt very happy when he recognized Iqbal Ghori. Yes this was the man. In the central part of the room a big and thick wooden log was holding the weight and balance of the big tin and wooden roof of the house. Major Iqbal Ghori was tied with rain drenched rope as the kinetic energy grip of a wet cotton is much stronger than that of a dry one. The other five had been tied through their waists in two groups in another place of the big room. Ten freedom fighters with firearms were keeping watch on the captives. To kill any kind of sounds, pieces of clothing had been pushed inside the captives' mouth under the instruction of Asad.

In 1206 AD, Md. Ghori, the Sultan of Delhi was killed as a consequence of a power conflict through a palace conspiracy hatched by his close relatives. During these tumultuous days Ghori's family

members took refuge in a nearby village called Gurgaon. Iqbal's parents used to believe that they were the descendants of that family as their family name is Ghori. This family earned a name in one particular act. That was showing mindless cruelty to anyone even without a motto.

At this hour Major Iqbal Ghori's *khaki* was drenched with rain and river water. His two arms had been tied so tight that any ordinary man would have started bleeding long ago but it had no effects on Ghori. Ghori was sitting on a wooden stool in a normal posture. There was no symptom of any fear or anxiety in his tiger-like yellowish eyes or carefree face. Asad told one of his boys to take the clothing out of Ghori's mouth. Ghori asked, 'why have I been brought to this place?

Everyone looked at him and tried to understand the question uttered in Urdu. Only Asad understood its meaning. Hazrat Ali asked Asad, 'What is he saying?'

Asad gave the answer in the vernacular. Hazrat Ali listened. His body complexion was pitch black. When he passed through darkness he used to mingle with it and so became almost invisible. He was a voracious eater also and his physical and mental strengths were unimaginable. Hazrat Ali had survived a number of operations against the occupation army unscathed. In that process he created a large stock of helmets, boot and combat-dress of the enemy soldiers killed by him. His home was at Puthia police station, ten miles north of Rajshahi district town. At this moment Hazrat Ali was wearing such a pair of boots and the upper part of the uniform of a slain soldier. Before Asad or anyone could guess anything, Hazrat Ali moved his right leg in an electric pace and hit Iqbal Ghori in the right lower leg with a tremendous strength and muttered,

-You will be fed milk from a bottle. That is why you have been brought here.

Asad watched and once again realized that he had committed a mistake by not briefing these people more thoroughly. He had seen even before that half-literate people enjoying the pleasure of possessing fire-arms for the first time in their life were indeed difficult to be disciplined. With a high temper Asad shouted at Hazrat Ali and said, 'Here I am the commander, it is nobody else. Keep one thing in mind. Nobody should make a single move without my Permission, right?'

Hazrat Ali's long experience, before the starting of the liberation struggle, was raising cattle and teaching very poor students simalteneously in rural primary schools. These educational structures were so dilapidated that usually they did not have even any roof. He got a little scared at the shouting of Asad. He realized that this urban boy though younger than him had a fire of personality in him. If the country became independent such men will become officers while he will possibly not be able even to be an ordinary soldier in the army. In an apologetic tone Hazrat Ali explained,

-Brother Asad, I am sorry for the mistake. Actually you told me about this guy before we started the operation and that angered me right away. Though in a primary school I am a teacher. Dr. Shamsuzzoha was also a teacher though in a University. Inspite of the very big social difference we belong to the same profession. Hearing the story of his killing prompted me to settle some score with this killer.

-OK, I realize that but be careful for the future. Remember we are in a military operation. A slightest mistake or emotion can kill all of us.

The impact of the strong kick made no changes in the expression of Major Ghori. Only a hushed 'uh' sound came out from his mouth. Asad was sitting before Ghori on a cane chair. Insufficient light from a kerosene lantern was throwing ghostly shades in the room. He stared at Ghori in the fearless eyes and asked, 'like to have some tea?'

-No.

-Cigarettes?

-No.

-Would you tell me where Lt. Col. Abbasi and Major Umor Raja of the F.I.U are now?

-I do not know them.

Asad could not really understand whether Ghori was telling the truth or not. Asad leisurely opened a small bag from the floor and took out a steel made tool. It was a small pair of pliers used by electricians and plumbers for fixing domestic appliances. He showed it to Ghori and said,

-Listen. First I will break one of your fingers with this. If you don't like that then answer my question before I do that.

Three seconds later the small finger of Iqbal Ghori's left hand fell down on the floor like the tail of a domestic lizard. A soft groan was heard from Iqbal's mouth.

Asad said, 'will you answer my question or do you like me to break the rest of your fingers?

-No. I know none of these fellows.

225

-OK. Let us turn to another issue. Why did you order the killing of Prof. Shamsuzzoha?

Iqbal did not show any diplomacy by asking 'which Zoha? Or where? He gave a straight forward answer instead.

-He was a very bad man. Always used to turn students against the government and was himself playing politics. So he was done away with.

-So what was wrong in doing that?

-There are rules against doing that. A government employee can't be involved in politics. Only teaching was his duty.

-Good. How then is your chief martial law administrator involved in politics? First of all how did he come to power? His job was to fight the enemy and defend the country only.

Iqbal got nervous but only momentarily as his iris showed a slight unpreparedness. Then he said, the chief executive has done the right thing.

-You did not answer my question as to how he became the chief executive. Now let us discuss something else. Do you have any idea how many innocent people your soldiers have killed here since last March and that more than ninety five percent of those were Moslems?

Iqbal was interested in this question in a way as if it was his cup of tea and enthusiastically said, we are killing infidels and that is for defending Pakistan.

-No, you are lying.

-I am speaking the truth.

-Never. Tell me, of the fifty thousand people killed at Vatiari near Chittagong cantonment how may were Hindus?

Iqbal kept silent and looked slightly thoughtful. There are some undeniable facts of life which even the best of the stage performers or diplomats cannot suppress. The face is thus sometimes, if not always, an index of the mind. The question on Vatiari was one such. Iqbal couldn't forget his role in that and that now that truth was reflected in his eyes. Asad started again,

-I know you will not answer that as you are a liar. The Biharees killed those fifty thousand Bengalees in a four month period. It was absolutely due to you and your forces' active support. We have all of this information with us. Another point, how do you look at the raping of Moslem women by your troops?

-I think that it would help upgrading your racial quality in the next generations. We Aryans believe that the Bengalees are inferior.

Almost none of the boys in the room understood the conversation. With the last answer of Ghori Asad got extremely angry but somehow exercised restraints on his emotion. He smiled and told 'Iqbal, let us start anew. Tell us where Abbasi and Raja are posted now. If you answer this question, we will tell you nothing more and arrange to send you back to your unit.

-I have told you I don't know them.

-Ok. I buy that. In that case take this wireless set, use it, talk to wherever is necessary and find out the location of those two men.

-With this set, we cannot talk any range bigger than three miles. So this is not good even for talking to Rajshahi Cantonment.

If Asad had been experienced, he would have understood that Ghori was telling lies. Neither Asad nor any of the boys had ever used this wireless-set. So they also did not know how to compel Ghori to use the set.

Asad felt indecisive. The night was advancing fast. Within another two hours the operation must be completed and they had to return to Kazipara camp before dawn. The risk was also increasing with the advance of the night. This might allow the news to leak and from ears to ears get to some dangerous place. Asad took the next decision and told Ghori,

-You co-operate with us or I will start killing those four of your men one after the other.

Asad looked at the rope-bounded soldiers and told Ghori to go ahead with the wireless set.

—Find out where Umar and Abbasi are now. One condition. Don't use a word other than Urdu while you communicate. Otherwise I will shoot you instantly.

This instruction was also a mistake which Asad did not realize. It was not known to him that whatever the consequences were, those soldiers would never go against their commanding officer. Accordingly each of the five men replied the wireless was not useable for the required distance. Asad nodded to Hazra Ali. Ali brought one of the captives before Asad. This man was the most handsome amongst all. He had a pink complexioned face and looked like the former President Field Marshall Ayub Khan. He had a beautiful nose and a pair of affectionate

eyes. After breaking his holy fast in the last evening the man used some kohl in the eyes. He had a well-trimmed beard around his cheeks and sideburns. In the Pakistan Television's religious talk show programmes like "The light of the holy Quaran" this type of persons used to take the role of the facilitator. He was the most aged soldier in the group. Two boys held the man in an erect position. Hazrat Ali held a sten-gun in his right hand standing on the left side, and using a splattering of Urdu asked, tell me how many of our men have you killed so far?

The man did not give any reply. Ali, with the barrel of his gun served a heavy blow on the man's bald head. Within seconds deposits of blood-stained brain matter and smashed bones smeared the ceiling and the sten-gun. The man named *Subeder* Kaif Ibne Majid sprawled down on the floor like the coil of a big reptile.

The other four were also given the same option. None gave any replies.

The instruction from Asad was pre-set. Now ten boys closed in on the soldiers. They started beating and stabbing them with knives, iron rods and bayonets. Two months ago, one of the boys watched his peasant father being shot dead by soldiers while he was working in his tobacco field. This boy now pushed a small iron rod inside the retina of sepoy Intezar khan and moved it around.

He gave out a ghostly scream and the man's torn soft tissues and blood gushed out from his sockets and stained the raincoat. Then the boy started hacking the man with a hammer on his head and kicked him on the navel.

None of the boys was using bullets. After ten minutes the floor at this point looked like a heap of blood, urine, stool, vomiting and mortal remains of five huge corpses.

A freedom fighter hailing from Raninagor area of Rajshahi district did not participate in the action. He lost consciousness after watching the scene. Ghori was staring in another direction. Asad now looked at him and said 'is there a change in your mind, man? Besides, let me ask you another question.

-How fair do you think it is that the army has been spending 60% of the national budget every year?

—I am not concerned with that?

—Why not? You are a beneficiary

—These are matters of politics.

—And your bosses are involved in politics but killing others here for doing the same thing. Don't you feel any remorse for this?

—There is no question as such.

—OK. I will make you an offer. Then we will close today's business. Consider if you can take it. You shall have to do nothing but only confess that shooting Dr. Shamsuzzoha was an offense. Next you will say in an audible voice here "Long live Bangladesh"—just these two things. We will take care of you as a special guest of ours and we will see to it that you will in no way be harmed. Major Iqbal listened attentively and everyone in the room heard as he chanted "Long live Pakistan" almost as a slogan.

With a calm face Asad opened his bag and brought out a small hammer and a big iron nail. In his mind the story of his parents' murder, sister's abduction, murder of 50,000 labourers at Vatiary, scene of Minoo's missing and Dr. Zoha's bullet—hit body got wiped out and transcended to a new realization, 'I imagined I knew them. Actually I was wrong. I now know them better'.

Asad did not utter a word. He took up the hammer and started maiming all the fingers of Iqbal's both hands. Then he placed the iron nail on Iqbal's head and with a thud from the hammer pushed that more than half way through to the man's head. Though hailing from the land of the Aryans, a much vaunted martial race Iqbal was not without a body and made of flesh and blood. He was also born out of a woman's womb. He tried to scream but it turned into a hushed groan. Within a minute the stare from the pupils of his eyes became fixed.

Right at that moment, eleven hundred miles away at the city of Lahore's Sultan Mahmood road the civil defense department was blowing a siren. This was for awaking pious Moslems from their sleep to have a meal in order to fast from sun-rise to sun-set for the next day. The month of Ramadan always follows that ritual. Ghori's mother was heating some food for the family in the kitchen oven. Ghori's father was offering the special prayer of 'Tahajjod' before sitting for the meal. Suddenly he started vomiting blood while seated on his prayer mat.

Asad took the iron-nail out of Ghori's head, wiped it and the hammer and replaced them without hurry. Everyone watched the scene. Each of those boys was a freedom fighter and was a survivor from dangerous missions. Human blood, exploded heads, dead body, amputated limbs, explosions, blood smeared bayonets and smoking firearms were familiar sights to them. Still two young boys started vomiting.

Ali spoke, 'brother Asad, did you see how tough they are? What a beating we gave to them still they did not yield!'

Asad realized Ali had seen only the physical strength of those soldiers and not their mentality. He told, 'Ali, let me tell you a fact which I heard from my father. It was 1944. The British were preparing to leave. A group of patriotic extremists kidnapped an English magistrate and his recently married wife from Churulia collectorate. They took them to their hideout and said they would be released on one condition. The condition was that the couple should utter "Inqilab Zindabad" (Long live freedom) and "Bande Mataram". Otherwise they would be killed. Even then the couple started uttering, "Long live the king." As a punishment they were killed then and there; still they did not budge.'

Ali did not know much of those stories. He said, 'but those English people never put fire to villages or abducted women like these Punjabees. On the contrary I heard from elderly people that their administration was far better and there was justice in society.

—Ali, you are correct. But see what these six people have demonstrated here today. They are so united, while many of us are collaborating with them in locating and getting us killed. What a shame!

—Brother Asad, you may appreciate their unity but to me they are dacoits and robbers. To hell with their ideology of togetherness. My target is only one. We will continue to kill the Punjabees until full victory is reached.

The night meanwhile had advanced further. Asad set everyone to their tasks and the dead bodies were thrown into the river. He thanked Ali and his brave boys. The group members greeted each other and departed for their respective destinations.

Colonel Ludhiani sitting at Rajshahi cantonment heard the news about the blowing of the the railway bridge and the killing of seven of his men and officers. That made him furious. He sent for his colonel staff and ordered, 'shoot everyone around the spot. Set fire to all the habitation.'

However he avoided forming any enquiry commission. Since March a lot of enquiry reports on similar and other incidents were lying piled up but it was not possible to take any action on most of them.

//

Winter had set in. It was the frontier state of Arunachol. The Aryan lady was on a visit to her Eastern provinces. In the British made red-bricked 'Writers' building' she was conferring with four of her Chief Ministers. The chief minister of Meghalaya told her, 'madam, the condition of my government is really bad. We are under heavy financial pressure from giving shelter and food to a million refugees. Ancillary social and law and order problems are also arising out of their presence here.'

The other three also expressed similar views. She listened to them and then asked.

—So what do you propose to resolve this?

—Take one of their border districts out and shift the refugees there. How long can we take care of a crore of refugees?

—Will not such a step make us an aggressor in the eyes of the world?

She was actually happy with the proposal as that was absolutely public opinion. On the contrary she could not be that undiplomatic as to express her pleasure at such a direct proposal. The four leaders, though belated, understood that they had made a mistake before that exceptionally intelligent world-class leader.

So they tried to make some amends and started explaining what they meant by their words. The talks could not proceed much as her private secretary took permission to enter the room carrying a message of utmost urgency and importance. Madam read the message and ordered that immediate arrangements be made to prepare her aeroplane for the flight to the capital city. The text of her speech was decided on board even before landing. At 9' o clock in the evening she addressed the nation through the official radio and informed the world that Pakistan had attacked her air bases at Jodhpur, Ambala, Pathankot, Gurudaspur and Jalandhar along the western frontier. Simultaneously their land forces had attacked her land border points.

The following day at Islamabad, the President looked despondent and desperate. He was also having a meeting with his prime minister. Of the military only Piru was allowed in. He whimpered,

—In every civilized nation the head of the government or of the state has a right to be advised by members of the civil society. Here nobody met me from that quarter. The *Nabab* of Larkana has always been only after one thing. He could advise me better on things I was not familiar with. But he never did that. Why is my big neighbour so interested in this affair? It is not for the Hindus got killed here in army action. It is something beyond that. They are looking for our markets in East Pakistan.

The prime minister thought suffering had made his boss wiser and to think and to talk better but was it not too late? The President continued,

—Piru also never advised me. When Podgorny advised me to exercise caution on the 1st week of April Piru did not allow the foreign secretary to talk to me because he was a Bengalee. Now the Soviet block is against us. I never knew how to talk in figures of speech. I have always been a straight-forward soldier, not adept in the zigzag way of politics. Except the Moslem world, nobody is supporting us. When Bengalee Foreign Service officers were demonstrating in Washington, I should have read the signs on the wall. I now realize that I could not play even my own cards well. The information department could advise me on the use of statistics in my speech regarding East Pakistan. If advised properly and well I could let the nation know how much money I put into the development of their province in the two years compared to a decade earlier during my predecessors. No body cited, as the General officer commanding there how much I did for the development of the garrisons? Everybody acted as quislings. Uncle Sam or the yellow friends are actually doing nothing in our favour. Now Mr. PM you are an exceptional person. Please show some light.

—Why do you think that I can do that?

—Because you were not in the bandwagon during the 1970 elections. You won it against the Awami flood. You have headed governments on earlier occasions also. Can you advise me now? I sense all Bengalees and their provocateurs from across the borders are planning to do something very bad. They are out to humiliate us. The PM silently said to himself, you are chasing the mules but not so much the traders behind them.'

Before the PM could say anything the PABX system informed the President that the US ambassador was due to see him and was waiting in the ante-room. With the long habit of depending on the west so much the President felt glad and told he could come in right then. The gentleman entered immediately. The President rose from his seat and was almost hugging him with a welcome, 'Hello my friend, how are you? This is a great relief to see you at this critical moment'.

Then the ambassador thought, 'has this man taken leave of all his senses?' Shunning any emotion the ambassador even avoided a smile and the hug and said wryly, 'I am not your friend but an ambassador only. I am here to tell you one thing point blank. We believe this is not going to be a place for any gentleman. That is one. Given the walkover that you have allowed to your armed forces in East Pakistan in dealing with civilians there, my government can no more support you. Good bye, Mr. President!'

With no more words or ceremony, the diplomat walked out of the room leaving a flabbergasted head of state behind in his office. The President started sobbing as the PM watched him silently. After a few minutes the President raised his head and said, 'Mr. Ameen, since there is none to advise me and everyone has stood off, I have taken a decision on my own.

—What is that?

—To exercise pressure on our big neighbour so that she eases her stranglehold on our eastern province, I have instructed my armed forces to strike hard on their western borders and they have already started doing that.

At Delhi, in her office the Aryan lady was sitting alone. She cancelled all appointments until further notice. She was watching and listening to the progress in the war zones along her eastern and western borders. She looked happy as her armed forces reported to be giving a thrashing to the enemy forces and were advancing in all sectors. She took a diary and noted,

"Irrespective of what I wanted in private, I never made that public. My father also liked this but Gandhi's so called humane approach towards our arch enemy prevented that in 1947. My side of the sub-continental population was against the partition of India. Even Khijir Hayat Khan, such an influential Punjabee Moslem, was against a separate homeland

for them. Azad was dead against this. The British were against this. What the devil was this two-nation theory? The majority supporters of the theory, the Moslems of Bengal are now undoing it. What a self contradiction only within 24 years. Now they are totally with us because they need us. Shall this softness remain when the job is done? The hangover of Pakistan—is that an easy thing to be evaporated away? The Farakka barrage issue is still unresolved. The same people raised slogans "Death trap Farakkah, blow it away". What shall happen to this issue just for a new friend? I can never compromise with my national interest. So bitterness is not far away. And, the corridors? My father was correct. Gandhi was not. He paid an exact price for his folly. If he had not agreed to the partition we would not have this problem for 24 years and also this enormous cost along the borders and the death of so many people."

She stopped writing and closed her diary. Her defense adviser phoned to tell her that the enemy's reaction was very lethargic. It was going to be a matter of days only before the conclusion.

///

It was the 7th of December. At a tea-stall of the township market at Gurudashpur, Lt. Colonel Faruque Shieer Mirja was enjoying a cup of tea. He was also reading a newspaper. Faruque was the commanding officer of 11th Electrical and Mechanical Engineers battalion of the 9th Indian mountain division stationed along Wagah-Khemkaran border. He was on leave for a week from Sardar Dorab Singh cantonment. It was 9 o'clock in the morning and the winter was indeed in full swing. His young son Arif aged 9 years entered the shop and said, 'Dad, you have an urgent call from the cantonment'.

Faruque did not finish the cup and returned home with his son. He attended the phone and told his mother and wife that he had to join duties at the cantonment.

The same afternoon Faruque and another three hundred officers and soldiers stood before a flag stand. The flag was tri-coloured with an indigenous weaving machine planted at its centre. Everyone stiffened to attention as the commanding officer stood before the podium. He spoke loudly and clearly, 'Men and officers, Pakistan has attacked us.

You are on a war-footing. You may have to be a part of the mobilization any moment from now.'

A stream of feelings and questions surrounded Faruque's mind even under that severe cold, 'who am I going to fight? I knew that in theory it could be Pakistan or China. In practice it is Pakistan. I am an Engineer, still a soldier. I will have to blow up bridges, culverts and water works with the same purpose of harming or killing soldiers and civilians who are Moslems. Shall I be able to do that? My employers here are skeptical about us. They also know that we also doubt them. Still I am earning my livelihood from them. Possibly now I am going to face the test.'

The same thoughts were active in the minds of other soldiers belonging to his religion. In early March they started disbelieving the East Pakistan cause. After the crackdown, it did not change to their favour but instead to the eastern wing. They thought the icon and lighthouse for Indian Moslems was under attack from the Bengalees on imaginary grounds of deprivation and exploitation.

Lt. Colonel Faruque went back to his officers' mess. At 4 o'clock, before sun rise he was still undecided though he was already in action. A shell from 11th Field regiment artillery of the enemy force hit him on his abdomen while he was dismantling the abutments under a bridge approaching Sialkot road. As the last rays of the earth faded away from his eyes Faruque thought, 'did I do a wrong by not opting for crossing the border during or after 1947? May be that is the cause of my death today.'

Far away at Dhaka the same day it was almost two hours past evening. Rear Gunner Jahanjeb Abrar was offering his post evening prayers. None of his much apprehended air strikes took place so far. Right at seven' o clock in the evening, all the sirens around the airport started ringing alarms at the same second. He was hearing this sound after a gap of six years. He heard the collective sound of gunners' rushing footsteps. Another serial deafening noise tore the tympanic membrane of Zahanjeb's ears within a few seconds. A true Moslem can't break his prayer even in such an hour as it will surely send him to hell without any mercy. The five soldiers behind and Zahanjeb standing on the prayer mat did not get any scope for thinking anything. Within seconds, the torn shoulders of one and amputated heads of the others flew from their bodies and then lay sprawled around the prayer mat and the adjacent open field. The green netted helmet from Zahanjeb's head flew a little further and then settled on the playground of the Air-force Shaheen Boys' high school. Above the sky, hell was let loose. Sixteen MIG-21 fighter bombers of the enemy air force were spewing fire and moving to the north, burning and destroying Abrar's whole unit to the ground. While exiting, the intruders strafed and created large chasms and crevices every twenty yards in the runway making it totally unsuitable for take-off or landing for any kind of aircraft.

At quarter past seven, Air-commodore Sharif, the local air officer commanding sent a coded message to Gen. Tarik saying, 'My air force and runway here have just come to an end.'

Tarik did not make any reply to this message. Basically he was not a brave man but when men like him put on a uniform, that is when an institute stands behind such men, they become brave. Even then the news of their bombardment and levelling of the runway did not seem to Tarik to be a cheerful one.

Naval commander Makhdum Shah hardly cared for this winter as his home was in a village neighbouring the Silk Road where the temperature at that time of the year usually remains at minus seven degree Celsius. Makhdum had received classified information from his sources that heavy attacks might be coming targeting his ports and ships any time after November. Immediately he cancelled all leave of the rattings and officers and sent a red-alert along the port and shore-line. Ten days had elapsed since the beginning of December, yet no signs of any such attack. That evening Makhdum was looking at the sky and the stars. He was wearing a woolen sweater hand-woven by his wife Hanafi. Suddenly even without the usual warning of the blow of sirens, a squadron strength of enemy bombers appeared from nowhere and started raining fireballs on his frigate and everything anchored in the port. Only front gunner Yunus Shams Khalili could quickly activate his Ack-Ack and shot one of the attacking planes down into the sea. The others, with their relentless firebombs smashed the frigate and its commander. The frigate fully eclipsed in the water.

At the same time, in the only air-field towards the north-east of Jessore cantonment, its base commander Irtazul Khan Quashim was almost asleep. A shrill whine of the siren woke him up completely. Six pilots under his command and Irtazul immediately made a rush to the F-16 Fighter bombers garaged in the hangar within walking distance. They were clambering up the iron-stairs into the Jets when a stream of extremely bright flood lights blinded them and they were unable to see anything. Volleys of bullets, exorbitant heat and blazing fire bombs started burning them and the fighters at a tremendous pace. Only two enemy planes taking highest risks had penetrated the base flying at a very low altitude. After completing the mission they flew out to the south. Squadron leader Quasim's parents had named their son after the great 8th century conqueror of Sindh Md. Bin Quasim. Quasim's target in this war was to destroy the enemy's Fort William garrison at Calcutta. Providence did not fulfill his dreams.

At 8' o clock commodore Inamul Haque, naval officer commanding Chittagong naval area, phoned Tarik to tell him that his last naval ship had been destroyed a few minutes ago. Tarik then sent two similar encrypted messages to the air and naval commanders which read, 'No army has ever won a war or battle with ships or firearms. The real asset in a war is determination and a strong mind. This is the hour when these ideas should be aroused in all ranks.'

Commodore Inam read the message and thought, 'A change in situation does not necessarily change a devil's devilry and it necessarily does not require one to be very intelligent to practice devilry.'

Inam understood, as he watched the accuracy of the attacks that those would not be repeated by the enemy. Their smartness tonight demonstrated that they always acted on confirmed information and on sure ground. They were then sure that their enemy was exhausted and they were wise enough not to flog a dead horse. Inamul returned to his bungalow at the naval colony. His wife Salsabil Tarannum asked him, 'Can you tell me why we have descended to such lows?'

Commodore Inamul had always been one of those handful wise gentlemen believing that it was most Islamic and rightful to hand over power to the majority party. On the very day the *Nabab* congratulated Kashmiri freedom strugglers for blowing up the passenger air-craft, Inam told his wife 'this statement of the *Nabab* will take us to grave dangers in case of a war with our enemy. In case we have to mobilize

in our eastern wing it will be extremely difficult to do that due to this air-embargo.'

Now to the query of his wife he replied, 'There is no more chances of dangers in my career. So let me now open my mind. To answer your question I must say the main reason of our insulting defeat today is the granting of a full autonomy to the armed forces. Every individual or institute in this earth has a guardian, with whom he can have consultation in hours of trouble. Our armed forces have no such guardian. The British, who created us gave one piece of advice when they left the subcontinent. That was, to keep the armed forces always under a civilian command, but we never adhered to that. Another big reason is we never learned the language of the majority population though we ruled them for so many years.'

Sitting in their village, Zahanjeb's daughter, son-in-law and wife were swallowing a news bulletin from Karachi radio station. The newsreader in a jubilant voice was informing them that 'the heroic Pakistanee soldiers were proceeding forward, destroying enemies, nobody should be misled by the baseless propaganda of the enemy. The whole nation was behind the armed forces and that their victory was certain.'

Tarik took refuge inside a sub-surface bunker at Dhaka cantonment. The enemy had been ceaselessly spewing fire from the sky since 7th December. He duly gave a situation report to headquarters. But there was nobody to receive even a phone call. Tarik sent a number of messages on the same issue but received no responses. After a strenuous effort Tarik could establish a connection with the President on the 13th of December. He said, 'Sir, all the cantonments except Dhaka are now virtually under siege by the enemy. The 9th infantry division is still somehow defending this city. The number of casualties on our side is now enormous.'

It was after many days that the President listened to Tarik patiently. He said, 'I do understand the situation you are in. You have been fighting like a hero. However, keep in touch with the governor and have my decision from him.'

With no more words the President hung up. Mughal informed that Rao Forman Ali and the chief of the collaborators Major General Jam shed Khan were waiting to meet him. He allowed them in.

A very crucial meeting started. Like many other meetings held earlier in this office, that meeting also did not record any minutes. The meeting decided some deadly issues and authorized personnel to implement those promptly. This province was being besieged by a foreign enemy who was not in possession of any visas or entry permits. Tarik had been condoning this gross insult to his profession but he spent only half an hour to decide certain things against a group of important local inhabitants who had always been innocent and had never broken any law. Following his green signal enthusiastic masked groups armed by General Jamshed gate crashed into many selected houses later on the early hours of the 14th. They picked up the listed people from those houses, blindfolded them and transported them to unknown destinations. They were the best of the intelligentsia of their community. People found their maimed and rotten dead bodies two days later at killing sites of Rayerbazar, a spot at the city's downtown.

At the southern port city of Khulna the number of immigrant inhabitants had always been heavy since 1947. That happened on two accounts. One was the influx of Bangla speaking Moslems from across the borders of west Bengal. The other one was the non-Bangla speaking Biharees and united provinces' people from the western borders. Those latter populace were usually famous for their knack in business initiatives and production industries. The port city, since the British days, created those facilities for the intending people.

The port area in the city was Nao Raton Colony. In English, 'Nao Raton' would mean 'new jems', a term used by the Moghul Emperor Akbar in the 16th century which was the name of a body of advisers for the court. There, in a very well off mansion, Begum Khosjahan had been arguing with her husband Ameer Khosru since last April about one particular issue. That couple emigrated to this part of Pakistan from the central provinces of India right after the partition. Khoshru turned into a business magnet by 1960s. He owned a shipping line. The wife used to ask her husband, 'Why are you not trying to go to a safe refuge?

Khoshru replied,

—Where shall we go to?

—Why? Karachi, Lahore or Islamabad.

—Do we have any relatives in those places? Besides what shall we do there for a living after leaving this flourishing business here? Here we will make a survival at the least. The locals are not all bad elements. We have good relations with all the educated people here. So what is the point of your worry, honey?

—That is correct but the way they have risen now against all non-locals is worrying me.

While this debate continued, Khosru kept himself informed of the happenings around. Confidants told him that the adjacent Poshur River was occasionally carrying rotten bodies and that they were non-locals mysteriously killed. Besides many Biharees had left their homes and gone to unknown destinations bag and baggage. Even lower animals can fore-sense if there is an impending threat or danger to their lives. Small animals like frogs and mice, which are on the food menu of snakes can smell and see the existence and movement of the predators. So Khoshru and Khosjahan continued thinking what to do though outwardly they were showing a brave face. Khoshru had questions about his family's security and the time line when this war would come to an end and with what consequences. He was certain about the answer to those questions.

The army units reached Khalishpur, an industrial belt near Khulna city, by the third week of April. The local Bengalee administration had decamped by that time. Khoshru had a Master's degree in Accounting. He never had the naïve belief that the army would ever defeat Hindustan easily. He also understood that the acceptability of people like himself to the army was just like the one of a country rattle to a king cobra. Accordingly, Khosru never tried to build a friendship with the local army camp. Suddenly Khosjahan asked, 'If the Bengalees really become independent how would they deal with us?'

Khoshru was startled receiving such a question from his wife who never made the 10th grade examination. He answered,

—I never imagined you could think so deeply. I still don't believe that they will be able to become independent on their own. Even if they can make it somehow their educated mass will be our reliance.

—I suppose you have no idea about their cruelty. That is why you are being so simplistic in your thoughts.

—Has anyone of them so far behaved rudely with us?

—No they have not. Still the looting and arson they have perpetrated at places like Syedpur, Rangpur, Mohammadpur, Mirpur and Chittagong are not negligible.

-Don't think I have not heard about those but that is not politics. In the matter of acquiring resources no Hindu spares another Hindu nor does a Moslem spare a fellow Moslem. I have always noted this. You should also not forget that this Punjabee army has killed Bengalees, ten times as much as the Biharees and non-locals killed at Bengalees' hands. I have no intention of moving elsewhere abandoning such big properties. Anwar Ali uncle at Dhaka has not deserted. He is still having a good medical practice as before.

Khosjahan understood that though what her husband was saying was not very preferable, but also that there was no better option.

At about the same time a few other families were having similar conversations at their Ispahani colony, Moghbazar, in Dhaka city. One such was Akiluddin Ispahani. He had a chain of production plants at Adamjee industrial area. His faith in the army's capacity was blind. From the first week of March his wife started asking her husband to sell the plants and move to Lahore. Akil replied that this state came into being to last until doomsday. Nobody other than a total idiot could ever think that the Bengalees with a few three-knot-three obsolete rifles were going to snatch their secession.

The same neighbourhood was also the habitation of Naqvis, Aga Khans, Alvis and Quereshis. The forefathers of these families all came from various areas of Iran, Turkey, West India and the Arab Peninsula. Their hobnobbing with the army was indeed intense. They also believed that so long as the army was there they had nothing to be scared of. They believed every letter of the official radio's report about the army's victory as true. From the thirteenth the rattle of the guns around and screeching of tanks started receding. On the other hand there was a continuous curfew. Telephone lines were disconnected. It was not possible to contact the acquaintances they had in the cantonment. They started thinking 'What the matter could be?'

In their Jhigatola residence Abul Hossain, Asad's uncle and aunt were having talks. Mrs. Hossain in a love mixed complaining tone told her husband, 'Could not you have any information about the only son of my elder sister?'

That was not the first time that his wife was making the complaint. Still Abul held his patience and replied, 'See, I have already told you what I have done in this regard. Tell me what else can still be done?'

—I also don't know what else could be or can be done. In any case I feel very bad. I never imagined that my only sister and brother-in-law would thus face the end of their lives. Such innocent souls they were! Then their only son's whereabouts is unknown. So I am keen to know if he is at least alive wherever he may be living.

Abul cautiously made all possible queries about Asad. He also wrote letters to his campus address but got no clue from anywhere or anybody. The only comfort he got was from making a phone call to the provost of the dormitory. He told Abul that this very student after attending some classes simply disappeared from his allotted room on his own. There was no evidence to show that anyone had harmed him or taken him away by force. Nobody could say anything beyond that much. Abul told this repeatedly to his wife but she still could not have any peace in her mind. She often continued to ask him, 'What do you think? Is he still alive somewhere?'

—I am afraid to utter what I think.

—Why?

—Because as the saying goes that 'even the walls have ears'.

—Still tell me what you think.

—I don't know why I think so. However, I have reason to believe, most probably Asad has joined the freedom fighters.

Abul was the chief Medical officer of the provincial government's research institute called Science Laboratory. Cautiously through the last 8 months, he had been listening to the foreign news agencies including the BBC. He had always the sense to believe as to which of the news they were broadcasting on the Pakistan crisis was credible. Abul added,

—He is a brave and strong boy. I can only hope if he survives we will meet one day. Whatever our own radio is telling us about the progress

of the war it seems to me that this is fiction. Their days are actually numbered now.

Mrs. Abul was never active in politics Nonetheless her support always leaned towards her sister and brother-in-law. She believed that one Pakistanee soldier was still equal to ten of the infidel enemy soldiers. So she did not feel confident in her husband's words. She asked,

—What do you mean by this?

—What I mean is clear. So much sacrifice of so many people cannot go in vain. This time something final is going to happen.

—That is impossible! I will never believe that. The so-called freedom fighters are a far cry. Even if they can get all the support of those they are depending on so much from across the borders, I will still think that yours or their dream is never going to be fulfilled. Under God's domain such an inequity can never take place.

Abul Hossain knew quite well how his wife looked at this freedom struggle. She did not accept it as anything nobler than a conspiracy aided by the Hindus for the break-up of the Moslem holy land Pakistan. He had also seen that it was impossible to make her understand the deep truth about the matter. He told,

—Well even if it is not a righteous cause according to you, science tells us one thing.

—How come science is relevant here?

—It is relevant. Science tells us that a mighty power will be defeated by a mightier one. So there is no question of ethics or morality. But one thing still puzzles me.

—What is that?

—Good fellows like your sister and brother-in-law got killed at their hands and you are still supporting them!

—Look. Nobody intentionally killed them. When a rebellion is suppressed by the army, some innocent people are likely to be killed in the process. Even during normal time some innocent people are inside the prisons or some others get shot by the police without doing any wrong, because they were in a crowd or near the spot of trouble. For these deviations you cannot argue for doing away with the police or the judiciary system.

—You like to describe this as 'a few'?

—Yes, a few. Tell me how many people have been killed by the army? How many women have they abducted? Why? Are you not attending office regularly? I have also not become old enough to detract the army. Have they done anything to us?

The couple had had similar conversation repeatedly. Mrs. Abul could never be convinced by her husband about the real situation going on in the province. Abul told stories he heard from colleagues and friends of young boys being picked up by the army and then never coming back. The burning of villages after villages and raping women also could not get any place in his wife's mind. She was always telling that those were highly exaggerated. Tired but not giving up Abul said,

—You had quite the same opinion with your brother in law. I am attending the office just for a livelihood. Internally my support is always with Asad's. Though young, he could foresee much better than any of us that these days were inevitably coming.

The conversation closed as Mrs. Abul moved towards the kitchen to arrange dinner.

///

Three hours had elapsed since evening set in.

It was the 3rd night of the continuous curfew. Abul heard a knock on the door of the drawing room from outside. Nobody could move without a 'hard to obtain' curfew pass at the moment. Abul thought, who could be outside, might be one of the neighbours from the upper storey. He asked without opening the door 'Who is there?'

—We are from this neighbourhood. A patient has become unconscious due to severe pain in his abdomen. If you will kindly open the door?

Abul Hossain used to attend patients as a general practitioner. The small chamber was inside their house. The tone of the stranger was rather docile. Abul opened the door. Three men wearing black masks were standing on the threshold. Abul did not feel any difficulty in recognizing the firearms held by those three young men. He kept a normal voice and asked

—'Where is the patient?'

The one standing in the front answered, At Maneswar road. A pass is not required to travel such a short distance. You see we could not have an ambulance now.

—But I don't attend patients on call. You have to bring in the patient here.

Overhearing the conversation Mrs. Abul Hossain approached from behind. The man on the front moved his sten-gun slightly upward. With a still friendly tone he said,

—Uncle, the patient is a freedom fighter. So we expect you to make an exception today and accompany us to treat him.

Mrs. Abul identified the second young man standing on the step of the half-dark stair and asked him.

—Hi, are you not Akram? Why have you put on a mask on your face?

—Aunty, since joining the freedom struggle we have created a few enemies around. So we have to move with some caution like this.

Actually Akram was working in the library and research wing of a highly fundamental and communal political party collaborating with the occupation army. Mrs. Abul was not aware of those things. She knew him as the son of a neighbour. The gang leader came forward and told Mr. Abul in an impatient voice, 'would you kindly hurry? We are getting late'.

Who was there, at that golden time of a big state not ready to show kindness to those with fire-arms. Dr. Abul said, 'let me bring my stethoscope and the medicine bag'.

—We have got all those things at our place but we don't have any doctor.

Mrs. Abul asked, 'Where is the patient? And who are these two boys?'

Akram answered, 'They are from our group of the freedom fighters. The patient is in our residence. Aunty, don't worry. Uncle will return soon.'

Mrs. Abul Hossain did not doubt the words of the boy. Seeing fire-arms at the boys' hands led her to believe that there was possibly some truth in the stories about the freedom fighters so often told by her

husband. She could not imagine that those boys were actually complying with the green signal of Tarik given a few days earlier.

//

The joint command of freedom fighters and the allies were proceeding further towards the capital city holding Tarik's forces at bay. Tarik was under heavier pressure in his sectors as the enemy had been intensifying her campaign in this province. Tarik was still in possession of sufficient heavy arms and ammo but his troops were decreasing everyday due to casualties. He needed soldiers to operate the arms but their strength was down to only 45,000. That was for the first time in his life Tarik had started criticizing the late father of the nation. He understood something only a few weeks ago and started having this adverse feeling. His first point was that it was not proper to have a state in two parts with an enemy territory in between spreading for a thousand miles. His second point was that the father of the nation failed in establishing the corridor connecting the two parts. Can an army fight in such a way bringing in reinforcements from such a distance? He was also feeling bad against the *Nabab*. He was the man who had prevented use of the direct air route from the centre to this province since February. And now on top of all there was nobody to give a decision on any important issues.

It was the eighth day of the war. The President used to reply to one or two messages from Tarik even a fortnight earlier. Thereafter he stopped that. In many districts Tarik's forces were falling. Tarik was at a loss as to what he should do about those. He was still trying to talk to a few people but they were showing helplessness. Major General Rao Forman Ali was his close acquaintance. He when contacted said 'I am Junior to you, how can I advise you. Plus I am responsible only for civil affairs of the province'.

Uncle Sam always expressed their likings for Tarik. Tarik went to their Consul-General. He told him, 'These are your internal affairs. How can I come to your help?'

Tarik tried to talk to the President, chief of staff, one by one but couldn't find either of them. He then phoned the governor. He replied, 'I am a dentist, what shall I do regarding increasing your soldiers' strength?'

After much assay, Tarik contacted a staff member of General Piru. Tarik insisted on talking to him but the staff member replied that his boss was busy playing squash at the moment. He would talk to Tarik later on. Tarik's commanders were all reporting the same thing from around Dhaka. 'The enemy is closing in on us from every corner. They are burning everything they are coming across. What should we do?'

Tarik was weeping. He was keeping away from the telephone, walkie-talkies and even the wireless system. He was also feeling, 'I have been betrayed by being sent here which I realize only now. What can I do? My bosses actually exploited my simplicity'.

On the other wing, enemy forces had penetrated deep into all sectors along the Punjab-Sindh border. Simultaneously strafing was continuing. Corps commander Lt. Gen. Tikka was looking for Gen. Hamid over the telephone. Hamid was not receiving the calls. Tikka knew he required more arms and soldiers to fight the war and to prevent the enemy advance. The stocks were there. He also required more fighter bombers. That stock was also not bad. Tikka was also looking for the Air-force chief Marshall Rahim Khan. He was remaining simply unavailable. Towards the south, enemy navy and air force had almost finished destroying the Karachi port along with its facilities. Admiral Muzaffar Hassan was a very noble soul but nobody could tell where he was at the moment. The need of the hour was only instructions but who would give those? Failing in his attempts Tikka asked his staff officer 'Munaem, you better go to their office and tell them that this is the situation down here. We need decisions.'

Major General Munaem with a quick 'yes sir' started out for the GHQ. It was a black-out from the front up to the capital city. Munaem proceeded with the headlights of his jeep off. After reaching there he found all the rooms well lit but none of the three was in their room. Munaem asked the subaltern 'Where are they?'

'They are all in the most honourable President's room, sir!' replied the man.

Munaem proceeded to the MSP's room and informed him of Tikka's message. The Military Secretary was not at all moved with the message and said' 'The four are in a meeting. You have to wait!'

—But the situation is real bad. Now Islamabad and Rawalpindi may be bombarded any time.

—I am not responsible for that. I can't do anything about that Munaem. I am not the President or the army chief, you know.

—I know that but you are one of my batchmates. You can at least tell the President or the chief of staff about this message.

—I have no such orders, friend.

—Then?

—As I said, wait. I will tell them about you when the President pushes the buzzer of the phone or sends for me for something.

Indeed an impeccable discipline was the only valuable matter at such hours!

Munaem took a chair and waited. Inside the palatial chamber, constructed by an American Engineer in the style of a medieval European pontiff, the four were sitting for the last four hours. They enjoyed the time watching a one day international cricket game between England and the West Indies. They were happy when England was defeated. This country had been supporting the Hindus and the Bengalees all through the crisis. General Hamid and Air-Marshal Rahim made soft attempts at influencing the President saying 'Sir, East-Pakistan is most probably gone. Please try to do something to save the west.'

The President replied, 'The soldiers are doing that duty. Is it the duty of Generals and Air Marshalls to go to the field and fight the war?'

Then he started drinking. Admiral Muzaffar said nothing. He only thought, 'Such a big occurrence, a province of a large country is seceding away from the centre, but the President did not even care to pay a visit there.' He did not think it to be a proper job. However Muzaffar kept mum for the fear of losing his job.

The President pushed a button and asked his military secretary to come inside. As he entered, the President opened a file and showed a note written inside. He pointed to a few words in the note and said, 'there has been a debacle' in East Pakistan! Who wrote these defeatist words? Get these corrected. It is only a temporary setback; there should not be any such negative remarks in a government file. Why do you people send something like this to me without examining it properly?'

The MSP told the President about the waiting visitor. The President told him to wait. After twenty minutes he was allowed inside. The President by then had almost lost self-control with the constant intake of pegs of whiskey. His Iranian Physique and fair complexioned face was more radiant. He with some indulgence in his tone asked, 'Munaem, are you out of your senses and forgotten everything about service discipline? You got in here without any formality and did not care that we are in an urgent meeting. Now tell me, what is so important that brought you to my office leaving the war-front?'

Munaem described Tikka's report. The boozing had made the President's voice more inarticulate and inaudible. The belt of his waist was also unbuckled, drops oozing out from the open zipper wetting his trousers. At this moment, a small but powerful Philips radio set placed on the desk started making an announcement from the enemy side, alternately in English, Punjabee and Urdu. All lent their ears to it. 'Commander Eastern command and commander western command, we call upon you to arrange to lay down the arms of your military forces and cesassion of all hostilities within the next twelve hours from now to our nearest commands. Otherwise we will intensify our campaign until we achieve full victory. We can be contacted through the following frequency of radio communication . . . .'

In the meantime two separate messages from Tarik and Tikka had been received by the cipher operator of the President. The President was drowsier now. The messages were placed before his eyes. He asked in a whisper 'What is this?'
—Sir, very urgent . . . .
The MSP explained.
The President started reading the messages. Both Tarik and Tikka had made the same submission in an imploring tone.
'Sir, the enemy is beating us heavily. We can't hold on any more as reinforcement is impossible now. For your kind information . . .'
The President instructed, 'Send them a message telling I have got nothing to say about this. Let them do whatever they consider best.'

//

The first day of the Bangla month *Paush* had been traditionally witnessing a lot of funfare in Bengal since its introduction about four hundred and fifty years ago by the mighty Moghul Emperor Akbar.

He did it for convenience of land tax computation on the basis of crop cultivation. Inhabitants of both parts of Bengal used to observe this day with preparation and consumption of various indigenous cakes. This year, today and since the last fortnight, Bangla speaking people were not at all looking for or enjoying any such things. Moslems, Hindus, Christians, Buddhists, agnostics, theists, irrespective of age, profession and social calling were keen to watch something absolutely different and new coming up. It was the expected birth of a new nation in its thousand year old history. The besieged population in the Eastern part and the free ones in west Bengal alike were keeping their eyes on the development and happenings at the city of Dhaka.

There, under the pale shadows of the short winter afternoon a group of people were standing, on a pale ground of the city center. This ground was constructed by the British in early 20th century for the pleasure of watching horse-races. The people standing were in 20s and 6s rows and each row accommodated sixteen people. They were all soldiers by profession. Soldiers, the world over kill unknown foreign colleagues to defend their own frontiers. But these soldiers, for the last eight months and twenty two days had killed a crisscross of children, women, men, old people and patients, Hindus, Moslems, Christians and Buddhists, who were the citizens of their own country. They were oath-bound to defend their citizens and the land. But today they were abandoning everything.

Now many of them were wearing worn-out shoes as their employers were running out even of shoe-shiners. Some did not have socks to cover their feet. To wear a woolen sweater or jacket over their uniform was one of the normal service conditions, but today many did not have that. Due to the tremendous and continuous attacks of the enemy on their supply line for the last thirteen days, these soldiers were even going without lifesaving drugs, drinking water and subsistence level food. Many were wearing cheap personal apparel and cambric made shoes.

The places where they were born and spent most of their livelihood were colder than the ground they were standing on. Still they were shivering. If there is a sunny day during a winter the temperature goes down instead of rising. For the last fortnight the clean blue sky above and the grounds below were releasing coolness mercilessly. So this was giving them additional affliction. On top of that, dust,unclean clothes and the mutual odor of sweat due to lack of baths were making everyone

unpleasant. When life is at stake, where is the time to ponder for a laundry or a clean bath?

Especially during the last five days none of these people could have a minute's rest or sleep. Their faces bore the expressions of that inhuman hardihood and fatigue. Everyone irrespective of rank was showing deposits of yellow mucous in the corners of their eyeballs. Their unshaved faces and chins were showing scattered black and gray stubble of beard instead of the usual greenish and healthy clean shine. What was mainly holding or compelling them feebly to remain erect on the grassless arid field was the rigorous and relentless professional training for the past twenty years. Otherwise they would not have this energy and could have given up earlier. Non-stop firing, strafing, rationing of food and drinks and excommunication with their families at home stretched them to the fringes of their fortitude.

The ethnic classifications of human beings inevitably generate some undeniably distinct mental and physical features. This was the second reason why they had not yet succumbed to their hard labour. Most of them were either Aryans, or Moghuls or Semitics. These races are well known for their patience, physical strength and a high capacity for survival under extreme stress and very adverse situations. By the inviolable dictates of fate or chance some of these people were transferred here to perform the professional call. Some came here six months while some others three months ago to witness this very day. At the time of their arrival they put on a smartly turned out show with clean and pressed uniforms. Their shoes used to glitter with the daily polish of cherry blossom shiner. They used to have a daily glow on their cheeks after a shave at the barber's hand. The officers' messes and soldiers' barracks satisfied their appetites and thirst daily by providing them a menu to their preference. War, then, seemed to be a child's play as the adversary was mainly a civilian population. From 3rd December, this game no longer remained a game and turned in to real war full of death, panic and deadly suffering. The adversary was also three fold mightier.

Standing at a place far away from their homes, these three hundred and twenty men and officers were awaiting an instruction from their superiors. A ceasefire with the enemy was passing its second day. Still most of them did not have the energy to hold the simple weight of their light firearms in their hands.

The first man in the third row was Saban Omarkot. His rank was Major. His name was the composition of two things. 'Saban' is the name of a holy month of the Islamic faith while Omarkot is the name of a place in India where the Moghul Emperor Akbar the great was born. To his right hand side was standing Lt. Colonel Dost Mohammad Khan. Saban looked at Khan and asked,

—Sir, do you know why we have been summoned here to this field?

—No, I don't have any idea.

—Sir, I feel there should be no more dragging on this conflict. This should be finally finished now. I have got tired of killing men.

—The condition is the same with me. I also don't feel any good dealing with women.

Saban in the name of a holy war killed three hundred people. Dost raped at least two hundred women and ordered troops to do the same to other women.

In the fourth row, four people familiar to one another were standing whilst staring at the sun. They hailed from Muzaffargarh. Their speciality was in bayoneting children and ripping their bodies apart from end to end.

Lt. Colonel Jane Alom Kaneja of the 31st Punjab infantry battalion asked Major Mia Hossain Fathoom of the education corps, standing beside him,

—There is no shooting for the last two days and then there is this sudden call here. Do you know what this is?

—I suppose there will be some fresh briefings.

Actually both guessed what this could be but they took recourse to this ruse. As if there was no harm if the war continued. The enemy was tightening their noose on the throats of this people. At such a time, they were not trying to prevent that, instead were indulging in the hypocrisy of briefings. Captain Shoaib Chunary of 29th cavalry was posted to Narayanganj just three days ago. He was summoned along with his tanks to this place yesterday. Chunari did not use his tanks even for once. Who shall he use it against? He spent two months at Tanbazar since his assignment started here four months ago. This area is out of bound for all ranks of this profession. But who shall punish who? Chunari's superior

Major Daniel Marhaba spent every night at Jamtala and Dhopapatti, two hotbed or pleasure spots for carnal satisfaction.

Daniel was a student of a Madrasha for four years at Gujrat where abstinence and self-repression were the only lessons. Nevertheless, this champion of Islam practiced something very different from what he learnt as a theory. That was 'not war but pleasure'. He took the self-ordained responsibility of changing this lowly untouchable race into a lofty Aryan one. So he never met with men or enemy soldiers but with women only. Are not women the mothers of the posterity of a nation?

Flight lieutenant Imam Hossain Thanvi of Mirpurkhash, Sindh, really had not even an inkling as to why he was called to this place. On the 4th of December, all the four of his saber-jet fighters got destroyed by enemy bombardment before they could be activated to take any action. So he had not had any duty since that day. He asked Lieutenant Rahbar Chagla standing next to him.
—Is it not a strange gathering?
—Why do you think so?
—Because I find there is not a single branch of the defense forces which is not represented here.

This dialogue was overheard by Major Shegufta Kanwar in the next row. He said,
—You are right; I have also noted the matter. All the branches like infantry, ordnance,armour, artillery, EME, AMC, signals, air force, navy, education corps, ISPR, medical corps, cavalry, legal corps, rangers, volunteers, scouts and even the bugle pipers are present here.

There was no hypocrisy in the words of these two officers. They had training on all issues relating to war in their academies but that did not give them any clue to the purpose of today's congregation. Like the dilapidated saber jets of Thanvi's, Chagla's gunboats were sunk by the enemy in the Meghna River at Chandpur port. Chagla fled to Dhaka the next day with a gang of fifteen rattings in a hijacked launch.
Drill commander colonel Fardin, station commander colonel Oaisee and Major General Rao Forman Ali were standing together and whispering something amongst them.

It was 18 minutes before sun-set. The cold was getting worse. Broken and vague conversation and sound of moving papers were becoming audible through a mike fastened atop a bamboo fixed in the field. Then gradually all the other noises died down and one voice became singularly audible. It was commander eastern command's. All sounds stopped immediately as he introduced himself,

-I, Lt. General Amir Abdullah Khan Niazi, NDC, PSC, SQA, WC alias Tarik Bin Ziad like to draw your attention.

Everyone stiffened to attention.

—Turn right.

Everyone turned to the right.

—Turn left.

Everyone turned to the left.

—Left, right, left, right . . .

-Stand at ease.

-Everyone followed his command.

-Halt.

Everyone halted.

Niazi alias Tarik looked at the faces of everyone he could see. Brigadier Bakar Siddique, Muin Chowdhury, Air-Commodore Sharif, Major General Rahim Khan. Brigadier Atif Mohammad and Major General Khushi Mohammad were all standing in front of him. Niazi moved his lips closer to the microphone. Seconds later his sonorous voice became audible,

—Lay down your arms.

Unpreparedness is a term alien to this profession. There was a sign of surprise in some of the faces. But that was momentary. They now understood it was the central-cum-ceremonial part of their total surrender signifying defeat to the steel-hard determination of seventy five million Bengalees, in spite of hyperbolic propaganda of victory even until this noon.

This historic city founded a little more than three hundred and fifty years ago during the Moghuls, was witnessing at this faded afternoon more history being made in its bosom. Earlier it had witnessed the forming of a political party, the Muslim League in 1906. That party later in 1940 made a specific demand for separate states for the Moslems of the sub-continent at Lahore. 1948 witnessed the only and first visit of the father of the nation to this province and to this city. In 1952 this city, then a small township, showed a remarkable protest against the clamping of a minority foreign dialect as the lingua franca on the majority population by the rulers. No nation on earth ever had seen demonstrators shedding their blood for the right to speak their mother tongue. Early at this year on the 7th March, the same city heard Mujib's inimitable thunder on this very ground, 'The struggle this time is the struggle for independence'. And finally today it was the birth of a new nation after the travails for almost nine months.

The symbolic fire arms of all three hundred twenty service men started falling softly down on the ground of the racecourse. The word surrender also includes the expression stooping. A jingle of gun metal with the hard winter soil rose and spread through the atmosphere. The stream of flashes of ISPR and foreign correspondents' cameras lit the dark evening every few seconds alternately. Niazi took his wireless set and said something in Punjabee to somebody. Within three minutes two men carried a table and a few chairs from the local Dhaka club office to the spot. These were put properly on the ground. Someone then placed a pen-stand and two pens on the table. Then a group of about thirty people followed Niazi from behind. They were soldiers and were wearing different uniforms. It was clear that they were the victors. A bearded and turbaned senior officer from that side and Niazi took their seats on the chairs. They took the pens in their hands and waited for something. Lt. Colonel Morsalin Daud of ISPR from the defeated side made an announcement without any ceremony, 'Now the Pakistanee forces of the Eastern command will formally surrender before the Indian Eastern command.'

General Jacob corrected him by saying 'No, they are going to surrender before the India-Bangladesh joint command.'

About twenty photographers and journalists started recording history dated 16th December, 1971, GMT 17 hundred 30 hours!

///

History, ageless as it is, was at work again. If not in every era this or similar incidents had happened in each century. After the end of the war the victor has always taken away possession of all assets of the vanquished. It was repeating at this hour today. As if this was a timeless warehouse of history. One could find anything here. Shoes, uniforms, sweaters, tunics, shoulder badges, epaulets, insignias, medals, helmets, berets, picks-up, waist belts, cooking pans, utensils, tents, canopies, mosquito nets, bedsteads, steel trunks, hold-alls, telephone sets and even a pitcher for toilet were in one side. On another corner sten-guns, bren-guns, rifles, light machine guns, sub-machine guns, howitzers, anti-air craft guns, mortars, tanks, ammunition of all measurements, bayonets and bullets were piled up neatly.

Colonel Jodhiram Tiwana from the victors' ordnance corps was taking an account of everything occupied by them. The handover was being made by Lt-Col. Hakikot Pilloo from the vanquished's side known as an extreme anti-Hindu.

Now the stiffness and formality between the two sides were gone as the surrender document had been executed. So both parties started exchanging something different beyond the taking over and handing over of the booty. They mingled with one another. Lt-commander Aurongjeb of INS Gandhi was telling Lt-Col. Akbar Khan of the station headquarters Dhaka cantonment that Sabiha is her first cousin. Sabiha was a top heroine of Pakistan's cine world. Akbar was told, 'After 1947, my cousin and uncle's family went to Pakistan but we chose to remain in India.'

Group captain Shameen Ahsan from Aurangabad air-base of the Indian air-force informed that Rear Admiral S. M. Ahsan, ex-governor of former East Pakistan was the husband of his mother's only sister. Colonel Jholmolia Khanna was standing behind an M-24 tank. He smilingly told Lt-Col. Nadir Khan Kasuri of Pakistan's 22nd Punjab that he often comes across with the neighbuors of Kasuri's family at Lahore.

Major Monohar Jha and Major Alimdad were telling everyone around them they were playmates since their childhood. Their families were in the same neighbourhood near Hossasiniwala ferry station and they used to fling water from the river Shotodru at one another as a part of a game they used to play as kids. Major Sunil Bhattacharya was pleased to share in clear Bangla language with captain Latif that both of them spoke the same dialect and that his village home was quite near this field in a police station named Dhamrai wherefrom captain Latif also hailed.

Wing commander Shahnewaz Khan Gharewal from the Himachal Air-base reminded naval commander Washim Lodhi from Sialkot that they had met during the 1965 war after the cease-fire agreement. General Forman Ali started talking to General Jakob in such an intimate tone as if he would be most happy now to get back to his grand parents' home inside Rohtak district in the Indian Punjab. Likewise, many of the victors recognized many faces from the vanquished and vice-versa. While making the reminiscences and revisiting connections mostly far-fetched, they exchanged hugging and handshakes. Some from the vanquished side mentioned that their descent was very high. Some of them were connected by blood to Kublai Khan, Chenghis Khan and Jalal Uddin Afghani, people who never knew what a defeat was. Today it was by mere misfortune that they were facing such an insult.

Simultaneously many from the defeated side started showing a deep interest in the musical talents of Lata Mageshkar and Mohamed Rafi, two world class Indian song stars. The first Nobel laureate from Indian Bengal, Rabindranath Tagore and his composition had always been a taboo throughout Pakistan and its military. The only reason was that he was a Hindu. At this moment Lt-Col. Musrat Mokaddam Khan from the Pakistanee army education corps gave a different interpretation of this genius's writings. He explained that the division of the human race on the basis of faith or religion was never important. What was important was humanity. What Tagore meant in his poem 'At the seashore of great humanity' was nothing but the harmony of human beings.

Colonel Saif Nasrullah of the Pakistan's EME was watching all of these. The laughter, reminiscences, jokes, talk-show on music and literature did not please him. He asked himself, is this place for exchanging these ideas! Is Hindu-Moslem-Shikh amity the theme of today? What a strange matter! Nobody from our side is saying that this cheerless evening is the last scene of a war, full of bloodshed and an utterly humiliating surrender. Nasrullah was an engineer and encountered no action as he was posted all through the troubles inside Dhaka garrison. Secretly, he had always been soft towards the Bengalees.

Nasrullah expressed satisfaction to God saying silently, 'O Allah' you have properly punished these Punjabee s.o.b.s. Who says poetic justice is not available on this earth?' Nasrullah was not fully correct. To his ignorance it was just-half an hour ago, Subeder Majari and his men were landing at Kamalapur railway station after finishing a journey from Sylhet as the unit was under order of transfer to Dhaka. No sooner had Majari stepped out of the big railway junction along with 25 of his troops then a brushfire from a freedom fighter's sniper hit him on the neck in the trachea. He breathed his last then and there while all of his men remaining unhurt. The only pastime of these men at Sylhet was women and especially Hindu women.

In another corner of the congregation Lt-Col Yaqub Malikee of the 49th Bengal was weeping to a Moslem counterpart of the victor. Yaqub came back from Comilla in last August to Savar, an outskirt of Dhaka city and was promoted to the rank of Colonel for his brilliant performance with 49th Bengal. He was telling the victor, 'tell me what the religion of Islam says about doing justice to men, the best creature of Allah, the most merciful? It is kindness, patience, and understanding. So long I was here I always showed highest consideration and kindness to the Bengalee soldiers and civilians. I was against the crackdown. How can a Moslem army fight its own Moslem civilians? I was against that also. But I am a small fry before so many top-notches and so was helpless. I can't advise them. Only you will believe me. After all you are a Moslem though an Indian. I with my small power and resources tried to save Bengalees as much as I could. That at times took me to high risks before my bosses. They were never kind to East Pakistan. But see how unkind Allah finally has become to them?'

Yaqub was not sure if this shedding of crocodile's tears was believed by the listener. An Indian is usually too intelligent to be understood easily by a Pakistanee. The former would show nothing in his countenance to indicate what he is brooding. So Col. Imran Dalmiah only curtly said 'Well now those days are over. Don't think about those anymore.'

Yaqub Khan, erstwhile commander, Eastern command was listening to the news of the fall of Dhaka while lying on a couch at the East Pakistan House, a government building in Karachi. He was happy with the latest information. He never subscribed to the President's thought about the province. Poetic justice did not show up for him also. He, after the start of the army invasion in the east, was demoted to the rank of a Major General by the President in April this year. So it was not only lack of poetic justice but victory of the farce at the same time.

Lt-Col. Abdullah Bakht Baluch from Quetta was telling his childhood friend wing commander Bakar Khan Hydery, 'This derogation is indeed intolerable.'

Hydery's home was at Mardan and Pathans are believed to be anti-Punjabee. He said,

'I have never had such an insulting affair in my life like the one I have suffered today along with these lousy and blockhead Punjabees. Still I am happy that those who were responsible have thoroughly paid for it. They should be ashamed. Fie on you suckers! Begging for life without a war! Spit on them!'

Abdur Raual Chowdhury, Lance Nayek, had only one thought in his mind, what shall happen to his wife?

None of the provisions of Geneva Convention mentioned the rights of such persons.

Brigadier Trilok Nath Chaturvedi, a psychiatrist from the victor's side was explaining to Major General Mitha Khan of the Pakistan commando, that Bible, Quran or Granthashahib all dealt with the same subject. That was surrender to God and indivisibility of the human race. General Mitha smiling like an idiot was agreeing fully with the brigadier.

There was no prospect of any personal profit due to the possession of the just now surrendered arms and assets for the victors. Still they felt extremely happy and satisfied. The feeling was similar to the one which a peasant enjoys viewing a ripe crop field before his eyes.

It is normal that a victor will show modesty and smile but the defeated were also smiling and showing utter humility before these foreigners. The only reason for this conduct was the strong urge for survival somehow. They knew that without these foreigners who were mostly infidels, they would be torn to pieces by the freedom fighters waiting everywhere outside the guarded race-course perimeter.

It was 8'o clock in the evening in Dhaka. The officers' mess and soldiers' lines were lit in such a way as if a national festival was being celebrated there. The victors had brought in with them enough food, drinks and even cooks for the occasion. After many days the defeated men, under the comfortable security umbrella of the victors' escort enjoyed the warmth of new uniforms, woolen pullovers, and socks. They fell on hot *tandoori, kebab* and steamed meat like hungry wolves.

Hot coffee in big metal mugs continuously satisfied them. The totally derogatory surrender was utterly forgotten by them within these three hours gap. Niazi had sent a last message to his employer saying 'the minimum value of the arms and ammo we have here would be 2500 million US dollars. What shall I do with these if I can't fight any more?'

His employer never replied to this query. None of the officers had the feeling of guilt about giving those enormously expensive assets up to the enemy bought out of the tax money of a very poor country. They were now turned into guests and started agreeing to whatever the host said though the host's condescending tone and looks were evident. They were talking to the host in the servile manner of peasants talking to their landlords. They were not showing even a fraction of the vendetta to the infidel host, compared to what they had shown to the countrymen of their own faith up to yesterday. These same people while taking the most popular figure and premier elect on the 25th of March showed him none of the respect to which he was entitled. No 'Sir' no 'Excellency' was in their lips on that night or later. Now they were very liberally using these superlatives and hyperboles to these hosts whom they always mentioned as the arch-enemy of their state in their propaganda machine since 1947. None of the feelings like, despondency, or guilt were demonstrated in their conduct now. Rather they looked like an honoured, relieved and glad group of travellers enjoying the meal and the festivities after a long strenuous journey. Nor did the last looks, groans or screams of innocent civilians and children killed by them make any impressions in the minds of these designers of innumerable death-spots. They had also totally forgotten the undeniable relationship with thousands of children yet to be born of innumerable molested Bengalee women.

The officers and men alike now the hosts' captives, behaved in the same manner. Soldiers looked for and found out Moslem colleagues from the host's side and attempted to establish intimacy with them. Their chief Niazi told his escort at the flag staff house that their chief Lt-General Aurora hailed from the adjacent district Rawalpindi very close to his Mianwali. He further informed his hosts that he was only two batches junior to Aurora from the British Indian Military Academy at Dehradun. He explained this in a way as if it was a big amusement and continued relishing his favourite 'reshmi kebab' and sharing obscene Punjabee jokes with the surrounding uniformed men.

A handful of the defeated ones demonstrated different behaviour and reaction. Captain Sher Md. Khan from Malakand agency in the NWFP, showed some self-respect. He refused to shake hands with Major Vojonlal Rotilal Jindal of the 11th cavalry.

Zindal told him that before the partition of the Punjab in 1947, his father was a close neighbour of Khan's. Showing no emotion to this fact, Khan grumbled,

'Put those damn words away. You are responsible for this insult today'

—You are for nothing blaming us, Khan. We are not responsible for this, but it is an invisible power that brought this day into being.

—Don't try to justify that philosophical theory.

—See, is not the state an invisible power? What value does an individual like you or I carry to its wishes?

—No, no, no. I feel I could commit suicide before this 16th December dawned but my religion Islam forbids me to do that.

To prevent the conversation getting further sour both stopped talking.

The evening was proceeding towards the night. The cold was also getting worse. The funfair of the surrender and victory being over, the fallen were courteously led to board vehicles to the cantonment. There is no harm in one who has the upper hand showing courtesy. A spokesman told the prisoners of war that they would have to spend a few weeks here and then be transported to camps in the land of the victors and live on their hospitality account until governments determined their fate by mutual consultation. This was said with a smiling face but none of the surrendered dared do anything childish but followed the announcement as the military police was escorting them from all corners. Everyone complied with the instructions. These very same people, during the last nine months, were stubbornly expressing their vow that they would never bow their heads to anyone on the grounds of this inferior riverine delta.

The central ceremony authorized all along the provinces' borders to surrender before the nearest joint command available. Most were relieved and happy. Only a few with some sense of self honour got infuriated. Major Jamil Ludhiani of soldiers' line at Jessore cantonment, 'the Stalingrad of the East' exploded with anger. 'What the hell of a decision is this? Surrender without any resistance?'

Lt. Colonel Nissar Sultan Jayedi standing behind him stopped him with his fingers on his lips and warned him by saying 'hold your tongue. If they hear it you will be put to a court martial'

Jamil retorted, 'Hell to your warning. How can one have the power to try someone when he himself has surrendered without a struggle?'

Aged Jayedi was ashamed at the young Jamil's words. Indeed who shall now put who to a court martial?' Actually Jayedi could not suddenly forget what he learnt through twenty two years of his profession. What he forgot was that both place and time had changed. Jamil said, 'We are not only the best army on the earth. Given the stock of arms and troops' strength we still have, we could continue to fight the enemy for at least another two months. I can't figure out why they stopped without trying for that.'

Major Jamil had had long working experience with the ordnance depot and regimental centers. His statistics about troops and ammo strength were very reliable. Jayedi also noted that in his address Jamil did not use even once the traditional honourable mode 'sir'. After the surrender discipline had broken down to a large extent. Decisions were being taken at the seniors' level. Accordingly juniors started giving pieces of their minds to seniors. Jayedi thought it safer not to say anything more now.

Along with the eastern theatre "the best soldiers on the earth" were laying down their arms to Indians troops at sixty points in the western theatre. This started from the north of the west Punjab down to the south of Sindh. The news of these falls did not take quite a while to reach Lahore, Rawalpindi, Karachi, Peshawar, Multan and other big cities in the west. Hamid summoned a briefing session for army officers to let them know the latest situation at the biggest 'counsel hall' inside the army headquarters. He could not speak much. A Major named Minhaj without taking permission, rose, almost touched the General's tunic and angrily demanded, 'we must know how and under whose advice was this decision to surrender taken? Four fifths of our soldiers are alive, three-fourths of our fire power are intact, and why were these not used at all?'

Such conduct is alien to the military profession and etiquette. Had this taken place a fortnight ago, the punishment would be unimaginably high. Today, Hamid and the seniors did nothing of the sort. He stared at the questioner, swallowed the brazen insult and without further ado left the hall forgetting to carry his pick-up from the table. However, Hamid had the answer but he thought, 'what responsibility do I have to make that? Legally the President is the only one to do that in a military government'.

Hamid used to keep silent earlier also. When the President exclaimed 'how can a civilian woman get the guts of sending her troops inside my territories with the intention of breaking it up? I must avenge this. If necessary, to do that I can even make compromises with the Bengalees.' Hamid never gave his boss any counsel or advice on issues like these. The President then took the personal decision to wage war.

At Jhelam, in a northern Punjab cantonment, Lt. Col. Shamsi Gama abused the President directly. He said, 'that the Bengalees did not support Niazi in the east is well understood.But here the whole population was behind us. In spite of this, why is this shameless compromise?'

At the capital city Islamabad, women flocked to the main streets holding broomsticks in their hands demanding capital punishment for the President and chanting slogans. An eminent poet Fazal also participated in the procession. The police stood a little away and watched the proceedings, but took no action. Gulzar Khan Fattah, an Additional superintendent of the Punjab police in charge of the contingent, in a soliloquy said, 'If I were not in this profession, I would also chant this same slogan!'

Wali Khan and Vice Admiral Ahsan also listened to the news with all intent, interest and felt happy with the thought that they could stay away from the sin and responsibility of this national devastation. However, except this handful men and fewer women like Mrs. Mahmoodee of Mohakhali, all Urdu speaking masses at Khulna's Nao Ratan colony, Dhaka's Ispahani colony, Khulna's Khalishpur, Syedpur, Chittagong, Mirpur and Mohammedpur and most of the people of the four provinces in the western wing did not sympathize with the news from Dhaka. They said, 'If these Bengalee rogues were destroyed right at the beginning of March, our dear motherland could be saved. Whatever the President and our patriotic armed forces have done has been an excellent job. All praises go to almighty Allah'.

It was like Emerson's view on everyone's prayer for God's favour to his side to win a war.

The leaders of the proletariat party at Jessore also heard the news. Selim said, 'Capitalism has once again been the victor. So we can't accept this. But this will be very short lived indeed. It is a matter of time only when the masses and communism must win.'

Baltu listened to the harangue and thought 'How long is that timeline? A thousand years?'

///

It was eleven and a half thousand miles away in the city of Newyork. Sitting on the glass covered balcony of a five star hotel facing the UN skyscraper, the *Nabab* also heard the news of the fall. He was wearing a sky blue suit made of best quality Hamilton woolen silk fabric. With a pink coloured silk neck-tie and a Dacron shirt he looked damnably handsome and healthy. He was toasting to himself by sipping from a glass of champagne of the 19th century. He thanked God and sensed his destination was not far away. He whispered to himself. 'This is bingo. I awaited this for the last six years. Yes patience pays, though in the long run. I have invested my whole life for this 'However he did not wish to see the short run. Mujib in custody at Mianwali gaol also heard the news. He looked somber imagining the mayhem his countrymen had suffered to reach this day.

The President came out from his boozing hangover and heard the news of the race course from Dhaka. General Piru was seated before him. He asked him 'Piru how do you feel?'

—Sir, I know Niazi for long. He is not the one to accept a defeat in a war easily. Possibly he accepted it for a better and bigger goal.
—You are correct. Actually we have not been a loser in this war. It has only been a tactical retreat. Laying down arms in a single sector does not determine the overall course of a war. We have seen this happening during the Second World War also.
—Sir, you are right.
—Besides, Piru, tell me another thing.
—What is that Sir?
—Have any Moslem forces ever accepted defeat before a different faith in the subcontinent's history?

—No, never Sir.

—Otherwise Pakistan could not have come into existence. Don't you think the saying, 'the pen is mightier than the sword', is a bogus one?

—You are right Sir. Soldiers have always won. Niazi also could continue the fight and win the war but that would take away hundreds of thousands of our Bengalee Moslem brothers and sisters' lives. So his decision has actually been a great moral victory to our side. We are a nation where we consider religion to be the foremost factor of life. Honesty, kindness and justice are its pillars'

The President's head was getting clearer now. He doubted some important parts of Piru's dialogue but generally liked it. No sense of remorse, defeatism, insult or even failure pricked his mind. Finally he said to this confidant, 'Should not we be happy that we did not have to hand over power to the bloody Bengalees ?'

Piru said, 'Absolutely Sir. There was no solution other than this one.'

The President felt once again that the *Nabab* had all along been hanging out for one purpose. That was the seat of power at Islamabad. Now he was going to have it. Still better, he was not a Bengalee, if not a Punjabee.

Two hundred and fifty miles away to the south at Bahawalpur, a Major-General was watching the developments at Dhaka. In the war concluded today, he was commanding a mountain division. He was relieved but not happy. In the eleven day long war he had lost not only soldiers and land but also honour. Usually he had always been a cool, calculative and introvert type. He was an in depth reader of political history, especially of this sub-continent. Since the last elections he was a keen watcher of the country's political developments. At his rank he never dreamed of approaching the President and making some specific suggestions about the country. Not a keen sympathizer with the Eastern wing people unlike Yaqub or Ahsan, he still did not like the decision about the 25th March army action.

Today as his men were busy withdrawing and packing their material for retreating tomorrow to the peacetime garrison, this military officer became thoughtful once again. He remembered his entry into this country from a town called Amritsar across the border of the East Punjab and then rising to a two-star general coming of a non-descript

refugee family. Nobody ever saw him smiling. Today this man named Zia-ul-Haque tried to make a smile which looked like a grin. Then he very quietly addressed somebody, 'You are responsible for this loss and ignominy. The long hand of the law tried to catch hold of you on previous occasions but yours have been longer. If I get a chance I will snare you. Who can say it will not be bestowed on me. Two of my predecessors have got it. May be I will.' Like Greek Zeus, providence smilingly approved his wishes but decided to snare him also at a distant future as it foresaw that Zia would also in the process commit enough sins.

Not very far away from this garrison town towards the east, at the metropolis of Delhi, one of the prime movers of this victory was sitting at her office. She consumed every bit of the proceedings at Dhaka. Diplomats of the highest order never let their faces show what they think inside. She did not smile. She only thanked her chief of staff, defense minister, defense secretary and the opposition leaders for their support in the war. They were dismissed shortly. She told her staff not to disturb her tonight. Now she was alone. She thought for half an hour and then opened the diary and took a pen. She started writing, 'My father committed a grave mistake in 1947. He was the best English-knowing man in this sub-continent. So what? He listened to Gandhi and accepted the partition of the subcontinent. Gandhi was humane but for whom? For the hooligans and the depraved! He sacrificed the interest of a vast majority at showing kindness to a miniscule minority. He agreed to the creation of this terror-state. These minorities were infiltrators. They vitiated a five thousand year old civilization by converting millions to a different faith and culture. In the process they killed many also. Even, their power politics always witnessed blood-bath and vendetta. All rulers starting from Md. Ghori, Tughlaks, Shahs, Abdalis, Sultans of Bengal, and Khiljis, usurped power by schemes, murders and treachery. The succession process always followed that. Kijilbash, Karranis, Dauds and Durranees all followed suit. Many Moghuls also killed and incarcerated their fathers, brothers just for sitting on the throne and enjoying life. Their co-religionists Harun did the same in Iraq. Now this time the *Nabab* of Larkana has done it for the same target. My sources told me 1800 of our soldiers got killed in the western sector only, 3500 to liberate Dhaka, and inside Bangladesh millions of civilians. Yes, this is their way of life. 93,000 prisoners of war and a million strength genocide for a throne? Is that going to be cost effective? Only history will determine that. For me, this is not the markets. Mediocre and average people think of markets. I am not a small fry. I look for greater things. I am a person of a large mould and politics is the most prestigious issue on earth. An army's clout is no match to that of a politician's like me. The pen is of course mightier than the sword. I here once again proved it. I have done it. I know these people are so jubilant today. No doubt they suffered a lot. Still the present hobnobbing and euphoria may not last long. They never trusted us, nor did we them. I am happy today. I have corrected the follies of my father and Gandhi. I have destroyed the two-nation theory. Above all I have taken retribution of a gigantic wrong done on us a thousand years ago and once again in 1947. History will not be able to give a verdict that I did this arbitrarily. No, never. The seventy five million people through their elected representatives lent their whole hearted support to me for attaining this. I am happy. This is the menu I have best relished in my life. I could not complete Berkeley but this is a better completion today than I have ever achieved in my life.'

She stopped at this point and thought for some time. Though she noted correctly the excesses inflicted on her communities by the outsiders, she wishfully forgot to note the atrocities perpetrated by her community on the Buddhists of the sub-continent on a very large scale. She did not appreciate that it was not faith but goodness or badness of rulers that matters.

Then she remembered a writing read a long time ago in a Greek tragedy, 'Hironimo'.
'First thoughts are sweet
Second thoughts are wise.'
She took her pen and it now dawned on her that she was too big a figure to record such thoughts in her diary though she felt them to be quite correct. She closed her pen and then tore the pages into pieces and put them down the lavatory. Then she thought. 'No kind of accounting invented by men will ever be able to compute the gains or losses to us had not the outsiders ever entered the subcontinent or materialized the two-nation theory. To a ruler it is the motive of hegemony. My ego has been satisfied. That is the main receipt. I have undone something which none of my forefathers could do.'

//

A few among those who had surrendered were not Moghuls, Pathans or Aryans. Their mother tongue was Bangla and their homes were somewhere in this land. Habilder Monser Fakir of Faridpur and Lt. Mushfique Chowdhury were two such men. Monser heard the continuous slogans being chanted from processions everywhere outside the cantonment board area. His liberated countrymen were full throated in their thunderous utterance of "Joy Bangla (Long Live Bangladesh)." He understood his motherland was now a free country. He in a low voice asked Lt. Mushfique, 'Sir, we have been taken as P.O.Ws, though we are Bengalees. Now what is the way of getting out of here?'

Mushfique answered, 'That is none of your business. The government will look into that.'

Monser immediately recognized the changes in the voice and manner of this army officer. During the whole war, Mushfique used to talk to him and behaved in the manner as a close relative. He shared many private issues with this non-commissioned officer. He always looked scared on two accounts. One, the freedom fighters might kill him anytime for treason and collaborating with the occupation army. Two, the occupation army could kill him any moment just for his being a Bengalee. Now Monser clearly saw those worries were gone from Mushfique's eyes and face and the authoritative, distant, cool and official superior's manner came back fully to his personality. This simple minded JCO Monser realized with dismay that there was no prospect of socialism being established in the near future and even if he could be free from captivity his livelihood would never be anything above a peasant or petty shop keeper. Earlier he had expected freedom would make him a commissioned officer.

Dropping out of school before completing the 7th grade, Habilder Monser could never be an avid reader of Charles Dickens'. Still the question coming to his mind at this hour was 'shall one tyranny be replaced by another one?'

//

Human civilization has evolved a class of people who are gifted with the power of imagination. They find meaning in meaningless phenomena; they find order in chaos and vice versa.

This genre of people could say on the beginning day of their nation's glorious struggle for liberty that Nature itself looked ominous on the night when the genocide started. Today also they could say that the morning dews were portentous, suggesting an impending cheerful conclusion of the war. Science however does not look at things with the fiction writers' vision. Accordingly though thousands of people were coming out to the streets of Dhaka singing Tagore's "My Bengal of gold, I love thee", "The sun has risen in the eastern horizon, it is blood red" celebrating the freedom of the 75 million people's nation, the grammar of science did not demonstrate any changes even on such an auspicious night.

The December night progressed, the temperature fell gradually like any other winter. The 10' o clock news of the official radio broadcast told that 10 old men, women and children had died due to cold and want of warm clothes that very evening at Lalmonirhat, a border town of this free country.

///

God, if there is some being like Him in existence, works in a way which seems very often inscrutable to his creatures. Believers take anything as the expression of His will while agnostics or freethinkers explain every phenomenon on the basis of cause and effect. Accordingly if there are four members in a family, Fate does not always make each of them unhappy by being cruel to them. For this or another inscrutable reason, Asad survived scot-free even after facing five encounters with the occupation forces while his parents, only sister and uncle Abul lost their lives. Besides, many of his co-fighters were killed at their first engagement with the Pakistanee army. Many lost their eyes, vital organs or other limbs whose cure would never be possible in this life even in the best hospitals of the earth.

Asad was called on 11th December to Jessore sector as the command was in dire necessity of the best boys there to assist the regular forces. He came back to the base after the last operation on 13th December. Then the proposal for surrender was put on the air. Then followed the process of armistice and surrender talks. Asad asked Captain Mohankumar Wadekar of his camp if he could go to Dhaka with one of the joint command units. Wadekar with a sympathetic smile told, 'Asad, you are

MASUD AHMED

one of the best fighters, no doubt, but a little simple. It is not men like me but of very high position from Delhi who decide such issues.'

Many freedom fighters with similar requests approached the camp commander and met with the same reply. On the 17th Asad said goodbye to his commander and host. A truck of the unit carried him and other survivors up to Benapole border of the new nation.

This truck was carrying twenty freedom fighters. Out of them, eight were familiar to Asad. After moving for a few miles the boy seated beside Asad started talking.

—Brother Asad, the path to our destination is still long. So please talk, smile and let us enjoy it. After all we are free now.

—You are correct. We are free. We have got what we longed for. Still, I don't feel quite good!

—Possibly we understand the reasons of your bad feeling. How can one forget such a big tragedy in his own family? Now we are hearing news that the troops have done the same thing to hundreds and thousands of people throughout the country.

—The reason is not only that. There are other things.

Another boy from the opposite bench said, 'Well if you do not have reservations let us share those.'

Asad replied, 'Have you thought about one matter? Such a big ceremony like the surrender but how many of us, I mean from our government, were invited to attend that? Especially our C-in-C should have been there. After all, this ceremony is ours. Besides, nowhere did they surrender before us and there is no signature from anyone of our side on the document.'

The boys started pondering. Then a young man, older than Asad quietly said, 'Well Asad, you are talking of an idealistic situation but I would prefer to consider the composition and conduct of the war. The two governments established the joint command and so we are represented in the document. It is not crucial who signed the document.'

Another boy younger than Asad told, 'We were so elated with their defeat that these finer points did not appear in our minds. Still this glorious struggle has taught me something very important. May I share those?'

Everyone nodded.

The boy said, 'Brother Asad, I realize your disappointment but will still argue that the barbarians have been compelled to lower their heads to our wishes. Our friendly and big neighbour largely helped us in materializing that. What is the harm in that? Don't we have examples like this in recent history? The French were liberated by the allies from German occupation in 1945. Do you think they could get out of their clutches on their own? For us also I don't know how long and what cost would it take to be free from Pakistan. On that account we should remain grateful to our benefactor.'

Everyone was impressed with the wisdom and maturity of this young fighter. Another boy from behind spoke out. He said, 'I am happy. I could kill three of them and still survived. Then I am seeing a free motherland. I am more than happy seeing that our enemy has realized how formidable the Bengalees are. A non-martial race could do such a great feat! That is enough.'

Asad took the floor and said,

—Do you remember how we used to quarrel among ourselves on issues like loans or the boundary of a land before this war started?

—Why? We used sticks, indigenous weapons and arguments.

—So see what we learnt through this war. We learnt that even a government can be ousted with firearms.

—So what is your point?

—My point is, this easy availability of firearms to millions of civilians is going to be dangerous for the safety and security of our society. It will be very difficult for any government to take these firearms back to its custody.

An elderly freedom fighter then said, 'I share your concerns. At the same time I wish to share my optimism with you in this regard. Many countries in Africa and Latin America have had their independence in the same way. Recovering fire arms was a problem but they did not fail finally. If a sense of ownership can be instilled into all of us by the leadership we will progress.'

At that moment the truck carrying them screeched to a halt. That was the Petrapole check post, the last point from the Indian side. The time was 3' o clock in the afternoon. Captain Raghabon of 2nd communication zone seated in front of the truck got down to see these guests off to their own country. He told Asad that after crossing the border into Benapole and then to Jessore cantonment, they would be carried to Dhaka by an army lorry of a Bengal regiment. A message to this effect had been given earlier by him to the Jessore cantonment. Raghabon shook hands with everyone and drove back inside the border. Asad and his group bought their lunch and then hired a mini-truck and started for Jessore.

Throughout liberated Bangladesh, in every locality, were it a rural market, community cafe, Union council office, shops, or home, people were talking about one issue only. That was, liberty, liberation war, and the atrocities of the Pakistanee troops. Everyone was in total agreement on those issues. A microscopic dissenter was there but they had either fled or been killed or in some rare cases taken into custody after a gang beating. The roads to Jessore were dilapidated in many places, bridges and culverts were blown up. To avoid those, the truck was often coming down to agricultural fields and farms and moving forward. Human congestion on many points of the road was also obstructing the easy passage of the truck. Off and on the driver out of curiosity was asking people, 'Brother, what is going on here?'

Someone from the multitude replied, 'A people's court is in session here. It is trying collaborators of the occupation army.'

Some of the scenes caught Asad's eyes. At one spot a bare bodied lean and thin man was tied to a tree and two young men were whipping him. In another place a group of men were beating an 18 year old boy with heavy bamboo sticks. In another place in a playground, three people dangling down from a foot-ball keeper's bar-post were yelling. A while ago a crowd gauged their eyes out of their sockets. A little ahead in the office of a local body, a man in his late fifties with a beard in his face had just been shot to death by a self-proclaimed judge.

The mini-truck proceeded further. The driver stopped and said to the passengers that he had a flat tire. He required half an hour to fix it from a local mechanic's shop. It was the last flank of a village. The time was four o'clock in the winter afternoon. Asad got down. The others also scattered to have some tea and snacks.

Asad found an old banyan tree and sat down under its shade. The sky above was blue, and a sun was yet dazzling. Alone in the land for which he staked his life and everything, after many days Asad almost broke into a howl. All the memories of his parents, sister and Minoo overflowed his mind with an uncontrollable force. He wept and wept, tears drenched his pullover's front side. Gradually he controlled his emotion and thought, 'Dear parents, dear Minoo, probably I am a selfish man. That is why I am surviving and I have not even received an injury from the war while you suffered terribly and died. You killed nobody, nor hurt anyone. And beloved Minoo, I gave you a commitment I would marry you. You trusted me and waited. I could do nothing to save your life, dear! I have killed at least a dozen Pakistanee brutes and am now breathing in a free motherland. Your souls are surely watching me and indicting me.' He touched the soil before him. Felt as if he was connected with the unknown graves of his parents, Minoo and only sister at vague and faraway places but somewhere within this free land.

Ten minutes passed by and Asad's bad feelings receded meanwhile. He realized nothing ever feels the same in life. He was never a fan of Nature though one of the papers in journalism was photography and reporting on Nature. At that moment Asad looked at the landscape in front of the village. So far as his eyes could see, the tilled lands of the village were smeared with greens and yellow colours of mustard plants. As if a big fabric woven with twines of those two colours were covering the whole village like a big blanket. Sunrays added an artistic aesthetics into the whole surroundings. Not many years ago Asad read one essay by Syed Ali Ahsan, titled "My East Bengal". Poet Nazrul also had fancied this land as Bangladesh, and Tagore wrote a lyric, 'O my Bengal of gold'. Looking at the scenic beauty Asad realized the relevance of those compositions. It seemed to him that after witnessing such a scene the poet Jasimuddin possibly had written his unforgettable stanza,

'The happy and veiled mustard dame,
Stooping with the yellow breeze,
And lowering her neck to kiss the peas'

Winter had squeezed the water bodies of the village and in many places, they got dried up. In a pond beside the main village street, where Asad was sitting, the clean water caught his eyes. A pack of blue-headed ducks swimming in the water was strutting and fretting their wings making a cackling sound out of their long beaks. Small red fishes were diving into the water and coming out along with small snails clasping in their bites. Suddenly a squadron of cormorants flew into the pond's surface, made a dive into the water and flew back away into the sky with small silvery fishes held into their beaks. Plenty of date trees were sprayed over the area. Earthen pots tied by peasants along the heads of the trees with jute made ropes were a common sight. Drops of date juice were dripping down and filling the pots. Asad looked at the cows and goats grazing on the gray bushes. A few chicken attired with red and violet tuft similar to Greek soldiers' helmet were moving to and fro on the field. Asad looked at the scene and it appeared to him that there was matchless beauty in all of those which he had not realized earlier. Meanwhile two ducks wet with water walked towards Asad from the pond and looked at this stranger. Asad felt a sudden urge to dive into the pond, mix with the sporting ducks and swans, fling water and mud and play with them.

Asad stepped slightly down the bank of the pond and lifted a handful of water. It felt very cold and his whole body shivered. Still this feeling, the winter blue sky and the aroma coming out from the mustard field filled Asad with a new sensation-' possibly these are the very invaluable cravings of the whole populace for which they have undergone so much pains and sufferings all through the last nine months.' After spending such a long time, almost every day and night amidst gunpowder and blood Asad had a really cheerful feeling at this moment.

A small shop across the village street was selling tea and stick-shaped cookies. Asad arrived there and ordered a cup of tea. A radio set was playing a popular and patriotic song composed during the liberation struggle,

"After a thousand years, I have come back once again
And am standing in the bosom of Bengal".

The lyric and the tune attracted Asad deeply. His attention was diverted as the driver requested everyone to board now. With a tired body, Asad fell asleep as the truck jerked to a start.

He was not aware of how long he had slept. After dusk a series of unknown soft noises awoke him up. Asad looked around and realized that flocks of crickets and fire flies flying from around the thick shrubs and bushes were making the noises. Simultaneously from behind the mini-truck, lightning bugs were racing forward focusing their beads of light in the dark. It was serene and tranquil all around the rural landscape. He felt that, this particular hour of the evening had a voice of its own. As if Nature was whispering,

'When all the lights of the earth fade out,
The manuscript arrays,
Then the lightning bugs shimmer colourfully towards the story,
All birds return to nests, all rivers to their sources,
All transactions of this life come to an end,
Only darkness prevails.'

The aroma of dust and vegetation made the place sensuous. Asad slightly shook his body on the seat and suddenly remembered this was the Grand Trunk Road through which the truck was proceeding. He recollected, 'my parents came to Dhaka in 1947 using this road. Minoo's parents and other innumerable men, women and children also had traversed the same road attracted by the dream of a new home. That mom is no more, that dad is no more and nor is Minoo or Jerin on this earth. What about Minoo's photograph and two letters, those invaluable mementos kept in my room number 111 with so much care and affection? Have these also been looted by someone along with thousands of dreams of so many people?'

With these memories Asad once again felt an emotional mood surging up within him and he came to tears. He felt, 'I am so near to you, yet will never see you. O parents, I could do nothing for you. Even during your last minutes of life I was hundreds of miles away.Oh, azure sky, silent night, oh twinkling stars, oh lovely moon, silvery dewdrops, convey to them this message—I loved them and still love them deeply. Your sacrifices have earned a free land, a free lake, the liberty I find in an unlimited sky, a grove of chrysanthemum and above all millions of elated souls.'Co-passengers could hear Asad's sobbing but guessed this might be something very personal. They didn't ask him anything.

The distance was only twenty two miles. Dilapidated roads,damaged bridges meant that it would take about one and a quarter hours to reach it. It was fifteen minutes past six in the evening when the truck reached the cantonment gate.

A new state had just emerged. The authorities were also novice. There was a liberal tempo even here. Asad looked for the station headquarters and asked Captain Akbar about the message of Major

Raghabon. Without any bureaucratic air, Akbar acknowledged receipt of the message, He then requested Asad and his boys in a friendly tone, 'Please board this vehicle. We will start sharp at seven o'clock.'

Four days had elapsed since there was a full moon. So the sky was dark for some time after the sun-set. The cold also had increased. A quarter moon now appeared through the thick branches of the woods behind the cantonment dispelling the darkness. The dewdrops on the wet leaves of the trees were glistening as moonlight fell on them. The fog was also becoming clear. There was serenity and tranquility around. The olive coloured lorry of the 1st Bengal regiment was waiting before the quarter-guard with its face eastward. Its destination was the capital city of a new born state. Before one minute to seven, Asad boarded the lorry visualizing the dawning of a golden day only hours away.

//

Written in Detroit, Michigan, Indiana city,
Indiana and Chicago, Illinois, USA, 2012

EPILOGUE

The protagonists of 1971 influenced the events of that year while the events also influenced the lives of the protagonists. President Yahya found him house-arrested by his beneficiary and died before ever becoming free. Feelings of frustration and treachery led him to make two attempts of committing suicide without success. Tarik-Bin-Ziad fought for his pension and died without receiving the same. The *Nabab* became the Prime Minister of a truncated Pakistan. He by dictates of Nemesis chose his own assassin Zia by superseding many in the Army list. General Zia-Ul-Haque hanged his benefactor after usurping state power. Nemesis did not spare Zia also. He was killed in a mysterious air crash at Bahawalpur. *Nabab's* daughter Benazir got elected to her country's premiership and was murdered mysteriously. Mujib alongwith members of his family got killed in a *coup-detat*. Madam was also gunned down by her own bodyguard. Her son, the elected Prime Minister of the country was also destroyed to pieces by assassins. In Bangladesh, General Zia took state power after Mujib's murder. He was also killed by his own bodyguards. All these took place within a span of a little more than a quarter of a century (1975-2007). The differences in historical and cultural traits and tradition of the two nations were demonstrated through the above episodes as well. While, Madam's and her son's murder did not effect a change in their country's political system, the other killings inside two neighbours were perpetrated by usurpers.